SALLOW BEND

SALLOW BEND

ALAN BAXTER

Cemetery Dance Publications
Baltimore
2022

Sallow Bend
Copyright © 2022 by Alan Baxter

Cover Artwork © 2022 by François Vaillancourt
Cover Design © 2022 by Desert Isle Design, LLC
Interior Design © 2022 by Desert Isle Design, LLC

All rights reserved. No part of this book may be reproduced in any form or by any electronic or mechanical means, including information storage and retrieval systems, without permission in writing from the publisher, except by a reviewer who may quote brief passages in a review.

Trade Paperback Edition

ISBN:
978-1-58767-832-5

This book is a work of fiction. Names, characters, places and incidents either are products of the author's imagination or are used fictitiously. Any resemblance to actual events or locales or persons, living or dead, is entirely coincidental.

Cemetery Dance Publications
132B Industry Lane, Unit #7
Forest Hill, MD 21050
www.cemeterydance.com

1

A SHARP RAPPING WOKE Caleb Jackson from a fitful doze. He glanced at the clock. Ten-fifteen am. He'd only napped a few minutes. Probably one of the kids had puked in the hall on the way to break or something. He sighed, hauled himself up from the sagging armchair.

He pulled the door open, bright sunlight flooding in, opened his mouth to ask what needed cleaning or fixing this time, but the words froze in his throat. Two police officers stood there, squinting into his gloom. Two of the four full-time officers in Sallow Bend. Mary Fitzpatrick, the school principal, hovered between them, slightly behind. Her friendly, round face held a nervous smile, but then she was always anxious. Floral dress billowing, iron gray hair perpetually in an untidy bun, she was warm and stood up for Caleb whenever she could.

Caleb winced under the tight scrutiny of the three people, the focused information from their faces, micro-expressions as loud as shouting to his over-sensitive eye. He looked at the floor.

"Caleb Jackson?" the Sheriff asked.

Caleb frowned. The man knew exactly who he was, just as Caleb knew the Sheriff was Freddie Holtz. Six-foot-four-inches of muscular ex-bully, ex-school jock, failed his exams, managed to pull himself straight and work his way up through the local Sheriff's Department. Not a bad guy anymore, but maybe still angry inside. Everybody in town knew Freddie Holtz's story and it was basically a good one, if you ignored the past and accepted the man had made good. Caleb and Holtz were of an age, guys just like Freddie had ridden Caleb mercilessly through school, though Caleb tried not to hold grudges against all their kind. He had been far away from Sallow Bend in his school years.

He stood a good six inches shorter and briefly squinted up at Holtz before looking away again. "Freddie..?"

"Official business, Caleb, answer the question."

Caleb hated the artifice of adult interactions. Kids were mean, but altogether more honest for that. He avoided adults and their social politics wherever he could, and was happier that way. He saw it all too clearly, could never play along like they seemed to do. He took a nervous breath. "Yes, Sheriff Holtz, I'm Caleb Jackson."

"May we come in? Need to ask you a few questions."

Mary Fitzpatrick leaned forward. "It's okay, Caleb. Just routine, you know?"

Caleb stepped back, left the door open. The three of them bustled inside and blinked until their eyes adjusted to the low light.

"Need a stronger bulb in here." Kurt Janssen, twenty-four, meanest of the three deputies under Sheriff Holtz. Tall, thin, arrogant. For all Caleb didn't get along with adults, he genuinely disliked Janssen. Holtz may have outgrown most of his bullying nature and become a decent guy. It didn't look like Janssen ever would.

"Bright enough for me. What do you need, Sheriff?"

Holtz looked around the small living space. Kitchenette in one corner, TV and tatty armchair opposite, small curtained-off area at the back with Caleb's unmade bed half-revealed. Cupboards, shelves, books randomly scattered. The only other door led to a small toilet and shower stall. It was more than enough space for Caleb, tucked under the school's assembly hall and rent-free as a perk for his double position as janitor and night security. He was happy. Possibly, he reflected, happier than most in town, but then he didn't crave the company of others or the pursuit of a career. So he only needed room for one.

Holtz's eyes found their way back to Caleb, so Caleb looked away. He saw a variety of things in Holtz's face, concern, determination, no little disdain. He saw that in most people's faces. "Clare Finlay. Thirteen years old. Good kid, smart, friendly, from a happy family."

Caleb nodded. "I know her. Student here."

"And Suki Tokugawa, same age, bit of a troublemaker, bit headstrong. But still a good kid. Good family."

"Yes, both here at school. They're best friends."

"You know a lot about the kids?"

Caleb shook his head, still looking at the ground. "Not a lot. I know who's who, some of the, you know, dynamics. I know those two are inseparable. Why?"

"You seen them today?" Holtz's voice was hard.

"Be nice to him," Fitzpatrick said, her voice high and wavery as usual, only perhaps more so. "He's not a suspect."

"Yes he is!" Janssen said, with a derisive laugh. "One of the most likely, the freaking weirdo."

"Enough!" Holtz's voice snapped like a wooden ruler slapping a desk. "Keep your mouth shut, Kurt." He looked back, caught Caleb's eye. "Answer the question, please."

Caleb saw warring emotions on the Sheriff's face, saw him trying to suppress a kind of fear. All the social lying and etiquette that Caleb simply couldn't understand playing out over and over with every sentence, every look. People pretended so many things while Caleb so often saw the opposite in the truth of their expressions and movements. He could never figure out how to balance those things. And his sensitivity to them, the simple overload of information, made any interaction exhausting. It was easier to remove himself from it all as much as possible. Now the scrutiny of these three was unbearable. "Suspect for what? What's happened?"

"Have you seen Clare or Suki today?"

Nerves rippled through Caleb. "No, not today. I was cleaning early, fixed the light over the main entrance. When the kids started to arrive I came in here and organized my roster of jobs, then had a nap. So I didn't see them arrive."

"Last night?"

"What about it?"

"You see them leave school?"

Caleb drew a deep breath, thought hard. "I was painting the window frames around the back of the English department all yesterday afternoon, so I didn't really see any of the kids leave. I wasn't out the front. But I did see Clare and Suki in their English class last period."

"Watching them through the windows were you?" Janssen asked, sneering. Where most wore disdain, Janssen's face betrayed genuine disgust, the promise of violence barely contained.

"You wanna go wait in the car?" Holtz asking, rounding on the deputy.

Janssen grunted, deflated a little. He looked daggers at Caleb.

"I wasn't watching them, no. But I saw them in there while I was painting. What's going on?"

"Miss Ransom told you Caleb was outside her English class," Fitzpatrick said. "She told you he was still there an hour after school when she finished marking. His story is the same."

Caleb nodded. "I came back here about five thirty or so. Long after school let out."

Holtz sighed. "Yep, it's all tight."

"What's happening?" Caleb asked again.

"Clare and Suki never made it home last night," Holtz said. "They haven't been seen since their English class yesterday. A couple of the other kids are sure they left school together."

"We can confirm it with security cameras," Caleb said. "At least, we can see if they left the school via the front gate and which way they went. After that it's up to you guys and the other cameras around town."

Holtz nodded. "Not too many of them. Okay, let's check yours first"

HOLTZ leaned back from the monitors in the small room behind the school office. "So they left and headed north. They both live south of the school. Where were they going?"

He stared up at Caleb, but Caleb avoided his gaze. He knew his inattention made people uncomfortable, but if it was their discomfort or his own, he would choose to protect himself every time. He theorized people recognized, on some level, that he saw through them. But there really wasn't much he could do about it except avoid them as much as possible. And they continued with their façades. "The carnival rolled into town yesterday," he said.

Holtz still looked at him. "I know. What are you suggesting?"

"Nothing. Just maybe they went there. Teenagers are headstrong, they take risks. And going to watch the carnival set up after school isn't even that much of a risk."

Holtz nodded, almost to himself. "Thanks for your help." He crammed his hat back on and strode from the room.

"We're still watching you," Janssen said.

Caleb forced himself to meet the man's eye, despite the almost instant headache it triggered. "Back off." Janssen flinched slightly and Caleb enjoyed that but had to look away from the flood of information from the young man's rapid expressions, which slightly ruined the moment. The deputy followed his boss without another word.

"I'll help with the search," Caleb said towards Fitzpatrick. "What can I do?"

She put a slightly trembling hand on his arm. He flinched a little but managed to hide it. "The teachers and parents are organizing search parties. School has to continue for now, but talk to Tricia Brent. She's one of the people getting everything moving. You can take the rest of the day off from your duties here if you want to go and help."

Caleb knew she was trying to make him feel better. He didn't mind, but also didn't understand why she would bother. Two young girls missing overnight was a big deal. He would like to help, if nothing else than to prove to Holtz and Janssen they had nothing to be concerned about with Caleb himself. He nodded. "Tricia Brent? She lost her son."

"Last year, yes. Toby. Went missing. Hasn't been found."

"Dead?"

Fitzpatrick's face crumpled in on itself in grief and Caleb quickly averted his eyes once more. "I honestly can't imagine what it's like for them."

"You think that's why she's eager to help here?"

"Maybe."

Caleb took a deep breath. He'd already talked and interacted more in the past half hour than he usually did in a week, even a month. It was exhausting, the headache pulsing behind his eyes. And now he'd have to do even more.

Fitzpatrick took his inertia as concern for the girls. "I know you care deeply for the kids here. Go. See Tricia, and offer your help. I'll write down her address."

Caleb swallowed, nodded. He took the slip of paper and hurried away, thankful to be free of conversation for a little while at least.

2

TRICIA BRENT BIT down on rising rage, tried to quench the fire of hatred that burned in her gut. Riley stood there, so drunk already he swayed slightly, his idiot face twisted in confusion.

"What do you mean, why does it have to be me?" she asked, voice low with the threat of explosion.

"Exactly that," Riley slurred. "What business is it of yours?"

Tricia looked her husband up and down, his burly frame gathering fat around the middle. He wasn't forty yet, but he was thickening, balding, increasingly bitter by the day. She was no teenage beauty any more herself, she knew that, but she kept better care of herself than he did. She was still fit even if she was a few pounds over where she'd like to be. And she didn't drink, not like Riley. No one she knew drank like Riley. Like he had ever since Toby disappeared.

"Children are missing," she said. "How can you not understand that?"

"I undersand it. I just don't know why you gotta get involved."

"Because they're fucking children, Riley! Because we lost our own son and you don't want me to care about that anymore!"

He took a stagger-step towards her and she rapidly backed up, bracing for a strike. He'd hit her before then begged forgiveness in a brief moment of sobriety. His logger's hands were rough and cracked, hard as the wood he felled. And his head was full of sawdust. He frightened her. "Those missing girls ain't gonna lead you to Toby!" He raised a hand, grimaced, let it fall again.

"How do you know that? And besides, I know how their mothers feel. If nothing else, we have to come together, as community. To help each other."

He sneered and turned away, snatched a bottle of Wild Turkey from the counter as he stumbled back towards his beaten old La-Z-Boy in front of the TV, drinking away his day off. "You do as you damn well please, woman. You always fuckin' do."

Tricia stood trembling, staring at the back of his pale head as he slumped into the seat and clicked the remote to show a football match. They'd been so in love, high school sweethearts infatuated with each other, both born and raised in Sallow Bend. They'd waited a long time to have kids, enjoying each other's company, then finally Toby was born. And that had been wonderful too, for a dozen good years more until Toby disappeared and Riley fell into a bottle and never found his way out. She'd lost them both, she knew that. But while Toby seemed gone forever, Riley was a bad smell that would never air out. She'd switch their places in an instant.

Her eyes roamed over the familiarity of their home, muted autumn colors in the soft furnishings, some of her artworks on the walls, worn but good quality furniture, the white and pine kitchen. The lived-in untidiness of it all. She felt as though she were looking through a screen now, as though she had been partially removed from her nest. Riley lived in the family home and she gently slipped away from it, watching it fade like the closing shot of a movie. They weren't well off, but they were far from poor. Riley made good money, though for how long given his current decline she couldn't be sure. She did okay at the grocery store four days a week. Even without Toby, if they held together they should have been able to weather the loss, keep looking for him as a team, never give up, and have each other and their comfortable home in the meantime. But Riley was drinking all that away.

"Fuck you," she muttered under her breath, swept her purse off the counter and left.

As she closed the front door, a man somewhere in his thirties, short dark hair over narrowed eyes, approached up the driveway. He glanced up and away often, seemingly unable to hold her gaze. He was familiar and he gave her the creeps, but she couldn't explain either.

"Mrs Brent?" he asked, in a tight voice. "Tricia Brent."

And then it dawned on her. The school janitor. The weirdo. But most people seemed to agree he was harmless enough. "Yes, that's me."

"I came to help look for the girls. Mrs Fitzpatrick said you were organizing something?"

"I'm just going over there now. We're meeting at the Town Hall and we'll start search parties. Your help is greatly appreciated. Mr Jackson, right?"

"Call me Caleb."

"All right then." She ran a tongue over suddenly dry lips. "You walked here?"

"Don't have a car."

"You want a ride with me now?"

"Thank you."

He still hadn't met her eye, though he smiled regularly, almost as if he was reminding himself to do it. His hands were calloused and stained with creosote, but his face was soft and kind. A wave of sympathy passed through Tricia as she watched him. "Come on, then." She blipped the car locks open on her scruffy red Ford and they climbed in.

It was only a few minutes' drive to the Town Hall, Caleb could have walked there from school quicker than getting to her house. "Mrs Fitzpatrick gave you my address?"

"She said you were organizing searches."

"Well, I'm hoping to help. Community has to come together at times like these."

From the corner of her eye she saw him nod. Silence settled uncomfortably and she felt the need to fill it.

"You know the two girls?"

"I know they're best friends. I see them at school."

"Of course."

The streets slipped by and Tricia willed the journey to speed up.

"Any ideas about where they might be?"

Caleb looked over at her then, but looked away again before she could meet his eye. "Not really."

She let out a nervous laugh. "I didn't mean you should know anything about them or, you know, where they might be. Just wondered if you had any guesses, anything like that?" She was babbling. Wasn't Caleb supposed to be the nervous one? Although he didn't seem uneasy or anxious, just dislocated, more confused by their interaction than anything.

"Carnival, maybe."

She hadn't thought of that. The carnies had rolled into town the day before, started setting up on Old Man Wilson's land on the outskirts of town. Same time every year, right before the summer holidays. Friday was the last day of semester, the carnival opened tomorrow, Thursday. Then it would be long summer days for all the kids, complaining of boredom at the same time as they ran and rode bikes, played video games and had water fights, living the absolute time of their lives. She swallowed all those thoughts away as Toby rose in her mind, his sandy curls and big, brown eyes, laughing and playing, the most beautiful boy in the world. "The carnival, yeah." She hitched a breath. "We should definitely ask there."

It was too much, more missing kids, thinking of Toby, trying not to bark into sobs and collapse. Sometimes it was all too hard, she could see the temptation to fall into something numbing like Riley had done. Then there Riley was, a barely living warning against doing such a self-destructive thing. She had to keep going.

"Must be hard."

She jumped, Caleb saying something unbidden a complete surprise. "Hard?"

"Missing children."

She let out a laugh. "You reading my mind?"

"Just your face. You're trying not to cry."

Damn, the man was blunt and completely right. "What's your story?" she asked, to deflect him. Put the discomfort back on him. She didn't want to face her own.

"Story?"

"The way you are." Two could be blunt. "Why?"

He shook his head, looking down at his hands clasped together in his lap. "I'm not autistic or anything, my parents had lots of tests done. I just see too much in people, struggle with the information overload. Over-sensitive to body language and micro-expressions, the doctors said, but they can't explain why. Nothing they can do about it."

She felt bad, realized she'd lashed out from grief. "I'm sorry."

"Why?"

She frowned. "For embarrassing you."

"I'm not embarrassed. No one ever asked before. It's just the truth. I've never really coped well around people is all, it's too tiring."

They drove on in silence. Tricia too uncomfortable on every level to risk more conversation. Caleb seemed entirely unperturbed by it all, his mood unchanged since he'd appeared in her driveway. They arrived at the Town Hall, the streets outside packed with cars and pick-ups, people milling on the steps, the Mayor moving between with an expression of determined concern.

Once the meeting got under way it turned out there wasn't much to talk about and Tricia didn't get to organize anything. The mayor and Sheriff Freddie Holtz took charge, explained where the police were focusing their attention and asked everyone to look wherever they could. Concentrate on forgotten places, Sheriff Holtz said. Look in barns and sheds, check creeks and ponds in the corners of properties, talk to everyone in case someone hadn't heard and might know something. Among the general hubbub of consternation, Sheriff Holtz yelled out, brought everything to a sudden and strained silence.

"I know everyone is concerned. I know you all want to help. So let's stop gathering wool here and just get out there, okay?"

"What about them carnies?" a voice shouted from the back.

Holtz raised his palms out to calm the sudden rise in opinions. "Now, let's not make any judgments or cause any extra strife."

"Pretty funny they arrive and those girls go missing the same time!" another voice called out.

"Not funny at all, just a coincidence." Holtz raised his hands again, and his voice. "But of course we'll be talking to them. Deputy Janssen and I are going over there right after this. Deputies Baker and Taylor are out searching in a patrol car, but all calls to the station are being redirected to them, so make sure you report anything, however seemingly insignificant. Now go! Get out there and let's find those children. I'm sure they're just two young girls being adventurous, and they've no idea the panic they've caused."

"Two young girls who've been gone all night!" a woman said.

Holtz nodded, mouth set in a flat line. "So let's find them."

People left the hall and the roar of engines rose and fell as vehicles went off in every direction.

"So I guess we pick a direction and go?" Tricia said. She wasn't entirely comfortable to find herself suddenly buddied up with Caleb Jackson, but it seemed to have fallen that way. She figured he wasn't ecstatic to be with her either. Then again, perhaps he wouldn't be happy with anyone and she could do her best not to judge him. She should be kind, he was trying to help, after all.

I've never really coped well around people is all.

What a terrible thing to admit to. What a terrible way to live.

"The carnival?" Caleb asked.

"Sheriff Holtz said he was going there."

"Yeah. But no one talks to the police. Not really. Do they?"

Tricia nodded slowly. "I guess you're right. I know Ashley a little bit from previous years, maybe she'll talk to me."

"Ashley?"

"She runs the carnival. And I don't expect she's especially fond of the police."

Caleb nodded once, then stood waiting.

"Okay then." Tricia left the Town Hall, heading for her car.

3

ASHLEY STRONG STOOD on the tailgate of her trailer, the carnival crew arrayed in a fan before her, all eyes upturned, expectant. The big *Strong's Traveling Carnival* sign arced over the end of the midway far across the field, all the rides and stalls and sideshows spreading out from it, filling the space between the sign and the crew trailers. Everything was nearly ready, bright colors and carved plywood, snaking cables and inert generators, lights unlit, ovens cool, everything neat and tidy and waiting to be fired up.

That short time between the completion of setup and the official kicking off of festivities had always been a time of pleasure for Ashley. *Here we are,* she would think. *Once again we've overcome the logistics and this is the peaceful moment, the calm before the storm.* But that sense of accomplishment, that pleasure drawn from the power of management she wielded, was compromised this time. Not quite ready and now this complication.

"My daddy would give you some big rousing speech about this," she said in a robust voice that carried over the still carnival. "He'd tell you how strong we all are, how much of a service we do, bringing pleasure town by town. You've heard all that old shit before." A ripple of nervous laughter and chatter passed through her people. "And he was right!" she added. "He was right then and if I repeated his spiel, I'd be right now. I remember it word for word, we all do. Maybe I should give the speech, go through the motions, but we know things are not the same today. Two little girls are missing."

Angry rumblings started in the crowd and Ashley raised her voice over them. "We know it's nothing to do with us, but who are always the first suspects when anything bad happens and the carnival is in town? Of course it's us. So let's just accept that we've arrived into a shitstorm and everyone in this backwoods town is going to be looking at us with narrowed eyes. If we did anything else but help out we'd only look more guilty of a crime none of us committed. And this is our long stay pitch, we're here for two weeks, not just a few days. So here's what we do. We make ourselves available, we offer to delay tomorrow night's grand opening, we help in the search, okay? I don't know about you all, but I don't want to think that we're ignoring the fact two thirteen-year-old girls are missing. So let's help and if they want us to open tomorrow night, we will."

"And if they don't?" John Barrow called out. His voice was powerful, belying his stature. But Ashley knew, little person or not, he had the heart and mind of a giant. Four and half feet of fiercely loyal friend under a mop of black hair, slowly turning to iron grey as he entered his fifties.

Ashley smiled. "Then we delay until Friday."

"We always open on Thursday night. We'd lose an entire night's takings, and all day Friday."

"If that's what it takes to soften the eyes of suspicion around us, then so be it."

Annoyed grumblings started up again and Ashley raised her hands.

"Your father would have insisted on opening tomorrow night," Barrow said loudly before she could speak.

Ashley pursed her lips. She knew what he was doing. Being the voice of her father, giving strength to the ghost she had competed against for nearly five years. One day they would forget about Joseph Strong and the carnival would truly belong to her, but in the meantime she had to continue to pay deference to the old man. For how long, she didn't know. And John Barrow would always give her the opportunity to show respect to Joseph while maintaining control. Barrow gave her a subtle wink, and a nod. She'd be glad to see him back managing customers in his burlesque show and bar tent, the infuriating bastard. But she did love him.

"My father would indeed have insisted on opening tomorrow night," she said. "He would have gone head to head with the police immediately, said we always open on Thursdays, and he would have fed off the energy of that conflict. My father was a powerful man, but he was headstrong and combative and made problems for himself day after day. You all know that to be true. I will offer to delay opening, but I will *campaign* for *no* delay. If we co-operate with the police, they will co-operate with us, I'm sure."

Further rumblings. They were coming to respect her more every year, but it was an exhaustingly slow process.

"Now I'm sure the police and at least some concerned citizens will be here soon. Let's help them. Organize yourselves into groups of two or three and start thinking about which direction you can go in search. If we're already out looking when the police get here, we'll immediately earn some favor. So go! Maybe concentrate on the woods and the river, as those are nearest to us."

She stepped down off the trailer, officially ending the meeting. She was a tall woman, with a flood of shining auburn hair that made her impossible to miss in a crowd, but everyone knew that when she stepped down, the meeting was over. The ride hands and stall holders, mechanics, roustabouts and security guards, everyone milled around chatting, gathering into small groups, then slowly drifted away.

John Barrow approached as the crowd thinned, his face serious. Saul Fallon and Sarah Carter followed, Sarah in her diaphanous Madame O'Reilly fortune-teller garb, jingling with rings and bangles, her tumbling blonde hair under a silk scarf of reds and greens. Fallon's tall frame, made only more impressive as he walked alongside Barrow, was stiff with annoyance, his dark blue mechanic's overalls clean and pressed. But he was no mechanic, no roustabout. His ridiculous sideshow brought in a decent amount of coin, but never enough to justify the man's perception of his own importance. He had dark eyes and dark hair, perpetually pale skin, his brow always drawn in a scowl. Ashley lifted her chin as the trio approached.

"You shouldn't kowtow to the police before they even get here," Fallon said.

John Barrow rolled his eyes, gave Ashley another wink that Fallon was too high above to see. "I agree with Ashley on this," he said.

Fallon scoffed. "Of course you do. You were a toady to her father and now you're a toady to her."

"Fuck you, Saul, you barely knew her father and you certainly don't know me."

"Enough!" Ashley snapped. "I won't have you all sniping at each other, not now. Not today. I've made my decision. If we delay opening, so be it. But I'm confident it won't come to that." She stared them down, wondering what it was they really wanted.

Saul Fallon and John Barrow exchanged a glance. Barrow raised his hand and Fallon reached out to bump knuckles with him. Ashley nodded once, pleased. She waited expectantly.

"It's some of the families," Sarah Carter said eventually.

"What about them?"

"There are a lot of kids among us, and the families want assurance their kids are safe."

Ashley blew out an exasperated sigh. "What the fuck am I supposed to do about that? They're as safe as they are anywhere else. Who knows what happened to those girls, they probably just ran off for a prank and they'll be back any time wondering why they're in trouble."

"We know that," Saul said. "But what are you going to tell the families to put them at ease?"

Ashley shook her head. "Nothing. I'm not buying into any fear or superstitious nonsense."

"You know the stories," Barrow said. "When the carnival comes to town and children go missing, it's the fey folk among us that are to blame."

"They'll be no children left by Sunday," Sarah said in her best Madame O'Reilly brogue.

Ashley laughed. "Kiss my ass, all of you. Let the families talk among themselves, but don't feed the paranoia. I meant what I said, let's just help the town look and see how this all pans out."

She looked up over them and winced as two police officers came walking along the still midway. She nodded, the others turning to see. "Here we go," she said quietly.

The man in front wore the Sheriff's badge, well over six feet of burly muscular ex-jock by the look of him. He had a rugged handsomeness to him, but a no-nonsense look in his eyes. She remembered him from previous years, but had never had cause to interact. Until now. Beside him walked a tall, thin deputy, couldn't be more than mid-twenties, an arrogant scowl twisting his mouth. Ashley, Barrow, Fallon, and Sarah walked to meet them halfway along the midway.

The Sheriff gestured back over his shoulder at the crew dispersing out of the carnival in every direction. "They told me you're in charge," he said to Saul Fallon. "Ashley Strong?"

Ashley laughed, shook her head. "I'm Ashley Strong."

The Sheriff turned a surprised look to her. "Oh, sorry. They said the tall one and I thought..."

"You assumed a man. They did that on purpose. It's fine, I get it all the time." She reached out a hand. "Good to meet you, Sheriff."

"Holtz," he said, shaking her hand. His palm was warm and calloused. "This here is Deputy Janssen." The young man gave a curt nod. "So you run this outfit?"

"I do. You're here about the missing girls." Cut to the chase, she had no time for small talk.

"That's right. You know about that already?"

Ashley smiled. "You know carnie folk. Gossip is our life blood." She pointed a finger randomly left and right. "That's where they're all going, teamed up to go and search. We want to help."

"Mighty kind of you. I'm sorry to sound clichéd, but I have to ask. You know anything about the missing girls?"

"Nope, sorry. We know from town gossip that two thirteen year-old girls went missing after school yesterday and haven't shown up yet. Understandable that everyone is concerned. So we're happy to help with the search. You have anywhere you'd like us to concentrate?"

Holt took off his hat, squinted around in the bright morning sun. The carnival stood on open fields on the north side of town, just over a mile from the small town center. The highway in and out ran up the west side of town the across between the last houses and the carnival, before turning north again on the east side of the dense forest. The Sallow River ran down that side of the forest, under the highway then past the east side of town, curving west then south again, the wide bend of water giving the town nestled there its name. Sun glittered off the river through some trees a couple of hundred yards from where they stood, the woods thickening the further north they looked.

Holtz sighed. "Honestly, they could be anywhere. We have a small town here, but a lot of country."

"I suggested my people concentrate on the woods and the river," Ashley said, gesturing vaguely north and east. "Seemed most likely given where we are. The locals will no doubt concentrate their searches in town and on properties."

"Yep, and the surrounding farmland."

"So anything else you'd like us to do? Like I said, we want to help."

Holtz put his hat back on. "Nothing I can think of. You definitely haven't seen two girls that match the description? They didn't come around here to watch you guys set up, maybe? Any of your people see them?"

"No, sorry. We had a meeting this morning and that's the first thing I asked, if any of my crew had seen any kids around. They all said no. If anyone sees anything, they'll tell me and I'll tell you, Sheriff."

"Okay. Thank you."

Ashley took a deep breath. "So we're supposed to open tomorrow. We always open Thursday night. You want us to delay that?"

Holtz smiled. "That's kind of you to offer, but I'm guessing it would cost you all a pretty sum."

Ashley nodded. "We do run on a tight budget. We could do without losing an opening night's coin if you think people would still come."

Holtz barked a harsh laugh. "There are plenty of people in town who don't care about two missing girls and will gladly come to ride the Ferris wheel and the bumper cars, and eat corn dogs and cotton candy. And you know how it is, people travel from miles around when you guys roll in. Besides, I hope we've found the girls before then anyway. You go right ahead."

Ashley breathed an internal sigh of relief, caught Barrow and Fallon's soft smiles. "Thank you, Sir."

"We'll be on our way." Holtz handed her a card. "Call me with anything you think is worthwhile, however vague."

"Will do."

Another patrol car pulled up a little way outside the arching sign and two deputies climbed out. A short, black woman and an older guy, a little overweight, his blond hair balding. They waved and stood waiting by the vehicle. Holtz shifted a little uncomfortably. "Now, listen, I mean no offense by this, but I'd like for my deputies to search through your stalls and rides and trailers. You can refuse and I'll need warrants, but that would be mighty inconvenient for us all."

Ashley opened her mouth, outrage showing on her face, but Holtz quickly carried on. "Not that I think the girls are, you know, held here or anything. Just in case they're hiding out somewhere."

Ashley drew a long breath to calm herself. "My people have already searched their places, Sheriff."

He shrugged. "Even still. It's procedure, I'm afraid."

Ashley pursed her lips, thinking. There was nothing she could do about it, not really. And she could trust her people to not have anything incriminating, couldn't she? She hoped so. "All right. But I want to be with them the whole time."

"Wait a minute!" Fallon's face was tight with rage. "You can't do that. That's against your own law."

Holtz shook his head. "It's not. I could get warrants."

"You'll have to get one if you want access to my place."

Ashley sighed. "Saul, shut the fuck up. What do you have to hide?"

He turned his fury to her and she raised one eyebrow, refusing to be cowed by him.

"That's not the point!" he said.

"So what is the point? You just want to be difficult?"

He glowered.

"We need to help any way we can, Saul. And we need to open on time."

"Then I'm gonna be there too."

"For your place, sure." Ashley tried not to let her relief show too clearly. She had wondered if Fallon would really dig his heels in and was thankful he hadn't. "Let's get underway," she said to Holtz.

"Absolutely, ma'am. I appreciate your help. The woman there is Deputy Baker, and the other one is Deputy Taylor. I'll let them know you're ready for them." He tipped his hat and turned away.

Deputy Janssen gave them a sneer as the two police officers turned and headed back down the midway.

"Nasty little shit, that young one," Barrow said, watching the deputy's narrow back retreat.

Ashley nodded. "The sheriff seems like a decent guy, but that young one is full of piss and vinegar. Thinks he's some kind of hot shit because he wears a badge. We'll have to watch him; he'll want to make trouble for us."

Saul Fallon stared after them, his eyes narrowed in thought.

"You don't start anything with him," Ashley said, slapping Fallon's arm.

"I won't." He walked away without looking at her and Ashley grit her teeth. Fallon was a good ally and he'd been around a while, but he could be a troublemaker too.

"I'll try to watch them," Barrow said, guessing her thoughts.

"Thanks."

"Folks'll be mad to hear the police were poking through their stuff."

Ashley sighed. She was mad about it herself. Her crew had every right to be as well. "We'll just assure them it's routine and nothing happened. Because nothing will happen, right?" She glanced down at Barrow. "No one has anything tucked away the police shouldn't find, do they?"

Barrow smiled. "I don't expect so. But I'll go and talk to the families still here, make sure people are aware."

"Thanks, John."

He left, leaving Ashley and Sarah Carter standing alone in the deserted carnival midway.

"You want to use your amazing powers of second sight and tell me where those girls are?" Ashley asked.

Sarah laughed, gave Ashley's hand a squeeze. "It'll be okay, one way or another."

Ashley laughed too. "That your psychic opinion or your hope? It bothers me we're here for two weeks. Anywhere else, we'd be gone in a few days. We can't afford trouble on this pitch, we're in the hole for a lot of money to Wilson for this land."

Sarah nodded and headed to her sideshow trailer off the midway, a painted up gypsy wagon that was her home and work all rolled into one.

Ashley watched her go then stood alone, lips pursed. She just wanted a peaceful and happy carnival, folks enjoying themselves, as few fights and crimes as possible. It didn't seem too much to ask, but there was always some drama or another. "Come on, girls," she said quietly. "Stop being little shits and go home." She walked to the main gate to meet the deputies.

4

CALEB DID HIS best to seem friendly with Tricia in the car driving out to the carnival. His chest was tight from so much interaction. He consoled himself with the knowledge that sooner or later he'd be back in his rooms under the school's hall, alone in the peace and quiet. He'd long ago learned he could correct his course with some time on his own. He realized Tricia was talking. She talked incessantly.

"I'm sorry, pardon?"

"I said, here we are."

Caleb looked up from his lap, saw they'd followed the highway the mile or so from the last of the town's gathered houses, past a few farms. Ahead of them the Sallow River glittered in the mid-morning sun as it emerged from the thick woods to the north of town and passed by on the eastern fringes. To their left were rolling fields, the biggest of them now home to the sprawling Strong's Traveling Carnival. Beyond the carnival, the woods stretched away, marching up the shallow rise of hill towards Sallow Lake somewhere deep in the hills and trees to the northeast, before mountains rose up even further away.

The carnival was a riot of color, bright wagons of food and trinkets along the midway, big circular rides covered in lights of every shade surrounding them, the giant eye of the Ferris wheel staring down over it all from the far side, right next to the river. But it was all still and dim. Caleb imagined it later that night, lights flashing, music blaring, thick crowds of townsfolk cramming the midway and screaming on the rides. He shuddered at the thought.

"You okay?" Tricia asked, looking over at him with concerned eyes as she pulled up in the field beside the carnival reserved for parking, not far from the brightly colored arching sign over the main gate. The only other cars were two police cruisers. Along the near side of the carnival they saw the all the workings, generators and portable toilets, cables and hoses. To the far side, right between where the fields ended and the woods started, stood several rows of carnie trailers. But the whole place seemed strangely deserted.

"I'm fine," Caleb said. "Don't like crowds."

"There are no crowds yet."

"I'm just imagining them."

Tricia gave a soft laugh, not unfriendly. She briefly patted his knee, then quickly drew her hand away. "It's okay."

Caleb caught a glimpse of her eyes, saw absolute sincerity there. He was often disappointed by the contradictory nature of adults, unlike the kids who were so open with their feelings and emotions. Adults hid, ducked and dived. But Tricia Brent, at least at this particular moment, was completely unguarded. "Thanks," he said, unsure of how else to respond.

"Come on." Tricia unbuckled her seat belt and opened her door. "Let's see what's what."

As they climbed from the car into the heat of the day, Sheriff Holtz and Deputy Janssen emerged from the main gate, and the town's two other deputies went the other way, heading in.

"What are you two doing here?" Holtz asked.

"We weren't sure where else to look," Tricia said. "So we thought maybe we'd come here."

"The carnies are helping," Holtz said. "Combing the woods, looking around the river and such. I guess you could help them."

"Okay."

"We're still watching you," Janssen said, pointing at Caleb.

Caleb chose to ignore him, watched the grass at his feet.

"Cut it out, Kurt," Holtz said.

"You leave him alone," Tricia said, stepping up closer to Janssen.

Caleb winced, she seemed so short against the deputy's tall leanness, tiny next to Holtz's broad bulk. The deputy must be only a couple of inches shorter than Holtz's hulking frame. She was a fiery woman.

"Or what?" Janssen said, looking down at her with his lip curled up.

Tricia reached up and slapped his shoulder. "I used to wipe the snot from your nose when you a damn baby, Kurt Janssen," she said. "I pulled you from the town pool when I was a life-saver there and you nearly drowned. Don't you act like some big shit around me!"

Kurt smirked, looked from his arm to Tricia. "I should run you in for assaulting a Sheriff's Deputy."

Holtz turned Janssen by his shoulder, pushed him towards the cruiser. "Shut up, Kurt." He looked back to Caleb and Tricia. "Thank you both for your help."

Without waiting for a reply he got in the cruiser and pulled away. As they drove by, Janssen looked out through the passenger window. His eyes were dark with anger. He pointed his index and middle finger towards those angry eyes, then stabbed them at Caleb and Tricia, then the car was gone.

Tricia sighed. "He is a nasty young man."

"You really used to wipe his nose?" Caleb asked.

"Yes, I did. Back in the day I worked at the child care center. And I was a life-saver at the pool for a while too. His mama and I are still good friends. But you know what, he's always been a vicious little shit. You're not supposed to dislike children, but I never liked him."

Caleb nodded. "I don't like him either."

"In all honesty, I don't think anyone really does and that's part of his problem. It's a cycle, you know? If he was nicer to people, then people might be nicer to him."

Caleb watched the last glimpse of the cruiser as it headed back towards town. "I guess if he's not a nice person, he can't be nice to people."

Tricia looked at him, eyebrows knitted together. "I guess not. Come on, let's go inside."

As they went in under the big sign they saw a woman at the end of the midway, great curls of bright red hair falling over her shoulders, talking to the two deputies. She wore denim dungarees with a white tee-shirt underneath, and scuffed black worker's boots. She was turning away as they entered, but stopped when she saw them and started back along, the deputies trailing her. They met halfway down the midway, a hot dog wagon on one side of them and a hoopla stall the other.

"Help you?" the woman asked. Then she frowned. "Tricia, right? Good to see you again."

"You too, Ashley. This is Caleb Jackson."

"Hi."

She shook both their hands, frowned slightly as Caleb couldn't meet her eye, but he was used to that. He'd practiced looking at people more directly, but never kept it up. Maybe he should try harder.

"We wanted to help look for the missing girls," Tricia said. "Thought we might come out here."

"To help us look or because you thought the girls might be here?" Ashley Strong's eyes were hard, her face set. She jabbed a thumb over her shoulders. "I have to accompany these two through all our stuff for the same reason."

Caleb realized that perhaps they should have thought this through more deeply. He felt a weight of guilt descend on his shoulders. He was only too familiar with people making judgments based on assumptions and it seemed he and Tricia had done exactly that.

Tricia smiled, laughed a little self-consciously. "I think everyone is a bit on edge and you guys arrived the same day the girls went missing. I'm sorry. But it's possible they came out here to watch you set up. The carnival is about the most interesting thing that ever happens around here."

"And you thought we'd show up and immediately abduct two curious teenagers?"

Tricia looked away, shook her head. "Honestly, I don't know what I was thinking. Just maybe they're hiding out here? A little over a year ago, my son disappeared. He was only twelve and we'll never give up hope, but this is all too close to home. I just need to do something." She looked up, met Strong's eyes. "You don't have kids do you?"

"No."

They fell to an uncomfortable silence, tension heavy in the air. A single tear breached Tricia's eye and rolled slowly over her cheek. Caleb watched in fascination as it reflected golden with the sunshine. The day was warming into a real scorcher.

Strong sighed, used one finger to wipe away Tricia's tear. "We have a lot of kids here, though. A lot of the rides and stalls are run by families, extended families. We've got one group of about sixteen people, all related somehow, but I lose track. Siblings and cousins, aunts and uncles, all that stuff. We've got more than twenty kids in their teen years or younger right now, down to babes still on the tit."

"And you all travel together, setting up and packing up, town after town." Tricia smiled. "That's the same as family."

"That's how it works. One big family, whether we're actually related or not. I get the trauma of missing kids, really."

"We really need to get on," Deputy Baker said.

"Hi, Val," Tricia said. "Sorry to interrupt you guys."

"It's okay. Won't take long, I'm sure, then we can all get on with searching elsewhere."

Ashley glanced up and sighed. "Shit."

Several more cars arrived in the parking field, a variety of locals, some carrying shotguns and rifles, poured out. Caleb wondered if it had taken them this long to arrive because they were busy arranging their posse and collecting their guns. It made him tense.

"Okay, everyone relax," Deputy Baker said. "Let's all just talk."

Ashley put two fingers in her mouth and gave a quick, sharp whistle. As the locals approached through the main gate, faces stern, a handful of burly guys and a couple of determined-looking women appeared from the trailers at the back of the site. One of the women carried a baby that couldn't be more than six months old. At least a dozen more kids of varying ages hung around near the trailers, moving left and right for a better view. Caleb felt suddenly sandwiched between the carnies on one side and the town posse on the other, with Ashley and Tricia his only allies. And the deputies, he supposed. Or perhaps only Tricia was an ally, because surely Ashley would side with her people and he expected the deputies would do all they could to remain neutral. Though at least they were armed. This was way more people than he liked to be around.

Ashley stepped forward to meet the approaching crowd. Caleb estimated there were at least twenty people.

"Good morning, folks," Ashley called out. "We heard about your missing girls. Most of my crew are already out looking."

"What do you know about it?" a large man in a red checked shirt said, stepping forward with a rifle held none too casually across his chest. Caleb vaguely recognized him, remembered the thick black beard. Barclay or Bentley or something like that, a father of a couple of the kids in school.

"We don't want any trouble here," Deputy Baker said loudly, but Caleb saw the concern in her face, along with nerves, adrenaline, determination. She was scared and he didn't like that. He had to look away. And he noticed the other deputy had moved back, offering his partner no support. He exuded nothing but weakness and something close to terror.

"Now everyone calm down," Tricia said before anyone else could speak. "We've been talking to Ashley here and she's been nothing but helpful."

"How do they know about the girls?" a woman called out.

"Some of my crew went into town early this morning for breakfast and overheard talk in the diner," Ashley said. "We immediately met about it and they've gone out looking."

Caleb glanced around, wondering if the tension he felt was genuine or not. He could never tell if adults were actually upset or if he was simply concerned about being in a crowd. But all of this felt like a genuine powder keg.

Two men from Ashley's crew had stepped up next to her. On one side a man whose dark skin glistened with sweat over bulging muscles, a grey tee-shirt stretched tight over huge arms. His head was bald and shining, thick legs clad in black jeans. On the other side of Ashley stood a tall man in clean, dark blue mechanic's overalls, his black hair and eyes at odds with skin like marble. Caleb frowned, further discomforted. There was something about the pale man that put his teeth on edge. Something predatory in the fellow's hard gaze. His was a face unlike anything Caleb had ever seen before.

Ashley put a hand to each of their chests and held them back while she stepped forward again. "Saul, Daniel, it's okay."

Caleb tried to remember those names. Daniel, the bald one, seemed like a strong but normal guy. Saul on the other hand, was the one making Caleb's stomach tight. And his headache worse. Next to them a small man appeared from one side of the midway. Caleb knew it was impolite to call them midgets, he wasn't sure about dwarf, but couldn't remember what the right term was. The man had a hard expression on his craggy face. Caleb looked down at the grass, the information overload headache making him wince.

"Tell us what you know," the big bearded local said.

Saul hissed quietly. From the corner of his eye, Caleb saw Daniel tense, the other carnies seeming to strain forward like dogs on leashes, waiting for Ashley to release them with a word. Tricia stepped closer to Caleb and held onto his arm. He gritted his teeth against the contact, but assumed she needed the comfort of it, so he bore it as best he could.

Ashley stepped forward again, within a yard of the bristling locals. "Honestly, that's all we know. My guys heard in the diner that two girls have gone missing since last night and the town is out looking. So I sent my people out too. Sheriff Holtz was just here and I told him the same thing. And these two deputies are just about to search all our tents and vans."

"Not all o' yours are out lookin'!" someone yelled, no doubt referring to the gathered roustabouts and others behind Ashley.

"And neither are yours while we stand here jawing," Ashley said, seeming to stand a little taller, a little belligerent.

Another ripple of tension swept through the group, crackling in the quickly warming summer air.

"You all need to get back in your cars and help search elsewhere," Deputy Baker said. "Or I'll start running you in for obstruction because me and Clive Taylor here are supposed to be doing our damn job!"

"And how good are either of you at your damn job?" someone yelled.

Other voices rose, some angry, some mocking. Caleb sensed the tension drawing tighter still. He wanted to be anywhere but right here.

A pick-up truck came roaring right through the main gate and up the midway, trailing a cloud of dust. Caleb squinted, saw Old Man Wilson behind the wheel. The truck skidded to a stop and Wilson jumped out.

"Put your damn guns down!" he yelled.

The gathered locals wavered, looked around at each other like guilty children. Deputy Baker looked positively relieved. Wilson was the kind of old resident who seemed a part of the very land Sallow Bend was carved from, like he'd been around forever, though most guessed him to be in his eighties. He moved and worked like a man half that age and commanded immediate respect. His pale blue eyes were piercing over a fall of clean white beard that reached halfway down his chest. Caleb didn't know the man's first name, wasn't sure anyone did, but everyone knew Old Man Wilson and respected him.

"These carnies are good folk!" Wilson said loudly, striding into the narrow space between Ashley and the rest. "I rent them my land for two whole weeks every year, and all of you enjoy the carnival. Don't be blundering out here like some kind of goddamned lynch mob!"

"I was just explaining that most of my crew are out looking," Ashley said.

"And Ashley is going to accompany us on a search of her carnival right as soon as you lot get out of here," Baker said.

Wilson nodded, patted Ashley's shoulder. His legs were a little bandy, but he seemed to stand tall nonetheless even though he gave away a couple of inches to carnival owner. "Thank you." He turned back to face the unsettled crowd. "Now you all get going too. Get out into the woods up there, get across the river and check right to the end of my east paddocks. There are creeks and ponds out that way and the ground can get boggy, even in summer. Instead of standing here being aggravating, go and find those girls!"

He stood scowling, waiting for a challenge.

"How do we know those poor girls aren't in here somewhere?" a voice called from the back, brave with anonymity.

As Wilson drew breath to speak, Ashley put a hand on his arm. "The police are right here!" she said. "They're going to search through everything, from the Haunted House to the Cotton Candy machine, and all our trailers. And I'm glad of it."

"So make yourselves useful," Wilson said. "Get on, all of you!"

The crowd reluctantly dispersed, muttered curses and accusations floating about on the summer breeze. Some trudged in the direction of Sallow River, others back to their vehicles to drive the highway home into Sallow Bend. The tension drained away like a plug had been pulled. Caleb realized he was trembling.

"Sorry about that," Wilson said to Ashley.

"Thank you for coming in. It's much better than me trying to convince them we want to help."

"They really going to search our trailers?" Daniel asked, clenching his fists at his sides, making his big arm and chest muscles pump.

Ashley nodded. "Don't be angry about it. It's routine."

Daniel growled in annoyance and strode off towards the back of the site, the little man jogging behind to keep up. The other gathered crew drifted off slowly, shooing children back with them.

"You cops better not touch my display," Saul said to the deputies.

Ashley rounded on him. Caleb was impressed with her strength of character. "Or what, Saul?"

The pale man grunted and walked away, leaving only Caleb and Tricia with Ashley and Wilson and the two deputies in the once again deserted midway. They all looked uncomfortably at each other for a moment, then Wilson sniffed.

"I'm heading back to my farm, keep searching the sheds."

He climbed back into his battered and rusty pick-up, beeped the horn twice, and reversed at breakneck speed straight back through the main gate. He bootlegged on the grass outside and roared away.

"Well, I guess things here are pretty well covered," Tricia said. She looked at Caleb. "Where should we go to search?"

Caleb swallowed, unsure how to respond. Old Man Wilson owned most of the land north of Sallow Bend and a good part of the forest too. His homestead was on the western end of the land and his property extended a good mile east of the Sallow River. "If Wilson is checking at home and that crowd are all around here and the river, maybe we can check Wilson's land between his homestead and the carnival?"

Tricia nodded, apparently delighted with the suggestion. "We'll see you tomorrow night for the opening if not before," she said to Ashely, and Caleb winced. The last place he wanted to be was at the carnival in full swing. She shouldn't speak for him, but then he was in no way obliged to do anything she said.

"Maybe now we can get on?" Deputy Baker said to Ashley.

Ashley gave a rueful smile. "Sure."

Tricia took Caleb's arm and drew him away. "Thank you for that suggestion," she said once they were out of earshot. "Smart thinking to get us away from the carnival. I felt terrible seeing the amount of distrust shown back there."

Caleb shrugged. It made sense to suspect the carnival, especially given the timing of events, but he recognized the discomfort of suspicion only too well. And people certainly were on edge. He'd be glad to search through open land for a few hours, ostensibly on his own. Maybe he could search far enough away from Tricia that she wouldn't be able to talk to him, for a little while at least.

5

FREDDIE HOLTZ PINCHED the bridge of his nose, a headache coming on, as Mrs. Tokugawa sobbed. Janssen sat stiffly opposite, uncomfortable in the floral armchair. The Tokugawa house was immaculate, a neat three bedroom on the south side of Sallow Bend. Mr. Tokugawa had gone out with the search parties, along with Mr. Finlay from next door. Mrs. Finlay sat with her arm around her friend and neighbor, both mothers remaining home in the hope their daughters would return, simply come tumbling through the door laughing and playing.

But Holtz had a bad feeling about this. It was too similar to a little less than a year ago when Toby Brent went missing, and that kid had never been found. Seeing Tricia before at the carnival had brought those memories back. Most of the town seemed to agree some itinerant had abducted Toby. Easier to think that than consider the possibility it might have been someone local. But now both Suki Tokugawa and Clare Finlay had vanished. It was happening again and, in a town as small as his, Holtz feared what kind of vigilantism it might stir up. He didn't want to have to call in city police, but if tensions rose, maybe he'd have to.

Finlay's eyes were red and puffy, but Tokugawa, it seemed, would never stop crying. Holtz cleared his throat. "I'm sorry, ladies, I can't imagine how hard this is for you both. But please can you answer some more questions?"

Mrs Tokugawa sat up suddenly, pinned him with her glare, tears still rolling. "We already answered your questions. We told you everything. Why aren't you out looking?"

"Lots of people are looking, ma'am. And we'll be back out there as soon as you can tell me a couple of things."

Suki's older sister, Akiko, came into the lounge room carrying a tray of cookies and freshly brewed coffee. She offered them around, Holtz and Janssen took a cup each simply to seem polite. Even in times like this, the niceties of society have to be observed, Holtz thought. Maybe they didn't have much else to do. He wondered if it might have been better to send Akiko along to school, but chose not to say anything about that.

"Mrs. Tokugawa, Mrs Finlay, did either of your girls say anything about the carnival coming into town yesterday?" he asked.

"They were excited for it," Mrs Finlay said. "All the kids are. Hell, most of the adults too."

"They say anything about going along? Watching them set up, anything like that?"

"Not to me. Hanae?" she asked the other girl's mother.

Hanae Tokugawa shook her head. "We both told our children the same thing. They could go to the opening night tomorrow, everyone wants to see the fireworks. But only for an hour, then they were to come home, it's a school night."

"So no reason they would have gone last night?" Holtz pressed.

"For what?" Shelly Finlay asked. "Unless some carnie met them in town? Promised them something?"

"Oh god, no!" Hanae said, devolving into sobs again. "Those people could have any kind of drugs, they could be rapists!"

"Now calm down!" Holtz said, trying to contain his anger. He didn't trust the carnie folk any more than the next guy, but the burgeoning threat of hysteria had him on edge. "I've been out there and talked to the owner. My deputies are searching every sideshow and trailer right now. The carnies are being very helpful."

"I told Clare she couldn't go tomorrow night," Shelly Finlay said quietly.

"What's that?"

Shelly sat up straighter. "Clare and I, and her father, had an argument the night before last about her grades. We said that she couldn't go to the opening of the carnival because she needed to work hard until the end of school. She could go on Friday night."

Hanae Tokugawa looked at her friend. "I thought we agreed on one hour tomorrow? For the fireworks."

"We did, and I'm sorry. I was going to tell you, but it slipped my mind."

"So wait a minute," Holtz said. "The girls thought they were going to the carnival tomorrow night, but then you changed your mind?"

"That's right. Clare needs to pick up her grades. You have to be firm with children, Sheriff Holtz. And Clare needs to set a better example for her little brother. Todd will be in high school soon enough."

"Fair enough," Holtz agreed. "So then yesterday the girls went to school and Clare would have told Suki that she wasn't allowed to go the carnival tomorrow."

"I suppose so."

"So maybe they did go last night anyway. Is that something Clare might do? Just to be, you know, contrary?"

Hanae nodded quietly and Shelly Finlay frowned. "Yes," she said quietly. "It's possible."

"Both of our girls would do something like that," Hanae Tokugawa said, sniffing wetly. "They're both willful."

"But *why* would they do that?" Janssen asked. "The carnival was only setting up yesterday, it wasn't open."

"Just to score points," Holtz said, looking to the mothers for confirmation.

"It's possible," Shelly Finlay said.

Freddie Holtz's phone rang, Val Baker written across the screen. "Excuse me." Holtz stepped out into the hall to answer.

His deputy's voice came through. "Sheriff, you got a moment?"

"Yeah, go on." He pictured her standing in the hot sun of the midway, short and slightly overweight, but powerful and well-respected. She faced a lot of prejudice among some of the older country folk for her dark skin and what they called "unnecessary sassiness", whatever the hell that meant, but she was a good cop. She was twice the deputy Janssen was, which was why Holtz always kept Janssen with him and let Val Baker run her own game, or cruise with Clive Taylor when Holtz had no excuse to keep Clive in the station.

"We were searching the carnival, nearly finished, actually."

"And?"

"And nothing so far, I think they're clean. But I just got a call from a couple of people searching the woods out near where the carnival set up. They found a grey cardigan hung up on a tree about a hundred yards in. About the right size for one of the girls."

Holtz swallowed. Was he more frightened of finding them or never seeing them again? Truth be told, he was most frightened of finding their bodies. Missing like Toby Brent was better than dead. Better for him and the department anyway, if not for the families. "Can you send me a photo?"

"Right away, Sheriff. They sent me a pic so I'll forward it to you."

"Thanks. And finish there, make sure."

"Will do."

He hung up and went back into the lounge. All eyes turned expectantly to him. As he sat down his phone beeped and the photo came up on the screen. A small, lightly knitted gray cardigan hung up on a low branch in among the gloom of some trees. He took a deep breath, turned the phone towards the mothers. "This familiar?"

Hanae Tokugawa howled and buried her face in her hands.

"It's Suki's," Shelly Finlay said, grim-faced. "What does that mean?"

"It means nothing more than Suki dropped her cardigan," Holtz said. "But now maybe we have a smaller area to search. We'll be going right away. Stay strong, you two. We'll find your girls."

He lead Janssen from the house and back out to the cruiser, wishing he believed his own words.

6

CALEB AND TRICIA had traipsed for nearly an hour through Old Man Wilson's fields, doing their best to ignore the curious cattle. The ground was dry in the summer heat, grass well cropped by the stock. They could see right across to the homestead, on a slight rise far to the west. The ramshackle house and surrounding sheds, vehicles, front end loader, and other farm machinery toy-like through the heat haze. Caleb was struck by the futility of their task, the great swathes of land, the vastness of nature when measured up against the tiny body of a thirteen year-old girl. Even against two of them.

What chance did any of them have of stumbling across the children? He supposed enough time and determination would pay out eventually if the girls were somewhere to be found, but that didn't count for abduction, which was another real possibility. He shrugged. He'd do his bit. Anything else was beyond his power.

Tricia had thankfully spent most of the time far enough from him that casual conversation was impossible, so he had managed to settle down a bit from the stress of the big crowd and the confrontation in the midway, his headache easing. Then they had run out of field to walk through and found themselves on the edge of the woods bordering Wilson's farm. To the east of them, about a mile distant out of sight behind undulations in the ground, the carnival stood. West was the homestead, behind them to the south the highway ran straight across about half a mile away. And to the north, woods, thick and old, getting deeper as they climbed the low slopes into the foothills. The forest continued, untamed, for several miles right up to where the distant mountains began. Caleb estimated that a forced hike directly north would take at least a full day to reach the mountains, probably more. He was tempted to make that hike now, except he was thoroughly unprepared for camping.

When he'd come to Sallow Bend it was for the small town peace and quiet. He knew that brought with it a certain lack of privacy, small town gossip, but when the live-in janitor and security position at the school came up days after he arrived, he figured it was fate. So far it had worked out pretty well. A decent percentage of the townsfolk were suspicious of him, but he accepted that. The vast majority were unconcerned, some even friendly. But most left him alone, and that was the most important thing. That's all he wanted. He hoped Suki and Clare turned up soon, so everything could go back to the calm boredom he preferred. Simple work and good books.

"We'll head into the woods for an hour or so," Tricia had said. "Then we'll head back to get some lunch, okay?"

He'd had no choice but to agree, so now they walked side by side through the trees, Tricia chatting casually about the pattern of bark or the color of leaves. It seemed to Caleb that Tricia used talk for security, wore words as armor, as though she were terrified to be alone with her own mind. Which was, he ruefully realized, the exact opposite of his own default preference.

The forest was gloomy, but the summer sun regularly pierced the thick canopy, lancing down to the leaf litter in bright shards alive with dust motes and floating pollen. Low, twisting vines and dark green ground cover swarmed over thick roots that made walking a treacherous effort if he stopped paying attention.

"Don't you think?" Tricia said, raising her voice.

He realized she'd asked him something directly. "I'm sorry, what?"

She laughed. "Caleb Jackson, you spend most of your life paying no attention to anything!"

He resented that. He wasn't paying attention to her, sure. But he was vibrantly aware of everything else. "Sorry."

"I was saying, it would be so easy to get lost in here. So easy to get turned around. You think that's what happened to Clare and Suki?"

"I guess it could be. They wouldn't come here though, would they? They wouldn't be allowed."

Tricia gave him a strange look, amusement and disbelief. "Of course they're not allowed. None of the kids are *allowed* in here, we all tell our children to stay away. How easy it is to get lost. But they all come anyway. I did."

"You did?"

"Of course! Every kid who grows up in Sallow Bend spends hours in these woods. This coming summer holiday, kids will spend most of their time either at the river or off among the trees playing crazy games, climbing and leaping, hurting themselves." She grinned. "Kissing and cuddling!"

Caleb let out a nervous, "Ha!", unsure how else to respond. Was all that okay or not? She said they weren't allowed, yet seemed to tacitly approve of the kids defying their parents.

Tricia's face grew serious again. "But we never went far, you know. Not too deep. Maybe Clare and Suki did. There are a lot of stories."

"What kind of stories?"

A crashing in the trees distracted them and a group of four men appeared through the thick, dark trunks. Caleb jumped, but immediately recognized a couple as fathers of some kids at school. Perhaps they all were, more searchers.

"Hey, Trish!" one said, and gave Tricia a rough hug. He was a large man, strong-looking, with a guileless, open face under a mop of dark curls. Caleb thought he was one of those rare adults who tended to present exactly as he was, no mask, no façade. The only kind of adult Caleb could ever seem to bear the company of for long, and certainly the rarest. He realized the same applied to Tricia, despite her propensity for chatter.

"Burt," she said. "Nice that you're searching too."

"Of course. You know Tony, Garret, and Steve?"

"Yes, yes. Hi everyone. You boys know Caleb, the school janitor."

The men all gave Caleb the kind of look up and down he was used to. He saw every version of the town's reaction to him in those four faces. Burt himself was open and smiling. "Hey, Caleb." He shook hands, too firm, too vigorous, but Caleb recognized it as the kind that wasn't unfriendly, just masculine.

Of the other three men, Tony, tall and rangy with a stubbled face and a bright red trucker's cap, frowned. Garret, a squat, robust-looking fellow with dark green eyes too close together, shook his head as though he didn't like something. And Steve, skinny, with not much chin and a thick, bushy moustache, limbs all elbows and knees as he walked, simply smirked. Caleb was used to the reactions. Frowns, denial and smirks seemed pretty common to him from the men around town. He nodded and looked at the forest floor, the other three men thankfully not reaching out to shake.

"Where you been looking?" Tricia asked.

Burt jabbed a thumb back over his shoulder, muscles stretching his checked shirt. "We set out early, headed all the way up to Sallow Lake."

"That's got to be an hour's hike," Caleb said, not looking up.

"Yep, about that. There's that old cabin on the lakeshore and we decided to head straight there and check it out. If the girls got turned around in the woods, they might've found the cabin and sheltered there."

"You think they could have got all that way?" Tricia asked.

"We figured no one else would search that far, so we decided to check. But it was a bust, nothing there. Now we're starving and heading back to town for a feed."

Tricia pursed her lips, turned to Caleb. "Maybe we should head back for food too." Before waiting for his answer, she said to Burt, "Mind if we walk with you?"

"No problem."

They turned and struck out, and Caleb winced, finding himself dragged into a crowd once more.

"Creepy ass place, that cabin," Garret said around gum he chewed vigorously.

Burt laughed. "You still going on about that? Just stories, man. We all remember the dares as kids."

"You ever go though? Before?" Garret asked.

Burt laughed. "Course not. We were all too chicken."

"They ain't just stories," Steve said.

"Seriously?" Tony asked.

Steve looked around the group, as if judging them for something. "You gotta not laugh at me, I tell you this."

"No promises not to laugh," Burt said. "But you go ahead. I'm ready to hear whatever it is."

"Well, it's actually my granddaddy's story. He used to own the property one west of Old Man Wilson, so his land bordered these woods too. Course, that was before my daddy sold up and moved into Sallow Bend proper, gave up the farming for fixing cars and trucks."

"And now you own the best repair shop in town," Burt said. "You're not trying to hit us up with some sneaky self-promotion again, are ya?"

Steve laughed. "Nah, just setting the scene. You all bring your vehicles to me already anyway."

"Like we could do anything else!"

Steve snorted a short laugh. "This was way back in '52, when my daddy was just a baby. See, the way my grandaddy told it, there was a slew of missing kids. Like three or four, teenage boys, all disappeared in the space of maybe two weeks."

Tricia caught her breath and Steve faltered. He put a hand briefly to his mouth in realization. "Shit, Trish, I'm sorry. I didn't mean to… you know."

"Is this about missing kids?" Burt asked.

"No, no, not really. Only it was some kids going missing that started events, but in those days strange stuff happened a lot, you know. You want me to not tell it?"

Tricia patted his arm. "It's okay. Go ahead."

"Sure, right. Well, you see, it was a little like this. Because kids were missing, the townsfolk set to searching, and my granddaddy and a couple of his farmhands went into the woods behind his place, searching just like we are now. They didn't find any of the kids, but in their roaming they came across that cabin on the lakeshore. You know, its been there more than a hundred years, maybe two. My granddaddy said it was there back in the 1880s and before.

"Anyway, they're looking and it's getting late, so they decide maybe they'll stay in the cabin overnight, rather than trek back and risk getting lost in the woods if it gets dark. So the three of them, they gather firewood, and they had some rations with them, bread and cheese and shit like that, and a big cut of ham. They set up a fire in that old stone fireplace, we saw it there in the cabin ourselves just a few hours ago."

"We remember," Burt said. "Go on."

Caleb kept his head down, trudging over dry leaves and tree roots that looked ready to snatch an unwary ankle. In all honesty he was glad of Steve's story because it forewent the need for any kind of regular conversation. He could happily spend time among people if one of them simply spun a yarn. That was just like a living book.

"Okay, so they set up a good fire, gathered what they needed, and settled in for the night. But when they unwrapped their food, something was stinking, ungodly-like. That ham was rotten like it had been left in the sun for a week. My granddaddy knew damn well it was fresh, he had cured his own self. It was fresh and good to eat that very morning when they went out. So they opened up the bread and that was stale and hard as rock. The cheese had green mold all over it.

"So of course, they were all a little perturbed by that turn of events and they were all hungry. It was getting dark, but they figured maybe they could go out and shoot something to eat instead. So they traipsed about the lakeshore and into the nearby trees, but there wasn't a living thing to be found. No birds or rabbits, they couldn't even hear the twitterings of birds or anything else. Like there wasn't another living thing but them, for miles around.

"It was getting late, too dark to fish and they had no poles or hooks anyway, so they figured they'd just have to go to bed hungry. They headed back into that cabin and the rotten food was stinking the place out, so they threw it in the lake and all lay down to try to sleep.

"Night fell, dark as pitch outside that cabin and though the fire was burning to give them some light inside, it simply would not warm up. Colder than an old hooker's heart, my granddaddy said. Anyway, they all dozed off eventually."

Caleb looked up as Steve paused in the telling, took in the woods around them. They weren't far from Old Man Wilson's fields again and he wondered what had interrupted the story. Steve was staring up into the branches above them, his neck stretched out under his lack of chin like a chicken's wattle. Caleb noticed the stubble on it reflected a little ginger in the shafts of sunlight, but the man's hair and thick moustache were chestnut brown.

"Go on, man," Tony said, pulling off his cap to swipe a sleeve across the sweat of his brow. The day was heating up, thick and buzzing with insects. "Why'd you stop there?"

Steve shook his head, brought his eyes back to watch where he was going. "The next bit always freaks me out. Scared the shit outta me when I was a kid and granddaddy would tell this story."

"You're a born showman," Burt said with a laugh. "Stop playing it up and just finish the yarn. It's probably all bullshit anyway."

"No it ain't. My granddaddy told it a hundred times that I remember, and I could see in his eyes every word of it was true."

"Well go on then!"

Steve took a deep breath. "Okay. The way my granddaddy told it, as he lay there trying to fall asleep he kept feeling these light touches. Like someone kept dragging a cobweb over his face is how he described it. He kept brushing them away, thinking it was midges in the air or something, and eventually fell asleep. A couple of times as the night got deep, he woke to strange noises. One he said sounded like a distant laugh, like a little girl giggling somewhere out in the woods."

"Probably a damn bird," Garret said.

"He even suggested the same thing himself, but remember they heard no birds, no life at all, when they went looking for it. Another time he heard a scratching, but said it didn't sound like no animal. Sounded more like fingernails dragging slowly across the floor or walls, lazy-like. Just for the sake of it.

"He kept refusing to pay too much mind to the noises, turning over, going back to sleep. Then he was woken by a voice, right in his ear as he tells it. Said he could feel the breath on his skin, smell a rotten stench like the worst breath you can imagine. Like whoever was talking had just dined on a big old plate of that rotten ham. The voice said, and this is the thing that always gave me the worst nightmares, the voice said, 'I can taste you where you lay!' The hell do you think that meant?" Steve paused, looked around the group. He was met with mostly blank stares, no one prepared to suggest an explanation, nor prepared, it seemed, to offer a denial. "What the hell do you suppose that meant?" Steve asked again.

"Was someone there?" Caleb asked.

Steve shook his head. "My granddaddy said he sat right up and felt as though something slipped away from his side, but couldn't see a thing. The fire was dying down, casting moving shadows on the uneven wooden logs of the cabin walls, and he says one of those shadows looked like a woman for a moment, that slipped into a dark corner and was gone."

"What were the other two doing all this time?" Burt asked. "The farmhands you said he had with him."

"Well, right about that point they were all awake. My granddaddy asked them if they seen or heard anything. One of them wouldn't answer, but the other said he heard a woman talking, thought it was dream. 'What did she say?' my granddaddy asked, and the farmhand said, 'She told me she could taste me.' And that's when my granddaddy said maybe they should go home, leave that place behind. But the one farmhand said surely it would be more dangerous in the woods at night and they were certainly all just spooked. The other farmhand, he just stared from one to the other and didn't say a word. So they decided to try to get back to sleep.

"My granddaddy said he must've fallen back asleep despite the cold and the spook, because next thing he was woken up sudden by that farmhand who wouldn't speak. The man had leaped up, screaming like his ass was on fire, and he ran out into the night. The others followed him, saw him vanish into the trees and my granddaddy said it looked like the man's hair had turned bone white. They chased him, called his name, but lost him in the trees. By then they'd both had more than enough and decided to head for home, the dangers of the woods at night be damned."

The small group emerged from the shade of the trees into the bright sunshine at the back of Wilson's land. Caleb was glad of the light and warmth, pleased to be out in the open. They tromped across the uneven grass, heading for the road.

"That it?" Burt asked. "That all that happened?"

"Pretty much. My granddaddy never went near that cabin again, he said. He and the one farmhand made it back okay, getting to his place just before dawn. But they never saw that other fellow again. I once asked for the names and my granddaddy told me the farmhand who was lost that night, he was called Luke Calgary. I looked it up a few years ago, and sure enough there are records of one Luke Calgary going missing the year my granddaddy said it happened." He looked around the group, defying them to say he was lying. "And you were there today. It's one hell of a creepy place, right? And did you hear any birds there? See any game? We couldn't wait to leave again once we saw it empty." No one answered him.

"Were any of the missing children found?" Tricia asked. Caleb noticed her skin was pale despite the exertion of walking.

Steve pursed his lips, shook his head. "Sorry, ma'am. None of 'em were. Not that time."

Tricia just nodded, looked at the ground.

"Not that time?" Caleb asked

Steve shrugged. "Well, Sallow Bend has had a few disappearances over the years, you all know that. A couple of times kids have been found, but not all the time."

Burt put a large hand on Tricia's shoulder. "It's hard to believe we're doing this again. I remember too well the way we all did it for Toby only a year ago. Don't you give up now."

"I won't." Tricia looked at the big man beside her. "But Riley already has."

"Yeah, and much as he and I have been friends since forever, I'm losing faith in that boy. He's gonna lose his job soon."

"Really?"

Burt gave her shoulder another squeeze. "It's only fair to tell you. I've worked with him for years, you know that. I've backed him all I can. But the boss is getting tired of his time off for sickness, when we all know he's drunk."

Tricia sighed. "What the hell will we do without his wage?"

"You tell me and I'll help all I can," Burt said.

"Me too," Steve said. "I've never worked with Riley, but he's always brought your cars to me, and my father before he died. I don't know him well, but you have a reputation in this town, Tricia, and it's well-earned. Tell me if I can help."

"Thank you, Steve."

Caleb noticed that both Garret and Tony were conspicuous by their silence. He glanced over at them and they both studiously watched their boots striding across the grass.

They reached the road where Tricia had parked and two large pick-ups were in a lay-by not much further along. They said their goodbyes and climbed into the car.

"You want to head into town and get some lunch?" Tricia asked.

Caleb thought maybe she wanted the company, but he certainly didn't. He wasn't sure if it would be rude to say no. "Maybe I should get back to school?" he said tentatively. "I can get some lunch there."

"Of course." She stared at the steering wheel for a while, not moving. Then, "You want to come out with me again this afternoon and look somewhere else?" She looked up suddenly, caught his eye. "Please?"

Caleb swallowed his surprise, tried not to let any expression show on his face lest it may be the wrong kind. Her desperation not to be alone was written all over her. After what she'd said about her husband, and the ghost of her missing son stirred up by events and that story, he couldn't blame her. "Sure, okay."

She squeezed his knee, then started the car. "Thank you."

7

SAUL FALLON STALKED through the deserted midway in the dark of night, a fingernail of moon casting a soft silvery glow across the grass, reflecting off metal stanchions between the stalls. He glanced up at the thick swathe of stars, glittering across a cloudless sky. It was shaping up to be a good summer, he could feel that in his bones. A long, hot, happy summer full of people only too pleased to socialize at the carnival instead of work their farms, or visit their families. Except for this debacle with the girls.

The damn woman running this show was giving too much leeway to the law. He was incensed they had gone through his things, through every stall and trailer. Poking around in people's private possessions like every crewmember was already a criminal. Well, they had found nothing and that might have frustrated them, but it was good enough for him. A gang of locals had ended up hanging around, watching like vultures while the two police officers went from one property to the next, apologizing and smiling like it was no big deal. But it was a big deal, this assumption of guilt. Ashley said they had to expect it, people always suspected carnies. Well fuck that, he was sick of being stereotyped. It carried greater risk for him than the others.

The girls were still not found and everyone had retired to their beds, at the carnival and, he presumed, in town. Sleeping fitfully, plagued by worried dreams, eager for the sun to rise and light their way again to search, however fruitlessly. There would be rich pickings out there tonight, but he didn't dare. Best to stay under the radar. Good advice for all the crew. Let the town suffer on their own. Could they have done more to protect their children? Might they have noticed something if only they hadn't been so busy working, drinking, fucking, whatever each person's personal demons of culpability suggested?

Anyway, for most of the last five years since her father had died, Ashley had made an okay job of things. But though he was relatively new to this outfit, by the way these people measured time and loyalty, Saul had been around carnivals in general for a long while. He had traveled the land for many extended decades. He remembered places, the taste of their energies. And he remembered this place with its long history of loss and grief. So many over long years. And so often children.

He smiled as he reached his tent off to one side halfway down the midway, behind Gail's tee-shirt stall. His show tent was large, dark green army surplus, his pickup parked behind. The sign outside was a work of art, large strong letters in bright red against a gunmetal grey background:

MENGELE'S SECRET

Come and feel the ghosts and horrors soaked into the very fabric of the secret lab Josef Mengele used for his hideous experiments at Auschwitz!

Inside the big canvas was a large camper trailer, round-ended on a tube chassis, like half a zeppelin on wheels. Painted Nazi grey, adorned with SS symbols and Iron Eagles. It was the most ridiculous and ostentatious display of faux-Nazi memorabilia he could imagine, but people bought it. As if what Mengele did wasn't bad enough, but Saul's whole shtick had to be mobile, so he'd invented this. They really thought this old thing was where Mengele had secretly dissected extra victims, had gouged the different colored eyes from the skulls of people with heterochromia iridum, one eye brown, one blue, or some other variation. Where he had unnecessarily amputated limbs, stitched living twins together, deliberately infected poor souls with typhus.

Saul chuckled. Good old Mengele had really done those things, of course, and more, but in a lab at Auschwitz-Birkenau. This camper, a 1948 Eurostream he'd picked up for a song at a deceased estate sale twenty years previously and carefully redecorated, had probably never seen anything more traumatic than a traffic jam. The paint job and his patter is what sold it, and then people would pay five dollars to step inside, to touch the worn bench seats where they were told children had cried moments before their deaths. To run their fingers along the small table where Saul informed them blood had spilled from living victims. And their fear and horror was what he needed. While they made faces at each other and grinned to hide their joy at the gruesome stories, while their adrenaline coursed, Saul fed. It was all most agreeable. Then he would pack up the tent into the trailer, hitch it to his pickup, and hit the road to the next location.

At the back of the large tent, behind the horrible artifact of his business, was a small sectioned off area containing his cot and cooking stove. Perhaps he would read and have a few shots of the good bourbon before he slept, try to shake off the annoyance those idiot cops had left dogging him.

As he pushed aside the canvas flap into the private area of his tent, he stopped, scowled.

"What the fuck are you doing here?"

"We need to talk," John Barrow said.

"I should break your midget back over my knee, coming into my space uninvited like this!"

Barrow raised one hand, palm out. "I know the codes I'm breaking, violating space like this. But I didn't want to be seen." He gestured behind himself. "I slipped in under the canvas, shielded by your truck."

Saul frowned, confused more than annoyed. "Why? What are you up to?"

"This situation could be problematical."

"The missing girls?"

Barrow nodded.

Saul stepped into his space, took a bottle of bourbon from a small cupboard next to his gas stove. He poured a glass, didn't offer any to Barrow. "Something you want to accuse me of?"

"Is there anything I *should* accuse you of?"

"Don't fuck with me!" Saul spat.

"People come from far and wide to give us money," Barrow said, like none of the previous words had been spoken. "Sallow Bend is a small town, but we'll get hundreds from across the county every night. That's why we always stay here extra time when the holidays start."

"Yeah, and? That's a good thing, we need the coin."

"Of course. But if these girls aren't found before we open tomorrow, there'll be a small local contingent in that crowd and they'll be angry, hurt, frightened. Looking for their missing children."

"So?"

"And in the crowds at a carnival, they'll poke around."

Saul began to see where the man was heading with this particular train of thought. "You think they'll let themselves into our spaces while we're working?"

"Exactly."

Saul nodded, poured another drink. "That may be so, but what can we do? We'll just have to pay attention."

Barrow shrugged.

"They won't find anything the police didn't find, and the police found nothing." Saul frowned. "Where the hell are you going with this, Barrow? Why sneak in here in the middle of the night to talk about something so fucking mundane?"

Barrow shrugged again and stood, moved around the cot he had been sitting on. "Just wanted you to think about it. Maybe think about anything you could do to prevent it, you know?" He lifted the back canvas of the tent and ducked out into the night.

"Fuck you!" Saul shouted after him. "You're as bad as the rest of them!"

He sat seething for several minutes, downed another few shots of bourbon. He had been angry enough with the police and their generalized suspicion. Now John Barrow comes creeping up in the middle of the night with his very targeted distrust? What an asshole. Saul knew he attracted a certain amount of wary perusal. It went with the territory. He had learned to live with it years ago. But it still smarted someone like Barrow would come to him like this. He considered the small bastard the closest thing he had to a friend in this crew, knowing full well that friends were not something he made easily or often. And he preferred it that way. But Barrow genuinely suspected him and came sneaking around with "friendly" suggestions, citing the well-being of the crew and their stuff as his reasoning? Asshole! Or perhaps he really did think there was something Saul could do about it, and that just showed a genuine lack of understanding between them. A lesser man might be hurt by it, but Saul was resigned to it.

He took one last shot then put the bottle away and lay down on his bunk. He was getting hungry and thought it best he go to sleep before anger drove him to do something he may come to regret.

8

RILEY BRENT WAS a man consumed by guilt, slowly drowning in alcoholism. He knew these two things to be true, and also knew he was too much of a coward to do anything about either one. And yet Tricia, his wife of so many years, made him furious despite these moments of self-awareness. Why couldn't she simply let it be? These girls may or may not come back. What difference did it make? He knew for a fact it would do nothing to return Toby to their home.

He swallowed, the old sensation like a rock in his throat, and turned his anger outwards again to protect himself from further self-reflection.

"What do you plan to achieve?" he demanded.

Tricia stared at him, brows creased in hurt confusion. She had been so beautiful when they were younger. She still retained the traces of that beauty, aged a little but no less striking. Except when she looked at him like this and that just made her ugly. "Achieve?" she managed finally.

"You're letting this shit consume you. They're gone. Two missing girls, so sad. They may come back, they may not."

"How can you not care?" Tricia shook her head, threw aside the piece of toast she had been holding as though her appetite had suddenly deserted her. "If nothing else, it's simply being a good neighbor!"

"They're not our neighbors!"

"Everyone in Sallow Bend is our neighbor, Riley! It's a small enough town as it is without losing more. Decent people care about each other, for fuck's sake!"

"Oh, and I'm not a decent person now, is that it?" Riley ground his teeth, he needed a damn drink. He'd take another day sick, work be damned. The boss had intimated that too many more sick days, or any more drinking on the job, would mean he had no more job to go to. So be it. Fuck that guy too. Fuck everything. Images of Toby flitted past his mind's eye, his young son's wide eyes and mouth open in a horrified O of shock. Riley bit back a sob.

"No, Riley," Tricia said in a dangerously low voice. "You are not a decent person. You used to be a strong man, a good father. Now? Now you're weak and broken and unkind." She stepped close, stared up at him with fury in her eyes. "You need help, Riley Brent. You need professional fucking help, before you drink yourself to death. See a psychiatrist!"

Red slid down over Riley's vision, a waterfall of rage. How dare she? He struck out, undecided between a punch and slap, so a half-open hand cracked into the back of her head as she frantically ducked. Something in his middle finger clicked, the knuckles of two more bending painfully against her skull instead of the face as he'd intended. She cried out, as much in anger as pain it sounded like.

Riley shook out his stung hand, angrier than ever, and clenched his fist tight. "You don't talk to me like that!" he yelled, and hauled back to hit her properly.

Tricia danced sideways and swung a savage kick up between his legs. He tried to turn his thigh against it, but only managed a half-block. The top of her foot ground into one testicle, nauseating pain shot into his belly. He half-yelled, half-gagged, went to one knee.

"Fucking bitch!" he managed, then something heavy crashed into the side of his head.

Blackness punctuated by colored lights sparkled across his vision and then the carpet was dragging roughly against his cheek. He coughed, blinked, tried to pull himself up again, but everything was watery and uncertain.

Tricia stood over him, the wooden chopping board from the kitchen counter held in one hand, raised ready to hit him again. He went onto one elbow, lifted the other arm to fend off the blow, but it didn't come.

"You never raise a hand to me again," Tricia said through tears. "You get out of this house, I don't care where you go. But you don't come back until you've got professional help and stopped drinking!"

He stared up at her, blinking through the pain in his head, the continued throb in his balls that made his stomach churn. Rage fell away and disgust rose, grief rose. Toby's face falling away from him over and over again.

"You have to face up to what happened!" Tricia said. "You need to deal with the fact that Toby has gone. You need to help me, we need to never stop looking, but you have to face it!"

If only she knew what he'd done. What he was. If only *he* knew what had really happened. Tears ran over his cheeks and Tricia's face softened slightly, but her eyes were still hard with anger. She threw the slab of smooth red oak back onto the counter where it landed with a surprisingly loud bang that made him flinch.

"If you promise me you're going to get help, you can stay," she said. "But if you won't, I want you gone before I get home. I'm going out again to help look for Clare and Suki. And I'll never stop looking for Toby."

She turned and left. After the front door slammed and the sound of her car's engine faded up the street, Riley collapsed to the carpet and sobbed like a baby.

TRICIA gasped for breath as she drove towards town, adrenaline coursing through her. Hands shaking as she gripped the wheel, heart hammering, she desperately tried to regain some control. She had never had a fight in her life, beyond schoolyard hair-pulling. She had never raised a hand in violence as an adult. And yet she had just floored her husband, almost twice her size. She gulped at the memory of bringing that heavy wooden board around into the side of his head, but she had genuinely feared for her safety. Thank god she hadn't cracked his idiot skull.

As her heart rate slowed and the adrenaline slipped away, nausea rose in its place. She pulled over, closed her eyes and rested her head on the steering wheel. She allowed herself to sit there at the roadside and bawl, all the fear and shock flooding out. She couldn't stop shaking. How could Riley not understand? How could he have given up so thoroughly on Toby? On life, even.

It felt as though a turning point had been reached. This day marked a significant juncture. From here, Riley would either get his shit together or fall forever into the pit of despair he had been digging for himself for nearly a year. She hoped for the former, but thought the latter more likely. Would he be gone when she got back? Would he refuse to leave, and instead drive her from the house? If it came to that, so be it. She'd go. It was a toxic environment with Riley and she couldn't bear it any more. She had friends who would put her up, at least in the short term. Or her sister, Carol. She could maybe stay there a while, though Carol's putz of a husband made that choice unpalatable. But she'd find somewhere if she had to.

She sat back, pulled a deep breath into her lungs. She needed to stay occupied, to help with the search, to be proactive. Swallowing down her pain, she pulled away from the curb again and continued on to the school.

She had parted ways with Caleb after he had agreed to let her pick him up again this morning. He was a strange one, but she was developing a soft spot for him. She'd heard every version of opinion about him from friends and strangers alike. Most agreed he was weird but harmless, some thought him more malevolent. But throughout the course of the day before she had come to realize he genuinely cared about the kids even if his interactions with adults were strained. He had been reluctant to join her again, but desperate to help. She would do all she could to make sure he didn't regret buddying with her. One thing she had learned was he found small talk incredibly uncomfortable. She had no problem with that. Companionable silence was fine with her.

She pulled up across the street from the school and parked. It only took a minute to head through the playground and around the back of the main hall. Caleb's small apartments were beneath it, a row of narrow windows at ground level along the back wall, his door down half a dozen cement steps. She smiled. Living half-buried in the architecture of the school seemed to fit his personality so perfectly. She saw his face looking out of one of the small windows as she approached. He spotted her and vanished from sight. A moment later the door opened and he met her at the top of the steps.

"Morning, Caleb."

He nodded, glanced once at her eyes, then quickly looked away. "Good morning." He stared at the grass, waiting.

"Okay, then. Let's head to the Town Hall. Sheriff Holtz said they'd have a map this morning showing all the places people had searched and they could divide up the areas still to be..."

Shouting and raised voices interrupted her and she looked around to see a crowd of people hurrying towards the school gates. Excitement seemed to run with them, students and teachers alike.

"Come on!"

She ran to catch up, caught the arm of the principal, Mrs Fitzpatrick, Caleb hot on her heels.

"What's happening?"

Fitzpatrick turned a glowing face to her, not stopping, but grinning. "They've been found! All three girls are found!"

9

CALEB'S HAPPINESS FALTERED along with his step. Three girls?

"Oh, what a relief!" Tricia said.

Caleb looked from Tricia to Mary Fitzpatrick and back again as they all hurried through the school gates.

"I know!" Fitzpatrick said. "Suki, Clare, and Hester are being picked up by Sheriff Holtz now. He's going to bring them briefly via the Town Hall and then to the police station."

Hester?

"Where were they?" Tricia asked.

"Some of those carnival folks were up early this morning, searching again, and one of them found the girls in the woods north of Old Man Wilson's place."

"Excuse me," Caleb said as the crowd hurried along the sidewalk. "Hester?"

Fitzpatrick turned a frown to him. "Yes. Hester Black. And Suki Tokugawa and Clare Finlay. All three are still together, thank heavens."

"Who's Hester Black?" Caleb had never heard the name, couldn't understand why others weren't questioning it. Two girls had gone missing. Not three.

Fitzpatrick laughed. "Hester Black! With the..." She gestured at the side of her head. "With the hair, the white streak. You know Hester, Caleb, for goodness sake."

He opened and closed his mouth a couple of times, but could think of nothing to say. The crowd hurried across the intersection at Prime Street and Forest Road and towards the steps of the Town Hall. A crowd had already gathered, several people Caleb recognized and dozens more he may or may not have seen around town. Voices blurred into white noise, the presence of so many gathered souls weighing heavily against him. His mind creaked under the weight of all the information flooding in from so many faces, a headache instant behind his eyes. Perhaps he could simply slip away, go back to school, back to his peace and quiet.

But *three* girls? That strange aberration kept him tolerating the mass of humanity. Without catching any eyes, he tried to listen in on the voices and it seemed like a fairly universal conversation was taking place. It boiled down to thank heavens the girls had been found and all three were okay. Not one person questioned the number. Caleb shook his head, confusion a physical pain alongside a burgeoning migraine. Suki and Clare had gone missing, no one else. They had been searching for two girls all along. Yet everyone acted like it had been three missing. Hester Black with the white streak of hair? He knew no one who matched that description.

The mood and focus of the crowd shifted and Caleb followed the massed gaze. Holtz's patrol car came slowly along Forest Street, the Sheriff's face visible over the wheel. Beside him sat the tall, sneering Deputy Janssen. Silhouetted in the back Caleb could just make out three small shapes. Holtz pulled up to the curb and jumped out right away as the crowd surged forward. He held up both palms.

"Stay back, everyone, don't crowd us, please!"

Janssen got out, moved next to Holtz to walk the crowd back.

"If you could all just move back to the steps, please," Holtz said. "I know you're excited, we are too. Of course you want to see the girls and I'm only stopping here because word spreads like wildfire in this town and you all knew we were coming. So you get one moment to see the girls, then we're going to the station. There's lots of formalities to get through and their families are meeting us there. So please stay back."

Janssen scowled at the restless group of residents as Holtz turned back to the car and opened the back door. Suki Tokugawa came out first, smiling but contrite, her hair, usually a black shiny, neat bob was tousled, her summer dress torn and dirty, smudges of what looked like mud and ash on her face and hands. She looked pale, tired, but she seemed uninjured. Clare Finlay followed, grubby and disheveled like Suki, her mass of tumbling strawberry blonde curls tangled and dotted with bits of grass and leaves. She too appeared unhurt, though bore a guilty expression a lot like her friend, and appeared equally worn out.

Then a third girl slipped from the back seat to stand smiling beside them. This, Caleb presumed, had to be the mysterious Hester Black. She was slim, athletic, a little taller than Suki and Clare. She had long, black hair, but the left side was bleached white a few inches wide, a streak that ran from her center parting all the way to the tips near her waist, bright in the morning sun. Her eyes were a deep, mossy green, her skin pale. She wore a white linen, tight-fitting dress that flared a little in the skirt, and had short black leather boots on her feet. She was as grubby as the other two, but managed to seem somehow less scruffy. She also appeared brighter while Suki and Clare were worn down, exhausted. Caleb had never seen her before in his life. And her features played through expressions he found hard to pin down.

Hester raised a long-fingered hand in a tentative wave, flashed a cheeky grin. "Sorry, everyone!"

The other two glanced at her, then matched her action, waved and echoed her words. "Sorry!"

"Where have you been?" someone called from the back of the steps.

"We got lost, that's all," Hester said.

Holtz stepped forward, ushered the girls back. "Okay, that's enough." Janssen herded them back into the car and shut the back door. "We have to take official statements, the girls' parents are waiting at the station, all that stuff. You've seen them, you know they're safe. Thank you all again for your help with the searching, and we're very happy this terrible situation has been resolved. Please, go back to your homes, your jobs, and be happy."

Without waiting for more, despite the sudden and clamoring rush of questions, Holtz jumped back into the car, gesturing with frustration at Janssen who startled with realization and joined him. They pulled away, heading towards the station two blocks over.

Tricia turned to Caleb and grabbed his hand. He frowned at the contact, but endured it. "Isn't it wonderful?" He saw sadness behind her joy. She was a strong woman indeed to be so genuinely happy that the girls had come back, while her own son remained missing. *Why can't it have been Toby?* was etched into the lines between her eyebrows despite her smile.

Caleb shook his head, struggling to understand. "Suki and Clare went missing," he said, as the gathered crowd began to disperse in every direction. Joyful conversations accompanied each progressively smaller group.

Tricia tipped her head to one side. "Yes. And Hester. But they only got lost, and now they're found."

"No, I mean *only* Suki and Clare went missing. We've been looking for two girls, not three."

"What?"

"I've never seen that other girl before. Why does everyone act like it was always three?"

Tricia laughed, but her brow remained creased. "Everyone knows Hester, Caleb. What are you talking about? You know, I wouldn't be at all surprised if she was the one who put the other two up to this. Wasn't I saying just that while we were tramping through the woods yesterday? She's a wild one, that Hester."

Caleb's stomach knotted. He knew he wasn't losing his mind. But was it really likely that everyone else was mad and he was the only sane one? He searched for something to say, something to ask that might help him land his dislocated thoughts. "Where does she live?"

"Hester?" Tricia shrugged. "I'm not sure, somewhere on the north side of town, I think."

"Where? Who's her mother? You ever see her at school?"

"Caleb, what's got into you? You're the one at school all the time, how can you say you don't know Hester?" Her face crumpled slightly. "Honestly,

I haven't been near the school much in the past year. It was difficult simply coming by to collect you this morning."

A new layer of discomfort added itself to Caleb's gut. "I'm sorry, that was insensitive of me."

Tricia smiled, a little sadly. "That's okay. So what now?"

"What do you mean?"

"Well, the girls are back, I'm sure we'll hear a lot more when the official paperwork is all done. So what shall we do now?"

"Oh, I see. Well, I suppose I should go back to work."

"Yes. Of course."

Caleb watched pain flutter through Tricia's eyes. It wasn't his job to fix it, but he felt bad nonetheless. "Mrs Fitzpatrick was happy for me to search, but now..."

"Yes, you have a job to do. I should get home anyway, I'm on at the supermarket from noon. I was going to skip it, but now the girls are safe, I should go in."

They stood in awkward silence for a moment. Caleb read her reluctance to go home and wondered about her husband. In a small town like Sallow Bend, Riley Brent's descent in unchecked alcoholism was no secret, but the men they had met yesterday had talked so openly that Caleb was in no doubt the man had a big problem. Perhaps being at home held challenges for Tricia.

"Walk me to my car?" she said suddenly.

"Er, sure."

They turned back toward the school, walking slowly along rapidly heating pavement. The day felt as though it was working itself up to be a belter. They didn't speak until they reached Tricia's battered Taurus, the red paint dulled by a fine layer of dust.

"I normally work noon until nine on Thursdays," Tricia said. "But I think I'm going to convince Bill to let me go early today, maybe at six."

Caleb wasn't sure why she had brought this up, but could clearly see her nervousness. "Okay," he said.

"Because, you know, the carnival opens tonight. Always a big deal, isn't it? When the carnival opens? They have the fireworks and everyone will be there. And people from all over the county."

It sounded exactly like Caleb's worst nightmare. "I guess so."

Tricia smiled. "So if I finish at six, maybe I could swing by here again and pick you up. You want to come with me?"

Caleb's breath caught in his throat, his eyes widened. Tricia smiled again, mistaking his horror at the suggestion for nervous excitement that she had asked him out. "I, er… I'm not good with crowds."

She tipped her head to one side again. "You really aren't, huh? People, small talk, human company. These things make you uncomfortable."

He nodded, unsure what else to say.

"Will you come with me anyway?" Her grin was cheeky now, playful.

Caleb's brain ran fast, trying to figure out a way to extricate himself from the terrible situation. "Your husband!" He winced internally at his almost triumphant tone.

Her eyes darkened. "What about him?"

"Well, would he be okay with it? You'd want to go with him, wouldn't you?"

Tricia's face fell, all her good humor draining away. "No. I wouldn't." She looked up again. "But that's okay, if you don't want to go. I wasn't suggesting a date, you know? Just thought it would be fun. I've enjoyed your company recently."

Tricia had been kind to him. She could have simply directed him to the Town Hall, after all. Fitzpatrick had told him to go and see Tricia, but Tricia wasn't doing anything more than any other citizen. He frowned, wondering why Fitzpatrick had sent him that way in the first place. Probably simple miscommunication. That was a thing so common with people, he had noticed, when they refused to be up front and open, explain exactly what they wanted or how they felt. And he realized the same thing was happening right here, with Tricia. She obviously needed some kind of distraction, some way to occupy herself. She had chosen Caleb, because he had come to her inadvertently. And he was harmless. She had been kind all along. The thought of carnival crowds made his hands shake, but maybe he could do something kind for her. The pale face flashed into his memory, green eyes, that bright white streak of hair. How could he ignore the fact that no one else seemed to notice a girl had appeared out of nowhere?

"What are you thinking about?" Tricia asked

He jumped, realized he'd been lost in thought for a long while. "Sorry. Was just thinking about that girl. Hester."

Tricia grinned. "That scamp will have a lot to answer for."

"Does she get in trouble a lot?"

"Well, you know Hester. Strong-willed, precocious."

Caleb knew nothing of the sort, and didn't know how Tricia possibly could. "How long has she lived here?"

"Here in town?" Tricia shrugged, shook her head. "Born here, I think."

"Always been here?"

Tricia's forehead creased in a frown, her eyes a little glazed like she was momentarily lost. "Sure. Always."

Caleb ran out of questions again and Tricia's frown melted away like it had never been there. "So you want to come with me tonight?"

He swallowed a rising mild panic at the thought and nodded. There was no way he could let this strange situation go, and that meant being among the townsfolk. If that was necessary, perhaps Tricia was his best shield for the activity. Her genuine openness seemed to act as a barrier between himself and other people. But would it be enough? "I don't like crowds though."

"It'll be busy there, but we'll find space for you. Maybe it'll do you good. I'll come back by here a little after six?"

"I'll be waiting."

Tricia let out a "Ha!" of happiness and climbed into her car. With a wave out the window, she drove away.

Caleb watched her go, then stood for a moment enjoying the quiet of the empty sidewalk. Eventually he sighed and turned toward the school.

10

SHERIFF HOLTZ SAT behind his desk, the three girls arrayed in front of him, nervously wringing their hands and glancing at one another. Uncomfortable silence filled the office, marred only by the occasional scuffing of feet and Clare Finlay's soft sniffs. She seemed most upset, Holtz noticed. Genuinely saddened. Suki Tokugawa appeared frightened somehow, but defiant, her eyes hard, lips tight. Both looked exhausted. Hester Black, of course, was casual as all hell and cool as a cucumber, but that wouldn't come as a surprise to anyone.

A soft tap at the office door made them look over, a collection of stippled silhouettes moving on the other side of the frosted glass. Holtz let out a sigh of relief.

"Come in."

The door opened and a small mob burst in. Shelly and Todd Finlay, both crying, swept Clare up into an almost violent group embrace. Hanae and Hiro Tokugawa rushed to crouch by Suki's chair, Hanae's face soaked with tears as she grabbed her daughter's hands. Hiro stood again once he'd seen his daughter was unharmed, his face stern. Babbling and tears filled the room and Holtz sat back and let it go for a while. His eye caught Hester's and she gave him an altogether too grown up smirk, rolled her eyes slightly as she toyed with the hem of her grubby white dress. Where was Hester's mom? he wondered. Had he ever met her parents?

"Thank you so much, Sheriff!" Shelly Finlay was suddenly in his face, launching herself at his chair with a blanketing hug. He struggled back, the chair rolling on its casters, and tried to return the hug and push her away at the same time.

"You don't need to thank me, I just picked the girls up. One of the carnies, a guy named Daniel, found them. Hell of a guy, he is, a great big muscle-bound roustabout. You should thank him."

"We will, we will," Todd Finlay said. "But where were they?"

Holtz guided Shelly back to the other side of the desk, both sets of parents dragging up chairs either side of their daughters. Hester sat between the two groups, alone, smiling. Through his still open office door, he saw Kurt Janssen, Val Baker, and Clive Taylor all huddled together behind Val's desk, craning their necks to watch proceedings. He gave them a stern raised eyebrow and they all frowned and moved reluctantly back to work. He closed the door.

"Let's start at the beginning, we've been waiting until everyone was here." He looked at Hester as he sat back in his large leather chair. "Where's your mama? You called, right?"

Each of the girls had taken a turn on Holtz's cell phone as soon as they got to the car out by the carnival, to call their parents in. He'd seen Hester call her folks, hadn't he?

"You know my mama," Hester said, flashing a sweet smile.

Holtz couldn't help himself smiling back. He raised his hands, wondering what to ask, where the woman was, when Hester laughed. It sounded like glass bells.

"I'll walk home from here. Mama will be too wasted already to come get me. It's okay, you know how it is."

All eyes in the office lingered momentarily on Hester and she let her soft smile slide over each of them. She almost seemed to enjoy their uneasiness at her family dysfunction.

"Where were we?" Holtz said.

"Where were you all?" Hanae Tokugawa said.

"That's it, let's have the story. Daniel, that carnie, said he found you deep in the woods north of Wilson's place."

"There's really nothing to tell," Clare said. "We got lost, that's all."

"You were missing for two nights!" Hiro Tokugawa said, brows creased like the words themselves caused him pain.

"We got to wandering in the woods and I guess we went the wrong way," Suki said. "We thought we were coming back, but there were just more trees and it got steeper and steeper, and we realized we were going up into the hills instead of back to town."

"It was Hester's idea that saved us really," Clare said.

All eyes turned to the slim, pale girl in the middle. She swept the long white streak of hair behind her left ear and gave a little shrug. "It's nothing special really. I just said that Sallow Bend is south of the woods, so we should always keep an eye on the sun as it goes east to west every day. That way we know we're going south and we'd find the road eventually."

"So we turned around," Suki said. "And then we found this old cabin and managed to rest there, get to sleep a bit. Then that big black guy came, smiling and laughing and asking if we were Suki and Clare. We said yes and he said the whole town was looking for us and he led us out."

Holtz's gaze slid to Hester for a moment, caught a flash of something in her deep, green eyes. He'd been about to ask her something, but it slipped his mind. "Where did you sleep the night before the cabin?" he asked instead.

"Under the trees. It's pretty warm at night now, but it wasn't very comfortable. We didn't sleep much."

"You must be exhausted," Hanae said, brushing her daughter's hair aside repeatedly.

Suki gently batted her mother's fingers away. "We're okay. I know everyone was worried, and we're really sorry, we didn't mean to get lost. But we're okay, I promise."

"We *were* scared," Clare said. "But we're okay."

"We looked after each other," Hester added.

"Why did you go into the woods?" Holtz asked.

Clare and Suki pressed their lips together, looked down at their shoes. Hester glanced from one to the other, then said, "It's my fault. I said we should go watch the carnival set up. Then, for fun, I dared them to go into the woods. We weren't going to go far, but we got turned around, that's all."

"That's all?" Todd Finlay said, voice rising in frustration. "You could have died, the three of you. You could have starved, or been eaten by a damn bear or something!"

"Okay, okay," Holtz said, patting the air with his palms. The girls' faces were crumpling towards tears, no doubt the weight of their folly finally hitting home. He didn't need family histrionics, let them mete out whatever punishments they saw fit at home. He just needed to establish a final fact. "You saw no one else out there?" he asked, trying to sound as casual as possible.

"In the woods?" Suki asked.

"Yeah."

"No, no one. Not until Daniel found us."

Clare shook her head. Hester shook hers.

"You're sure?" Holtz pressed. "No one at all? Even if they said, you know, that you shouldn't tell anyone? You know that if an adult ever tells you not to tell your parents something, or not to tell the police something, that adult is almost certainly a bad guy."

Hester let out a startling peal of laughter. "You mean a pedophile? Is that it? You think someone coaxed us out there and told us to stay quiet about it?"

"I just need to make sure," Holtz said, feeling stupid in the face of this thirteen year-old's mirth.

"We know better than that, Sheriff." Hester shrugged. "We're not little kids any more. We know about predators."

Holtz looked to Suki then to Clare. "That right?"

They both nodded. "Honestly, Sheriff, we saw no one," Clare said. "That was the scariest part. There's really no one out there."

"Okay." Holtz stood, gestured towards his door. "I think these girls need to go home and have a good hot bath. And something to eat. We gave them donuts when they got here, which they devoured, but I reckon you could all use a square meal, right?"

"We are so hungry!" Suki agreed.

The two families headed for the door, but Hester hung back with Holtz. After a few awkward farewells the parents shepherded Suki and Clare through the main office.

"See you tonight!" Hester called after them.

"Tonight?" Todd Finlay asked, looking back.

"The carnival. The fireworks!"

Todd's face darkened. "I don't know about that. You girls are safe, that's the main thing, but you're not out of trouble. I don't know if Clare is going anywhere any time soon!"

"Awww, Dad!"

"Out, young lady. We'll talk about this at home."

Suki turned wide eyes to her parents, but her mother looked away.

"At home!" Hiro said, his voice low but firm.

Both girls looked back at Hester, who shrugged and waved.

Once they were gone, Holtz looked down at her. "Your mom really not coming?"

"Looks like."

"Things okay at home?"

"Sure, as far as they ever are. You know how it is."

"Okay. You can talk to me if you ever need to, you know that, right?"

"It's okay. Thank you, Sheriff. You've been very kind."

"You want me to drive you? Or Val? I mean Deputy Baker. I can ask her to drive you."

"No, really, I'm fine. I want to walk, remind myself I'm really out of the woods."

She headed across the office for the door, Kurt Janssen and Val Baker watching from behind their desks, Clive Taylor's eyes were closed as he napped. Val's brows knitted slightly, Kurt's usual sneer slightly softened.

Hester breezed out into the mid-morning sunshine and the door swung shut behind her.

"There is something wild about that girl," Val Baker said quietly, almost to herself.

Holtz sighed. "Well, you know Hester."

He heard Val *Mmm-hmm*-ing as he went back into his office.

TRICIA had driven aimlessly for a while after dropping Caleb, too scared to go home. She imagined Riley lying there in the kitchen, a deep scarlet pool spreading from his head. She knew she hadn't killed him, that he'd been hurt but conscious when she left, yet still she worried. What if it had been a delayed reaction and he'd collapsed into a coma right after she drove away? What if he was stumbling around with a crippling concussion?

That wasn't the only reason she was scared to go home. What if he hadn't lapsed into a vegetative state there on the linoleum, but was in his chair, and drunk, and even angrier than ever. The way he hauled his fist back right before she kicked him terrified her. He had had every intention of punching her square, like he was brawling with fellow loggers at Gil's Tavern. On the highway right at the edge of town, that place was all about country music and masculinity, bikers and loggers and drinking and fighting. Just lately, if Riley wasn't drunk at home, he was drunk at Gil's. And it seemed the atmosphere of that awful bar was spreading into their home, like blood soaking through a checkered shirt. She often wondered if one night he'd leave Gil's, turn right instead of left and end up in the Sallow River. She also wondered if that would be such a bad thing. But that was evil thinking and she didn't mean it. She loved Riley with all her heart. No. She had loved him. Not any more. She hated what he had become. Losing him, losing what he had been, what they had been together, hurt like knives in her gut. So soon after Toby it was almost too much to bear.

Tricia had stopped for a coffee at Bev's Café, then stayed for a sandwich, but she'd run out of reasons not to go home. And work started at noon, so she didn't have much time left to go and change. She started the engine outside Bev's and pointed the car west, back across town. It didn't take long until she was pulling up onto the driveway and a kind of shuddering relief washed through her when she saw Riley's pick-up truck had gone. It had been there when she left. The empty spot by the garage seemed to be a kind of punctuation mark in their marriage. The words she'd yelled at Riley that morning came back to her.

You get out of this house, I don't care where you go. But you don't come back until you've got professional help and stopped drinking!

She had honestly expected him to challenge that ultimatum, and maybe he still would. Maybe he'd only gone to Gil's to drown his rage in more bourbon and beer. Perhaps he'd come back more sour drunk than ever and then who knew what he might do? A tear escaped over one cheek as Tricia considered her thoughts and realized she was genuinely afraid for her safety. Afraid for her life even, at the hands of her own husband. How could they have come to this? No couple should ever have to deal with the loss of a child, but surely not every man would descend like Riley had. Well, if he came home again, she'd have to deal with it. Keep that damn chopping board handy and floor the fucker again if he came at her.

She went inside, began getting ready for work. When she went into the bedroom, she stopped, heart racing. The drawers in his dresser stood open and empty. She went to the closet and his boots and other gear was all gone too. In the garage, she discovered his fishing gear and a bunch of his tools also missing.

She stood on the cement floor of the strangely quiet garage, cool air tickling over her skin, hands on her hips. "God damn," she said quietly. "He really left."

She wondered if he would ever come back, and alongside that thought was another one. Did she want him to come back? Was that it, Tricia and Riley over and done? The perfect couple shattered and dissolved completely?

She licked her lips, trembling slightly at the possibilities. Where she might go from here. It was all too much to process. She would have to ask around, she knew that. Where the hell would he go anyway? She'd ring his friends. She'd call Gil's. But in the immediate future she had to get to work and then finish early to pick up Caleb and go to the carnival. The implosion of home life was too immediate, too big in her mind, and she needed time to process it all.

"God damn," she said again, and went back into the house.

11

ASHLEY STRONG STOOD in the midway beside the motionless carousel, hands on her hips. Her relief that the three girls had been found was palpable, as though a yoke had been lifted from her shoulders. The carnival bustled, everyone finally back at their stations and focused. The last bunting was tied, several crew checking all the midway lights. Stalls and rides were undergoing last minute running tests. They opened at six, the big welcome fireworks display at eight. She would be glad once that was done and the regular routine underway.

With a soft nod to herself she turned back towards her trailer, checked her watch. Nearly three pm, time for the final crew pep talk. She winced internally as Saul came at her from the side, emerging from his tent flap like a trapdoor spider.

"Got a sec, boss?"

"Walk with me. What's up?"

"Just wondering if anyone had come to you with, you know, complaints."

Ashley frowned. "About what?"

"Me."

She couldn't help snuffing a short laugh. "Saul, people always complain about you. You're a sour and disagreeable asshole sometimes."

"Hey!"

"And the rest of the time, you're downright horrible." She laughed, showing it for a joke even though they both knew she wasn't really ribbing. Many a true word in jest and all that.

"I just meant with this missing girls thing."

"Someone been up in your face about it?"

"Only because I crouched down."

This time Ashley's laugh was genuine, and a grin broke out on Saul's face. He could be a great guy, Ash reflected, if he wasn't so torn up inside by whatever it was that darkened his heart and soul. She'd tried to talk to him about it a few times when she first took over, but quickly gave up. His secrets were staying locked away and it wasn't her job to safe break for them. "John Barrow cares too much, that's all," she said.

"He's a fucking busybody."

"Yes, he is. Because he cares too much about things running well. I'm sorry if he gave you a hard time. Honestly, he hasn't said anything to me."

Saul grunted, nodded once. "Well, just so you know about it. If he gives me too much grief…"

Ashley stopped, turned to pin Saul with a fierce eye. "What?"

"Well…"

"Well nothing, Saul. I'm sick of this macho posturing bullshit around here. Suck it up. Barrow can be a pain in the ass, but you can be the bigger man. It all comes from a good place, so just accept it. You have nothing to hide, so rise above it."

They stared at each other for a moment, then Saul nodded again. Ashley would be damned if she'd let these fools antagonize each other. Seemed like she spent half her time putting out spot fires sparked by personality clashes. She supposed it went with the territory. "Anything else."

"I guess not."

The summer sun had baked Old Man Wilson's fields hard, the grass downtrodden and yellowing. Dust motes and bugs danced in the air, birdsong rang out from the woods behind them. The air smelled of grass and pollen and the hot Sallow River. The heat of the day had set in, like it slowed down time, and everything felt right, ready. It felt like carnival time. Ashley drew a deep breath and smiled. "You're all set? Any other gripes among the crew?"

Saul shook his head. "Not that I've heard. Everyone's pretty relieved the girls were found."

"Yeah, we owe a lot to Daniel."

Saul nodded ahead of them. "Talk of the devil."

"Hey, Dan!" Ashley called out.

The man startled slightly at his name, looked up at her, and then slipped through the busy crew to meet them. John Barrow and Sarah Carter, the latter in her Madame O'Reilly garb again, caught the exchange and wandered over too. Fallon and Barrow exchanged a wary nod.

Ashley reached up and put an arm around Dan's huge shoulders, grinning at the absurdity of the position she found herself in. "I just wanted to thank you personally," she said, and stretched up to kiss his cheek. His dark skin flushed, and he couldn't look at her.

She took her arm back from its precarious perch. "I'm serious. The specter of those missing kids was going to haunt us. You finding them saved us from a whole lot of trouble. But!" She turned her attention the small impromptu group. "People in small towns like this are quick to anger and slow to settle. Those girls are fine, they just got lost in the woods and thank fuck you found them, safe and sound. But the locals always look at us with side-eyes and they'll only be even more on edge until things truly calm down. The way we make sure things settle is by having a smooth and flawless opening night. So no tricksters, no marking, no fighting, no rip-offs! I need you guys to spread that word quietly, okay?" At their frowns she raised an eyebrow. "I know damn well that every one of you fuckers is as honest and upstanding as a priest. Well, we all know how damned untrustworthy fucking preachers are!"

"We'll spread the word," Barrow said. "But I don't think we need to. People get it already."

"Sure. Even still. This is our long pitch, two weeks we need to make coin here. We gotta start right."

"I'm glad you happened by, actually," Daniel said. "I talk to you minute?"

"Sure." Ashley looked expectantly at the others, hoping her eyes conveyed the idea that they should be getting on with their work. Saul smirked, stalked off back towards his tent. Barrow and Sarah lingered.

"I don't mind these two sticking around. They might help." Daniel's eyes were scrunched, like he had a bad taste in his mouth.

"Come on." Ashley led them to a picnic bench she kept beside her trailer to enjoy meals in the sunshine. And to stop people from wanting to come inside whenever they decided they needed a chat, which seemed ever more frequent lately. She sat and the other three joined her. "Go on, Dan. What's eating you?"

Daniel frowned, took a deep breath. He interlaced his fingers, placed them on the old silvered wood of the table and stared at them. He shook his head slightly, licked his lips. Ashley watched him silently, having long ago learned that people would speak when they were good and ready, and pushing them only made them clam up. Her crew were her family, her responsibility, however irritating many of them could be. Barrow and Sarah sat quietly too, watching. Sarah's brow was slightly creased, head tilted to one side. Ashley let a smile tickle her lips. She liked it when Sarah wore that expression, it suited her. She had yet to decide, even after all this time, whether or not Sarah really had supernatural powers or was simply a fine actor. In truth, she wondered if Sarah knew, that perhaps she fooled herself. Ashley didn't hold with superstition and other nonsense, but she also wasn't arrogant enough to think she knew everything, so she kept an open mind. Just not so open that her brain might fall out.

"I dunno how to tell it," Daniel said then, pulling her attention back.

"Just start at the beginning."

He looked at her, brown eyes soft in his dark face. His skin had a slight sheen of sweat that glistened in the hot sun. "Well, okay. I was bothered by those girls missing, like everyone. I wondered how far they might have gone. Everybody was talking about how they were probably abducted, probably already sold into sex slavery in the next state."

"People were saying that?" Barrow asked, horrified.

Ashley laughed. "You can always trust people to think the worst. Go on, Dan."

"Well, I got to thinking that maybe they'd wandered off into the woods and got lost. It seemed the most likely, with us here and all. We're interesting to young kids, right? Especially small town kids."

"Sure."

"So I thought maybe I'd set out real early and go deep into the woods. Man, it's thick and wild in there. The further you go, the spookier it gets. It's like something from an old fantasy novel, you ever read those? I loved them growing up and they always had shit like Mirkwood or The Dark Place, you know?"

Ashley nodded, smiled. Was Dan really spooked by a dark forest? Surely it was more than that.

"Anyway, I kept going, looking around. I started to think it was pointless, because the whole place was so damn big and thick and dark. There are trees in there so wide and gnarled you could believe they've been growing for five hundred years. I coulda walked right past those girls, no more than ten feet away, and still not seen 'em. But I kept going anyway, deeper in and getting desperate. I was kinda scared, you know? It was just so damn creepy. But I'm not a superstitious man, Ashley, really I'm not.

"Then I came to this lake. It's big, gotta be a mile across and so still. It looks deep, the trees all around it like a wall. The banks of the lake only head about half a dozen yards or something before the trees start. But after the forest, it suddenly seemed so bright, so much sky over the water, the clouds reflected in it. It should be beautiful, but it wasn't. It felt… wrong somehow.

"Then I saw a wooden cabin not far around, just under the edges of the trees. It looked old, all worn down and moss covered. The shingles of the roof were kinda half curled up and crooked, like the skin of a dead old lizard lying in the sun. But I thought, hell, if those girls got lost and were scared, looking for shelter, they might have gone there. So I went around the lake to see."

Daniel stopped, swallowed, stared at his clasped hands again.

"What happened?" Sarah asked in a soft voice. "What did you see?"

"I didn't see anything, but I felt… I heard…" He paused, shook his head. "As I got closer, I noticed a change, but couldn't place it at first. Then I realized it was too quiet. That forest is old and full of life, you know. Birdsong everywhere, things scurrying through the undergrowth. Rabbits and shit, I guess. But as I got near this old cabin, there was nothing. Not a sound, not a bird. It all felt still and…" He shrugged. "And dead. But I carried on, and looked inside that shack. It has a door that's a bit crooked, but hanging on. Only a couple of windows, all battered, with shutters on the outside, but the shutters were open. The glass is all cracked and grimy and covered in lichen and moss and shit. The door was ajar, so I pushed it open and leaned in. It was real dark inside, took my eyes a while to adjust. Then my heart skipped a beat, cos I saw these two shapes on the floor.

"I ran inside, and next to this big old stone fireplace were two of the girls. They were lying there like they were dead and I panicked, nearly screamed."

"They weren't just sleeping?" Barrow asked.

"Well, yeah, it turns out they were. But when I saw them, laying on their backs with their mouths half-open, skin pale as milk... I'm telling you, they looked dead. Then a voice said, 'Someone's found us!' and I spun around and there was Hester. I hadn't even seen her as I ran in, I guess I was focused on the other two, but there she was, right by this rickety old table near a window. I have no idea how I missed her, especially with that bright white streak of hair, but like I said, it was real gloomy in there.

"Then the other two are jumping up and grabbing me, crying they're so happy someone has found them, and they're crushing me while Hester just stands there and smiles. And they didn't look dead at all, they had color in their cheeks, though they were dirty as hell, of course."

"And then what?" Ashley asked.

"Well, then I said I was happy to have found them too, and they should come with me, I'll take them back. And I did. But I'm telling you, Ashley, when I first saw them girls lying there, I was sure they were dead. I mean, I was *certain*. I've seen corpses before, and those girls looked like 'em. Then

Hester spoke and I looked at her, and when I looked back, those other two were bright and perky and totally alive. The whole thing freaked me the fuck out."

Sarah reached across the table and laid a hand over Daniel's intertwined fingers. Her skin was china pale against his. "I can sense the wrongness of what you saw," she said. "It lingers on you."

Barrow looked from Daniel to Sarah and back again, brows knitted. Daniel's eyes were wet, haunted.

"Okay, that's enough of that," Ashley said. She looked at Sarah and shook her head subtly. Sarah squeezed Dan's hand once more, then withdrew her touch.

"You had a frightening experience, there's no doubt about it," Sarah said.

"And you think something stayed with me?" Daniel's voice was a little too high, a little wavery.

"Sarah," Ashley warned in a dangerously low tone.

Sarah didn't look at her, but held Daniel's eye. "There's a cleansing ritual we can do to remove the lingering presence of that awful place from you. Come back with me and we'll do it now, you'll be fine."

Ashley let out a sigh. "All right, you guys go ahead and do that. Will that make you feel better, Daniel?"

"Yes, I think it will."

"Okay. This has hit you hard. I'm glad you came to tell me. But let's not get carried away with too much nonsense, okay? You go with Sarah, let her cleanse you. And if anything else is bothering you, you come and tell me, okay?"

"I will."

"You promise?" However much Ashley thought this situation was completely garbage, Daniel was clearly perturbed by it despite his protestations that he was not a superstitious man. She needed her crew to be sharp and balanced. If he believed it, that was good enough for her. If he also believed Sarah could fix him, even better. Perhaps Sarah had been quicker to realize a good solution than Ash had. Again she wondered how much of Sarah's shtick was real and how much deliberately contrived. She knew beyond a doubt that Sarah was a smart and caring person. That was usually enough.

"I promise. I feel a bit better just for having told you guys."

"Good. Now run along with Sarah and she'll make it better still."

Ashley caught Sarah's eye as they stood, raised one eyebrow as Daniel turned away. Sarah smiled softly, gave Ashley a wink. Was the woman suggesting she was simply humoring Daniel's spook, or was that wink a knowing *I've-got-this* kind of reassurance. As the two of them turned and headed for Sarah's colorful wagon, Ashley decided she didn't much give a shit, as long as everybody ended up happy and working. She knew she would have to keep one ear on crew gossip, though. This was the kind of thing that would most definitely be talked about, and it'd spread through the crew like a brushfire. There was nothing these guys enjoyed more than a good story, especially a spooky one.

"You believe him?" Barrow asked, once Sarah and Daniel had gone.

Ashley shrugged. "I honestly don't know. I believe he certainly got spooked up there. Beyond that, it doesn't much matter. The girls are all back, the town is happy, the carnival opens tonight. Let's concentrate on that."

Barrow smiled, nodded. He swung his legs around on the bench and hopped down to the grass. As he went to walk away, Ashley said, "Oh, John?"

"Yeah?"

"Try to see to it that Daniel and Sarah don't stir up any crazy talk with this story, will you? Head off any nonsense you hear around the camp?"

Barrow smiled again. "Sure thing."

"And John? While you're at it, stop stirring up Saul."

He paused, the smile frozen halfway to a frown. "What do you mean? He been complaining about me?"

"Just be a force for calm, John Barrow, instead of an antagonizer. You think you can manage that?"

He bowed theatrically, doffing an imaginary hat. "Whatever my lady so desires."

She laughed. "Fuck off."

As he walked off towards the midway, Ashley looked over the carnival spread out before her. She didn't hold much truck with superstition, but she couldn't shake the feeling this site was going to bring nothing but trouble. Previous years had been just fine here, but something about this time was different. A little off-kilter. Not that there was anything she could do about it except wait for any trouble and deal with it as fast as possible. They were in the hole to Old Man Wilson for a lot of rent money. Only a busy stay would fix that and keep them all paid. But still, she thought perhaps she would be glad when they moved on in two weeks.

12

CALEB DREW IN a deep breath as Tricia pulled into the field beside the carnival. Hundreds of cars were already there, in neat rows like automotive grave markers. People milled everywhere, between the cars and on the already rough-trodden path leading to the big, arching *Strong's Traveling Carnival* gateway. Beyond the sign, lights and movement rushed, rides spinning. Whoops and screams drifted to them on the hot summer air, muffled through the closed car windows. Twilight had begun, the sky softening to golden yellows ahead of the indigo before night.

Tricia killed the engine and glanced over at him. "You okay?"

"Sure."

"Why are you so sensitive to people? Nobody can tell you? You said you had all kinds of tests when you were young."

"Yeah. The doctor said I had an oversensitivity to things like facial tics and body language. That my mind constantly processed a lot more information than most people do and it's overwhelming, wears me out."

"And that's why you look at the ground a lot, don't meet people's eye."

"Yeah."

"And they kinda judge you for that and think you're a bit weird."

Caleb had been staring at his hands in his lap, but looked up at the amused tone of her voice. She was grinning at him, deliberating ribbing him. *Have we come this far already?* he thought. *She thinks it's okay to have playful digs at me*. He wasn't sure whether he was okay with that or not, but if he was honest with himself, it didn't smart too much.

"Something like that," he said, giving her a small smile back. "That's why I came to a small town, without many people. It's why I do a job where I'm on my own most of the time. It works better for me that way."

"You haven't managed to, I don't know, fix it? Treat it?"

He shrugged. "Sure. I tried other types of jobs, to push past it, ignore it. But I always got so tired, got headaches that would last for days. I saw psychiatrists, hypnotists. They all had ideas, but none of them worked. So I fixed it by removing myself from the worst of the triggers. Exposure to people never gets any easier, especially in crowds, around lots of noise, so I put myself elsewhere."

"And here I am making you come to the busiest event in the Sallow Bend calendar. Should I take you home?" Her face betrayed genuine concern. She would drive away immediately if he asked her to, but she didn't want him to do that.

"It has some advantages," he said. "It means I can't be lied to, for example. I always know when something isn't truthful."

She tipped her head to one side. "Huh."

"And you need the company right now, don't you?"

She swallowed, realizing the trap he'd set. She couldn't lie to him. "Yeah. I do. But I don't really want to talk about why."

"Fair enough. But you must have so many other friends in town. You can't hang out with them?"

"Everyone is such a gossip. They always want the dirt, want to dig."

Caleb nodded. "Kinda like I'm doing now?"

"Up until now you haven't. You've been good company."

"And you've been kind to me, where most people are at least wary. So it's okay, you don't need to take me home."

He meant what he said. But he also wanted to learn more about Hester, to hear what people were saying about her. This place was probably the best opportunity to hear gossip, see what people thought. The girls themselves would no doubt be here, if they weren't grounded. Regardless, he needed to learn what he could. And, if the chance arose, he wanted to find out which carnie had found them and talk to that person too. He could only do all that by coming to the carnival. He swallowed. "I want to be here, be company for you, see what's happening. But don't judge me if I look at the ground a lot."

Tricia's face lit up in a smile. Relief shone through it, and a little guilt. She was clearly hiding from something, or trying to not think about it, and the distraction of Caleb had become her focus. That and the carnival itself. So be it. They were playing a game here, only Tricia had no idea of his side of it. People constantly manipulated and cajoled others around them, sometimes not even realizing themselves what they were doing. He thought perhaps Tricia didn't realize she was using him to hide. No matter. It was all means to ends.

"Let's go then!" she said. "And listen. If it gets too much or if we get split up in there somehow, just come right back here to the car. As soon as I realize you're not right beside me, I'll come back and find you, okay?"

"Okay."

Tricia jumped from the car and Caleb joined her. The summer evening was hot, the air thick and close after the air-conditioned vehicle. Aromas of grass and night blossoms on the breeze were overburdened with extra scents of metal and diesel, cotton candy and hot dogs. They joined the loose mass of people heading into the carnival, Caleb true to his word, watching the flat, yellowed grass pass under his feet. He kept Tricia in his peripheral vision, her white sneakers and tight, pale blue jeans. The noise increased exponentially and he paused just inside the midway, rocked slightly on his feet at the sensory overload. Lights of every color whirled and flashed, crazed rings and clangs and claxons and buzzers and the growl of generators fought with wild calliope music and stallholders hawking their games and wares. Raised voices shouting and laughing, screaming and calling, like a thousand gulls at a beach all clamoring for food.

"You okay?" Tricia had one hand lightly on his forearm, her touch hot against his bare skin.

He took a deep breath as the maelstrom of noise and input began to level out, his mind finding its equilibrium. As long as he avoided too much observation of people, he'd be fine here. He could do this. "Yeah. What now?"

Tricia laughed. "Oh, I don't know. Maybe let's have some fun? This way."

She led him along the midway and he glanced left and right, took in the face painting and Catch-A-Duck, Whack-and-Smash and Corn Shack, Waffle Dogs and carousel. Beyond them, the bigger rides spun and rocked, the Tilt-A-Whirl and Helter Skelter, the Pirate Ship and Bumper Cars Arcade. At the far side near the river the Ferris Wheel turned lazily, carrying swinging buckets of people high into the air where they pointed and laughed, before swooping down again, only to repeat, around and around. Near the back, before the trailers and camp of the carnival's crew started, was a large black and grey house, all crooked angles and gothic gambrel roofs, with *The World's Most Terrifying Haunted House* in big flashing lights across the front.

"Hey, check this out!"

Caleb looked to where Tricia pointed, an excited grin on her face. On the midway was an open-fronted yellow tent, carrying the sign Gail's Shirts and Hats. Inside were racks of tee-shirts, and more covered every inch of the internal walls. Wolves and dragons, movie and cartoon characters, wrestlers, musicians, a thousand other things Caleb had no hope of identifying.

"You want to buy a tee-shirt?"

"No, silly! Behind it."

He moved over to see she was pointing past Gail's shop, at the next row of larger tents and vans. One was a brightly colored old Romany Gypsy wagon with spoked wheels and a rounded roof, a curving set of steps leading up to a beaded curtain. Sitting on the steps was a beautiful woman in layers of colored silks. She was hung with bangles and about a dozen different necklaces. A sign beside the steps said *Madame O'Reilly – Fortunes Told*. Next to O'Reilly's was a tattoo artist, offering temporary henna tattoos and genuine forever ink. His machine was buzzing away, a young man who couldn't be long out of high school grinning drunkenly as his friends egged him on. He seemed to be getting some kind of hot rod design on his upper left arm.

But Tricia was pointing at the next attraction along. A large, dark green army surplus tent. The sign outside read:

MENGELE'S SECRET

Come and feel the ghosts and horrors soaked into the very fabric of the secret lab Josef Mengele used for his hideous experiments at Auschwitz!

Caleb looked from the attraction back to Tricia, saw childlike joy on her face. "Really?" he asked.

"I love this stuff. I've always been a sucker for the macabre."

"You don't really believe this is Mengele's though, do you?"

Tricia shrugged, still grinning. "I seriously doubt it is, but for the purposes of fun, I choose to believe it might be."

"And you want to go in?"

Someone bumped into Caleb, mumbled an apology as popcorn rained down over his feet. He winced, seeing complete insincerity in the man's face and body as he pushed on by.

"There'll be less people in there, if nothing else," Tricia said. She wore that cheeky half-smile again.

"It's wrong to take advantage of a person's disabilities." Caleb tried to replicate her expression and knew immediately he had failed. For all his ability to see through people like fine glass, he was hopeless at conveying his own feelings or emotions.

"Do you think of it as a disability?" Tricia asked.

"No, not at all. I'm joking. It's a disadvantage. An inconvenience."

"I don't know. By every metric, it is a disability. I hadn't thought about it like that, but it does affect your life."

"I was only joking. We can go in if you like."

In the open flap of the large tent a man stood observing their conversation. He was tall, well over six feet, wearing dark blue mechanic's overalls. He watched with dark eyes, black hair neatly combed over a bone-pale face.

Caleb realized it was the man who had made him feel so uncomfortable during that tense gathering in the midway the day before. The carnival owner, Ashley, had called him Saul. He was too far away to hear their words over the noise, but had spotted them considering his attraction. As Caleb made brief eye contact, the man gestured with one hand, inviting them in.

Caleb startled slightly at Saul's presence when he moved. There was that predatory nature again in his eyes, something aggressive in his physicality. Caleb had never seen anything quite like it before. A clarification of the previous day's discomfort, it only heightened his concerns. He immediately regretted suggesting they could go in, but Tricia was already moving forward.

"Good evening, fine lady," the carnie said. "You've chosen a very interesting exhibit and you won't be disappointed. But can you handle the horrors of the presence of the Angel of Death?"

"Didn't Mengele do his experiments on people in a big lab?" Caleb asked. "Not a tent."

Saul gave him a sardonic half-grin, and Caleb shivered. If a shark could smile, it would look like this. "Inside my tent is Mengele's secret trailer, which he kept just outside Auschwitz. Most experiments he did in his lab, of course. Others, he brought to the trailer. To take his time with them."

"I'm scared already!" Tricia said, though she sounded, looked, and acted excited.

"Five dollars each to go in and feel the evil! Are you up to it?"

"I've got this," Tricia said, pulling a ten from her purse. She handed it over and the carnie stepped aside.

Inside the tent was dim, low red-hued bulbs hidden somewhere gave everything a blood-soaked sheen. In the center was a large trailer, round-ended on the far side. A set of three steps led up into the darkened interior. As Caleb and Tricia mounted the steps, sudden screams of agony rang out from inside. Tricia jumped and let out a scream herself, that became a laugh. Saul stood behind them, grinning, like he had had nothing to do with it.

"Go on, if you dare," he said quietly.

Tricia turned back and entered the trailer, Caleb close behind. The carnie followed them, stood in the doorway blocking their exit. It was unusually large, lit blood red like the tent outside. On a worn bench seat along the near wall sat manikins of two children in 1940s school uniforms.

"This is where they would cry tears of hopelessness," Saul said. "Moments before their deaths. Some would watch their siblings sliced open and gutted, but they would be too drugged to run away. Or too resigned to their fate."

"This is terrible," Caleb said quietly to Tricia.

She nodded, brow creased. "This is a hell of a way to make your living," she said to the carnie.

"Better that people never forget the horrors of the holocaust. We can't allow such a thing to ever happen again."

Before Caleb could question the man's commodifying of the holocaust, he went on. "That table is where Mengele would perform his atrocious surgeries. The cupboards you see at the back contained the cleaned bones of children that he used in occult rituals to gain the favor of dark gods."

Caleb wondered if Tricia should put herself through this, the loss of her own child so recent. Was it somehow cathartic? He saw her body give way to a kind of primal fear as she imagined the things the carnie described. He felt it himself, the truth of Mengele's possible inhumanity. The predatory nature of the human animal. Caleb also felt something else. A kind of drawing away, as though something inside him was being sucked out. On one side of the large space was an old wardrobe, mirrors on the doors. In one mirror he saw Saul's hands stretched forward, one towards him and one towards Tricia. The carnie's eyes were hooded and his mouth worked slightly, like he were tasting something. Swallowing it. Dizziness crept over Caleb, like a sudden tiredness washing softly through his mind. He realized Tricia was swaying slightly as she looked around the horrible place. He grabbed at her elbow, made her cry out in surprise. Saul gasped in satisfaction.

"We should go," Caleb said, pulling Tricia back towards the door.

As they turned, Saul quickly dropped his hands and smiled benignly. "Your fear is palpable," he said with a chuckle.

Caleb couldn't help thinking the man actually meant edible. He had never seen a person quite like this guy before, hadn't encountered mannerisms and expressions like his. The slight incongruity profoundly disturbed him. But the carnie stepped aside and let them climb down ahead of him. Leaving the trailer, Caleb spotted an SS uniform hanging on the back of the door. It looked long, tailored for a thin man. Someone exactly Saul's size, he guessed.

As they headed for the tent flap, Saul called out, "Come again! And tell your friends!"

The bustle and noise and bright lights outside were like a shower of fresh rain after the close and ruddy exhibit. Dusk had darkened towards evening and the air was beginning to cool.

"What the hell was that like?" Tricia asked, laughing.

"It was utterly wrong," Caleb said. "I don't think I will come again."

"Me either."

"Did you sense anything wrong with that guy?"

"Well, he was creepy as hell, but that's his job, right?"

"Sure, but more than that, I mean."

Before Tricia could answer, a confrontation on the midway rose above the general noise and commotion.

"Where did you come from?" a man's voice stridently demanded.

Caleb and Tricia stepped out past Gail's tee-shirt stall to see a small crowd quickly gathering. In the center of the crowd was a man in his forties, balding on top, grey and brown stubble a shadow over his face. And next to him, looking bewildered and scared, was Hester Black.

Other voices quickly rose.

"What are you doing, man?"

"Hey, leave the kid alone!"

"You're drunk as hell, Kirk!"

Hester looked left and right, eyes wild like a trapped animal.

"Who are you?" the man called Kirk demanded, jabbing one meaty forefinger at Hester.

He was drunk, Caleb saw that. But he was scared too, confused. Horrified bewilderment danced in his eyes. He saw through Hester's strange appearance too. Finally, someone else to back him up.

"It's Hester, Kirk, for God's sake. What's wrong with you?"

"Dude, leave Hester alone. You need to go sober up!"

Several people surrounded the young girl, guided her away, several more dragging Kirk back as he protested loudly.

"Doesn't anyone else get it?" he demanded. He shook off the hands holding him and stalked off between the rides, heading towards the river, the opposite direction from where the friendly hands had guided Hester.

"What was that all about?" Tricia asked.

"Let's follow him," Caleb said, already starting through the crowd.

"What? Why?"

Tricia's voice fell back a little, but Caleb was desperate not to lose sight of Kirk. Hoping she would follow, he pushed on, gritting his teeth against the seething mass of people, ignoring the headache flaring behind his eyes. A gap opened up, Kirk somehow finding clear passage where Caleb repeatedly bumped into knots of bodies, had to make apologies, came across groups of friends gathered in broad circles.

As he came around a teacup ride, he caught sight of Kirk again, some twenty yards ahead. But now the man was moving altogether differently. Where he had been belligerent and headlong before, now he was tall and stiff, walking in a slow, stuttering gait. As Caleb watched, trying to get past the throng, the man approached the back of the Ferris wheel. It was surrounded by four-foot high metal fencing, a gate in the north side that lead the line of people to a small booth where cash was taken and the ride operated. Up close, the Ferris wheel towered huge over everything, moving faster than it appeared to from a distance. Unseen by the operator or the people waiting their turn, Kirk climbed over the low metal railing.

Caleb yelled out, but his voice was lost in the hubbub of carnival fun. People in the Ferris wheel cars, two, three, four in a row, holding the metal bar lowered over their laps, sailed around, all looking south, no doubt getting a fine view of the town of Sallow Bend from the top. And they all came around facing the open section inside the fencing, where Kirk now walked, standing tall. He clambered over a second security fence, awkwardly, his face strained like he was trying to resist his own movements, then dragged that fence forward. He clambered stiffly onto it, balancing precariously as he stood up. A group of three teenage girls sailed over the operator's booth and screamed, all hauling their feet up, as Kirk straightened up in of them. He wore an expression of pain, of effort, like the face of a man trying to lift a weight he would never budge. Then Kirk drove his head forward to meet the swiftly moving seat carrying the girls and it slammed into his face, lifted him off the fence, and threw him back to lay sprawled on the grass. Blood flooded from his crushed nose and mouth, the skin of his forehead split open to expose the shining white of his skull. More screaming, from on the ride and all around it, as people realized what had happened.

A tall, skinny carnie with almost no chin and an Adam's apple like an extra knuckle driving out of his throat, hit the emergency stop button and came running around the operator's booth, face a mask of horror. More screams and yells rang out as the Ferris wheel shuddered to a halt, every seat of swinging back and forth in place with arrested momentum. A family in the car right before the sprawled body of Kirk twisted under their restraining bar, the two parents covering the eyes of their young son and daughter even as they looked on in horror themselves. The three girls, now above and past the fallen man, twisted in their seats to look back and down, crying and hugging each other.

Caleb stopped a few yards from the fence, staring at the supine form of Kirk. Others gathered around him, pointed and chattered. The man's chest hitched erratically, still alive but badly wounded. One leg twitched and danced like electricity was coursing through it, the fingers of both hands clenching and stretching out spasmodically. Blood leaked from his ears. Caleb turned slowly, eyes scanning the crowd. Some quickly converged to get their macabre thrill, others hurried away, distraught. Moving off between two other stalls, Caleb caught a glimpse of a pale linen dress, black hair with a flash of white as the breeze lifted it, then she was gone. Voices came to him through the noise.

"What was he thinking?"

"Was that a suicide?"

"He was out of his head, man, he was just yelling in the face of some kid back there a minute ago."

Jerry and Jill Yonker, local husband and wife paramedic team, ran up, vaulted over the fencing and crouched by the man, quickly rummaging in their emergency packs. Jerry stood and pulled out his phone, called for an ambulance.

"What's going on, Caleb? Why did you run off?"

He looked around to see Tricia beside him, face concerned. She looked at the crowd, then back to him. "What's happening?"

"That guy, Kirk? The one who was hassling Hester?"

"Yeah?"

"He just walked in front of the Ferris wheel, let it hit him in the head."

Tricia's hand flew up in front of her mouth. "Oh! Is he… is he dead?"

"Not quite."

"Why would he do such a thing?"

"I don't think he wanted to do it."

Tricia frowned at him. "What?"

Caleb shook his head, uncertain. The headache pounded inside, made thinking hard. Tricia shook her head. "That poor man. Come on, let's not stay around here. It's wrong to gawp at stuff like this. Come on, the fireworks will be starting soon."

13

RILEY BRENT WOKE with an aching back and a pounding head, cold hard floor beneath him. He groaned and rolled over, stomach protesting at the movement. He tried a couple of times to open his eyes, before the back room of Gil's Tavern swam blearily into view. The previous night came back to him in flashes and sounds. Too much beer, too much angry ranting. He had burned up a lot of goodwill in Gil's last night, drinking bitterly and growling at anyone who would listen about the injustices of life, pointing at his bruised head. Gil had shut him in the back room with a blanket after confiscating the keys to his pickup, but he had nowhere to drive to anyway. Anything that mattered to him had been packed into the back of that truck and he might as well just drive it into the Sallow River and be done with it.

He sat up, groaned again as he pushed the blanket away. The hangover was inevitable, but he worried about concussion too. Though what did it matter? He deserved nothing but pain. Boxes and crates filled the space, summer sun leaking in through grimy, barred windows. A small office in the back had a toilet beside it and he staggered to it, bladder threatening to burst. As he pissed, he thought back over the night's ramblings, patchy and inconsistent though they were. But he had kept his darkest secret to himself.

Perhaps he shouldn't have. Maybe it was time to come clean, blurt it all out and let them lock him up. But what would they jail him for? How could he even explain it? He went into Gil's little office and put on the coffee pot in there. The tavern owner had always been a good pal, looked out for Riley and a handful of others. It wasn't the first time he had woken up in the back room and made coffee ready for Gil's arrival some time around ten.

He fell into the tatty leather office chair, leaned it back and threw a forearm over his splintering eyes. Then something else about the conversation of the night before came back to him and his heart stuttered against his ribs. The girls had been found, all three of them. That was good, right? But something else. Suki, Clare, and Hester. Riley made a sound halfway between a cough and a sob. His brain struggled to target his discomfort. Missing kids obviously made him think of Toby, but why Hester in particular?

He remembered that awful Saturday in blistering detail, almost a year ago.

"Hey mom, I'm going to Jack's."

"Jack Wallace?" Tricia called from the kitchen.

"Of course Jack Wallace!"

"Okay, just making sure."

"We're gonna play D&D. Dinner at six?"

"Yep, no later. Love you, sweetie."

Toby mumbled something that may have been about love, then pulled the front door shut behind him. And Riley made a sudden decision that would change everything forever. Toby and his nerdy damn friends playing those stupid games in basements all the time. When Riley was Toby's age he used to ride billy carts and fish, get into fist fights and steal his parent's booze. His own boy was into nothing but dragons and computers, it drove him crazy. But like a flash of light behind his eyes, as soon as Toby had said he'd be out until six, a plan fell fully formed into Riley's mind. His fishing gear was already in the pick-up, he'd been planning to go that day anyway.

He grabbed his boots and went to the kitchen door. "I'm going fishing, love."

Tricia looked up, hands and apron covered in floor as she stood at the workbench. Her dark chestnut hair hung over her eyes as she smiled. "Already? Planning to make a day of not catching anything?"

Riley laughed. She was beautiful and cheeky and he loved every atom of her. "Sure, why not? Get a head start on next week's pointless sitting around on the riverbank, right?"

"Have a good day."

He crossed the floor for a kiss, her lips full and warm against his. "See you for dinner," he said, and left.

He drove the pick-up to the next block, turned right, and there was Toby only a hundred yards ahead, strolling along, backpack full of rulebooks and dice hanging off his narrow shoulders. Riley pulled up to the curb beside him.

"Hey, champ! What's up?"

Toby jumped. "Hey, Dad."

"Hop in."

"Nah, Jack's is only two minutes away. I'll walk."

Riley leaned over and pushed the passenger door open. "Hop in. I've got a suggestion to run by you." He would toughen his son up one way or another, and this idea was inspired. Toby would thank him for it one day.

Toby frowned, but swung his bag off his back and climbed in, his tumbling brown curly hair flopping over his eyes. He brushed it away, and smiled. "What suggestion?"

Riley drew in a deep breath. He loved this boy more than life, could never stay mad whenever he did get angry, though the lad drove him to distraction sometimes. Truth was, they both needed this. "How about a father and son adventure?"

"What do you mean?"

"I've got something exciting to show you. Been saving it up for the right moment." He realized that wasn't entirely a lie. And he knew he had been saving it for himself too.

"What about Jack and the others? D&D?"

"You can do that any time. They won't miss you that much, will they?"

Toby pursed his lips, shrugged. "I guess not. A bunch of us loosely planned to play today, but if I don't show I don't expect they'll care."

"Good. Because I have a secret to show you, but you can't tell Mom, okay?"

Toby's face was alive with excitement at the sudden thrill of defiance and outrageous behavior. It would do the boy good to get a little wild. It'd stop him getting too crazy when he was older and the leash was let off. Tricia wasn't expecting either of them until dinner anyway. Riley smiled. If they did get found out, there'd be trouble, but he was prepared to take the risk. Family life could be so damned restrictive sometimes, it paid to drop a grenade into it every now and then. He imagined Tricia, screaming at him about how irresponsible he was, and it gave him a subtle buzz. But they wouldn't get caught. "You up for it?" He knew his excitement was contagious.

"Sure!"

"Come on, then."

He gunned the engine and headed for the highway. As they passed the western side of town, heading north towards the woods, Toby asked, "So what's the secret?"

"You gotta be a tough guy, okay? You gotta be brave. Can you do that?"

Toby's face blanched slightly. "I guess."

Riley remembered his own attempt, at around the same age. But he'd been with two friends and they'd all three chickened and ran long before they got close. If he'd been with his old man, he'd have been brave. "I'm gonna look out for you, okay? You're safe with me, aren't you?"

"Of course."

"We'll be like two heroes from your game of DD. Swashbuckling rangers or something."

"Daa-aad!"

Riley laughed. "Yeah, I know, I don't get that stuff. But we'll be like that. Brave adventurers."

He followed the highway around and crossed the Sallow River. Only a hundred yards after the bridge was a small dirt road between the trees, so dark and overgrown you'd miss it unless you knew it was there. He turned in and the pickup bounced and crunched along the track. Another few hundred yards and he pulled up into a small open gap between two trees and killed the engine.

"Is this all an excuse to take me fishing?" Toby asked. "That's not an adventure."

"No, son. This is entirely different."

They climbed out and Riley shouldered his own small pack that he always took fishing with him. It had a couple of bottles of water, some chips and muesli bars. More than enough for a few hours in the woods. "Now, you gotta be fit and strong. We're gonna walk for about an hour or so, following the river. It'll be a bit rough in places, but it's mostly easy enough through the trees."

"That sounds like a long way."

"It sure is, but you don't find adventure without a little journeying. Come on."

He set off, striding into a good pace to make sure Toby followed without any further protest. Toby ran to catch up and his eyes were alight again, the promise of adventure slowly pushing aside his trepidation.

The day warmed up, birds sang, sunlight lanced between the trees and dappled everything in soft green shades. Riley made jokes and Toby danced excitedly around, acting more like a little kid than the surly teenager he was becoming of late. They saw a stag that turned magnificent antlers towards them before bounding off between the trees, Toby delighted with the sighting. Riley pointed out different birds, told Toby what they were, identified their song. They saw rabbits and once something much bigger than a rabbit, but neither saw it clearly enough to guess what it was. Riley smiled to himself, happy with the decision. They were bonding, they were out in the world instead of buried in stupid gaming books. He made a promise to think of more excursions like this.

After a little over a half hour, Toby complained of tired legs.

"Just a little further, champ. We'll rest when we get to the lake."

"Sallow Lake?" Toby asked, eyes wide.

"You've heard of it?"

"Sure, hasn't everyone? There's all kinds of stories about it."

"And you've heard about the cabin there?"

Toby's brows knitted. "No…"

Riley grinned. "That's what we're going to see." The cabin he'd been too chicken to see with his friends twenty years before. The cabin he had been secretly promising himself he'd come back to one day. A promise so secret, he hadn't even realized until the idea came to him that morning. They walked on in silence.

The woods seemed darker, like the sun had gone behind clouds. And cooler, the air damp and chill instead of warm and loamy as it had been. Their feet crunched over leaves and twigs but there was no other sound.

"What happened to the birds?" Toby asked in a quiet, nervous voice.

Riley smiled, but it was forced. "I don't know." He saw a sheen of something ahead through the trees. "There it is!"

They pushed on and came out from under the thick canopy at the lake's edge. The body of water was huge reflecting the sky above in a deep blue, hinting at depths far greater than might seem reasonable. Everything was still, but for a light wind sighing through the leaves. Riley pointed. "See it there?"

Toby stepped around his father to look. The cabin stood just under the trees, old wood darkened with age, covered in moss and stains. Two grimy windows like open eyes, shutters hanging and broken, either side of a tatty door that stood ajar. A stone chimney took up the end wall, rising above the shingle roof.

"Dad, that is a creepy place."

Riley enjoyed the nervous thrill that tickled through him. There really was a cabin, like so many people said. He'd heard plenty of stories, talk of it being haunted, talk of people dying there. Stories about wayward travelers camping there and never being seen again. Who would travel through thick forest like this? But that was the point. Bring Toby here and scare him, scare them both. Create a bonding experience, a secret from Tricia, something just for them to laugh about and remember when they were safely home again. Proof of life beyond rulebooks and dice and video games.

"Let's go inside!"

"Dad, no."

"This is what we're here for, champ. This is the adventure. An act of daring." He looked down at Toby, wiggled his eyebrows. "You're not chicken, are you?"

Toby laughed, but it was strained. "I am a bit, actually."

"You know what? Me too. Let's be men. It's just an old cabin, Tobes. There are no ghosts or monsters really."

Toby licked his lips, a nervous smile making his cheeks flicker. He took a deep breath. "Okay, let's do it."

"Yes!"

Toby pushed his father forward. "But you first."

"Okay, fair enough."

They set off, two brave adventurers in single file. The air had a chill to it that raised gooseflesh on their arms, their footsteps strangely loud. As they got close, Riley felt as though even the woods held their breath. Tension hung in the air, a sensation of taut expectation. He glanced back at Toby and the boy's eyes glittered with swirling fear and excitement.

Riley reached out and pushed the door open, his heart hammering despite his rational adult mind assuring him it was just an old cabin. The wood was cold and slimy to the touch, lightly furred with mold and lichens. It moved silently in and he stepped into the dark interior. Toby quickly followed, holding onto his dad's arm like a child even though the near-teenager stood up to Riley's shoulder already. They stared and blinked for a moment, waiting for their eyes to adjust. The light through the two windows was wan and patchy, making puddles of illumination on the flagstone floor. The fireplace at one end was huge, taking up half the wall, the hearth and mantel around it made of large stones, neatly put together. They moved into the middle and turned a slow circle. The ceiling above was dim, cobwebbed joists supporting the weather-stained shingles that clearly leaked in dozens of places, even let shards of light in here and there. Still, cold, inert, damp, but nothing more. A rickety table stood against one wall, two broken chairs beside it like cadaverous guards. In the far corner was a crooked box cot, one leg canted sideways. Tattered and stained rags across it like mold. A handful of pitted and rusted pots and pans littered the ground beside the hearth, some on their sides, all hung with cobwebs. More webs stretched across the windows, under the table and cots, like gossamer bridges between the crippled chairs.

Riley looked at Toby and grinned, his heart rate calming. "Bit of an anti-climax after all that, eh, champ?"

Toby laughed, nodded, his curls flapping. "Yeah, I was really scared there for a…"

The cabin door slammed shut.

They both jumped, Riley let out a bark of surprise even as Toby's words become a terrified shriek.

"Just the wind, Tobes." He went back to the door and grabbed the curved wooden handle. When he pulled against it, the door didn't budge.

"Open the door, Dad!"

"I'm trying. It's stuck." He hauled against it again, leaning his not inconsiderable weight back, but it was like the wood had been nailed in place. "Must have swollen up with damp and jammed now its blown shut."

"There wasn't any wind, Dad."

"We changed the air pressure by leaving the door open or something." He didn't really believe his own words, but what other explanation was there?

"Let's be men…" a woman's voice said.

Riley spun around, saw Toby looking left and right, but they were alone.

"Let's be men," the voice said again, whispery and mocking.

"Who's there?" Riley yelled, fear lending unexpected volume to his words.

"Always have to be men, hmm? Always men are the problem."

"Who's there? Show yourself!"

The voice seemed to echo all around them, like it came from somewhere above and reflected back off the roof. Almost, Riley thought absurdly, like the cabin itself was speaking.

"Planning to make your child into a man, were you?" the voice said. It had an old-fashioned tone to it, an accent that spoke of age and history. "A man like you? Are you so very much worth emulating?"

Toby was turning in circles, tears streaming over his cheeks. "Dad! What is it?"

"I don't know, son. Help me here." Riley turned back to the door and got both hands locked into the wood and hauled. He grunted with the strain, but it wouldn't move.

"*DAD*!"

"Toby, help me here!" Riley looked back over one shoulder as he strained against the door and cried out to see Toby sliding backward over the flagstone floor. The boy was on his butt, arms up and flailing like someone had him under the armpits to drag him along, but there was no one there. His face was stretched in horror, his fingers scrabbling the air for Riley.

"*DAD*!"

Riley ran across the cabin. The huge fireplace, which before had been plain and solid grey stone, was a wide open darkness. A hole into nothing. And Toby was rapidly retreating toward it, dragged by unseen hands. Riley dived forward, grabbed hold of Toby's left foot, but the boy jerked suddenly and Riley's hand slipped free. He scrabbled to hands and knees as Toby was pulled into the dark mouth of the cavernous hearth that had been solid stone moments before. Bruising his knees, grazing his palms, Riley surged ahead and caught sight of a figure in the darkness, hands reaching forward like she was waiting to receive a parcel. Or a child. He couldn't focus, couldn't tell if it was a middle-aged woman hunched over or a younger girl standing up. Her mouth twisted in hateful glee. Darker patches striated her form, like gaps at her shoulders and hips, at her knees and neck, her limbs shifting as she swayed like some hideous marionette.

Riley gasped, stunned at the sudden presence, and paused for one horrible, final second. In that moment of shock, Toby vanished into the darkness and the woman seemed to close over him. Riley howled and rushed forward, only to crash into hard, cold, unforgiving stone. His vision crossed, stars and spots burst behind his eyes, and he fell heavily onto his side. He lay there breathless for a moment, trying to figure out which way was up while his ears sang. He finally managed to get onto his knees and frantically played his hands all over the hearth, digging his fingers into every gap, but it was solid rock and mortar, the base a single gray slab. Old, hardened, undisturbed for decades.

He stumbled to his feet, kicked and pushed at the stones, at the mantle, yelling and crying incoherently. He staggered back, looked all around. "Give me back my son!" he screamed.

The cabin door creaked open, watery sunlight making a wedge on the dark floor. Bubbling, mocking laughter rippled out from all around him, as though the cabin, even the woods themselves, were amused.

"Give me back my Toby!" Riley yelled.

He ran out of the cabin, around to the end to where the back of the fireplace stood out from the wall, rising up to the broad, square chimney above the roof. He kicked and pulled at the stones, but they were strong, still fixed fast. They would stand for decades yet.

"Where is he?" he cried.

"Gone," whispered the trees.

For hours, Riley scrabbled at the stones and the wooden walls. He dug at the earth around the chimney until his nails were broken and his fingers bled. He shouted for Toby's return, he begged, he offered himself in Toby's place, but the voice didn't say another word. There was nothing but the cold lake, the old cabin, the silent woods all around. Riley was alone in the world. His fault, his stupid idea, his ridiculous plan. Toby should be safe in Jack Wallace's house, rolling dice to determine the fate of some imaginary warrior, but instead he was gone forever. Riley railed and sobbed, but there was nothing he could do. He considered getting back to town, getting a party out to search, but it made no sense at all, no one would believe him. He had watched Toby dragged into darkness, had seen his son taken by some force beyond nature and he knew, without any doubt, in his bones he knew that his son was gone. He had lost his boy.

Eventually he lay on the lake side and sobbed, staring at the broken down old cabin. He had been in and out a dozen times or more, but there was nothing but wood and stone and silence. As the light began to dim, he knew it was over. He knew as well that whoever that woman was, she could surely have taken him as easily as she took Toby, but had chosen not to. She deliberately left him to suffer. And in that dimming late afternoon, something in Riley Brent stretched beyond its bounds and snapped.

He stumbled to his feet and followed the river back south. As darkness fell, he made his way half by seeing and half by listening for the flow of the Sallow River over rocks and tree roots. No one knew he had picked up his son. No one knew of his impromptu adventure. Did that creature back there know that as well? Was that her punishment? No matter, no one knew. He could never tell a soul, they would think him mad. Perhaps he was mad, but Toby was really gone. It had really happened. He eventually stumbled into his truck in the dark, climbed inside and drove numbly home. As he pulled up onto the driveway, he saw a police cruiser parked at the curb and Tricia came running from the house, eyes red and swollen from crying.

"Where have you been?" she screamed, clawing at his shirt.

"Just fishing, at the river..."

"Toby is missing!" she sobbed. "He never even made it to Jack's this morning. No one knows where he is!"

Riley jerked back to the present, rocking forward in Gil's tattered office chair. The coffee pot bubbled and boiled as he sank his face into his hands and bawled, for the millionth time. A thousand times he had berated himself for not telling anyone, for not coming clean. And every time he didn't admit what had happened, it became a harder thing to do. How could he ever explain such a thing? Who would believe him? They would lock him up, thinking he had done away with his son. And a thousand times he had considered that a viable option, but was too much of a chickenshit to allow it to happen.

But the talk in the bar the night before, the girls coming back, had made all those feelings fresh and raw again. They had been found up at that cabin. Apart from the obvious horror of what had happened to him there, why was it that the three girls being found there filled him with such discomfort? He scrunched his face in grief and concentration, tried to catch the elusive thoughts flitting through his pounding, hungover mind. That hideous vision of the creature who took Toby, that woman. Her seemingly dislocated form, her long dark hair, a flash of something white. His eyes popped wide. It wasn't just the girls coming back, but particularly one of them. Clarity faded again in a new swirl of headache and nausea, but one thought remained. Hester coming back. There was a connection, one he couldn't grasp, but which lingered nonetheless. He felt an inexplicable but powerful urge to talk with Hester Black.

14

ASHLEY STRONG STOOD surrounded by a couple of dozen members of her crew, all restless. The hulking presence of Sheriff Holtz beside her did nothing to ease tensions. The crowd had gathered around Holtz as he walked along the midway only to mill nervously near her trailer.

The summer sun beat down hard on them, already hot and not yet nine in the morning. They were in a for a stinker of a summer, all dried grasses and hard, cracked earth. Normally that would fill Ash with hope, hot nights where people wanted to stay out late, spend all their money at the carnival. The kind of nights when people wore very little, teenagers lusting after each other in the summer break, dating each other at the carnival, trying to outdo one another with gifts of rides and candy and tee-shirts and soft toys. It was all grease in the wheels of her life. But that strident heat seemed to carry a warning with it instead of hope. She berated herself for allowing superstition and worry to imbue something as simple as weather with some kind of malevolent intent. Yet she couldn't deny the feeling.

"What can I do for you, Sheriff?" She knew he was here about the accident, but had no intention of making it easy for him. She was still sore about them going through everyone's stuff.

"Wanted to talk to you about the accident last night."

"Weren't no accident!" The voice from the back of the small crowd rang out loud and belligerent.

Ash couldn't be bothered to try to work out who it was. It didn't matter, one speaking for all. She opened her mouth to speak but Sheriff Holtz stepped forward, tipped his hat up a little revealing a brow glistening with sweat. "Now I know it wasn't exactly an accident, but can anyone tell me what happened?"

"Paramedics asked all the questions already," someone called out.

Holtz's face hardened. "And now I'm asking them again because Kirk died in the hospital last night."

A ripple of unease passed over the crew, a few made crosses on their chests, a couple made older signs to avert the evil eye.

"Was a suicide," Clyde Raymond said, quietly but loud enough to be heard.

Ashley pointed him out to Holtz. Tall, skinny, chinless Clyde with his protuberant Adam's apple. Like always, he wore jeans and a bright, clean white tee-shirt, with red Converse hi-tops on his feet. "He runs the Ferris wheel," she said.

Holtz crooked a finger. "Step forward, son. What did you see?"

Clyde moved out from the rest of the crew, raised his voice. "I inherited that wheel off my daddy and we never had a single accident until last night. And that was no accident!"

"No one's in trouble here, we're just trying to understand."

Clyde licked his lips, looked around, nodded almost to himself. "That guy was crazed, some said he was steaming drunk. However you look at it, he did that to his-self. I didn't see him climb over, but there's two fences and still the wheel is too high to hit anyone, it's designed that way. But that fella he climbed on top of the fence and stretched up." Clyde pushed up onto his tiptoes as he talked, acting the part. "He deliberately put his head in the way of that car. The man was suicidal."

"So it would seem," Holtz said.

"So that matches the other reports you've had?" Ashley asked, loud enough to be heard by all. She needed her crew settled, no rumor, no speculation. One idiot suicide and nothing more. It was awful, incredibly sad, but it needed to be done and finished. She wished the damn fool had chosen somewhere else. Jumped in the river, hanged himself in his garage, anything rather than bring this heat down on her carnival. Again. Heartless though it sounded, it was extra hassle she didn't need.

Holtz nodded. "It's what a bunch of people told the paramedics, and the same as what we've heard. We don't understand it, that's all. Kirk was known to enjoy a drink but he's a happy family man. *Was* a happy family man. Good job, loving wife, three kids."

Ashley felt a surge of guilt at her previous thoughts, but pushed it aside. "And no indication he was depressed or anything like that?"

"Nope. Kirk was always a little odd. Some said he was on the spectrum, you know? Had a hard time with social cues sometimes, stuff like that. But he's never been down about it as far as I know. Kirk's a respected citizen in this town, and he had no reason to kill himself."

"I guess sometimes we simply don't know a person's mind."

Holtz frowned. "Guess so."

She sensed his discomfort, but it wasn't hers to bear. She did need to mollify him though. She turned back to her crew. "I know you've all been one hundred percent on top of your safety routines, but I want every hand to go over their health and safety protocols again before we open at noon." She raised both hands at the sudden swell of protesting voices. "I know it's a royal pain in the ass, and I know last night was no accident, and it wasn't Clyde's fault. But let's not tempt fate, okay? Everyone, please, one more check."

"Maybe it's not the kind of thing we can check for," Saul Fallon said. His pale face was bright in the morning sun, his scowl dark.

Ash internally cursed him. "What?"

"Perhaps there's something bad in this town." He turned, tall enough to be seen scanning the crew. "Missing children, now inexplicable suicides. Who knows what's next? Perhaps bad energy lives here." He smirked as he looked back to Ashley.

She stared hard at him, wishing a sudden heart attack would drop him on the spot. There was something callous and vulturine about Saul, he seemed to always enjoy fear and superstition. He was the one who told scary stories when they had bonfires to sit around. He was the one who read out macabre news from the paper as they ate breakfast in the big staff canteen tent. And he reveled in the discomfort he caused. She could always rely on him to stir up the crew. Asshole. Shutting him down quickly was the best option, but she knew he'd already planted his seed. "Shut the fuck up, Saul. The girls were found safe and sound, they just played too far in the woods. And like I just told the Sheriff, sometimes you can't know a person's mind. Kirk picking the carnival for his check-out is simple bad luck."

Saul shrugged, still smirking. He seemed to be drawing long, deep breaths. Ash ground her teeth. Freak.

"Now please, go and make your checks. Everything will be in order and we'll open at noon with no more mishaps and nothing but fun."

She wasn't surprised to see the crew disperse to leave only John Barrow and Sarah Carter, who came over to join her and Holtz.

"Anything we can do to help?" Barrow asked.

Holtz let out a humorless laugh. "What is there to help with? Kirk lost his mind last night for some reason we can't explain, and because of that he lost his life. Thank you all for your time." He briefly lifted his hat, then walked off along the midway, heading for the gate and his cruiser beyond.

Ashley turned to Barrow and Sarah. "You two got anything you want to tell me?"

Sarah lifted one hand, bangles jingling. She squeezed Ash's upper arm. "I know you don't have much truck with my talents, and I know Saul's an asshole, but..."

"But what?"

"But there is something weird going on around here."

Ashley sighed. "Weird how?"

"I don't know. Nothing I can really put my finger on. But there's a bad vibe in the air."

"Well, if you manage to put a finger on it, you be sure to come and let me know."

"You want me to talk to Saul?" Barrow asked.

Ashley shook her head. "You already annoyed him once doing that. John, it's not your job to fix this stuff. It's mine. And sometimes the best way to fix something is to leave it the hell alone. Things will settle down."

She turned and went back to her trailer, but felt their skeptical eyes on her back the whole way.

15

CALEB WATCHED THROUGH the narrow ground level windows of his rooms as the children streamed into school. His was a unique perspective, staring across at grass level, the rear door of the school to his far left, out of sight, but the entire playground and sports field beyond spread out before him. Several trees and a series of scattered low benches filled the foreground of his vision, a patch of shade and comfort where students regularly gathered to eat packed lunches and gossip and play. Usually the territory was controlled by one group or another, and the boundaries changed as years went by. It had been the domain of the jocks for a long time, then the mean girls, who shared it with the jocks for a while. For a time last year, one entire semester, it had been the corner where the goths and weirdoes sulked, before they were driven out by a pack of raucous metalheads. Caleb enjoyed watching the politics play out from his subterranean viewpoint, though he was careful not to stare for long. Enough people thought him creepy enough as it was. Besides, more than a couple of minutes would start the headache, and he always avoided that where he could. Right now, the area was under a seemingly shifting ownership, with no particular group claiming it as their province. A time of geopolitical flux.

Before long the bell would ring and the kids would all pile into class, the mayhem he watched now suddenly still and empty. It was always a strange thing to see, the way the students flexed between ordered study and chaotic play through the course of their day. Much as he despised the falsities of adult interaction, much as he preferred the open and more honest socialization of the kids, it meant they were capable of incredible cruelty to each other. If adults pretended to like someone they hated, that was dishonest. But a child would be entirely candid, tell another they were hated and exactly why, and Caleb had witnessed many times the damage that caused.

He'd occasionally hear the kids be entirely honest with what they thought of him too, sometimes when they knew he could hear them, other times when they thought they were alone. Once, through his open door, he had listened to a small group on one of those low benches as they spent an entire morning break discussing all the ways he was dangerous and weird. By the end of that particular conversation they were all giggling madly at the sure knowledge that Caleb abducted and ate babies every chance he got. One of the kids suggested that if you were locked into the school accidentally overnight, you would never be found again unless the police checked Caleb's freezer and unwrapped the individual portions of chopped up student in there. On one level it hurt his feelings, but they were just kids. More than anything he was impressed with their imaginations.

Then he saw the reason he was peering from his windows on this particular morning. The first indication was the sudden attention of everyone already in the play area towards the back doors. Though he couldn't see them, he could see the last of the steps leading down to the path, and all eyes turned that way. A small crowd quickly gathered and Suki, Clare, and Hester stepped into view. They all talked and hugged and flapped their hands at each other, the crowd bombarding the three girls with questions. At first it was a maelstrom, but it slowly resolved into a more organized gathering. The three girls moved to one of the benches under the trees and sat down. Others milled around, the gaggle of voices too indistinct for Caleb to make out any particular words despite leaving his door half open.

After a couple of minutes more the initial excitement waned. Kids could always be relied upon for a short attention span if nothing else. A core group of a dozen or so, mostly other girls, sat around on the summer-hardened ground or on nearby benches, the three returned girls at their center. Of the three, Hester sat in the middle, of course, like a queen holding court. Caleb narrowed his eyes to see better through the grubby, narrow pane. Though pale, Hester looked bright and vibrant, those moss green eyes sparkling. But Suki and Clare still appeared exhausted, drawn out. It looked as though they could both use a solid week of sleep.

As the initial squealing slowed, Caleb began to pick out the words of the conversation.

"...you must have been so scared!"

"It was pretty frightening," Hester said. "But we looked out for each other."

"Who found you? I heard it was one of those weird carnies."

Hester laughed. "His name is Daniel. Suki liked his muscles."

Suki's mouth dropped open in horror. "Hester!"

"That's what you told me."

"But you weren't supposed to tell anyone else!" Suki's pale cheeks had brightened scarlet and she looked around, unable to hold anyone's eye.

Clare laughed. "He was pretty gorgeous though. He was huge!"

More laughter, more ribbing.

"That what really happened? You spent a couple of days sucking carnie dick?" The new voice was a boy's. Caleb couldn't see where at first, then a tall, gangly kid with a shock of dark hair stepped past a tree. He wore a black metal band tee-shirt under his school shirt and carried a candy bar in one hand. He took a bite of the candy, grinning around his distended cheek as he chewed. Caleb recognized him. Reece Gossett, one of those kids who acts like a hard-ass but wasn't really tough. Better to act like a bully than risk being bullied, perhaps, until his bluff was called. Reece's family were pretty poor, if Caleb remembered correctly, and he had several siblings. A lot of mouths for his parents to feed. But none of that excused the kind of misogynistic comment the kid had just made. It caused Caleb to grind his teeth. Jokes like that tended to embed themselves and make unpleasant adults of the hapless teens. He would try to find an opportunity to talk to Reece about it, but right now he was more concerned with Hester.

"Shut up, Reece!" Suki said. "You're such a pig."

The boy shrugged, still grinning. "That why you're all pretending you just got lost? You can't admit the truth?"

As Suki opened her mouth to speak again, Hester said, "That all you got? Lame dick jokes because you're intimidated by women? You want to be careful you don't choke, talking and eating at the same time." Her voice was low, barely above a whisper, but it cut through the day like torchlight through a dark room. Even Caleb, tucked away more than ten yards distant, heard her clearly.

Reece frowned at her. "You fucking freak..." he started, then coughed.

Hester stood, took a step towards him. "You know, you could die, choking on a candy bar. Imagine how embarrassing that would be. What a ridiculous way to go."

Reece coughed again, panic replacing the sneer he had been wearing. He opened his mouth, gagged, coughed and clawed at his throat.

"Something stuck in there?" Hester asked, as casual as if she was asking for the time.

The others were almost motionless, staring as though lost in a dream. Caleb, wincing against a sudden, pulsing pain behind his eyes, started for the door, wondering why none of the others had said a word. As he pulled his door fully open and started up the steps, the back door of the school banged open and Mr Daley, the physics teacher, ran out. He grabbed Reece from behind, lifted him up and locked his hands beneath the boy's ribcage, ready to apply the Heimlich manoeuver. Caleb stopped halfway up his steps, watching neither the teacher nor the unfortunate Reece, but Hester. Her face had fallen from cruel amusement to disdain. She turned away. Reece sucked in a huge, gasping breath and staggered away, dragging harsh gasps into his tortured lungs. His face was red, eyes bulging.

Daley's brows were creased in confusion, but relief washed across his face. "Why did none of you do anything?" he demanded. "You didn't even call for help! If I hadn't seen him from my window..."

"We didn't know what to do!" Hester said, a whine in her voice.

Reece cast her a terrified sidelong glance, then scurried away between the trees. Daley's face softened. He put one hand on Hester's shoulder, stood a little closer than Caleb thought appropriate. Hester's lips dipped downwards in disgust.

"Don't be scared, okay?" Daley said. He brushed one finger down her cheek. "But next time, call for help. Call me whenever you need me."

Hester twisted out from under Daley's hand and took a couple of steps back. The look she gave him was acidic. As she opened her mouth to say more, the school bell rang sharply. Caleb had never liked Daley, never found him trustworthy, but hadn't been able to put his finger on why. The man always seemed to be trailing a cloud of grease behind him. Seeing that little interaction had given Caleb an insight that scared him. He thought the man should not be allowed anywhere near a school.

At the sound of the bell, the kids grabbed their bags and headed for the building. Hester was the last to leave, and Caleb saw she had no bag.

As Caleb quietly backed into his rooms again, Daley said, "Go on, now, Hester. Run along." And he playfully slapped her butt. Caleb drew breath to speak, then thought better of it. But he would certainly report that to Fitzpatrick. Hester watched the physics teacher from under lowered brows for a moment, then slowly walked past him and up the steps to the school's back doors. Daley turned and watched her go, hands on his hips, a half-smile tugging at his lips.

Caleb went back inside and closed his door. As he headed for his desk to check his work roster, he caught sight of Daley still standing there, elbows out to either side. The man's face was twisted into a strange expression.

Caleb hurried to his window, wondering if he was imagining it. But he wasn't. Daley's face contorted like he was trying to work out a particularly difficult mathematics problem. Then his eyes darted left and right, his shoulders trembled. Caleb frowned, the headache surging back. As he wondered what was wrong with the man, a loud crack sounded from somewhere high above. At the same moment, he realized where he had seen a facial expression like that before. Kirk, as he had climbed, wobbling, atop the fence behind the Ferris wheel. But Caleb had no time to consider the revelation as a huge branch dropped from above and smashed Daley to the ground.

Caleb let out a cry of shock and ran back to his door. He pounded up the steps and pushed his way through the sudden foliage that sprouted from the fallen tree limb. He pulled smaller branches left and right, fighting his way through, to reveal Daley lying beneath the thick main limb that had fallen. But Daley was gone, only his body remained, his neck canted brutally to one side, his left ear pressed into his left shoulder, wide blank eyes staring glassily, still conveying a last moment of impotent terror.

16

CALEB STOOD BY the fallen tree limb, trying to ignore the emptiness in his gut. Police tape surrounded the scene, the students all sent home early in a cloud of gossip and macabre excitement. One thing he had seen more than any other was a kind of suppressed glee. Not that there had been a sudden death at school, that carried the kind of shock he would have expected, but that it had occurred to Mr Daley. It appeared almost every student thought it couldn't have happened to a nicer guy. Perhaps Hester had done them all a favor. And he was in no doubt that somehow Hester had been involved. Kirk under the Ferris Wheel, Reece Gossett choking, now this? But therein lay that empty hole in his insides. The gap between his sure though inexplicable knowledge and everyone else's obliviousness in the face of the cause.

The paramedics had arrived swiftly in response to his frantic call, Jerry and Jill Yonker stony-faced in the presence of another horrible accident so soon after the last. But Caleb knew it was no accident. And the Yonkers had left again as quickly as they arrived, faces darkened by the grim ending before them. Daley was dead, they said. Nothing more to be done. His neck snapped like a twig, as Caleb had seen, but more than that, his midsection had been crushed flat, like a fly under a timely palm. His hips and thighs were out of sight under the large fallen tree limb, but that rough wood was pressed hard into the earth. Daley's lower legs protruded at erratic angles from the other side, partly obscured by smaller branches and foliage.

Freddie Holtz had been by almost on the heels of the paramedics, the horse-faced Janssen in tow as usual. He'd accepted the tragic accident story, of course. After all, what else could it be? And he'd left Caleb waiting for Burt Lebowski, the logger Caleb and Tricia had met in the woods near Old Man Wilson's place. Burt would remove the broken tree to allow the paramedics to return and retrieve the body.

While he waited, Caleb moved around to the other end of the fallen branch. It was massive, a good twenty feet long, nearly three feet in diameter at the thickest point. The part that had landed square on top of the physics teacher. When it had first fallen, the branches spreading from the limb were healthy, thick with a summer growth of green leaves. The broken end where it had torn away from the trunk was clean and white, beaded with sap that leaked like blood. A fresh, healthy limb, not something old and dead. But in the time he had waited, as paramedics and police had come and gone, the thing had aged. Not fast enough that he could see the changes happening, but the bright green leaves were old and brittle now, the clean, bleeding end had dried and browned.

Caleb's mouth was dry too, his mind churning. He *knew* Hester had caused the accident. He'd watched Daley freeze up like Kirk had at the carnival. And where Kirk had been guided by some unseen hand under the Ferris wheel, Daley had been pinned to the spot while a perfectly healthy tree limb detached itself from a vibrant tree and crushed him to death. Hester was the only connection, but how could he even explain, let alone prove, that to anyone?

The sound of an engine revving echoed across the empty schoolyard and Caleb stepped out from behind the fallen branch to see Burt Lebowski pull a large pick-up around the corner of the school hall. He waved and Burt stuck one hand out the window in acknowledgment. Towed behind the pick-up was a dented and rusted wood chipper. Burt made a series of complicated maneuvers until he'd parked up alongside the branch, in the shade of the trees. He climbed from the truck and walked over to Caleb, hand outstretched.

Caleb shook, hiding his wince at the strong, vigorous pumping his arm received. "How are you, Caleb?"

"Good, given the circumstances. Thanks for coming out."

"Well, I wish I didn't have to. As you say, given the circumstances. Hell of a thing to have happened, eh?"

Caleb nodded, uncertain how to respond. He couldn't simply spit out the truth.

Burt paused a moment, then nodded once, as if acknowledging Caleb's discomfort. He pushed the smaller branches aside and moved towards the main limb. "Jesus Christ." His voice was low, slightly pained. "Look at the poor bastard. Tim Daley, right?"

"Yes. Physics teacher. Sheriff Holtz told me to call him when you arrived," Caleb said. "He wants to be here, oversee things."

"Okay. You do that while I start on all these smaller branches. It'll take me a while to get the main part cleared."

Caleb went into his rooms and dialed Holtz from the landline there. He had never had a cell phone and hoped to avoid the need to ever get one. The idea that he could be contacted or tracked anywhere he went made his stomach tighten.

"This is Holtz."

"Burt Lebowski is here." The whine of a chainsaw started up.

"That him cutting already?"

"Yeah, he said it'll take a while to strip the thing down, to get in close."

"Okay. I'm on my way."

Burt was busy, grubby ear protectors over his equally grubby Redsox cap. He expertly used the tip of the small chainsaw to trim the smaller branches, tossing them back towards his truck as he went. Surprisingly quickly the fallen limb was denuded and Caleb realized it had aged further still in the short time he'd been inside. Brown, dead leaves littered the ground, the previously healthy branches silvered and brittle. In less than fifteen minutes, Burt had stripped the thing down to the one main branch, Daley crushed beneath staring sightlessly at the canopy above. Hot summer sun lanced down through gaps, speckled the ground with lazily shifting spots of light.

Burt wiped sweat from his face and fired up the chipper, the sound deeper and harsher on the ears than the chainsaw had been. He paused, came to stand close to Caleb.

"You want me to carry the chips away?" he yelled over the engine noise. "Or let 'em pile up there and you can use 'em to mulch the beds?"

It was such a mundane question. Caleb thought perhaps using a branch that had killed a man to mulch the flowerbeds was some kind of sacrilege, but he wasn't generally given to superstition. He was pragmatic above anything else.

"Let them pile up, I guess." He pointed to a spot behind the benches, between several of the trees.

Burt nodded and backed the chipper up, then all chance of conversation was lost in the whine of branches being reduced to sawdust, spraying from the funnel of the chipper like blood from an arterial wound.

As he finished up, Holtz pulled in beside the pick-up. He climbed out and looked at Daley's crushed body under the stripped branch. He pushed his hat back, rubbed his forehead. "Holy shit, man."

Caleb had tried not to look at Daley the whole time, but as Burt came to stand next to Holtz, both staring down at the corpse, Caleb decided he needed to join them. There seemed to be some kind of necessary ritual happening, some moment of respect.

"Old Willy Hendon's church organized a candlelight vigil tonight for Kirk Branton," Burt said eventually. "Reckon they might make it a twofer?"

Holtz shook his head. "I don't know. Seems unfair to Kirk's family to draw attention away. I guess they'll have to have another one tomorrow for Daley here."

"You going tonight?"

Holtz sighed. "I'm an elected official, I'll have to make an appearance. I never know what to do or say though." He looked at Caleb. "You going?"

Caleb jumped, surprised to be addressed. "I didn't know about it."

"Not a church-goer?"

"Not really."

"I know Kirk wasn't all that easy to get on with, his autism or whatever, but make an effort to show if you can. Community is important, right?"

Caleb nodded. "Autism?"

Holtz shrugged. "Actually, I don't know. Maybe that's not right. But he never quite got social interactions, old Kirk. You'd tell a joke and he'd stare like he didn't get it. Or you'd throw him a wink and he'd frown at you. Stuff like that. Never seemed to see people quite like the rest of us. But he was a great guy."

"That right?" Caleb said quietly. His mind raced with possibilities. Holtz didn't seem to draw a comparison between Caleb's own 'weirdness' and Kirk's difficulty with social interactions, as he'd put it, but maybe that's just because Caleb made a point of avoiding such interactions as much as he could. But the similarity didn't escape him, nor the fact that only he and Kirk seemed to see through Hester's spell.

The other men's attention drifted back to the atrocity before them. Daley's blood had darkened the sun-hardened ground in a small pool around the limb where it flattened him. Caleb saw a displaced bulge under his shirt, stained dark brown. He gulped and looked away when he realized it must be something from inside the man forced out.

"He's gonna be pizza under there," Burt said quietly. "How you want me to proceed?"

Holtz shook his head. "Fucked if I know. Holy hell, what a thing to happen." He looked at Caleb. "How could you not have seen this huge dead branch up there? Bad enough it killed a man, imagine if twenty kids had been sitting here in the shade!"

Panic rilled through Caleb as he found himself the center of blame. The truth was that twenty students had been sitting there moments before, but there was no way the branch would have fallen until Hester willed it. He had to suck up the accusation. He looked up, pointed to the thick umbrella of healthy leaves.

"It came from high up. All the trees seem in good shape. I wouldn't have seen that branch unless I climbed up there."

Burt followed Caleb's finger. He sniffed and nodded. "Man has a point. I can't understand why just one big limb like this died back enough to snap and fall. Maybe it got a borer in it or something."

"You see any evidence of that?" Caleb asked.

Burt moved around, checked the broken end. "Not really. Just looks dead. Damnedest thing. I wouldn't have spotted this either, Freddie. Not from down here."

"And I do check," Caleb added, telling the truth. "Each spring I make sure everything is healthy. It was fine before now, I assure you."

Holtz blew out a sigh. "Well, can you get up in all these trees before school starts back after the summer? I want you to make sure each one is in tip top shape, every branch healthy and strong. Or I'll order the whole lot taken down."

"I can do that." And he knew he would, to be certain. But he was also sure he would find the entire copse in rude health.

"Good." Holtz rubbed a hand over his face. "Kirk last night and now Daley? This town is too small for accidents so close together."

"Not both accidents, the way I heard it," Burt said.

"Well, maybe not. Seems Kirk put himself in danger and I have no idea why. But this is tragic and two deaths in two days is two too many for any town. Especially a little place like ours."

Caleb swallowed, determined to try to push their thoughts in the direction of Hester. "Not to mention the missing girls."

Holtz looked up at him. "And I'm fucking glad those three were found."

"I'm glad that carnie went back up to Sallow Lake," Burt said. "You know, me and some of the guys went up there the day before. We figured the girls might have got lost and found shelter in the old cabin. But there wasn't a soul anywhere."

Holtz nodded. "Seems they wandered aimlessly and found the place that night. That carnie, Daniel, he found them the next day."

"You ever go up there before?"

Holtz laughed. "Hell, no. We all made the dares as kids, same as everyone. But none of us went. It's too damn far and too damn spooky. Then I never had the inclination as an adult. You went before?"

"Nah. Nor as a kid, same as you. But we got to talking about where those girls might be and it turned into a kind of grown up dare to go and check the cabin. I think we all felt like we had unfinished teenage business." Burt barked a short laugh. "It is a genuinely creepy-ass place."

"And *both* girls could easily have wandered that far in the time they were lost," Caleb said. He watched the other men's faces closely.

Holtz nodded, lips pursed. "Yep. It's a good thing they stumbled onto the place. They could have wandered until they died of exposure otherwise."

Burt glanced at Caleb, wearing a slight frown. Had he caught the word 'both' Caleb had used. He tried to push the confusion. "Where does Hester live?"

"Some place north of town," Holtz said absently, looking back at the fallen branch.

"She lived here long?"

"You reckon we can lift that limb if you cut it into sections of, say, three feet each?"

Burt nodded. "Yeah, especially with all three of us. We can load it into the truck and I'll take it to the yard to break up for firewood."

"Was Hester born here?" Caleb pressed.

The other two looked up, brows creased. "What are you talking about Hester for?" Holtz said.

Burt had already turned to his truck and lifted out a second, bigger chainsaw. He pulled his ear protectors back down and his shoulders bulged as he held it one handed and yanked the starter cord. It roared to life, drowning out any possible chance for further conversation. In six howling cuts, he divided the limb up and killed the chainsaw's motor. They lifted each section up into the truck, grunting and heaving under the weight.

Puffed out and sweating, they left only the piece about three feet long laying over the crushed and gaping form of Tim Daley, legs crooked out one side, torso and head out the other, neck at that wrong and ruined angle. With everything else cleared they saw a large abrasion where the limb had first struck Daley's head, tearing the skin like tissue paper down one side of his forehead and cheek, snapping his neck like a chopstick. Caleb thought perhaps, if he were lucky, Daley had died the moment his neck severed like that and had avoided the subsequent crushing pain.

"Fuck me, but this is grim," Holtz said.

"Poor bastard," Burt agreed. "Gonna be worse when we lift that piece."

"Let's get it over with."

Caleb paused, unsure how he would fit in as the other two took an end each. A nub where a larger side branch had been cut away stuck out, so Caleb got a hand under that to help with the weight. As they lifted, Daley came up with it, arms and legs flopping, head lolling in a brutal, disconnected circle on a neck suddenly a couple of inches too long. Blood ran and dripped and the stench of shit rose up like a cloud.

"Ah, fuck," Holtz said. "Caleb, pull him off!"

The two men groaned under the weight and Caleb had no choice. He dithered for a second, wondering how to do it, then bit down his bile and pushed quickly against Daley's chest. A wet, sucking sound accompanied the flattened section of Daley as it peeled away from the rough bark. His shirt and pants shifted and loops of intestine slapped into the freshly blood-soaked earth, then the body smacked into the wet patch of ground, twisted even further out of any human shape. Daley's middle was little more than crooked blood-soaked clothing, flattened and creased. His head, which had been pressed against one shoulder, now lay crooked under his back, staring upside-down directly at Caleb.

"Jesus fucking Christ," Burt said, his voice low as a growl.

Caleb staggered back, turning away. The bile rose again and he swallowed it. The truck bed rang as they dumped the section of branch into it. Burt Lebowski hauled a crackling blue plastic tarpaulin out of the cab and threw it over Daley's broken corpse. Then he and Holtz came to join Caleb, their backs to humped tarp and the desecration it now thankfully concealed, gasping to catch their breath.

"What a fucking thing," Holtz said eventually. He reached up, patted Caleb's shoulder. "Well done. That was horrible."

The three men stood breathing deeply for a few moments, blessedly downwind of the death stench of the unfortunate teacher behind them.

"He got a family?" Burt asked eventually.

"No," Holtz said. "Single guy, lives across town near the supermarket on his own. We have to check the school records for next of kin to inform. Fitzpatrick's doing that. She'll come back with someone for Val Baker to call."

"That deputy of yours is worth her weight in gold," Burt said.

"Yep. One of her is worth ten Kurt fucking Janssens or Clive sleeping Taylors."

They both laughed, clearly using these banal details to remove themselves from the experience they'd just endured. All Caleb could hear was that wet tear and slap, repeating over and over in his mind.

"I'm going to call the Yonkers back in, they'll take it from here." Holtz squeezed Caleb's shoulder again. "Can you make sure no one else comes near until they get here? I don't think they'll take long."

"Sure."

"Good. And thanks again for your help there."

Burt Lebowski reached over and crushed Caleb's fingers again, pumped his arm. "You're a good man, Caleb."

"Thanks."

The three men stood watching each other for a moment, clearly sharing something unspoken. Caleb realized he was seeing an expression in their faces he was unused to. Respect. The three had been part of an experience no one else would understand, a thing only they could know. It bonded them somehow, and both Freddie Holtz and Burt Lebowski looked at Caleb with fresh eyes. He allowed a wavery smile, unsure how to react to such an alien interaction. But part of him liked it, particularly how it seemed so entirely normal compared to the ordeal they had just endured. They returned tight smiles of their own, then shook each other's hands again and turned away. The moment of camaraderie burst like a bubble, but Caleb knew they would always have this connection. He only wished they could share his burden of the cause as well.

The two big men returned to their vehicles and drove away. In moments, silence descended on the empty schoolyard, everything eerily still and inert. Usually Caleb enjoyed the desolation of school during the holidays, but this time it was unnaturally premature, heavy with unspoken truths that no one else would believe. He needed to figure out this Hester thing, because it seemed no one else would. How could they if they didn't even know it was happening?

But right now, all he needed was an evening to himself, away from everyone, to think and recharge. He'd be glad when the paramedics had taken Daley's body away. He'd hose off the ground, take some painkillers for his headache, then enjoy the rest of Friday and all that night on his own. Maybe lose himself in a good book. Everything else could wait.

17

RILEY BRENT DROVE slowly through Sallow Bend, frowning in confusion. Kids seemed to be on the streets everywhere, laughing and playing like school vacation had already started. But he was sure this was supposed to be the last day of school. A lump caught in his throat, lodged there like a stone. Only a year ago he would have known for sure, on top of the semesters, the homework, the teachers, and which of them Toby liked and loathed. And so quickly all that had changed.

His head pounded, as much from the clout Tricia had given him with the chopping board as from the self-abuse he had administered the night before with alcohol. His balls were swollen and tender still from her kick. As he drove, he kept a wary eye out for her red Taurus, and for Tricia herself. The last thing he wanted now was to see her. The night before he had left in a wounded rage. By this morning, the rage had been replaced with fresh grief and tearing confusion.

He had intended to drive by the school around lunchtime, see if he could spot Hester and her friends, maybe find a way to have a quiet word with her. He had no idea what he would say, but the collision of his memory of that horrible day at the cabin and Hester's appearance dogged him. In all this time, Hester all over town since… well, since forever that he could remember, he had never made the connection before, and that put painful lines of disparity through his thoughts. Regardless, all he could think of was talking to her. Maybe seeing her in the flesh would trigger some idea of what to ask. Just because she and the other girls had sheltered in the cabin, been found there, meant nothing in terms of his experiences with Toby. Yet he was determined, even compelled, to talk to her.

And now what? Kids everywhere, clearly school had quit already. A large group of ten or more teenagers were standing around outside Ken's General Store. They always loitered there, only a block from school. Often in their lunch break, after school, sometimes even before school. Ken was a decent guy, he ran a store that seemed to have anything you could desire. If you found yourself needing a Hi-Vis Vest or a quart of milk, a foolscap envelope or a trashy paperback, Ken would have it. The kids loved Ken's because he stocked all kinds of candy and comic books and those little foil packets of collectible cards they loved to play and trade. And he had a slushy machine with six different flavors and only charged two bucks a cup. A sign hung always on the door:

Help me help you! Only three students at a time, please.

Riley pulled up into a space among the small strip of parking out the front of Ken's. He had both windows down and his truck ticked over roughly but not so loud that he couldn't hear teens gabbling to one another about anything and everything. He stared at the dark screen of his cell phone, pretending to be occupied, as he listened for any hint of what was going on. It didn't take long before he had a full accounting of the gossip. Tim Daley was dead, crushed by a falling tree limb right there in the schoolyard just after classes started.

Holy shit. Riley knew Tim Daley. Not well, but they'd drunk together at Gil's often enough. The man was what Tricia would have called a career bachelor, and sometimes Riley had envied that. But he'd also been a little wary of the physics teacher. Nothing significant, but enough that he'd think twice about inviting the man into his home.

That lump blocked his throat again and he swallowed it down. Did he have a home anymore? Tricia had been furious and deadly serious about him not coming back unless he got help. Well, maybe that's exactly what he was doing. If he could get answers from Hester, maybe that would go some way towards help. And if she could in any way cast light on exactly what had happened to Toby, it might be enough for him to take to a genuine psychiatrist. Have something he could sanely talk about and then perhaps Tricia would open the door for him again. Maybe Hester could even give him an idea of where Toby had been taken that day, and that opened the possibility that Riley could go to some place and get Toby back. A ripple of panicked laughter caught at the back of his throat and he quickly derailed his thoughts. The thing in him that had snapped that day still whipped loosely around the back of his mind, like a broken powerline in a storm. If he lingered too long on thoughts of that awful day, it always snaked forward and tangled up his rational mind. Only alcohol ever seemed to keep it at bay, but right now he needed to focus.

He slammed a mental door. Why the hell would Hester have any kind of answers? It made no sense. He had to admit Toby was gone, there had been nothing so final in his life as that moment when he had dived forward only to plow headfirst into hard stone. If he allowed himself hope that Toby was alive somewhere, it would destroy the fragile wall he'd built around everything that had happened since. There in the woods, as the trees whispered at him, the last strand of hope he would ever have for anything had snapped like fishing line under the weight of too large a catch. He shook himself, climbed from the cab and went inside to buy a cold can of cola from Ken.

"You look rough, Riley." Ken was an elderly guy, but the sort of person who had always been old. Riley remembered Ken from when Riley himself was a teenager and Ken seemed just as old then as he did now. His head was almost perfectly round, his cheeks permanently rosy, his hair a gray circlet under a polished dome of skin patched with livery marks. His body matched his head, almost completely round, stretching out the buttons of a white shirt. And he seemed to be always smiling, even as he told Riley how awful he looked.

"I've had a rough couple of days." Riley handed over money for the drink.

"Not as rough as day as Tim Daley. You heard?"

"Killed by a falling branch."

Even Ken's smile wavered. "What a hell of thing, eh? Man wasn't even forty years old."

"I'd be surprised if he was much over thirty, really," Riley said, wondering if Daley had been older or younger than he and Tricia. Did it matter?

Ken handed over the change. "Just goes to show, you gotta live every minute. You never know when your number's up."

"True enough." Riley left the store, wincing against the heat and bright sunshine punching into his hungover eyes like steel spikes. He got back in the pickup and backed out, thinking he'd maybe cruise the town for a little while and see if he could spot Hester and her friends. If he couldn't find her, he no idea of his next move. He didn't know where she lived, and, now he came to think about it, didn't know who her parents were. In a small town like Sallow Bend, anyone with kids within about five years of each other in age tended to know one another. Meeting outside the kindergarten, pickups and drop-offs, PTA meetings. He couldn't ever remember meeting Hester's parents but figured he must have at some point. He shrugged it off and drove slowly through town, down past the school heading south. All the way he kept one eye open for Hester and the other on the lookout for Tricia.

After about ten minutes he reached the south side of town, where the Sallow River curved west then south again, to run alongside the highway. The town nestled in that large sweeping bow of water, wrapped in the arms of the forest to the north and the river bending around to the south. Several blocks of housing filled the space between town and that east-west stretch of river, and Riley knew for a fact two of the missing girls, Suki Tokugawa and Clare Finlay, lived nearby each other somewhere in that sprawl of tract housing. He couldn't say where exactly, but Tricia would know. Regardless, he wondered if Hester lived that side too. He couldn't recall ever knowing one way or the other, but something told him that Hester lived north of town. Maybe on one of the big properties near Old Man Wilson's land? But he was speculating wildly. What he did know was all three girls were friends and at least two of them lived this side. As he turned north again, heading through the housing towards Prime Street, he gasped, his heart slamming an extra beat against his ribs. On the front lawn of a neat and tidy house, he'd caught a flash of black and white hair catching the sunlight.

Sure enough, the three girls were there, standing in a close huddle. Suki and Clare looked pale, shoulders a little stooped, still exhausted from their ordeal, perhaps. Hester seemed bright as a button. The front door opened and Suki Tokugawa's mother leaned out. Her face was stern as she snapped something and the girls separated. Suki ran for the front door as Clare jogged across the driveway to the next house along.

As Riley cruised by he heard Clare calling out, "…grounded too today. But Dad said I could go the carnival tomorrow. Let's meet there!"

Suki said something to her mother, but the woman pulled her inside and shut the door. Hester waved, shouted back, "See you there at noon!"

And then Riley was past, watching in his rearview mirror as Hester strolled along the footpath alone, swinging her arms gently. He pulled up to the curb about hundred yards further on and hunkered down into the seat. Hester walked past on the opposite sidewalk, swaying slightly from side to side as she went as though listening to some internal song. Riley swallowed hard, suddenly at a loss. There she was, right there, on her own. Maybe she knew stuff about what happened to Toby, even though he had no idea why he had come to such a wild assumption. And what the hell was he supposed to do about it?

He pushed himself back up in his seat and watched through the windshield. She got to about twenty yards past him, then turned quickly. She stared right at him, pinned him with those deep green eyes. They seemed to glow suddenly brighter. Riley's breath stilled in his throat, his heart hammered. She lifted one hand, palm out, and danced it left and right in a kind of mocking wave. She grinned, her expression somehow far too adult for a thirteen-year old face. The white stripe down the left side of her head shone bright in the sun, the softer white of her clean linen dress a contrast to the rest of her jet black hair. Then she lifted the other hand and crooked her index finger at him, once, twice. *Come on.*

Riley gasped, like the first breath of a man who'd thought himself drowning. Dizziness swirled through his mind and his vision crossed. He blinked. Blinked again. Hester was more than two hundred yards away. Strolling along as casually as before.

What the hell?

He put the truck in gear and pulled away, drove up slowly behind her. As he got close, she looked back over her shoulder, coy, smiling winsomely. She made a strange, complicated gesture with one hand and the dizziness swelled through Riley's mind again. He blinked, rubbed his eyes, and she was gone.

He sat forward, staring out over the steering wheel, and caught sight of her turning into Prime Street several hundred yards ahead. He gunned the engine, shot after her, and when he turned into the street behind her she was another two hundred yards away. He followed. When he got close, she gestured. Dizziness made him sway, he braked until it cleared, and then she was far ahead again. He knew she was toying with him, had no idea how she did it, but he was committed now. He couldn't give up on talking to her. The strange game of catch and follow continued through town. He became vaguely aware of traveling past the Town Hall on his right at they crossed Forest Street, then she led him eastwards for a block or two before heading north again. As he drove hard to catch up for seemingly the hundredth time he realized he was passing Gil's Tavern, the highway dead ahead. She'd drawn him diagonally across the full length of Sallow Bend.

Every time the dizziness left him feeling a little more hollowed out, a little more disconnected from reality, but he pushed on. As though persisting through a dream, he drove mechanically, operating on auto-pilot, simply waiting for each dizzy spell to pass enough that he could drive on as fast as possible before the next made him slow down, stop, wait. And he knew where she was leading him.

They turned right onto the highway, Hester strolling the edge of the road, carefree in the sunshine. They passed the carnival on the left, bright but still in the morning light. Then over the old Wilson's Bridge to cross the Sallow River. A hundred yards further on she turned into the small dirt road between the trees and disappeared into shadows. It had been a year since Riley was last here.

He turned in, bounced along the track until he reached the open gap he'd used so many times before on fishing trips, the last time with his son that was no fishing trip, and parked. He killed the engine and silence fell like a lid closing. He sat in the pickup's cab, breathing heavily, trying to will the fog from his brain. Staring hard into the dimness between the trees he saw a distant flash of white, far ahead beside the river. He swallowed, nodded. Okay. She was leading him back to the cabin, it was beyond a doubt now. Toying with him, a fucking child playing with him like she was a cat and he the hapless mouse. But was she the one who had taken Toby? That was surely no child. A woman grown, he had thought. At the very least, Hester must know something, have something to tell him that might clear away the painful mystery. Toby's absence was a knife in his heart, constantly twisting. He would do anything to ease that agony, even if meant going back to the cabin he had promised himself then he would never set foot near again. So be it. He climbed from the truck and set off through the trees, following the river, knowing he followed Hester too.

18

THE DAY GREW ever hotter as Riley pushed through the thick brush beside the river. Sometimes the way grew clearer, gaps between trees enough that he walked at ease, work boots crunching on dry twigs and leaves. Other times, low scrub between narrow trunks was so thick that he clambered over it or ripped it aside. His hands and arms bore scratches and insect bites, sweat rolled down his face, despite the shade the canopy provided. Out in the town, away from the enclosing arms of the forest, the day would be working its way up into a real scorcher.

But he refused to rest or slow down. Committed to the course of action, he had to get to the lake, to the cabin, as soon as possible. How Hester stayed ahead of him so easily was just another mystery among many and one he didn't put any brain power toward. There were clearly many unnatural things about that girl.

He figured it for about noon as he found the trees thinning slightly, then saw the glitter of the lake ahead. He paused, his sudden stillness confirming his realization that there were no other sounds at all in the woods around him. Not a single cheep of a bird or flap of wing. No rustle in the undergrowth or the leaves above. No breeze to stir the air. And it was cooler. The sun beat down over the lake as he emerged from the cover of the trees, but though it should have been sweltering, the air remained cool, almost chilled.

The cabin stood squat, old and run-down just as he remembered it, not fifty yards away.

He looked down and saw his shadow, thin and watery despite the fact that he stood in full sun. Something in him quavered and he yelled, "Where are you?" The harsh sound of his voice a blasphemy to the stillness, and silence seemed to swell and engulf him as the words died away.

He swallowed, did his best to ignore the trembling in his hands and knees, and approached the cabin. The stillness was total, a complete lack of any life, Riley himself the only living thing anywhere near. Even the trees felt dead, like they were carved from stone rather than grown from seed. The cabin door, crooked on its hinges, stood slightly ajar. He leaned forward to peer into the dark gap. The air that leaked out chilled his face, raised goose-flesh on his arms and neck.

"Where are you?" he shouted again, but this time his voice sounded strained, weak.

Memories of that awful day kept flooding past his mind's eye. Toby sliding back across the flagstone floor, shoulders hitched up by invisible hands under his arms. His face, screaming, calling for his dad. The gaping darkness where the hard stone hearth had been. The feel of Toby's ankle tearing from Riley's grasp and the boy sliding into that blackness. The impact of stone knocking Riley half-blind as he dived after his son. Then hours of sobbing terror, clawing at every stone, every log, scrabbling in the dirt where the chimney stones met the earth. The trees whispering, *Gone. Gooonnnnne...*

"I know you're here!" Riley said. He also knew he would have to go inside again. Where else could she be?

He pushed the door open suddenly, braced, holding his breath. It swung in, banged against the wall and sprang halfway back. The empty cabin lay beyond. Cold air washed out like he'd opened a refrigerator. "The fuck are you?" he demanded, letting anger mask his fear, and strode inside.

He reached the middle of the single room and turned in a full circle. The broken table and chairs, the crooked cot, the battered pots by the huge hearth, all as he remembered it. Untouched. Unchanged. He stopped, staring at the cold gray stone of the fireplace, remembering. Tears ran over his cheeks. It was a good five feet square under the mantel, receding back from the hearth at least three feet. The stones curved forward for the smoke shelf right before the dark gaping hole of the chimney angled up and out of sight. But it was all so normal. So solid.

He walked to it, hands trembling worse than ever, as though he were struck with a palsy. He crouched on the hearth, leaned into the fireplace to press his hands against the stones of the back, just as he had that day. And they were as hard and unyielding as they were a year ago.

"Such idiots, you men."

Riley barked a noise of surprise and staggered back out of the suddenly constricting space to spin around. Hester sat on the edge of the cot at the other end of the cabin, toying with a grubby linen doll, it's eyes simple stitched Xs. She shook her head sadly, an all too grown up expression of disdain on her face.

"You shouldn't have come, you know. I gave you so many chances to simply go to sleep and forget."

Riley's mouth was dry, instantly drained of moisture. He worked his lips, tried to breathe down the blood rushing in his ears, the pulse hammering against his chest and neck. "How could I..." He gasped, the words like barbed wire in his throat.

Hester laughed. "How could you not follow? That's just it, isn't it? You men can never simply let go. Always have to know, to control, to *insert* yourselves."

"Was it you? Last year?"

Hester tipped her head to one side, an almost compassionate smile pulling up one side of her mouth. "Did it look like me?"

"I don't know." Fresh tears started, and Riley ignored them. Couldn't stop them. "What do *you* know?"

"Me?" She laughed again. "I know everything."

"Did you kill my son?" Riley yelled, straining forward like a dog on a short leash, but his legs wouldn't move. He couldn't have approached her if he'd wanted to.

"Yes."

Riley let out an *Agh!* of grief and dropped to his knees. His chest deflated, the air stripped from his lungs like he'd been opened to the vacuum of space.

"Did you still harbor some hope he'd be alive?" Hester asked, a note of wonder in her voice. "I suppose some credit is due for that kind of blind optimism. That must be borne of deep love."

Riley sobbed, face in his hands. Despite what he had insisted to himself all these months, he realized he *had* harbored that hope. Secretly, deep inside. And now she had torn the last of him away. There was so much he wanted to say, but grief disabled him, unlocked him.

"Yet you never told a soul, did you?" Hester said, mockery replacing the wonder. "You were too weak to admit any part of it."

"What the fuck should I have told them?" Riley spat, finding his voice as he looked up, hate pouring from him. "That my son vanished into a fireplace?"

Hester tipped her head back and laughed, a crystalline, glittering sound entirely at odds with the environment, and the subject of her mirth.

"I thought I was mad," Riley said, voice weakening again. "Even though I knew what I'd seen, it couldn't be true. Toby just… he vanished. He was gone. How could I tell anyone that?"

Hester made a soft ticking sound with her tongue, looking towards the end of the cot where it met the wall. A scrawny rat, grey and nervous, poked a twitching nose over the headboards, then came slowly to her outstretched hand. She picked it up, let it crawl from one hand to the other, over her forearms, playing with it gently. Riley jumped when she looked up and pinned him with her gaze again. "You didn't even make up a story."

"What do you mean?"

"You could have admitted to all of it, that you'd secretly taken him on an adventure. Then you could have simply said he'd run off into the woods, that you'd lost him."

"How would that have been any better?"

She sat forward, face twisted in anger. The rat, he noticed, had gone. Vanished like it was never there, as was the doll. "Because at least then you'd have taken some responsibility. Admitted your part in things."

"I didn't think of it like that."

Hester made a noise of derision. "Of course not. You were too busy thinking about how you needed to toughen him up. To infect him with your toxicity. But when it all fell apart, you were proven weak and scared and useless. All the things you thought you needed to force out of him."

"I just wanted him to share with me..."

"Share what?" Her words were like whip lashes.

"I don't know!" Riley devolved into tears again.

"You're all so noxious. You gave me Toby right on the cusp of his manhood, that sweet precipice between innocence and poison. He was delicious."

"I didn't give him to you!" Riley wailed.

She let out that glassy laugh again. "Men like you..." She didn't finish the thought, simply sat with that mocking smile making dimples on her cheeks.

Riley gasped, tried to still his tears. Rage slid in where grief tore holes in him and he staggered to his feet. He forced himself past the inertia that gelled his limbs and ran for the cot where Hester sat but she wasn't there. He stumbled, looked left and right, saw the cabin door swinging back from where it had been opened again.

He ran out into the day, the wan sunlight under the forest's edge making him blink rapidly after the dim interior. Hester stood in the lake, the water up just over her knees. Her arms were out to either side, that ugly doll clutched again in one hand, its X eyes staring at him. Her other hand had fingers spread wide. She tipped her head back as Riley ran from the cabin and then her free hand shot forward, grabbing at the air.

Something hard and rough smashed into Riley's shoulder, sent him sprawling onto the dirt. His arm sang with pain, pins and needles in his fingers, as the branch that had struck him flexed back up into the tree from where it grew. As he stared, Hester gestured again and he was struck once more, from the other side. The second branch, from a different tree, sent him face-first into the mud and his teeth punctured his lower lip. He tasted blood and dirt as it washed back over his tongue.

"Please…" he managed through a painfully dislocated jaw.

Hester paused, looked at him as he bled on the lakeshore. "Please? No."

She gestured with both arms and the trees leaned in, like some arboreal congregation bowing to their master. Dozens of smaller branches wrapped like vines around Riley's arms and wrists, hauled him upright. More snaked out and snared his legs, crushed tightly across his torso.

"Fuck you!" Riley howled as he was carried high into the air, then branches began whipping in from all around, battering and slashing at him. Pain lanced and blossomed in every inch of his body as the trees held him high above the ground. He writhed against the attack but was powerless to stop any blow. Blood flowed freely from gashes in his head and face, and from where the rough bark of the branches twisted around his limbs and body in their death grip. He stared down at Hester, now up to her waist in the lake, smiling as she walked slowly backward. Her form seemed to ebb and flow as the lake water lapped at her. It rose to her chest, she never once taking her eyes from him as the trees beat and lashed his head and body. The pain became overwhelming and consciousness fled, Toby's face the last thing he saw in his mind's eye, and he hoped desperately for an afterlife where he might gather the boy in his arms and apologize forever. But some terrified part of him feared that would never come to pass and only darkness waited.

19

ASHLEY SAT ON her trailer's tailgate, letting her feet swing lazily a foot or two above the dry grass. Night lay quiet all around, stars glittering in a clear sky, the summer warmth finally seeping out of the day. She took a long, slow breath, leaning back on her hands, and let her gaze fall over the dark, still carnival. Fading aromas of popcorn and cotton candy carried on the soft cool breeze along with the scents of paddocks and forest. These hours after the rides shut down and everyone went to sleep were always her favorite time of day. She shifted her weight and took up the small square tumbler that sat beside her. The bourbon inside was dark and rich, honey and vanilla tones warm on her tongue.

Opening the night before had gone well enough in terms of trade, but the poor bastard suiciding on the Ferris wheel had marred everything. If she looked past that, things were off to an okay start. But the Friday after opening on Thursday was always a better indicator of how things might go. They'd opened at noon, to a line of people already waiting by the gates. The place had been packed from then until closing at eleven. The crowd had been extra swelled by the presence of dozens of school-age kids and teens, all turned out early thanks to some accident at the school. A teacher had died, so the gossip went, crushed under an old, rotten tree branch.

She shook her head, sipped again. That poor soul's misfortune was her crew's lucky break, all those extra teenage dollars dropping on the stalls and rides all afternoon. The night had been busy, especially with the added youth from across the county. If she ignored one suicide on her doorstep and one strange death on the other side of town, she could almost convince herself everything bode well for their stay. John Barrow had tried to rile her up before he went to bed, suggesting that bad luck hung over Sallow Bend this year. She wouldn't give in to his, or anyone else's, superstitions.

She refilled her glass from the bottle beside it, then climbed to her feet. Back inside her trailer, she put the bottle on her dresser and slumped onto the leather two-seater couch. Her bed was rumpled at the far end, beyond the small kitchenette and shower/toilet cubicle. Sleep would be good, but she was a little too wired just yet. She needed to earth herself with some normalcy.

She pulled her cell phone out and tapped a message – *Still awake?* – and hit send.

The bourbon warmed her belly as she sat quietly, letting her mind flatline. Then she felt the soft movement of someone mounting the steps beside her trailer's tailgate, followed by a quiet *tap-tap* at the door.

"It's open." She reached for another glass as the door opened and Sarah Carter stepped in, smiling slightly.

She wore loose track pants and an over-sized tee-shirt, her blonde hair pulled back in a half-effort at a pony-tail. Out of the ostentatious Madame O-Reilly garb, she was more vibrant, more beautiful than ever. "You called?" Her eyes sparkled in the low light of the standard lamp behind Ash's couch.

Ash filled the second glass and held it out, then lifted hers in a toast. The high ring of the glasses meeting was the only sound, then they both swallowed the contents down in one. Sarah lowered herself to sit sidelong on the cushion and Ash reached up her free hand, laid it against Sarah's warm, smooth cheek. She sat up and Sarah came to meet her, their lips hot and firm together.

For several minutes they lost themselves in each other, then Ash pulled away to refill their glasses. No words were needed. They drank the bourbon down once more and fell into each other's arms. Ash slowly relieved Sarah of her casual clothes and Sarah unhooked the straps of Ash's overalls, let it fall to her waist and peeled up the tight white tee-shirt beneath. Before long they were moving in only their underwear from the couch to the bed and nothing else existed as the night rolled indifferently by outside.

"I'm glad you're feeling more yourself again," Sarah said afterward, as they sat propped up on pillows, taking time to sip the bourbon now.

"I wasn't before?"

"Well, you're always tense before opening, that's normal. You have a lot of responsibility. But this time you seemed more strung out."

Ashley laughed. "Not one hundred percent mellow like you?"

"I'm far from mellow sometimes. But this pitch feels different this year."

Ashley rolled the glass gently between her palms, enjoying the edges of its slightly rounded corners. A gentle breeze through the open window beside them rippled the light curtains and tickled cool across her sweat-damp, naked skin. "Barrow tried to tell me there's bad juju here this time."

Sarah nodded, her face serious. "There is."

"Aw, come on, you don't believe that horse shit, do you?"

Sarah shrugged. "I know you don't believe I'm really a medium. You think it's all an act, and that's okay. I accept your skepticism." She smirked at Ash.

"Get fucked," Ash said with good humor.

"Already did. A lot of what I do is an act, I've admitted as much before. Cold reading is a pretty easy mug's game to play when they want to believe so badly. But I'm not entirely insensitive, Ash. I see and feel more than most, and Barrow is right. There's a weight around here this year. A malevolence."

"One guy killed himself, another had an accident. That's how life and death goes. Nothing extraordinary."

Sarah nodded. "Oh, I agree. But it's not just that. There's something in the air. Something weird."

"And what are we supposed to do about that?"

"Nothing."

"So why worry about it?"

Sarah looked over again, smiling. "I'm not the one worrying about it. You are."

"Fuck! Barrow is the one going on about it, and it's Saul feeding him. I'm just annoyed people can't concentrate on their jobs for all the gossip."

"The incident at Clyde's wheel hasn't helped any."

Ash spat a soft noise of annoyance, refilled their glasses. "I'm sympathetic to that poor man's plight. I mean, someone has to be out of their mind, you know? They have to be in a pretty bad place to end up suicidal, especially so publicly. So..."

"Violently?"

"Yeah, exactly. But for all my sympathy, I wish the fucker hadn't chosen my fair."

Sarah didn't reply, just nodded.

They sat quietly sipping for several minutes, enjoying the warmth and closeness of each other. Night birds hooted, a semi on the highway across the fields rumbled distantly by.

"Saul's enjoying it," Sarah said eventually.

"Enjoying it?"

"The disruption. The anxiety." She looked over and Ash saw genuine concern in her lover's eyes. "The fear."

"I know Saul is an asshole, Sarah. But enjoying the fear?"

Sarah chewed inside her cheek for a moment, then sipped more bourbon. Eventually she took a deep breath. "I know you're skeptical of my sensitivities, but there is something off about Saul Fallon. Everyone knows it, most put it down to him being an asshole. And yeah, some people are like that. Just assholes. But not Saul. He *is* an asshole, but he's also something more. Something broken. I can't explain it, most of my shit is an act." She flashed a self-deprecatory grin. "But I'm not making it all up and something is not right with him. Barrow gets it too. He doesn't realize it, but he's sensitive as well."

"John Barrow?" Ash barked a laugh. "That fucker is psychic?"

"You know I don't like the word psychic. It tries to claim too much credit for itself. But Barrow gets vibes more than most people, it's why he's always at loggerheads with Saul."

"They always make up though, fist-bumping and shit. They're like idiot brothers or something."

Sarah shook her head. "That's the act Barrow maintains, keeping his enemies close. Saul Fallon does it to keep you happy."

"Me?"

"Sure. He wants peace. He wants to avoid your scrutiny."

Ashley frowned. "Why?"

"Because then he can get on with what he does best. Sowing discord, making people frightened. He feeds off that."

"I think you're giving *him* too much credit."

"Look at the damn freak show he runs, Ash! Mengele's secret lab."

Ashley lifted one palm. "And? The public love that macabre stuff."

"And it gives Saul the chance to scare them, and suck that fear right up." Sarah shifted on the bed, waved a hand to cut off Ashley's further protest. "Look, I know you think I'm all hippy dippy about this. But just promise me something, okay?"

"What?"

"That you'll watch Saul closely. John Barrow will. I will. But we're both largely powerless. Will you watch him too? For me?"

Ash leaned over and pressed her lips to Sarah's. "For you? Sure."

"And don't write off this gossip about bad luck around here. We need to not get complacent. Hopefully it'll come to nothing, but stay aware, okay?"

"Okay." Ashley swallowed the last of her bourbon, the heat spreading into her limbs, its soporific effect had long since mellowed her mind. "But right now, everything's okay?"

Sarah smiled. "I guess."

"Good." She nodded to Sarah's glass and Sarah swallowed down the contents. Ash rose up from the bed and sat on her lover's lap, and pulled their bodies together.

20

TRICIA BRENT SAT at the kitchen counter in her strangely quiet home, thoughtfully sipping coffee. Still no Riley. He'd taken her absolutely at her word and vanished. She'd rung Gil's Tavern the night before. Gil said that sure, Riley had been there Thursday night and really put away the juice. He'd become belligerent, but not dangerously so, and Gil had packed him off to the back room after closing. Riley had been out cold as Gil shut the door. And the next day, Friday, he was gone before Gil opened up again, just left a note on the office desk saying thanks.

"He didn't come in last night?" Tricia had asked. "He always goes there Fridays."

"A-yup," Gil said slowly. "But he wasn't here last night."

Tricia frowned, sipped more coffee. So where was he? On the one hand, she didn't care. But it bothered her how totally he had taken her at her word. She'd called around a couple of his friends and work colleagues after talking to Gil and they all confirmed what the tavern owner had told her. Big Burt Lebowski said Riley hadn't been to work since Tuesday.

"I'm sorry to tell ya, Tricia, but Riley doesn't have a job to come back to anymore."

"Well, shit," Tricia said.

"You call me you need any help, okay?"

She needed to call Freddie Holtz next, but that made her nervous. She'd need to admit Riley had left after a big fight. Did she tell Holtz about the violence? The phone rang, and she stared at it for a moment, then took a deep breath and answered.

"Tricia? It's Caleb Jackson. The janitor from school."

She laughed softly. "Yeah, I know you're the janitor from school. How are you?"

"Okay, I guess. You hear about Tim Daley?"

"I did. Terrible thing."

There was silence for a moment and Tricia was about to ask if he was still there, when he drew a quick breath and said, "You want to come out to the carnival with me this afternoon?"

"You're inviting me out among crowds, Caleb? This is a big turnaround."

"I need someone with me, I think. I trust you. I need a witness."

A cold rock grew in Tricia's belly. "A witness to what?" Images of Kirk Branton with his head peeled half open on the grass flashed across her mind.

"I need to check something and I'd appreciate some help, that's all."

"Okay, sure. I can come." She could put off calling Holtz now, for a little while anyway. Good timing, Caleb Jackson. "You really okay? What's up?"

He breathed quietly for a moment, then, "Daley's death was no accident."

CALEB remembered Tricia's discomfort about coming to the school, the memories of her missing son it triggered, so he had said he'd come to her place again. She tried to insist it was fine, she'd pick him up, but he honestly didn't mind the walk. It only took twenty minutes or so and the exercise was good for him. She'd relented and said she would see him around noon.

As he walked along Wilson Street about a quarter hour before noon, the sun almost directly overhead was incandescent and brutally hot. The day scorched, dry and blistering, blinding light reflecting off car windshields as they cruised by. Some other people were out and about, shorts and tee-shirts all around, some in big hats and sunglasses, others squinting against the glare as their exposed skin pinked under the assault. Caleb wore light cotton long pants and a long-sleeved white button-up shirt, open at the collar. A floppy, dark green canvas hat with a wide brim all around shaded his face, though his head sweated underneath it. He passed a short strip of shops, a tan dog fast asleep on the step of the dry cleaners, and felt the welcome air-con breeze coming from the open door of Ken's General Store. He stepped in and bought a cold can of soda, enduring Ken's incessant banter with a polite smile, avoiding his eye, then walked the rest of the way to Tricia's, sipping the drink.

She opened the front door as he walked up her driveway. "Morning. Saw you coming."

"Hi."

"You want coffee?"

He gestured with the empty can. "I just had this, thanks."

She took it from him. "I'll throw it out for you. Come in."

He hesitated on the porch, unsure whether he wanted to go in, but saw no way to suggest otherwise.

"I won't bite, Caleb. And Riley isn't here."

He nodded, followed her inside. The house smelled of coffee and toast, and lemon furniture polish. Everything tidy and organized, neat like a show home. Or a home without kids, he thought, with a pang of sympathy for Tricia.

"Is Riley working this weekend?"

She went through to the kitchen and dropped his can into the trash. "No. He's… not here." When she turned back, Caleb read a sharp anguish in her expression. Had he left her?

"Everything okay?"

She paused, seemed to consider her answer. "No. In truth, it's not. Hasn't been for a long time. He hasn't been coping since Toby went missing."

Caleb watched her throat working as she held back tears, saw the rapid progression of emotion across her face. He looked away, overwhelmed. "I have heard, of course. Small town gossip."

"We had a big fight and I told him to get out and not come back until he'd found professional help."

"A shrink?"

"I guess. Something like that. Seems he took me seriously."

"Oh. I'm sorry?" He wasn't sure why he'd made it sound like a question. The headache was coming back already.

Tricia let out a bark of laughter. "You're really shit at this stuff, huh?"

He grinned nervously. "It's why I tend to keep to myself."

She shook her head, gathered her purse from a chair at the dining table in the space beside the kitchen. "Shall we go?"

"Sure."

The car was like an oven when they climbed in, sitting in the full sun of the driveway. Tricia cranked up the AC and opened all the windows trying to push the heat out for the first couple of blocks. As the AC got into its stride, she closed the car up again and the cool, calm interior was a balm.

"This is going to be one hot summer," she said.

Caleb thought about the strange occurrences and how a stiflingly hot summer seemed to somehow fit together with that, but had no way to articulate the idea. "Sure is," he said instead.

"You said Daley's death was no accident." Tricia glanced at him, brows furrowed, then turned her attention back to the road.

"I know you're not going to believe me. I think you'll even have trouble concentrating on what I'm about to say, but will you try real hard?"

She glanced over again. "Yeah, sure."

"I don't think Kirk's death was a suicide. I *know* Daley's death wasn't an accident." He took a deep breath, watched the side of her face as she drove while he said, "Hester Black caused them both."

Tricia's brows knotted tighter than ever and she started to say, "What?" but it petered out. There was silence for a second, then she said, "Man, it's going to be a hot summer."

"Tricia, did you hear what I said? Hester caused those two men's deaths."

"How could a child do that?" Her frown this time was almost a wince, pained.

"There is something unnatural about her," Caleb pressed on. He had thought long and hard about it all the day before, unable to really concentrate on the book he tried to read, unable to relax and take some time out like he'd intended. He had no idea how to push through the bizarre response to talk of Hester, the way attention seemed to slip off people like rain off a tent.

"Unnatural?"

"Tricia, think hard about Hester. You see her in your mind's eye? That streak of hair, that white dress with the short wide skirt, the low-top black leather boots."

"Of course, everyone knows..."

"Have you ever seen her wear anything else? Can you remember her as a little girl, say eight years old? Or ten? Can you see her any other way than you see her now?"

"She's been here all... She's always had..."

Caleb watched the certainty crack and drain from Tricia, saw the discomfort of realization soak through her.

"Have you ever seen her parents?" he pressed on. "Do you really know where she lives?"

"Somewhere to the north of..."

"Do you remember at the carnival? Do you remember Kirk shouting at her, asking 'Where did you come from?' and 'Who are you?' He didn't know her, did he?"

Tricia shook her head like she was trying to clear a ringing in her ears. "But everyone knows..."

"Everyone knows Hester?" Caleb asked. "Do they? Why? How? How long have you known Hester?" He leaned forward to see her face, and her eyes were scrunched, like she was in some kind of agony. He recognized the expression. Kirk Branton had worn it as he clambered atop the security fencing. Tim Daley as he stood immobile in the schoolyard and the tree limb had cracked above him like a gunshot.

Tricia shook her head again, looked down at her lap, the car veering sharply toward the curb. With a cry, Caleb grabbed the wheel and pushed them back into their lane. Tricia gasped, sat up straight like she'd been shocked, sucked in a breath as she reset her grip on the wheel, knuckles white.

"Jesus, Caleb, I'm sorry. I felt suddenly faint for a moment." She swallowed, let out a long, slow breath. "It's passing." She threw a contrite look his way, then looked back at the road. "I've been drinking coffee all morning. Maybe I've had a little too much and not enough to eat. Let's get a hotdog or something when we get to the carnival, yeah?"

"Sure." Caleb realized he was hungry too. He also knew the breakthrough he had thought was coming had vanished like smoke in the wind.

"What were we talking about?" Tricia asked.

Caleb smiled, shrugged. "I don't remember."

"Ha. Me either. Definitely too much coffee." They drove on in silence for another five minutes before Tricia indicated and pulled into the field reserved for parking. It was already filling with cars, lights and movement in the next field over showed the carnival in full swing for the day.

When they opened the doors and got out, music and laughing and aromas of cotton candy and popcorn and hot dogs accompanied the oppressive heat that slammed into them.

"You said Daley's death was no accident," Tricia said as they walked towards the big arched gate. "And that you wanted to check something. What are we checking?"

Caleb decided he would only get through to her, if at all, by showing her incontrovertible evidence. "I'm hoping Hester and Suki and Clare are here today. I expect they will be. I want to watch them."

Tricia laughed, gave him a strange expression of confusion and concern. "What the hell for?"

"Just humor me?"

"Okay. I guess."

They entered the already bustling carnival and Caleb kept his head down like he had last time. He found he was learning to stem the flood of information from the crowds around him, benefitting from his experience of a couple of days before. Tricia's presence certainly helped, a kind of shield, an anchor against the flood. If he kept the majority of his attention on her and avoided direct eye contact with the throng, he could resist the overwhelming sensations of pressure and panic that crowds usually instilled in him. He didn't like the environment, thought it likely he never would, but he appreciated the developing ability to better cope with them. How much he wondered, would he cope without Tricia's armoring presence? That was something he didn't relish discovering.

They went first along the midway, checking the various food stalls until Tricia saw some strange combination of Mexican and hot dog concoction. A *Chili Dog with Xxxtra Bite*, according to the garishly painted sign hanging beside the service window. Caleb said he'd have whatever she was having, that way avoiding the need to talk to the vendor or engage in any kind of small talk. He gave her a twenty and insisted she let him pay, as she came out for him, and drove them.

Moments later they were strolling aimlessly along taking bites from the huge dogs, grinning and huffing at each other as their cheeks reddened with the spices. The sandwiches were indeed fiery and damned tasty. They ate the last of them and wiped their fingers and mouths on the accompanying napkins, then went in search of chilled bottled water. Sweat trickled down Caleb's back, soaked the rim of his hat, and made his hair feel thick beneath it, but he felt good. Sated. And the whole time he glanced repeatedly around the crowd, looking out for that tell-tale flash of white hair. Despite Tricia's presence, the familiar ache behind his eyes remained, though perhaps not as bad as it might normally be.

"Let's go on that!" Tricia said, pointing.

Caleb saw her pause, raise her eyebrows at something. He followed her gaze, saw a look of disapproval on the faces of two other women not far away. Then they turned away from Tricia's challenging look, mouths tight.

"Small town gossip," Tricia said, with a small shake of her head.

"Riley?" he asked, not sure what she meant.

"Sure. And me out with you. Only in small town America can a woman not have a friend of the opposite sex without being judged."

He shifted uncomfortably from foot to foot, unsure how to respond. The idea they were friends was strange enough. That they were being judged for it made him feel completely out of his depth.

Tricia laughed. "Come on, fuck 'em. I want to ride that."

The ride she indicated looked terrifying. A crazy contraption of several arms stretching out from a central hub like a rigid steel octopus draped in lights of every color. On the end of each arm, a set of three cars hung in a triangular configuration. Those triangles spun hectically on the end of the arms, while the arms themselves rotated at ridiculous speed, the whole thing tilting up and down like a spun coin that seemed like it would never come to rest.

Are YOU brave enough to ride the Waltz'n'Whirl? a giant flashing sign challenged.

Caleb grimaced. "I don't know that I *am* brave enough."

"Come on, don't be chicken. It'll be fun!"

"It'll be *Mex-i-hot Chili Dog* all over everyone else, maybe."

Tricia laughed, a high, musical sound of genuine mirth. "I dare you, Caleb!"

The ride slowed, screaming aboard reducing to laughter as it came to a halt and the cars emptied, people staggering and grinning, some looking decidedly unwell. Tricia grabbed his hand and hauled him forward.

"Two, please," she said to the smiling carnie, handing over the cash.

Before he could formulate a believable resistance, she had pushed him into a seat and pulled the restraining bar down tight across their hips. The cars were hard red plastic, shiny and glittering with embedded silver flecks, like a carved half-circle. Four people could fit into each one, but Tricia had claimed them one privately, and they sat in the two central indentations, one empty to either side of them. Other people flowed in, filling probably three-quarters of the ride, then the carnie climbed back up into his clear Perspex booth. He leaned forward to a microphone and his voice brayed out over the blaring R&B music from the ride's speakers.

"Hold tight, ladies and gentlemen, boys and girls, here we go, here we go!"

The machine jerked slightly then began to rotate slowly. It remained level with the ground and picked up speed, the bunches of cars at the end of each arm staying put as the larger mechanism spun. It moved ever faster, the colors and noises of the carnival around them becoming a blur.

"Let's waltz!" the carnie yelled, and the machine suddenly tilted to an angle of about thirty degrees.

Caleb's stomach lurched, his hotdog threatened to come back for a visit and he swallowed it down. They whipped around, the ground coming terrifyingly close then strangely far away in rapid, hard to fathom sequence. Just as Caleb opened his mouth to say maybe it wasn't so bad after all, the carnie yelled, "And now we whirl!" and the little group of three cars suddenly spun, as if it had cut loose from the articulated arm above and sailed off across the midway. Caleb's words became a yelp of shock and Tricia's high, screaming laughter was ripped away on the wind as they spun around in complicated small and large rotations that stripped any sense of direction Caleb could have hoped to retain. He gripped the lap bar like his life depended on it, which he felt it maybe did. He tried closing his eyes, but that only made the disorientation swell and his hotdog rose again. He whipped his eyes open, tried to look beyond their immediate surroundings where perhaps distance would give his eyes something to hang on to. Images flashed and whipped like a strobe light of every hue, but as his equilibrium became more used to the incredible momentum he found his stomach and heart rate settling and began to actually enjoy the hectic motion of the ride. The tilting became a kind of rush, a tingling buzz that fired his senses, made his skin tingle, forced a smile onto his face that he couldn't suppress no matter how much he tried.

He picked out the tall faux-gothic roofs of the Haunted House, the giant circle of the Ferris wheel pulled into an oval by his compressed eyeballs every time it whipped past. Tricia's laughter rang out, punctuated with occasional exclamations of "Holy shit!" and "Oh my God!"

Caleb tried to look over at her, but the centripetal force of the ride kept his head pressed back into the red cushioned back of the seat and he realized why that cushioning was there.

Then a flash of white hit his eye like a sunbeam. Like the brightness of those car windshields as he'd walked to Tricia's house that morning. It came around again, and he'd missed it before he realized it was coming. Then again. He held his breath, concentrated, and then he saw it once more. Definitely Hester and her friends, lining up for the bumper cars arcade across the way from the Waltz'n'Whirl.

"Let's turn around!" the carnie hollered, and the ride slowed so fast Caleb was thrust against the hip bar, nearly smashing his face into his knees, then it quickly accelerated back the other way. Howls and screams rose again and Caleb had no choice but to sit back and swallow and try to reprocess all the new information as his body rebelled at the change in direction.

He breathed deeply, re-found the equilibrium he had lost, and before long the ride slowed again, more sedately this time. It leveled out, the little bunches of cars locked into place while the greater wheel turned lazily, the music rushed back in as the buffeting wind of speed eased, then the whole thing came to a gentle stop.

Tricia gently slapped his knee, letting out a soft, "Whooo" of relief. "That was something, huh? And you kept your dog down."

But Caleb was already lifting the bar, standing to see across to the bumper cars, their flags fluttering as they zoomed around like so many random flies. Except where flies miraculously avoided collisions in their hectic aerial dance, the bumper cars actively sought them. He wobbled, willed his jelly knees to hold him up, his eyes to stop flickering with the memory of motion. And then there they were. Clare and Suki, pale but smiling, in one car with Suki driving. Laughing and cutting across them at every opportunity was Hester, alone driving her own car.

"Caleb, you okay?"

He looked down. "Yes, sorry. You're right, that was kinda fun." He meant it too. They stepped from the ride and he staggered sideways, shoulder barging Tricia into the security fence surrounding the ride as they headed for the gate.

She grabbed him, pushed him back upright. "Steady on there! Slow down."

"Sorry." He took a couple of deep breaths, slowed his stride as he got his land legs back. He pointed to the bumper cars. "The girls are over there, I saw them from the ride."

"Holy crap, Caleb, you've got some stamina! I could barely keep my eyes open on that thing, let alone spot anyone."

He moved through the crowds and stood off to one side, watched the girls laugh and bump and squeal.

"What now?" Tricia asked. "You realize this is a little weird, right? A grown man like you watching three young girls."

"I know. But I promise you, something is up here. It seems I'm the only one who can see it, and I want to know why." He bit his lower lip in thought. "Well, there was someone else who saw it. Kirk Branton, he knew something was up." He pinned Tricia with his gaze. "But Hester killed him."

"Hester what?"

"She made him step up in front of that Ferris wheel. I know she did."

"That's insane, Caleb. How could she?"

"I don't know. That's what I want to find out. You don't think there's something strange about Hester?"

Tricia laughed. "Of course. Everyone knows she's a whacky kid."

"How does everyone know that?"

"What?"

"How does everyone know Hester? How does everyone know she's a whacky kid?"

Tricia frowned, that furrowing of the brows slowly descending into the expression of discomfort Caleb had come to recognize. "A kid like that, she gets noticed..."

"You remember what she did at the carnival last year?" Caleb asked. "You remember any stories of her exploits at school?"

Tricia's expression of pain intensified. "Caleb, I don't understand what you're asking."

"That white streak in her hair. Is that natural? Or is that something she started doing one day? When did that first happen?"

"It's natural, I think. Or is it?" Tricia stared at the ground, head shaking slightly from side to side in uncomfortable denial.

Caleb watched her, wondered if he'd said enough this time, ignoring the pulse of discomfort behind his eyes. He decided not to risk it, drew breath to push the point further, but her head came up quickly, a slight smile on her lips. "You want to ride the Ferris wheel? You can see almost clear across the county from up there."

And it was gone again, like a reflection in water shattered by a thrown pebble.

"I want to watch Hester and her friends, remember?"

"Oh yeah, of course. You know, that's a pretty weird thing to do, Caleb. They're thirteen."

"Have you noticed how whenever we talk about Hester, you change the subject as soon as you have to think too hard about her?"

Tricia tipped her head to one side. "Do I?"

"Everyone does. Everyone except me."

"Really? Why?"

"That's what I want to know."

The bumper cars all came to a swift standstill and the *Awws* and *Ahhs* of the drivers rose up. The carnies hopped from car to car, helping people up, directing them to the edges of the arcade. Hester, Suki, and Clare all clasped hands and half-walked, half-danced off one side.

"Come on." Caleb tugged at Tricia's hand and she fell into step beside him.

"I'm not entirely comfortable with this," she said.

"Please, just trust me? For a little while? I want to watch the girls, see what they do, who they talk to."

"Okay."

The three friends walked up to a cotton candy vendor and each bought a stick with a cloud of candy on it bigger than their heads. Suki and Clare both still looked drawn and pale, like they had yet to catch up on the rest they needed. Caleb moved to the front of the next stall along, began aimlessly looking at complicated dreamcatchers and other appropriated items of Native American culture.

"Can you believe Dirty Daley is dead?" Suki said, a note of excitement in her tone.

"Crushed to a pulp," Clare said. "Like pizza."

"Ewww!" Suki made a gagging face.

Hester just smiled.

"Couldn't happen to a nicer guy, though," Suki said around a mouthful of sweet cotton.

"You think?" Hester asked.

"He never creeped on you? He did on me. You too, Clare?"

"Of course! He always stood too close behind your chair in class. Kinda leaned over and pressed his hips against your back."

Suki shuddered, gritted her teeth. "Exactly!"

Hester smiled. "So you're glad he's dead?"

"I dunno about glad," Clare said, scrunching up her freckled nose and brow in thought. "I mean, I don't really wish anyone dead. But I don't think he'll be missed by many people, do you?"

Suki nodded, face set. "I'm glad he's dead. I wish all the creepers in the world would get crushed under trees."

"I can only work one at a time," Hester said with a laugh.

An electric shock pulsed through Caleb's chest and he held his breath. Her friends knew?

"What do you mean?" Clare asked. Suki frowned, stopped chewing.

Hester laughed. "Nothing, come on."

Both her friends faces softened, that same slipping away of awareness Caleb saw every time he pressed Tricia to realize and she gave in to whatever it was that prevented her. Hester manipulated her friends the same way.

Caleb swallowed, looked down at the tacky trinkets to catch his mental breath. The effort of watching, of observing the interaction, drowned his thoughts, made his head swim. The information overload was too much, the thing he always avoided in company. The whole reason he'd moved to quiet little Sallow Bend. His head pounded.

The girls wandered away from the cotton candy seller and Caleb took a deep breath, moved to follow. Tricia walked alongside, frowning. Had she heard the interaction just then too? Caleb sensed a slight crack in her obliviousness. Some hint of realization briefly surfacing like the smooth hump of a whale's back in a dark ocean. He tried to grab at it. "Did you hear what Hester said? How many times have I told you I think something is wrong with Hester, and how many times have you forgotten that?"

She shook her head. "It seems like a lot."

"She's doing something to everyone. Making everyone forget about her."

"Why? How?"

Caleb watched the moment of clarity slip back beneath the waves. "When the girls went missing," he pressed. "It was only Suki and Clare. We were all looking for *two* missing girls. Then when they were found, three came back. Hester came with them. That's the first time Hester has ever been seen in this town, Tricia. She came out of nowhere!"

Tricia winced, looked at Caleb with narrowed eyes, like she was resisting a headache of her own. That familiar expression intensified, Kirk as he stood atop the railing, Daley as he struggled to step out from under the falling limb. "You're right," Tricia said, so quietly he almost didn't hear her. "Where the fuck did she come from?"

Excitement rose in Caleb like sunshine after a long night. He'd got through. He opened his mouth to press the point, then all the air rushed out of him with an *Ooof!*

"Jesus, sorry," a big bearded man in a lumberjack shirt and too short shorts said, grabbing Caleb by one shoulder to stop him falling. "You okay? I don't think either of us were looking where we were going."

Caleb sucked breath back in, gathered himself from the shock of the sudden, unexpected impact. “I’m fine, sorry. You okay?”

“I think I outweigh you by a hundred pounds, friend. I reckon you came off worse.”

The big man laughed, slapped a meaty palm onto Caleb’s shoulder then moved past.

Caleb shook himself, looked back to Tricia. “You get it now,” he said, but his fears were instantly realized.

“Get what, Caleb?”

He was too tired to start again, but he had got through. For a moment he had cracked whatever it was that held everyone in thrall, given Tricia a moment of clarity.

Hester, Suki, and Clare strolled along the midway sucking the last of the candy off long wooden sticks when Hester pointed off to one side. The girls grinned at each other and turned towards Mengele’s Secret. Caleb stopped at the corner of the tee-shirt shop in front of the macabre sideshow to watch. Tricia wandered into the stall, looked lazily through the racks of colored, printed shirts, oblivious once more.

The three girls went into the Mengele’s Secret sideshow and the tent flap fell closed behind them. Caleb remembered his own encounter there with Tricia, the weird carnie, Saul, and the strange sensations of drawing and dizziness. *Your fear is palpable*, the carnie had said, and Caleb had thought the man really meant edible.

After several minutes, the three friends emerged again, chattering quietly to each other. Suki and Clare both looked cowed, somehow even paler than they had been before, even more drained. Hester looked fine, except she wore an expression of concern, like she had got something more from the experience than the others. Caleb saw a touch of respect in her eyes as she glanced back towards the tent flaps as they fell closed.

“That was horrible,” Clare said as the three passed Caleb and headed back along the midway.

“Creepy as hell,” Suki agreed.

Hester continued to frown.

As they walked on past the tee-shirt shop, Caleb watched Hester's back and whispered to himself, "What is it about you?"

Hester looked back sharply over one shoulder, pinned Caleb with a searing gaze. Her deep green eyes brightened, glittering in the blistering sun. She stared into him, through him, and he felt his legs turn leaden, his feet meld with the hard, dry earth beneath the crushed grass. He couldn't have moved a muscle if he'd wanted.

There was no way she could have heard him. Panic washed through him, visions of Kirk Branton climbing the railing, Tim Daley grimacing as the tree limb fell. Hester's eyes narrowed and Caleb's fear became a howling gale, tearing through his soul. She could kill him with a thought. He forced every image from his mind. He couldn't tear his gaze away, but he would give nothing through it. He counted frantically to ten, picturing nothing but the numbers before his mind's eye, then immediately started over at one. Suki and Clare continued on for a few paces, then stopped and looked back when they realized Hester was no longer with them. Caleb counted to ten again, tried to think of nothing but numbers, give no fear away, not let a single suspicion of Hester's true nature leak out.

"What's up?" Clare called out, taking a step back towards Hester.

"You okay?" Tricia asked at almost the same moment, moving out from behind a rack of shirts to put a hand on Caleb's shoulder.

He looked past her, past Hester, stared into some empty middle distance, counted over and over again.

"Hester?" Clare called again. Suki turned as well.

Tricia shook his shoulder. "Caleb?"

Hester blinked and turned away and Caleb staggered forward one step. The pressure on his mind gone, Hester's attention vanished like it had never been there. Had he avoided her scrutiny? He couldn't help but feel somehow marked, touched by some unseen, unseeable hand.

"Caleb, are you okay?" Tricia asked.

He desperately wanted to point to Hester, to draw Tricia's attention to what had happened, but he didn't dare awake Hester's interest again. "I'm fine, sorry. Just dizzy a moment. The heat, maybe?"

"Let's find some shade and a cold drink."

"Good idea."

He went to step away and saw the owner of Mengele's Secret, Saul. The tall, pale, dark-haired man had come from this tent to stand at the corner of the tee-shirt stall. He watched with narrowed eyes, looked from Caleb to Hester as she continued along the midway with her friends, all laughing and joking like nothing was wrong. The carnie was clearly perturbed, genuine fear in his eyes. Caleb wanted to ask him what he was thinking, what he suspected. The man watched Hester like a mouse watches a cat. No, not quite. Caleb shook his head, adjusted his assessment. The carnie watched Hester like a cat watches another cat. Two predators forced to share an overlapping territory. Caleb remembered the carnie's outstretched hands, the way he had seemed to drink in their fear. He wondered what the man might have just tasted from Hester. And what he might have seen during those moments when Hester held Caleb pinned in the midway like a bug to a display board.

As Tricia took his hand and drew him away from the rows of tee-shirts, Caleb wondered if perhaps Saul, who would be moving on soon anyway, might not be an ally against the strangeness of Hester and the likelihood that she wasn't going anywhere. And he wondered if he would have any chance to do anything about that, given the way Hester had just held him with her gaze and left some kind of stain upon him.

21

DEPUTY VAL BAKER drove slowly along Wilson Street with the windows up and the AC blowing an arctic gale. She hated the heat of summer, but despised the cold of winter more. One day, she thought, she'd learn about a place that had a steady springtime climate and badly needed a police deputy and she'd pack her bags that night.

She grinned, imagining her dad. He had been a cop and a damned good one by all accounts. But he took two bullets in Atlanta, one to the knee and one to the chest. The chest wound had nearly killed him, but healed up leaving nothing but an ugly scar. The leg wound was never life-threatening, but it destroyed the joint and left him with a limp and a walking cane, and bad case of bitter recriminations. He had never held it against the job, but against his inability to continue with it. Pensioned out when she was still a kid, he eventually accepted defeat and retired to Sallow Bend, bringing his relieved wife with him. Safer than the city where he got shot, maybe, but dull as hell for his kids.

Val's mother had become a valued member of the town, though Val herself never really felt like she belonged. Arriving at fourteen years of age, she immediately cemented her position as outsider and went off to college first chance she got. Her older brother moved back to Atlanta after less than a year in Sallow Bend. But college life never really suited Val and her father was appalled when she came back and followed him into the police. After more than ten years serving the community of Sallow Bend, they had learned to respect her decision. Getting old now, they were proud of her. And that's why she found the thought of moving away amusing. Her dad's façade would crumble and fall if she took her gun and badge to anywhere bigger than the sleepy town she had finally called home for thirteen years. She imagined he only respected her choice to be a police deputy because the risk levels in Sallow Bend were about as low as they could get. She didn't mind the idea of being a big city police officer, it sounded quite exciting, but if she was honest with herself, she was a little chickenshit too. In thirteen years, she had never pulled her service weapon in anger or need. Only ever on the range, for practice she hoped to never put into use. Long may that situation persist.

Her radio hissed and Janssen came over the waves, sounding surly as usual. He was the one who most often got to go out with Holtz while Val and Clive manned the station, but every once in a while Holtz would grow sick of Janssen's acidic company and leave the young man on desk duty to give Val the second squad car, and a day or two out in the fresh air. Why he never took her along with him like he did Janssen always confused Val. She would enjoy spending the day next to that hulking, beautiful man. She let out a small laugh. Maybe he sensed that and kept his distance.

Janssen was squawking again and she decided she'd ignored him for too long.

"What's up?"

"What took you so long to answer? I bet you weren't outside the damn car on a hot day like this."

"What's it to you? I was busy singing a damn song. What have you got?"

Janssen let out a muffled curse, knowing better than to insult her outright. "We got a call there's been an accident at the river, on Wilson's Bridge. Ambulance is en route, so we'd better show up too. I couldn't raise Holtz, so you're it."

"Okay, mark me as attending. But make sure Holtz gets the message too."

"Yeah, I know. I'm not new here."

"And wake Clive up."

"How'd you know he was sleeping?"

Val laughed as she ignored any further communication. Kurt thought himself a police deputy, but he couldn't solve a Sesame Street mystery. Honestly, she had no idea how he even got the job.

She set the lights flashing, sirens wailing, smiling at the group of teenagers who nearly jumped out of their skin in front of Ken's General Store. *Guilty conscience, kids?* she wondered, and powered out towards the highway north of town.

Wilson's Bridge was the last part of Sallow Bend a person saw going north, or the first part heading south. Val passed the carnival on her left, packed with cars and people sweltering in the afternoon heat. No one could pay her enough to spend any time there on a cold day, let alone in the summer. She would never understand the attraction. Less than a mile past the carnival, the road curved slightly north and Wilson's Bridge came into view. The road humped, the bridge itself three wide stone arches that spanned the Sallow River, their thick footings disappearing into the deep, slowly flowing water. Either side of the bridge had a shoulder about a yard wide for pedestrians, should anyone be fool enough to come walking all the way out here, then low walls of carefully locked together gray stone, patchy with weather and lichen.

An accident on Wilson's Bridge most likely meant one of three things. Either two vehicles had collided, misjudging the available width in each direction. It was no different to the highway for several miles to either side of the damn bridge, but the sudden presence of something different in the road seemed to make some people extra stupid. Often, a driver would move subconsciously into the center of the road and clip or even directly head-on with a vehicle coming the other way. Second most likely was a pedestrian being hit by a passing car. While anyone simply walking along the highway so far from town was both unlikely and stupid, it was pretty common for people to drive out to Wilson's Bridge, then sit on the low wall and fish. Why the damn fools didn't go down to the riverbank was something Val Baker would never understand, but in her years of policing she had learned one thing beyond all others: people were damned fools. The third possible reason for an accident on the bridge was the most likely on a day like this. Kids would come out here and leap from the bridge the fifteen feet or so into the river, then swim to one bank or the other and do it all again. Now for all the truth that people were damned fools, Val herself had engaged in this idiot pursuit on many occasions in her youth and had fond memories of those days. She had fond memories too of making out with various boys in the shade under the bridge, hands exploring goose-fleshed skin inside bikinis and bathing shorts. But sometimes a kid would jump badly, or too near one bank or the other, or any number of other small mishaps that could occur with stupid teenage bravado. And there was the crossover with cars hitting kids like they sometimes hit incautious fishermen.

As she pulled over onto the hard dirt just before the bridge, it seemed the latter was the cause of the call out. The ambulance had already arrived, Jerry and Jill Yonker huddled with a group of almost naked teenagers on the near bank, just below the bridge footing. Others gathered along one side and leaned over to leer.

Val climbed out of the car, letting go an involuntary, "Oof!" as the heat of the day hit her like a punch. She left the blue and red lights flashing, but killed the siren and engine.

"All of y'all!" she yelled at the people rubbernecking off the bridge. "Get down from there and stop blocking the road. We don't want another accident when we already have one to deal with."

People milled, looked at each other.

"Move now, before I start handing out tickets for obstruction!" she yelled, and people scowled but finally started moving. Some returned to vehicles parked nearby, others walked back towards the carnival, while a few moved with Val down to the riverbank.

"Get back, everyone, let's clear a space here."

As people moved away, she crouched beside the paramedics. Jerry and Jill Yonker had driven the local ambulance for more years than Val had lived in Sallow Bend. Both in their fifties at least, with almost matching ash blond hair and rangy, athletic bodies, they were universally liked and respected. Both their faces were pinched as Val saw the pale, inert form of a young man on the muddy bank between them. Their crisis bags were open, but the level of inactivity made a stone drop in Val's gut.

She recognized the boy, but couldn't place him. "What do we have?" she quietly asked Jill Yonker.

"Drowned," Jill said. "It was already too late when we got here."

"We know how?"

Jill nodded towards a group of five teenagers gathered close together, many crying, all consoling each other.

"You got this?" Val asked.

Jill nodded as Jerry pulled a thin sheet from the side of his bag and unfolded it to lay over the young man's body. Wails and sobs rose up with a rush of conversation as he covered the boy's face. "Coroner is on his way," Jill said. The woman's eyes tightened and she said, "Too many. What's happening?"

Val had no answer for that. She gave Jill's shoulder a gentle squeeze, then stood and moved over to the group of friends. "What happened?"

They looked at each other, then one girl seemed to be silently anointed as the spokesperson and she swallowed and took a step forward. "He couldn't get out of the river," she said, her voice cracking.

"Let's get some names first." Val pulled out her notepad. "I'm sorry for your loss, and this is a traumatic time, but let me get some details while it's all fresh in your minds, okay?"

"I'm never going to forget a second of this," the girl said, fresh tears pouring over her cheeks.

"You're Angela Franks, right?"

The girl nodded. "You know my daddy, he's the janitor for your station and other stuff."

"That's right. And who..?" Val gestured back to the bright white sheet, starkly clean against the brown mud. The shape underneath it thin and small-looking, somehow obscene.

"Reece Gossett, he lives south of town. His dad's a logger, don't know about his mom."

Val remembered the family, not well off, a little rough around the edges, but all decent people. She remembered Reece too, a kid who tried to hide his anxieties by being a hardass and a smartass though he was neither hard nor smart. But he was angry, and she'd chewed him out once for some awful sexist comment he'd made while she was in earshot. She hadn't expected him to learn from it though. He had helped Val once when a bunch of teens got into a crazy brawl outside Ken's store one night. Complicated kid. And now he was gone, dead, just like that. He couldn't have been more than fourteen years old.

"He nearly choked to death at school yesterday," one of the other kids said. "And now this."

Val raised an eyebrow. A complicated and unlucky kid. "So tell me what happened."

"We were just fooling, you know? Jumping off the bridge, swimming, hanging out. Reece has jumped off this bridge a thousand times, and he's a good swimmer. You know he swims for county, right?"

Val didn't know that, but it only made everything worse.

"He's not just a good swimmer, he's a potential champion," another of the kids said. "Was a potential champ, anyway. He was going to state next year, hisons coach said."

"So how does a world-class swimmer drown in Sallow River?" Val asked, keeping her voice as gentle as she could despite the butterflies that chewed at her gut. Something felt way off about this whole thing.

"I don't know," Angela said. "We were all jumping, then he stood on the wall up there about to jump, but paused." She scrunched her brow, trying to remember the sequence of events. "He paused and looked over there," she pointed to the road leading to the bridge, "and said, 'What do you want?' to Hester."

"Hester was here?"

"Yeah, with those friends of hers, Suki and Clare, and a couple of others. They just came wandering along the road. From the carnival, I guess."

Val lifted her hat, wiped the sweat off her brow with a sleeve and put it back. The afternoon heat was making her impatient and she took a deep breath. Give Angela Franks time to get out the story in her own way. "Okay."

"And Hester said she wasn't doing anything, and then Reece kinda flinched."

"Flinched?"

"Yeah. I was down here in the water, I'd just jumped, and I was teasing him to catch me, you know, before Hester came along."

"You two are..?" Val prompted.

Angela twisted one side of her mouth, both cheeks flaring with color. "No! He's kind of a sleaze." She blanched. "Was. I was just winding him up, I guess."

"Okay."

"Anyway, he flinched and then just stepped off the bridge. He usually jumps, does flips, all kinds of stuff. He's a show-off, you know? But he just stepped off, almost like he didn't really want to. And when he hit the water, he went straight under. Didn't swim or anything. At first we laughed, we thought that was his shtick, you know? He was playing dead, just falling in and not coming up. Then it went on too long. A few of us started diving, trying to find him, but it's muddy, you can't see anything in this river. I was kicking around under there where he fell, people started screaming and shouting." Angela hitched a breath, rubbed one hand over her mouth.

"Take your time, honey."

"Then he just floated up over there." She pointed to the river's edge about ten yards from where they stood. "He was face down, arms and legs out like a star, not moving. We grabbed him and dragged him onto the bank, Terry tried CPR."

"I learned it for First Aid at Scouts," said a gangly teenager at the back, his red hair tousled, a spray of freckles across his nose and cheeks. "I kept it up till Jill and Jerry got here, but I knew from the moment I started it was pointless. I could tell he was dead."

"He was under so long!" someone else said.

"What do you think happened?" another kid asked, her eyes pleading with Val.

"I don't know. Maybe he got tangled up in something under there? Some branches maybe?"

"I couldn't feel anything," Angela said, her voice hollow. Shock seemed to be setting in as she unburdened herself of the tale. "It's just mud and rocks."

"Maybe he hit his head on one of the rocks?" Val suggested.

"He went in feet first."

An awkward silence fell, no one sure what else to say with the body of Reece Gossett under a sheet not three yards away.

"Okay," Val said. "I want you kids to all gather up your stuff and get home, okay? But you each come and give me your name before you go, just so I have a list of everyone who was here in case we get more questions." She looked around the group. "Where's Hester and her friends?"

Angela shrugged.

"They left again," another kid said. "They went back that way." He pointed down the highway towards the carnival and town beyond it.

"I guess I'll talk to them later. Many others leave already?"

"A few, I guess."

"Okay."

She spent ten minutes collecting names, watching the kids walk off or get into cars parked back from the road on either side of the river. By the time Freddie Holtz pulled up there were only a handful waiting dolefully for lifts home. The coroner was not far behind Holtz and went straight to the riverbank and Reece's body as Val filled Holtz in on all she'd learned.

Holtz shook his head. "Another death. Something in the fucking air this summer?"

"You know," Val said slowly, finally voicing something that had been bugging her ever since Jerry Yonker laid down that white sheet. "There have been times in Sallow Bend's history like this before."

"What do you mean?"

"I've read about it. Time's when there's been a spate of accidents and unexplained deaths."

Holtz narrowed his eyes at her and she tried not to feel a little inflamed. "Times like when?" he asked.

"You must know the rumors? Every few decades death comes to Sallow Bend, stuff like that?"

Holtz let out a gruff laugh. "Small town superstition, Val. Don't buy into that bullshit. I know you've been around a little while, you and your family, but you're still kinda new here. You get used to people spilling that kind of nonsense. It comes from a lack of education and you're too smart to let it get under your skin."

She felt a glow of pride at the inadvertent compliment he'd paid her, but couldn't help rankling a little about the "new here" jab. Just not born here, that's what he meant. And something about the last few days still bugged her. "I guess so," she said anyway.

"And besides," Holtz went on. "You start talking about stuff like that and you scare people. The last thing we need to do is scare people. They do dumb things when they're scared."

She had to admit he was right there. They did dumb things when they *weren't* scared. People were damned fools after all. But the niggle about those spates of deaths, the rumors she'd heard obliquely all the time she'd been a resident of Sallow Bend, *had* got under her skin. She thought maybe she might do a little more research as time allowed. If for no other reason than to put her mind at rest about how much it was nonsense after all.

"There *are* strange stories about our town," Jerry Yonker said, stepping up beside them.

Holtz sighed. "Strange stories?"

"You seen Old Man Wilson around much the last coupla days? He's usually all over the carnival, strutting up and down. He's got some stories."

"I haven't spent much time there," Holtz said. "He not around?"

Jerry Yonker shrugged. "Maybe someone ought to go and chat to him. Check up on him." He smiled, like it was all nothing to really worry about it. "We're done here. Bill will let you know when he has what he needs and he'll take the body."

"Okay, thanks." Holtz turned back to Val. "Get on back to the station and fill out the forms. I know you don't like the heat, I'll stay here until Bill down there has finished up."

"Yes, sir."

Holtz pursed his lips a moment, then said, "And if you get a chance, drop by Old Man Wilson's, check he's okay. He is an old man, after all, and lives alone up there."

"Will do."

Val headed back to her car, already anticipating the cool kiss of the air conditioning. But a chill of a different kind was tickling the base of her spine. Her old dad would call it police intuition.

If you don't remember anything else, he had said when she graduated, *you remember this: Whenever you get that gut feeling, the ice at the bottom of your spine, you treat that like a telegram from God. You treat that like the new Gospel. You never, ever ignore your intuition.*

Val nodded to herself as she got into the cruiser and fired it up. She remembered Jerry Yonker's words, *There* are *strange stories about our town.*

"You got it, Daddy," she whispered, and pulled a U-turn off the shoulder and headed back toward the Sheriff's Office.

22

THE AFTERNOON HEAT made a haze of the air. The sky, a pale blue like distant linen, speckled with high-flying birds spiraling in cooler updrafts. Caleb had reached the end of his ability to remain among people, the headache stabbing like an iron spike.

"I don't know where they've gone," he said as much to himself as to Tricia.

"Who?"

"Hester and the others?" He phrased it like a question, realizing Tricia had mentally lost her grasp again.

"Oh, that's right. Maybe they've gone home."

"Maybe. Time for me to call it a day too."

Tricia smiled, took a bite from her cotton candy. Caleb watched it vanish the moment it entered her mouth. "I'll drive you."

"Thanks."

He had enjoyed observing Tricia enjoy the carnival. They'd had a lunch with undoubtedly low nutritional value that had left Caleb feeling slightly nauseated, but had been delicious despite his misgivings. On top of the chili dog it was surely going to do terrible things to him. Tricia had since relished sodas and candies, dropped dollars on all kinds of sideshows and games. She'd convinced him to try his hand at Hoopla and, to his amazement, he'd snagged her a two-foot tall teddy bear with a big red and blue spotted tie around its neck. She carried the prize casually under one arm, but her elbow was clamped down tight. He had to admit they'd had some measure of fun, even if he had to repeatedly stand aside and stare at the flat-trodden grass to let the massive information input from the crowd ease. He was amazed at the grounding effect of hiding behind Tricia's genuine and guileless presence. It was something he had never experienced before, never even considered. Though he suffered now, he had lasted way longer in a crowd than he ever had before.

But despite the fun she'd had, something clearly tickled the edges of Tricia's good mood. Some weight she bore no matter how hard she tried to enjoy herself. Almost as though she were forcing it aside with the myriad distractions to be had. She'd told him that morning about her fight with Riley, how her husband had taken her at her word to get out and not come back. How much of that had she meant, he wondered? He had no way of knowing their history. Did she really want Riley gone? Was she tense now because he had gone, or because she had sent him away? Or in case he came back? People's lives were convoluted and infuriating whenever they intertwined in his experience.

But he had his own problems, despite current discomfort. The day was growing long, and he had no more idea of Hester's activities than he did before. Except that strange interaction with Saul, who ran the Mengele's Secret sideshow. Maybe that was enough, perhaps he could talk to the guy and figure a new course of action. He needed to do something, and soon, because the hard perusal from Hester right afterward had left him rattled and marked.

Tricia had moved away, talking animatedly to a group of others. They seemed to be parents like her, or adults of an age at least. Tricia's hand was up, covering her mouth in shock, all the other faces serious and strained.

He stepped forward. "What's happening?"

"A boy drowned," Tricia said, her voice tinged with disbelief. "Down at Wilson's Bridge."

Only a mile or so from the carnival, the kids always played there in summer. Accidents weren't unheard of, but drownings were rare. Caleb couldn't remember one happening before in his time. Another death. His stomach became heavy and cold. "Who?" he asked.

"Reece Gossett," said one of the women. "Sal's little boy."

The group descended into strained and tight chatter once more, but Caleb let the sound wash away. He stepped back, shaking his head. Too much of a coincidence. It had to be. After he'd watched Hester stalk toward that boy the day before, closing his throat with her mind while so many other students sat by as if dreaming.

Caleb found himself looking directly at a small group of girls walking along the midway. Hester, Clare and Suki, chattering with two others whose names escaped him. But he recognized them from school. Had they been at the carnival all along, or had they just got back? Because if they'd been out to Wilson's Bridge, that was all the proof Caleb needed.

He tore his eyes away as they drew nearer, eager not to attract Hester's attention again.

"...always was a douche," one of the girls was saying as they passed.

"No one will miss him," Hester said. "The world is better off with one less guy like that in it."

"Did you see though?" another girl said. "He just didn't come up for ages. I can't understand why."

Hester laughed, a high, glassy sound. "Who cares? He's gone. Good riddance."

There were gasps and suppressed giggles at the sheer decadence of Hester's attitude to death. Caleb risked a glance and saw both Suki and Clare were tight-lipped, pale and drawn. They clearly needed sleep, the only real color in their skin the deep purplish blue of bags under their eyes. He wondered if their experiences were keeping them awake at night.

The lowering sun made their shadows long across the grass of the midway, merged with hundreds of others, and with the shapes of the stalls and rides. The low golden light glittered off chrome as the colored bulbs on the rides began to gain prominence.

"Look at the time!" Clare said. "It's nearly five. We have to go." She pulled at Suki's sleeve and the other girl seemed to wake up, nodded.

"You can't stay longer?" Hester asked.

"We're grounded in the evenings still," Suki said. "We're allowed out in daytime as long as we're never late."

Clare pulled Suki back towards the entrance. "My dad's picking us up at five," she called back, and they were gone into the crowd.

Hester shrugged, grinned. "See you later," she said to the others, and those girls wandered off too.

For a moment Hester stood alone, looking around with narrowed eyes. Caleb looked away again, terrified she would notice him. From the side of his eye he watched her short black leather boots, then she turned and headed north. He moved to watch her weave slowly through the crowds, then bear to the left around the trailers where the carnies lived. He lost sight of her as she headed for the trees beyond the carnival grounds. He was entirely unsurprised that she'd gone that way and wanted to follow, but fear chewed his gut at the mere thought of it. Following her into the forest was surely a death sentence. Also not surprisingly, no one else seemed to have noticed Hester leave or see where she had gone. Caleb felt frighteningly alone in a packed crowd.

He swallowed, looked back the other way, then glanced at his watch. A few minutes before five. He moved back to Tricia.

"Hey, I'd like to talk to Suki and Clare before they head home."

"What for?"

He suppressed annoyance. "Humor me?"

"Okay."

She said strained goodbyes to the others nearby then fell into step beside him.

"You know I think something is up with Hester, right?" Caleb said slowly. "You remember that?"

She nodded, face set in concentration. "I do remember that. You said something earlier today..." She shook her head, smiled. "No, it's gone."

Her face softened and he watched the realizations slip away again. He needed to keep chipping away at the mental armor Hester had wrapped around everyone. If he could get through to Tricia eventually, maybe he could get through to more people too. And perhaps there were more like him around, like that poor bastard Kirk Branton. He had no idea why so few seemed to see through Hester's glamor. If nothing else, he and Tricia together must have a better chance of convincing others, or finding more like he and Kirk. And that carnie was still an ace card he might yet play. Saul knew something was up. Perhaps there was a chance of blowing this weirdness wide open yet. Suki and Clare stood just beyond the carnival's main entrance, talking quietly to each other as they waited. For the first time, out in public but not chaperoned by Hester.

"Come on," Caleb said. "Let's ask them about stuff."

Tricia shrugged. "If you insist."

The girls looked up as he approached, both developing instant matching frowns. Caleb recognized it as the face young people put on when approached by the truly old and uncool.

"Hi," he said simply.

"You're the janitor," Clare said.

"That's right."

"We're waiting for her dad," Suki said, pointing to Clare. "He'll be here any minute."

Caleb heard the implied threat, tried to smile again to reassure them. But he knew he wasn't very good at smiling. "Are you two feeling better since your couple of days in the woods?"

Suki shrugged. "Yeah. Still pretty tired."

"You look a bit run down. Maybe you need to get more sleep."

Clare let out a short laugh. "I sleep all the time lately. Doesn't seem to make any difference."

Caleb swallowed, decided to go all in before Mr Finlay arrived. "Do you remember when you first saw Hester?"

The girls both snapped their gaze to him. "Years ago?" Suki said, but her voice had lost its bored defiance. The suggestion came out like a question.

The girls looked at each other, faces strained. Clare began to cry silently. "We've known Hester forever!" she said after a moment, but it sounded like an accusation.

"I want to go home," Suki said. "Where's your dad?"

"There!" Clare's face brightened as she pointed.

Caleb glanced around and saw a newish green sedan cruising up towards the gate, Todd Finlay frowning at them through the windshield. Disappointment sank through him. They had been close, but maybe it was best not to push these girls too hard. A pulse of panic washed through him as he imagined them telling Hester he'd been asking questions. But the girl's dismay had slipped away in that fashion he was becoming so used to.

Todd Finlay parked and climbed out. "Everything okay here?"

"Fine," Caleb said, but saw Todd's concern, his fatherly urge to protect surfacing. Caleb looked away, breaking eye contact. His head felt like it might literally split down the middle.

"Get in the car, girls."

Suki and Clare scurried for the back seat, but Todd walked towards Caleb and Tricia. "Why are you talking to my girl?"

"It's fine, Todd," Tricia said. "We saw them waiting here and were just asking if they were okay. If they had a lift. They said you were coming."

"That right?"

Caleb continued to stare at the ground.

"I think we're all a bit edgy since… you know." Tricia gave a small, nervous laugh, and squeezed Todd's arm. "Everyone feels the need to keep an extra eye on the kids."

Todd grunted, gave a reluctant shrug. "You hear about Reece Gossett?"

Tricia blew air out. "Yes, just now. What a terrible thing."

Todd grunted again, turned back to his car. "Thanks for watching out for the kids," he said, and got into the driver's seat before Caleb or Tricia could reply.

They watched the car bump up onto the highway, then Tricia tugged at Caleb's arm. "Come on, I'll drive you home."

Her car was hot again from standing in the sun all afternoon, but Caleb barely noticed. He felt lost and alone and uncertain. Where did he go from here? What did he do? Tricia pulled up across the road from the school and smiled at him. "I had fun this afternoon, thanks."

He nodded. "Me too."

"You okay?"

What else could he say? "Sure, just tired. Overwhelmed from all the people. Headache."

She looked like she wanted to say something else, then thought better of it, patted his arm. "Get some sleep."

"I will, thanks." He got out of the car and turned to watch her pull away. She threw a wave out the window, then turned a corner out of sight.

His small room under the school hall was cool and quiet, gloomy as the evening came on. A thorough relief. He left the light off, the TV off, swallowed two painkillers with a long drink of water, and slumped into his tatty armchair, wallowing in solitude. For several minutes he simply stared at the ceiling.

"You think I hadn't noticed you lurking and spying? Why do men always think we don't see them watching us?"

Caleb barked a shout of surprise, ice flooding his gut. He hadn't seen or heard her open the door, but the young girl's silhouette was unmistakable outlined by twilight. Trembling set in, but he couldn't move a muscle. That same inertia that had gripped him in the midway now pinned him to the chair.

"It's funny," she said, stepping into the room, her glowing green eyes and the white stripe in her hair the only bright things about her. "Always someone interferes. Every time. Maybe it's just some kind of universal balance at play. There are always one or two who notice, but I deal with them."

Caleb's throat worked, he gasped, tried to speak but couldn't. She turned and walked back out, up the steps to the area where Daley had so recently died. Unable to resist the urge, Caleb stood and followed, stepping awkwardly like he was trying to remember how to walk, but incapable of holding himself still. Hester's will drove him like a puppet. Outside, darkness had fallen, the space under the trees quiet and still. The entire school empty, a ghost town for the holidays. How would she do it? Caleb knew he had no chance now and tears squeezed from his eyes. He didn't want to die, but more than that, he didn't want anyone else to die either, and once he was gone, there was no one left to stand up to Hester. But no one could stand up to her anyway, that much was apparent by his own unwilling actions. Guided by her, he turned and a sob of horror escaped him at the sight of a loop of rope hanging from one of the lower branches nearby. A saw horse stood under the noose, one of several he kept around the side of the building.

Hester stood behind it, her pale linen dress spectral in the low light. A smile bowed her lips and she raised one hand, palm up, as if inviting him to dance. He would be dancing in a moment, that much was certain, his feet a good yard above the hard-packed earth.

He stepped up onto the saw horse, every muscle straining as he tried to resist her silent orders. His face hurt, cramped from the grimace that he knew was identical to the one he'd seen on Kirk Branton's face. And Tim Daley's. The rope was rough and heavy as he lifted it and dropped it down over his head. It hit his shoulders like a benediction.

"Goodbye, Caleb," Hester said softly.

"Noooo!" The voice was high and horrified, pitched almost to a scream.

Hester whirled around and Caleb felt the grip on his body fall away, like he'd been doused with a bucket of water. He staggered and tottered, nearly hanged himself anyway, but grabbed the thick knot of the noose and hauled himself upright. He threw the loop of rope off as Tricia barreled out of the darkness and knocked Hester sideways with two outstretched arms.

She suddenly stilled, stiffened, as Hester regained her balance. The young girl's face was a mask of fury. "Don't interfere!"

Tricia stood tall and straight, trembling as she grimaced, trying to resist Hester's control. And Caleb realized he still had command of himself. He recalled the conversation he had overheard earlier. Suki saying *I wish all the creepers in the world would get crushed under trees.* And then Hester, *I can only work one at a time.*

"Hey!" he shouted. "Leave her alone!"

Hester turned, face lowered as she glared at him from beneath her brows. He took one step forward, mind racing. Could he simply punch her to ground? Knowing she was something unnatural was one thing, but he was looking at a thirteen-year-old girl. Tricia let out strangled sounds of frustration.

This damned creature had almost made him hang himself. She was no young girl. Caleb surged forward and Hester shot out one hand, palm towards him. He gasped as the air rushed from his lungs and he sat heavily in the dirt, even though she was still ten feet from him. But Tricia had staggered forward, Hester's hold on her lost. Tricia dragged in breath, hands at her throat, eyes wide in horror. Caleb tried to pull himself to his feet, but his limbs wouldn't respond.

Hester grinned. "Who would believe you? Who will you tell? Better watch your back!" She turned and ran into the trees, swallowed by the shadows.

Tricia rushed to Caleb as his ability to move returned. He looked into the darkness, knees shaking.

"Let her go," Tricia said. "We can't chase her through the night."

He turned to face her. "If you hadn't come along..."

"I know. I came back to ask if you wanted to have lunch tomorrow or something. I wanted to repay you for your kindness, helping me to not think so hard about Riley today. Then realized I didn't have your number."

He shrugged. "I'm glad that was a by-product, but it's not what I was really doing."

"No. You needed a witness. I remember now. But I wasn't anything of the sort."

"Until now."

Tricia nodded, staring off between the trees. "Until now. What the hell is she?"

"Something new. She came back with Suki and Clare."

"Yes. It's obvious now. How could I not have seen that before?"

"The whole town can't see it. But you can now?"

Tricia laughed. "Clear as day."

Caleb rubbed a palm over his throat. "Well, that's something."

23

DANIEL CLARKE STRETCHED as the sun gained height and the heat of the day made itself known. Another hell of a day on the way for sure. The kind of day his grandma used to call a Jesus cook pot of a day. Whatever that meant. She just needed to get Jesus into everything because any aspect of life without the Messiah was anathema to that old lady. Daniel smiled as he massaged his large biceps, pumped and trembling from his workout. He missed his grandma, but took great solace in the knowledge that she was with her beloved Lord now.

"What if I get up there and He finds me wanting?" she'd once asked Daniel, in a moment of rare self-doubt.

"Grandma, if the Good Lord finds you wanting, the rest of us are going straight to Hell."

She'd cackled and slapped him at the same time. "You watch your mouth, Daniel, but bless your heart."

He crossed one arm over his wide chest, pressed into the elbow with the opposite hand to stretch his shoulder joint. He was justifiably proud of his body, his enormous strength. There was vanity in it, he knew, and he would never apologize for that. But there was need too. Life as a roustabout demanded it, lifting, fixing, carrying, loading. It all required fitness and physical power, and he had those in excess thanks to his daily hard work. Nothing came to those who weren't prepared to work for it, so went another of his grandma's wisdoms. But his exercise today had been distracted, half-hearted. The simple truth was his visit to the woods, finding the girls in that creepy-ass cabin, had deeply disturbed him. He remembered what Sarah had said, that something had come back with him, some lingering presence. He was not a superstitious man, but he was not arrogant either. There was divinity in the world, and there was evil. Surely it was possible that some of it might brush up against a hard-working man like himself, just through sheer bad luck.

He'd saved those girls, he knew that was a fact. That *had* to be a fact. That was a good deed, but another of his grandma's snippets of wisdom came to him then. No good deed goes unpunished. Sarah knew about that stuff, she was closer to the veiled world than most, and she'd done a ritual to him. She'd lit a thick bunch of sage and wafted the heavy smoke all around, told any bad spirits to be gone. It had smelled like magic, and it seemed powerful. At the time he felt a lot better, like she'd done just what she said she would and cleansed him. But that night there were nightmares. And the next night. And then last night again. Three nights in a row he'd had the same dream, of that cabin in the woods.

The day had been bright and hot, but in his dream, as he entered that old shack, his breath had misted with the cold. He smelled rotten meat and those two girls were lying there dead on the chilled stone floor, mouths agape, eyes staring blankly at the cobwebbed ceiling beams above. Just those two, no sign of Hester. Then when he walked back outside the cabin, it was suddenly night, and freezing cold, frost all over the trees and the grass, the lake a solid white slab. And his eye caught something moving, far out across the other side. So he tried to focus on it, and realized it was a leg sliding under its own power somehow, slipping to him across the ice. Then another, then an arm, and a head and a torso, and another arm. From all directions the body parts came, heading toward each other and heading toward him. As they got close they began to twitch and dance, then they slammed into each other and became a woman of indeterminate middle age, naked and beautiful, skin pale as snow in the moonlight, just like the single white streak through her long black hair, her eyes shining green. As she came together, she stood, reaching forward with clawing hands. But this was a woman grown, no child, her body full of desirable curves. Her mouth fell open and she screamed, the sound rattling, piercing his ears like nails, too loud to be natural. And when Daniel began to babble and stutter, try to say something, anything, as urine spread hotly through his black jeans, she had tipped her head back and laughed, deep and loud and long. Her hands reached, she was almost upon him, when she snapped her gaze back to his, locked eyes, her teeth pressed together as she snarled.

And Daniel woke with a start, sweat-soaked. And piss-soaked too, having wet himself in bed just like in the dream. A grown damn man of thirty-five years, pissing his bed like a child, in genuine fear. Three nights in a row. And each time, he had been too afraid to go back to sleep and dawn had been close, so he rose and exercised.

Was he going mad? Perhaps he should go to see Sarah again and ask her for help. Maybe it would take a shitload more sage than she had used the first time. Or maybe burning damn herbs wasn't the answer.

"You okay, son?"

Daniel turned to see John Barrow standing just beside the small trailer Daniel called home. He moved over and lifted his barbells and dumbbells to one side to make room.

"Sure, I'm fine."

Barrow stepped forward. He had on heavy chinos and a collared shirt, the usual attire the man affected, and tough-looking boots. He wore a wide, flat cap over his thick black-going-to-gray hair. "You sure? You looked a little spooked there."

Daniel drew a deep breath, licked his lips. "Truth is, I am a bit."

"That thing with the cabin you told us about? Finding the girls?"

Daniel nodded, unsure what else to say.

Barrow stared up at him for a while, clearly thinking, so Daniel let him think. Then the small man nodded once. "Let's go back."

"What?"

"I'll go with you. Take me there, show me around. For one, I'm intrigued. But also, maybe it'll help you shake off this spook. When you see it's all fine."

Daniel frowned. “And what if it isn’t fine?”

“I’ll be with you.”

Daniel’s frown popped into an expression of amused surprise. Barrow raised one hand before he could speak.

“I may be small of stature, not six foot four of muscled mahogany like your good self, but don’t underestimate me. Besides, I also have this.” He reached into a small satchel that Daniel hadn’t noticed he was carrying and pulled out a revolver almost as big as his head.

“That a damn Magnum?”

Barrow smiled. “Yep. Blow a hole through anything, this will.”

Daniel sighed, shook his head. “I don’t think whatever lurks up there is going to be bothered by bullets, however big they are.”

Barrow shrugged, put the gun back. “Still. I want to go. Will you take me?”

“It’s quite a hike, more than an hour. You’re like, what, a hundred years old?”

“Fuck you, I’m fifty-one.”

Daniel grinned. It felt good to joust good-naturedly with Barrow, it was a sport they had enjoyed for a long time. “And it’ll take you three hours to walk one hour for me with those stumpy-ass legs.”

Barrow nodded, raised his eyebrows. “So now it’s a challenge then? Let’s go, I’ll show you how capable this stumpy-ass fifty-one year old is.”

“You’re serious, huh?”

“I am. And no joke, I’m fit. I’ll keep up with you. There’s something up, isn’t there? Something weird about this town. Saul Fallon is all out of sorts and while that makes me kinda happy, it also disturbs me. Because if that freak is upset, then we should all take notice.”

“What’s he upset about?” Daniel had never liked Saul, never trusted him. But he agreed with Barrow that the man was a kind of barometer for weirdness.

“I’m not sure. I did have a bit of a row with him the other day, though not really any big thing. I tried to talk to him again last night and he’s genuinely cranky about something. Told me to fuck off and didn't even seem like he enjoyed it. That's not like him."

"And you think it's to do with these girls? With the cabin I found?"

Barrow shrugged. "I don't know. Every time I try to think about it, it's like my thoughts are oil and they slip right around in my brain. But the one thing I do remember is that tale you told us, and I want to see that place for myself."

Daniel wondered at his own sanity for a moment, then decided that besides Ashley and Sarah, Barrow was probably the one other crew member he could truly trust. "I've been having powerful nightmares every night since I found 'em."

"Have you?"

"Yep. Exactly the same nightmare every time."

Barrow moved forward, leaning his head way back to look at Daniel. "Let's go up there."

"I'm honest with you, John, I'm scared to. What might happen?"

"I don't think anything will happen. If *I'm* honest with *you*, I think a lot of superstitious nonsense is taking a grip of this camp and I want to put a stop to it. Ashley asked me to put a halt to any gossip. But I feel like something is wrong. So I aim to go up to that cabin and prove to myself that it's all bullshit. I'd really like you to show me, because I don't know how to find it."

"You can just follow the river. It's a long way around, the but the river will lead you up to the lake."

"I'm not built for long ways around, Daniel."

Daniel smiled, nodded. He trusted Barrow, he didn't want to be superstitious or mad. And he didn't want any more nightmares. He didn't want to be this scared any more. It made sense to confront the source of his fear and find it impotent. *You get bullied by big fools,* his grandma had said, *you front up to those animals and you tell them you have no fear of anyone but Jesus. And you put them on their ass if you need to!*

He wasn't sure he'd be able to put actual fear on its ass, certainly not with a punch, but perhaps simply facing up to it was enough. "Okay," he said. "I'll take you. Should we take anyone else?"

"No, let's keep this between you and me. It's only just after six, we can be there and back easily by ten, and we don't have to work until noon. Easy, right?"

"I guess. Let me get ready."

He had a rinse down from the water tank next to his trailer, put on clean black jeans, boots, and a fresh tee-shirt. He ran a hand over his shining, shaved head, then grabbed a trucker cap to keep the sun off, even though he felt the trees would provide more than enough shade. "You have water?"

Barrow hefted the satchel. "Water, some candy bars, and a big fucking gun."

Daniel nodded, filled his own water bottle and held it in one hand. He didn't have a satchel, but he didn't mind carrying it. "Okay, let's go."

Daniel had to admit he was impressed by John Barrow's fortitude. They set off behind the camp and entered the trees at a slow stroll, Daniel assuming that would be a pretty tough pace for Barrow already. But the small man powered along and soon enough Daniel was walking at a pace good enough to feel his stride stretch and a sheen of sweat stipple his skin as the heat of the day increased. Within about ten or fifteen minutes, the trees thickened, the air cooled and shaded. It felt good, somehow natural and honest away from the presence of humans. The undergrowth and tree roots slowed their progress a little, but Barrow continued on.

"You really are damn fit, man."

Barrow grinned. "You want me to slow down for you?"

"Hell no, I can keep up. I'm impressed, that's all."

"You spend your life trying to survive in a world made for people twice your size and you learn to toughen up to it." Barrow shrugged. "Anyway, I'm an impatient man. I can't be going everywhere at the pace these legs naturally allow."

After half an hour or so, Barrow was puffing and Daniel's fatigue made his legs feel swollen. Sweat ran over them both. That comment from Barrow about surviving in a world not made for him had hit Daniel somewhere deep inside and it pained him a little. "I need a rest. I'd only just finished my workout when you showed up and then this forced march…"

Barrow looked at him with narrow eyes. "*You're* tired?"

"I just need a moment, a drink of water." Without waiting for a response, he sat on a fallen log and stretched his long legs out, uncapped his water bottle.

Barrow hopped up onto the log beside and pulled off his cap to mop his brow. His black and silver curls were soaked with sweat, stuck to his forehead where the hat had flattened them. He blew out a breath and drank. "Halfway?"

"About that."

They sat in companionable silence, listening to the birdsong and the rustle of summer breeze through the leaves high above. Sunbeams lanced in here and there, dust motes dancing like pirouetting stars. After no more than two minutes, Barrow jumped down again and set off without a word. Daniel let out a small laugh of resignation and followed.

Another twenty minutes and the woods were thick and cloying. Daniel remembered telling Ashley about how they seemed like Mirkwood. He got the feeling again, a sudden switch from nature's beauty to oppressive and dangerous.

"We're nearly there." His voice was little more than a whisper.

Barrow stopped, turned in a slow circle, frowning. Daniel waited for him to realize what the problem was, glad that it wasn't something only he felt. He remembered it from last time.

"Where are the birds?" Barrow asked, whispering too.

Daniel nodded. "Not a sound, huh? No birds, not even the wind. Feels dead, doesn't it."

He saw Barrow's Adam's apple pulse as the man swallowed. "You said this before, but I thought you were, you know, kinda embellishing."

"I didn't make up a single bit of that story." He pointed. "We'll come out of the trees any minute and you'll see the lake right up there."

They pushed slowly on, walking carefully now as if hunting. Brightness between the trees appeared, then they seemed to suddenly part and the huge expanse of the lake spread out before them. The sky was pale blue with high, scudding clouds, the day scorching hot already and it was barely eight am.

Yet somehow there still seemed to be a shadow laying over everything, the air carried a chill.

"It's like when you stand by the door of a store with air-conditioning on a hot day, trying to cool down," Barrow said.

"You think the water does that?"

"I guess so. Why else would there be a chill in the air?"

Daniel had an answer, but he didn't voice it. He stared out over the lake, imagined it solid white ice, body parts slithering across, gathering together as they rushed forward, then the woman with the white streak of hair screaming. His bladder felt suddenly full so he turned away, pointed along the lake shore. "There it is."

Barrow followed his gesture to look at the cabin a few hundred yards away. It looked the same as before, ragged and abandoned, offering little in the way of shelter. And yet it would have appeared a godsend to two little girls lost in the woods for a day and night. Daniel frowned. Three little girls, not two. He'd seen two first, then Hester had been behind him. And why did that frightening apparition in his dreams look like a grown up Hester? Was he seeing her mother? Her future?

"John, before we go around there, I want to tell you something."

"Okay." Barrow looked up at Daniel, his eyes concerned. "You okay?"

"Not really."

"This place is spooky as fuck, Dan, I won't lie to you. But it's all pretty normal."

"Is it? So where are the birds? Why is it cold?"

Barrow drew a breath, held it for a second, then had nothing to say. He blew it out again. "What did you want to tell me?"

Daniel licked suddenly dry lips, tried to swallow, but his throat felt like a sandpit. He gulped water, realizing too late that he'd drained his supply. He knew damn well he wouldn't be refilling his bottle from the lake. Never mind, he'd survive until they got back. His mind touched briefly on not getting back, and he pushed it aside. "These nightmares I've been having."

"Yeah. You said it was always the same."

"Three nights in a row now." And he told Barrow all about it. Except the bit where he pissed the bed. He figured he'd retain that dignity if he could.

"Hester's future self?" Barrow asked.

"Well, maybe. People sometimes say dreams are premonitions, right? You think of another explanation?"

Barrow shrugged. "Dreams are often completely nonsensical, Dan. People haven't been able to–"

A scream ripped through the trees, echoing unnaturally loud, ululating like a speaker that can't handle the frequency. Both men ducked instinctively, faces crunching into winces as they slapped their hands over their ears. Daniel's bladder almost let go and he went onto one knee beside Barrow. The scream stopped abruptly, silence falling like a rock.

"The hell was that?"

Barrow shook his head, looked around. "Some kind of bird?"

"That was no fucking bird, man! How big would a bird have to be to make that much noise?" His hands shook, his stomach watery and loose.

They slowly lowered their hands and Daniel stood back up. They both turned towards the cabin. "We have to go and look," Barrow said.

"This is a bad idea, John. We shouldn't have come."

Barrow opened his mouth to reply, but another sound beat him to it. Wind hissed through the trees behind them, stirred the leaves.

shouldn'thavecomeshouldn'thavecomeshouldn'thavecome

"Did you fucking hear that, man?"

Barrow nodded, staring into the darkness between the gnarled trunks. "A woman's voice."

Daniel wanted the trembling in his knees to stop. "Let's get out of here. You've seen it now, you know I'm not joking about it being spooky as fuck. I tell you what, I can't wait to move on. The sooner we're done with Sallow Bend, the be–"

A soft sound rose up, from far away, drifting to them on the gentle breeze that had begun to push along the lake shore. A song. A woman's voice, soft and lilting.

Golden slumbers kiss your eyes,
Smiles await you when you rise.
Sleep,
pretty baby,
Do not cry,
And I will sing a lullaby.

The voice was beautiful, low and slow and mesmerizing. Daniel's skin rippled with gooseflesh, his breath caught in his throat like it was on a hook. "We gotta go, John. Now!"

"The hell..?" Barrow whispered.

The voice seemed to come nearer, but there was no one to be seen.

Cares you know not,
Therefore sleep,
While over you a watch I'll keep.
Sleep,
pretty darling,
Do not cry,
And I will sing a lullaby.

Daniel let out a groan that wanted to be a scream. The trembling had risen from his knees to his whole body. Cold sweat sheened his face.

"We have to go, man!" He pulled at Barrow's shirt near the shoulder, caused the small man to hitch his arm, but Barrow pulled away.

"What's that?" He pointed towards the cabin.

Daniel swallowed what felt like broken glass. He didn't want to look but was compelled almost against his will to follow Barrow's trembling finger. The voice died away, almost a sigh of resignation, the breeze fell with it. Everything hung in still silence. Beside the cabin something lay lumped and dark. It looked like an animal, asleep on its side. Or maybe… Daniel dragged in a breath, dizziness reeling away as he realized it was the first breath he'd drawn in since the first word of the soft, crooning lullaby.

"Is that..?" He swallowed, tried again. "Is that a person?"

"We have to go and look." Barrow started towards it, but Daniel pulled him back.

"Fuck that noise, man! Let's just hurry back and call the police."

"We can't leave it there. It might get dragged off by wild animals or something."

Daniel gestured expansively with both arms. "There's nothing fucking here! This place is a dead zone!"

Soft laughter rippled to them as if from across the lake.

Barrow broke into a run, heading for the cabin. Daniel spat out a curse and followed. In seconds, studiously ignoring the cold, inert shack beside them, they stood looking down at the dead body. The man was tall and well-built, balding, dressed in jeans and a heavy cotton shirt. And he was covered with blood. He had been beaten almost unrecognizable, his face split and broken, nose flattened. Gouges like rope burns had flayed the skin from his wrists and legs, left wet, red welts across his chest.

"The hell could do this to a man?" Daniel whispered.

"He's been beaten to death," Barrow said. "Tied up and beaten by several strong men."

Daniel looked down at Barrow incredulously. "Several strong men? You still think there's anything about this so easily explained? What the hell were a bunch of fucking strongmen doing out here, beating folk up?"

Barrow shook his head, still staring at the corpse. "Small town justice? The mob? A cult group?"

"Who the fuck cares anyway? John, let's just get out of here."

"Isn't this, like, a crime scene or something?"

"I don't know, man."

Barrow finally turned away from the dead man, looked up at Daniel. "We have to call the police."

Daniel blew air out, nodded. "Yeah."

That soft, female laughter rippled through the air again and Barrow spun around, trying to look everywhere at once.

"Let's just get the fuck out of here." Daniel took long strides away from the cabin and into the trees. He heard Barrow's rapid steps catching up behind.

24

TRICIA SLEPT IN late, surprised she'd managed to fall asleep at all. She and Caleb had agreed that until something could be done about Hester, they had to stay together. It seemed to be the girl's only weakness, that she could control just one person at a time. If Tricia and Caleb watched each other constantly, they could always interrupt any control Hester might try to gain. So Caleb had returned home with Tricia. They'd discussed Hester at length, how she had come out of nowhere, what she might want, and what they could do about it. And they had come up with no answers and no plan. Only fear.

Shivers rippled through Tricia despite the hot morning. It felt as though she had fallen face-first through a mirror and where before she had seen only her own reflection, now she saw a greater world beyond. A place that hadn't existed but was now undeniable. How could she possibly have not remembered that only Suki and Clare had gone missing, yet they had returned with Hester? And everyone knew Hester, she was a town fixture, the cheeky girl with the white streak in her hair. That old part of her, the part that knew Hester, still lived somewhere deep inside. That person had been real. But that person had also shattered like mirror glass and Tricia could no longer accept anything but the truth. Hester had managed a powerful glamor over the entire town, but it seemed that once it was cracked, it stayed gone. How could they show everyone?

Hester had come out of nowhere. And she was responsible for at least three deaths. Almost four if she had had a few more moments with Caleb. Just what the hell was going on? But though disbelief pushed at her, cajoled her, like it wanted to move in and remove the new fear in her mind, she couldn't let it. One thing throughout all of this that had been constant was Caleb. She looked over the side of the bed and he lay on the floor in a sleeping bag, eyes wide.

"You're awake?" she said, stupidly.

"Have been for a while."

She nodded. "You okay?"

"Not really."

"Me either."

Tricia sat up, moved around to see him more clearly. He pulled himself to a sitting position too, leaning against her bedside table. "How come you knew all along?" she asked.

Caleb shook his head. "It was plain to me from the very start. And to Kirk Branton, which is why Hester killed him."

Tricia let out a humorless laugh of confusion. This stuff didn't happen in the really real world. Yet she knew her mind had refused to see Hester for what she was until plain evidence forced the issue. And *what* was she? Even now, with the glamor burst, Hester was still only a thirteen year old girl, albeit with a far more adult personality. The phone rang on the bedside next to her and Tricia yelped. She looked at the screen as it buzzed on the polished wood surface. Her sister.

She flicked a smile at Caleb, then tapped to answer. "Hey, Carol."

"He home yet?"

Tricia laughed. "Straight to the point. No, he's not." Her thoughts returned again to Riley. Where the hell was he? Even if he had taken her at her word and gone for help, or even gone for good, he could at least have sent a text. "I'm torn between being worried and furious at the asshole."

"I believe you. I still don't want to believe he got violent, but I did warn you."

Tricia sighed. "Carol, I know you did. So did everyone when he started drinking so much. But marriage is a partnership, I had to try to hold it together. Toby's disappearance hit him hard." She swallowed for the millionth time the stone of grief that Toby's memory put in her. He was not dead. One day she would see him again. One day. "But you were right. Riley is an asshole. A weak, pathetic asshole."

"It hit you both hard, but he didn't cope." Carol made a dismissive noise. "Anyway, I'm not ringing to give you a hard time. Of course you stuck with your husband. It's what we would all do. I was hoping to hear he'd come back and you'd hit him with the damn cheeseboard again."

Tricia could see her sister's face in her mind's eye, those lips twisted in a wicked grin. She couldn't help laughing. "Chopping board. But yeah, I kinda wish that was the case too. At least I'd know what had happened to him."

"It's been three days now, and not a word?"

"Not a thing."

"Ass. Hole."

Tricia shrugged, realized Carol couldn't see that. "I just hope nothing terrible has happened. I half-expect to hear that he got so drunk at Gil's that he drove his pickup into the river or something."

"You should be so lucky."

"Carol!"

"I'm sorry. I'm angry, that's all. I'm sure you are too. I bet he's just on a bender somewhere, thinks he's making a point by making you suffer. Probably expects that you'll beg him to come back when you realize how empty life is without him blah blah blah."

Tricia wished it was that simple, but she knew Riley better. That wasn't his nature, to be vindictive that way. That was more Carol's husband's toxic personality. He was the kind of guy who got off on manipulating women, spent half his life gaslighting his wife and it drove Tricia mad. But her sister couldn't see it and their life was relatively stable for all that. Given that her own husband was a missing alcoholic, perhaps Tricia should try not to judge. "How's Peter?" she said anyway.

Carol huffed softly, recognizing the subtle dig. "He's good. We're booking a trip away actually. He's taking me to New York for a long weekend. Can you believe that? Four days in the big city. We're gonna see a show on Broadway and everything. For our anniversary, obviously, so a few months away yet. Trish? You listening?"

Tricia heard the words but she wasn't listening. Out the window she saw a car pulling onto her driveway. As she shifted for a better view, she realized it was a police cruiser. Freddie Holtz climbed out. Ice water ran through her veins and she knew it was bad news.

"Carol, I have to call you back."

"Trish? You okay?"

"The police are here."

"Oh, shit. Trish."

"I gotta go, they're knocking. I'll call back, tell you everything." She hung up without waiting for her sister to say more and put the phone back on the cabinet.

Caleb looked at her with wide eyes. "Should I..?"

"Just stay here and stay quiet. Right now we don't know what to do about Hester, and I don't want more town gossip that you stayed the night. This… I don't know what this is."

Her knees were weak, hands shaking, as she climbed from bed still clothed from the night before and headed down the stairs. She opened the door. Holtz stood with his eyes downcast, holding his hat self-consciously by the rim.

"Oh fuck. He's dead, isn't he?"

Holtz pressed his lips together, then said, "Tricia, can I come in?"

"Freddie, is he dead?" Tricia shouted.

"Yes. I'm so sorry that it's my sad duty to tell you that we found Riley Brent. I'm afraid he's died."

The line was obviously practiced, Holtz no doubt going over and over in his head on the drive how he would deliver the news. But it echoed emptily in Tricia's ears. She turned away from the door, left it open, walked to the lounge. She collapsed onto the sofa, elbows on her knees, heads in her hands, and all the strength she'd been relying on for days, maybe even for the year since Toby had disappeared, drained away, and she sobbed.

She had no idea how long she sat with her face buried in palms wet with tears. It might have been two minutes or two hours, but the floodgates were open and nothing was closing them again until they were eventually, temporarily, empty. When she finally looked up, Holtz was in an armchair opposite, looking patient and grief-stricken himself. As soon as she caught his eye, Holtz rose and came to crouch next to her. He put an arm around her.

"I'm so sorry, Tricia. No one deserves the kind of luck you've had."

"Luck."

"There's not a word for what you've endured."

She looked up, gave him a weak smile. "Perhaps I'm in hell, Freddie. You ever think of that?"

He nodded softly. "And I'm right here with you, for whatever that's worth."

She kept trying to imagine Riley dead and it both filled her with grief and simultaneously refused to compute. Like the memory of Hester and the knowledge the memory was fake, her husband was both alive and dead. "He's really..?" She couldn't finish the sentence.

"He is. No question."

Tricia drew a shuddering breath. A movie played in hectic fast forward in the background of her mind's eye. Her and Riley young and in love, getting married, Toby as a baby, Toby disappearing, Riley drinking more and more, *whack!* as the heavy chopping board slammed into his head. Over and over it went in random profusion, coupled with the searing knowledge that that was it. He was gone. Forever. Snuffed out. The last thing she would ever remember of him was his bleeding, stunned face on the floor, looking up at her in miserable confusion as she screamed at him to get out and not come back until he got professional help. She'd killed him. As surely as putting a gun to his head, making those demands of him in his weakened state had finished him. Had he taken his own life after that? More tears came, her heart stuttering in her chest like a trapped bird. She might not be able to cope with that knowledge.

"How did he..?" She swallowed. "What happened? Car accident?" Perhaps if he had been drunk and crashed the pick-up, maybe that wouldn't be quite so much her fault. That kind of idiocy was all on him.

Holtz drew a deep breath. "Tricia, this is going to be hard for you to hear, and I apologize in advance that I don't have more information."

"What?" She looked at him, his face wavery through a veil of tears.

"We're still waiting on official word, but it's pretty clear that Riley was beaten to death."

An empty wind sailed through Tricia's mind. "Beaten? By who?"

"We don't know. But there's more than that. You know the carnie who found the three girls? Hester, Suki, and Clare?"

At the mention of Hester's name a new fear pulsed briefly to the surface then vanished under Tricia's ocean of grief. "What about him?"

"He and another carnie decided to go back to where they found the girls. They said there was something spooky about it or some shit. You know those kinda folk, they're superstitious, easily confused. Anyway, they went back up to Sallow Lake, to the old cabin up there where the girls were found. That's where they found Riley's body. State police went up right after they got back and confirmed, sealed the scene."

"What?" None of what Holtz had said made sense, but disconnected thoughts clashed and fired through Tricia's mind like summer lightning.

"I wish I could tell you more. I don't understand either. That's all I can say now because I don't know more."

"Why the hell was he out there?"

Holtz shrugged, moved from his crouch to sit beside her on the couch. "It's possible he was beaten and then dumped out there, that's one theory."

"By who? The carnies? Why? And why dumped there? Fuck, Freddie, if someone was going to go to the trouble of hauling Riley's heavy ass all the way out there, they'd bury him in the trees, not just dump him in that scary old cabin!" Anger at the situation had pushed Tricia's grief slightly askew and her brain began to work harder at putting threads together. Caleb had said something about Hester going into the woods. The girls had been found at the cabin. Hester must have come from somewhere nearby, if not the cabin itself, she and Caleb had decided that much the night before.

"Outside the cabin, not in it."

"What?"

"They found him on the lake shore outside the cabin."

Tricia shook her head. "That makes even less sense. At least if they put him inside, maybe they'd think it'd be unlikely anyone would go in and find him." She wiped a hand across her face. "Freddie, this is all bullshit. None of this makes sense."

"I agree with you. It's a mystery. But our job is to solve mysteries. I've sent Kurt Janssen and Clive Taylor out to the cabin with the state police. They've taken the case, of course, but my guys are there as observers. So we can hopefully know anything they find. The carnies refused to go back, but they've given us all the information we need to have a proper look. Maybe there'll be some evidence nearby that sheds some light."

"Maybe those carnies did beat him to death!" Tricia said, though she wasn't sure she believed that the moment it was out of her mouth. They had an undeserved reputation. They were decent folk in her experience. And surely they wouldn't find the body if they meant to cover up a crime.

"Another theory we're looking at," Freddie said. "They've been nothing but cooperative, and we currently don't have any reason to believe they're lying. They're not going anywhere. Do you know anything that might help? Riley didn't argue with any of those guys or anything like that? Or anyone else?"

"No! Not that I know of." She wanted to say something about Hester, about the cabin, but knew it wouldn't make sense to Holtz. It didn't make sense to her yet, but there was something in it.

Holtz nodded, gently squeezed her forearm. "There's time for all this later. We'll do our job, Tricia, I promise."

Tears breached again, any more words trapped for the moment in her throat, so she just nodded.

"Is there anything I can do? Anything I can get you, someone I can call for you?"

Tricia shook her head, drew a shuddering breath to find her voice. "I'm okay, Freddie, thanks. I was on the phone to my sister when you came. I'll call her back when you go."

"You're sure?"

"I'm sure. Thanks."

Holtz stood, gripping his hat nervously again. "I'm so very sorry, Tricia."

"Me too. Thanks for coming yourself."

"This isn't something a Sheriff should delegate. Especially with a friend."

When she had seen him out, Tricia's mind began to harden with resolve. Too much coincidence to ignore. Caleb stood at the top of the stairs.

"I'm sorry," he said simply.

"It's gotta be her, right?"

Caleb shrugged, shook his head. "But why?"

"Maybe he was onto her too, like you and Kirk."

"Maybe. But could she beat him to death?"

Tricia hitched a sob at the words, the mental image they triggered.

"I'm sorry," Caleb said again. He came down the stairs, awkwardly patted her shoulder. She realized what a massive step that was for him and it eased the grief just fractionally.

She sucked in a long breath, then blew it quickly out. "Right."

She went back up for her phone, messaged her sister, *Riley is dead. I can't talk now. I'm okay.*

And she was, she realized, kind of okay. The grief was huge and that made it impossible to grasp, so she simply let it sit there, deflected herself from it with other concerns. Hester-shaped concerns. She ignored the phone when her sister immediately rang back, put on shoes, and grabbed her bag.

"Come on," she said to Caleb. "I need to not be at home right now."

25

DIAGONALLY ACROSS WILSON Street from Ken's General Store stood Bella Donna's. It had borne many names over the decades it had serviced the populace of Sallow Bend, but for the last fourteen years, Jacqueline Sharp and Sandra Welling had worked the counter and the kitchen, served burgers and sandwiches, breakfasts and lunches, coffee and milkshakes. When they took over the diner they had named it Bella Donna's and to their mind that's what it would always be.

From a booth by the front window, Caleb watched the proprietors, busily shuttling between the counter and the kitchen behind. Now in their mid-forties, Jaqueline ("call me Jack") Sharp was tall and willowy with short black hair, a long sharp nose and fingers like a concert pianist. Sandra ("just Sandy, darling") Welling was the complete opposite. Short, wide-shouldered, blonde and pale, with a warm, friendly face and a smile for everyone, any time of day or night. The pair had arrived in Sallow Bend to take on the diner, weathered a good couple of years of gossip and disapproval from certain more conservative members of the community, but slowly become a part of Sallow Bend fabric with their quiet professionalism, excellent food, and long opening hours. The two women ran Bella Donna's from six in the morning to eight at night, seven days a week except Christmas and public holidays. Whatever they may or may not do in whatever small amount of spare time they had, residents could forgive it or ignore it for that kind of reliable business. And they had always employed a handful of local teenagers to bus the tables and clean up, and those kids were well looked after and paid a fair rate.

One came to Caleb and Tricia's table, a redhead girl of about sixteen Caleb recognized from school, but her name escaped him. He watched the clear play of concern and disapproval play across her face as she saw him, recognized him, considered him somehow out of place in public instead of his hole under the school. But, he knew, he was partly to blame for that perception. She put aside the fleeting set of expressions on her face with a forced smile.

"What'll it be, Mr Jackson?"

He thought about saying *Call me Caleb*, then wondered if that would be inappropriate. Her face changed again as he paused, discomfort coming back. This was why he avoided people. Interactions like these were always broken somehow. "Coffee. Thanks."

"Mrs Brent?"

"Same, coffee. Thanks, Callista."

Caleb nodded internally. Callista, that was it.

"You want I should leave menus?"

"Sure, thanks."

She scooted away, came back in moments and dropped two laminated menus on the polished wood table, and was gone again without a word or a second of eye contact. Caleb sighed. He watched Jack and Sandy behind the brushed chrome counter, busily taking orders, sending them out. The row of red vinyl topped stools in front were mostly taken, as were the majority of booths along the window and the smaller tables and chairs in between. The lunchtime crowd already filled the place with the clatter of cutlery on crockery, the hubbub of conversation. Rock and roll music played from the classic jukebox in the corner, now converted for CDs. Dark wood and bright, primary-colored light tubes, with that strangely Art Deco design.

Caleb turned his attention back to Tricia. She had on some makeup, but he saw the anguish beneath it. Her eyes were red, swollen from crying, and there was a set to her mouth that spoke of deep pain. He could easily understand it all.

"I think Hester happened," she said.

She took Caleb's wide-eyed silence as a cue to continue.

"To Riley, I mean. I don't know why, but what else is there?"

"I don't know. I think you're right. I just wish we knew more."

The red-haired waitress came back and they both ordered a hamburger and fries. They sat in stunned silence, Caleb happy not to talk, Tricia seeming to seethe with anger that blocked any conversation. Their food arrived and they ate mechanically.

"Why was he there?" Tricia asked, pushing aside her half-eaten meal. "Why did she kill him?" She took a deep breath, swallowed. "I wonder if it's about Toby."

"Your son?"

"He's been missing a year. What if Hester had something to do with that too? What if Riley knew? Or suspected it?"

"But Hester only just appeared. We know we've never seen her before she came back with Suki and Clare, right?"

Tricia shrugged, nodded. "But just because that's the first time she's come to town, it doesn't mean she hasn't been around longer. Who knows how long? I can't think of anything else. It could be a coincidence. Riley is stupid enough sometimes, certainly drunk enough, to get in who knows what kind of trouble. Maybe he just ran afoul of some bad dudes and they use that old abandoned cabin or something."

"But to just leave his body lying there on the lake shore?"

Tricia shrugged again.

"I'm sorry," Caleb said suddenly, remembering the social graces he had been taught.

Tricia smiled sadly. "Thanks. But I can't even really process it right now. I don't know how to feel."

Caleb remembered something his aunt had said when his mother had died. Caleb had only been fourteen, his mother chewed to the bone by cancer before she was forty. His aunt, red-faced and almost spherical of body, had crouched in front of him, put one hand on his shoulder as he stared into nowhere. "Caleb, honey, however you're feeling right now, that's okay. And however you feel tomorrow and the next day, and the next, that's okay too."

It had been strangely comforting at the time.

He looked up at Tricia, tried to hold her eye. "However you feel, that's okay."

Her face brightened in the first genuine smile he had seen all day. She reached across the narrow table, put one warm palm on the back of his hand and squeezed. "Thanks."

A tightness built between Caleb's eyebrows, too much information from Tricia and others around flooding his mind. He took a deep breath and looked out the window as Tricia took her hand away from his. And looked right into the frightened eyes of Suki Tokugawa. For a moment they stared at each other, the glass of the window the only thing between them, almost intangible. Caleb read fear in her face, but also exhaustion, confusion. He raised a hand tentatively, gave a little wave.

Tricia followed his gaze, made a small, "Oh!" of surprise. She stood and went to the door. Caleb watched her pause and talk to Suki, then lead the girl inside.

As she passed the counter, she called out, "Sandy, can we get a chocolate milk?"

"Sure thing, honey!"

Tricia brought Suki to sit at their booth. Caleb chose to remain quiet, he simply gave the young girl a nod and a quick smile. She looked nervously from him to Tricia, then yawned expansively. The redhead arrived with a milkshake and Suki eyed it suspiciously.

"My treat," Tricia said. "You look like you need it."

Suki sipped at the drink, nodded, sipped again. Tricia caught Caleb's eye, raised her eyebrows. Caleb shook his head slightly, at a loss for anything to say.

Tricia turned back to Suki. "You okay, sweetheart? You looked a little spooked out there."

"I was walking past and looked in, saw you two sitting here. It made me feel weird and I didn't know why. Something about yesterday. At the carnival."

"We asked you about Hester, you remember that?" Tricia said softly.

Suki's face creased up like she was about to cry. She shook her head, stared at the table top, her milkshake forgotten.

"It's okay," Tricia said. "We know something's very wrong. We want to help you."

Caleb ignored the nerves tickling around his gut, kept his mouth shut while Tricia was doing such a good job.

"I don't feel right," Suki said, almost a whisper. "I'm tired all the time, I sleep half the day." She looked up. "Clare's just the same."

"Since you got back from being lost in the woods?"

Suki nodded, looked back at the table. "My mom says it's just the stress of what we went through, but I don't know."

"What about Hester? She feeling it too?"

Suki's gaze snapped back to Tricia, anger and defiance in her eyes. "Hester is fine!"

"She's a good friend?"

"Yes. She kept us safe. She found the cabin."

"What do you remember about the cabin?"

Suki's mouth tipped down at the edges. "The fireplace was so cold. So dark. It was like a hole in the ground, a never-ending pit. And she was there."

"Who was there?" Tricia's voice was nearly a whisper. "Hester? Is that where she came from?"

Suki gasped a short breath, sat back. "She looked after us."

Tricia licked her lips, glanced at Caleb, then back to Suki. "But did you know her before you got lost?"

Tears trickled over Suki's cheeks and she hitched a couple of quick sobs. "I don't know!" she said, almost a wail. "And every time Clare and I try to think about it, or talk about it, we get so tired." As if to illustrate the point, Suki's mouth stretched in another massive yawn. She put her arm on the table and rested her head on it. It took Caleb a second to realize she was already asleep.

"That's quite some self-protection trick," he said.

"And what's the betting she won't remember any of this conversation when she wakes up."

"We have to do something. Maybe more and more people will wake up to what's happening here, but maybe not. And how many will die in the meantime?" Caleb ate the last of his fries, pushed the plate away. "I think there's maybe one ally we can call on. You remember the weird carnie with Mengele's Secret? His name is Saul."

Tricia's brow knitted in confusion. "What's he got to do with it?"

"I think he's onto Hester somehow. Or suspects, at least. And I think there's something… different about that guy. I can see it in him. We should talk to him. I don't think he's going to be willing to help, but we should try. You know, the enemy of my enemy and all that?"

"Maybe we can find out more first. Arm ourselves with knowledge."

"How?"

Tricia shrugged. "A town like this, it's full of gossip, old-time stories and superstitions. But maybe some of that stuff is true. Growing up in Sallow Bend you hear about times when death came to town. Lots of people dying all at once." She frowned. "It was always just stories, but it's like that right now, isn't it? Maybe we should search through town records, find news clippings, see if there's a pattern."

"Maybe even see what made it stop before?"

"Right!"

Caleb gestured to the sleeping girl. "What about..?"

Tricia gently shook Suki's shoulder. She sniffed, startled slightly and woke. "I fell asleep again?"

"You did. You were having a chocolate milk."

Suki looked at the half-empty glass. "I'm supposed to meet Clare and Hester."

"Okay, have fun."

Suki looked at them both, clearly confused. She opened her mouth as if to ask a question, then shook her head and stood. Tricia moved to let her out of the booth and she was gone in a flash. Caleb turned, watched through the glass door of Bella Donna's as Suki hurried off down the street, and he wondered how safe she was. Were her days numbered too? And Clare's?

26

ASHLEY STRONG TOOK a deep breath and slowly counted to ten. Then she looked up and held Daniel Clarke's eye again. "You definitely haven't told anyone else?"

He shook his head. She turned her attention to John Barrow, raised an eyebrow.

"Nope. Not yet."

She nodded, chewed her lower lip for a moment. The sounds of the carnival came muted through the walls of her trailer, all the curtains drawn to try to keep back the heat. In the gloom everyone's face was a patchwork of concerned shadows. Sarah squeezed Ash's thigh once under the small table, used her other hand to brush back a stray strand of hair. Ashley patted her lover's hand in acknowledgment.

"When do they want you back in for questions?"

"They don't," Barrow said. "We told them everything, like we told you, and they said they probably had all they needed. But we can't go anywhere and they'll come back with more questions, probably."

Ashley let out a mirthless laugh. "Probably?"

"What do you mean?"

"Come on, John! You two are both in the frame, you'll be suspects numbers one and two. They'll be back."

Silence settled around them as they all considered the truth of that. Ashley couldn't believe how much hassle this site was presenting, and how fast. She was furious that Dan and John had gone back there, yet she understood the urge. "When you say you told them everything..?"

"Everything about going there out of curiosity and finding the body," Dan said. "We didn't talk about the weird shit we just told you about."

"Good. They'd think you mad."

"There is more going on than we can see," Sarah said. At Ashley's flash of anger, she shook her head, raised a hand. "No, Ash, I know you don't like this stuff. And I'm not saying I understand it. But there is bad energy here. Bad stuff is happening to Sallow Bend."

Daniel nodded emphatically. "She's right. You can't deny it!"

Ashley looked at John Barrow and he lifted his shoulders and let them drop. "Neither Dan or I are lying about what happened up there. Like Sarah, I can't explain it, but it's happening. Whatever it is."

"And what should we do about it?" Ashley demanded.

Daniel looked at each of them in turn, then said, "We leave! Move on to the next site."

Ash laughed again. "We can't do that. You said yourself, the police told you not to. Besides, we're in the hole to Wilson for a lot of money on this site and we're not booked into the next for over two weeks. We can't afford to just move on. And where would we go?"

"People will find out about Riley Brent," Sarah said softly. "Small town gossip, crew gossip. By close tonight everyone will know there's been another death and they'll know Dan and John found the body."

Ashley sighed. "Even so, we still can't afford to move on. And the police." She gave Barrow and Daniel a dark look. "You should have just left it well alone. Left him for someone else to find." There was a knock at the trailer door. Ashley's face darkened. "What now? Come!"

The door opened and Saul Fallon stood there, tall and pale in his usual dark blue overalls. "What's going on?"

Ashley's brows knitted. "Why do you think something is going on?"

"You all have been holed up in here for a while and I can tell something is up."

"You can tell?"

Saul stepped in, closed the door behind him. "Who died now?"

John Barrow rounded on the tall man, his voice tight. "How do you know stuff like this, Saul? Huh? What is it with you?"

Ashley stood and moved between them. "All right, settle down. I've had enough of everyone. You all need to get back to work."

Barrow and Fallon both started to talk, to protest. Ashley opened her door and stood by it. "Out!"

Reluctantly they left. Daniel rose, wringing his hands together.

"I'm not happy, Ashley. I think things will only get worse."

She reached up and put a hand on his shoulder. "You may be right. But there's nothing we can do. It's only two weeks. Let's just keep our heads down, do our jobs, and if anything does happen, let's hope it keeps happening to the residents of Sallow Bend and not to us."

Daniel pursed his lips, nodded, but seemed entirely unconvinced. She had nothing better to offer him, so just smiled. He left quietly.

Sarah rose and started to gather her things. "I'd better go to work too."

"Yeah."

"I'm sorry this is happening, Ash, but it *is* happening. We can't ignore it."

"We can't do anything about it either."

They were silent for a moment, then Sarah planted a kiss on Ashley's cheek and left. Ashley stood in the middle of her small home, for a moment simply enjoying the lack of people, of voices. She glanced at the bottle of bourbon on the bedside table, then quickly walked out into the hot day before the temptation to fall into it grew too strong.

JOHN Barrow dragged on Saul Fallon's hand as they headed back down the midway.

Fallon turned on him. "What?"

"You need to back off."

Fallon barked a laugh. "That right? And what are you going to do about it, little man?"

"Don't underestimate me. And just leave things well enough alone unless you intend to be part of the solution."

"And how can I do that when your private little club in there won't tell me anything?"

Barrow stared at his infuriating crew mate, wondering how much there was to tell. What good it would do. "There is something not entirely normal about you, Fallon. We all get it and we all ignore it. Just weird old Saul Fallon, he's harmless. But sometimes I wonder if you *are* harmless. And if you're not, maybe you can direct some of that potential malice at whatever is going on around here."

"What *is* going on around here?"

"I wish I knew. But people are dying, and Sarah says there's bad energy in this place."

Saul smirked. "She's a two-bit circus act."

Barrow's eyebrows shot up. He raised his hands, gestured around them. "No shit, Sherlock. She's also got something going on I can't explain, but I trust it."

"And?"

"And I don't trust you. But perhaps you can prove your worth by maybe looking into what's happening in this weird-ass small town, and then maybe you can do something about it. Before the deaths start coming closer to home."

Fallon looked down at him for a drawn-out moment, enough that Barrow began to grow uncomfortable. Eventually, Fallon said, "You overestimate me." He turned and stalked away.

Barrow watched him go, wondering if he'd done enough. Would the strange man retreat into his shell and keep his head down, or had Barrow got under his skin, to maybe trigger Fallon into some kind of action? He could only hope he had, though what that action might reveal was anyone's guess. With a sigh he ducked off the midway to his large red and white tent to check the stage lights were all set and his dancing girls were ready to entertain.

27

CALEB AND TRICIA had sat poring over old newspaper articles and scanning microfiche in giant light boxes for hours. Caleb's back ached, his neck stiff with a tension born of waiting for some kind of hammer to fall. It could only be a matter of time before Hester tracked him again. In such a small town, he could only hide for so long. Certainly he would avoid the school, but did she know where Tricia lived? Would Hester make the connection and come for him there? Tricia had suggested they find somewhere else to stay and he had agreed. But for how long? They needed a more proactive plan than hiding. His life felt like an hourglass that had been turned over and nailed down, no way to turn it back. All he could do was wait for the sands to run out. Frustration clawed at him.

"We're wasting time here," he said.

Tricia backed away from a microfiche viewer to see him. "Are we?"

"Have we learned anything useful?"

She shrugged, scooted her wheeled office chair over to the table behind them. "We've got a lot of evidence of patterns forming. I've been working backwards through the records, but between us, look at this stuff." She pulled a notepad over, spidery scrawl covering page after page. She pointed to one stack of papers, then jabbed her pencil at the pad. "2008, April. Three teenagers go missing, two girls and a boy. The boy was never found but the girls were. During the ten days of their disappearance, at least six deaths by suicide or misadventure were recorded. Then here, 1997, September. Seems to start with one middle-aged man going missing. He was never found, but over the next two weeks, eleven deaths were noted, a variety of accidents, and three suicides. Then 1984, July. Four children missing, all boys, never found. During the weeks that followed, eight deaths by misadventure, and six suicides. This is not in any way normal for Sallow Bend, Caleb!"

"But how does it *help* us?"

She scowled, flipped the page. "February 1972, two missing girls, both found just over two weeks later. In that time, nine deaths. I couldn't track which might be accidents or suicides, I just wanted to keep looking. I found it again, in March 1966, a young couple reported missing. The woman was eventually found, out of her mind, and she never fully recovered. She was sent to a secure psychiatric facility, authorities suspected rape and torture drove her mad. The man lost with her was never found. In the days following their disappearance, at least ten deaths by accident, some reported as 'bizarre', and four suspected suicides. I'm going back again and I bet I find more."

Caleb reached out, put a hand on her pad. "I'm sure you will. We don't need convincing of this stuff. You're fifty or sixty years back already, who knows how much further it might go. But how does it help us? Here. Now."

Tricia slumped back in her seat. "The original disappearances are a mix of adults and kids. It seems that boys and men are never found, while girls and women usually are. And in that time there's a disproportionate number of deaths in Sallow Bend."

"And it's happening again right now. It'll keep happening, I guess. We could just let it run its course, like it has all those times before, but who else might die before its over?" He leaned forward, knew his face betrayed fear he couldn't hide. "Whoever else does die, I'll be among them. Maybe not you, you're a woman, but who knows? You saved my life, Tricia, but how long can we hide? How long can you protect me? And in the meantime–"

Tricia tapped her pad with her pencil. "Occasionally a woman has died during those periods."

"There you are then. That could be coincidental, or maybe those women found Hester out. Either way, it still doesn't help us! Or anyone else right now." He held up a hand to forestall her protest and pointed to his own notes of research. "I've been trying to find something out about Hester herself. I can't find any record of her at all, nothing in any birth or death registries. I only found one mention of her name, and that was in an article from a newspaper dated *eighteen-seventy-nine*." He watched Tricia's face, saw the shock beginning to register as she did the math.

"It can't be the same one," she whispered.

"Maybe not. But there's no record of any other. And this entry is in an obituary about one Cyril Linklater, a man who rose to some prominence nearby and had a reporter attending as he died. His reported final words were, 'I'm worried I'll be damned for what we did to Hester Black.' The reporter says that when he pressed the townsfolk in an attempt to understand those last words, they 'all clammed up, like some mass secret had been agreed upon'. I cant find any other reference to her name. I'm thinking maybe they simply missed this one, having expunged all others."

"Why? What did they do to her?"

Caleb shrugged. "But again, we're faced with the same problem. None of this helps us now. Any of this *could* be purely coincidence. And even if it wasn't, we're not gaining any new knowledge. Nothing we can… weaponize against Hester."

Tricia frowned. "Maybe we should go to the police. At least try that and see what happens."

"And tell them what?"

"Everything. Explain what's happening, try to get them to see the patterns. If nothing else, we'd have more people on our side. We can challenge Hester in numbers."

VAL Baker watched Freddie Holtz closely as he talked. She tried to concentrate on his words, but couldn't help admiring the stretch of khaki pants over his thick thigh, the bugle of shoulder in his shirt. And other bulges she daren't stare at. She realized she was also using her strong attraction to the boss to avoid thinking too hard about the subject at hand.

"We're a small town department," Holtz said. "There's only four of us full-timers, for God's sake. I don't want to have to call in the part-time deputies."

"Those weekend warriors are more trouble than help," Kurt said, with his usual sneer.

Val bit back a response. When it came to useless policing, no one could outplay Kurt Janssen. But there was no point in crossing that ground again.

"Anyway, state police are up at the lake and maybe that will lead to the FBI."

"What? Why?" Clive Taylor's brow creased, in genuine confusion.

Val sighed. Freddie claimed there were only four full-timers, but when you took into account Kurt and Clive, it was really only two. Her and Freddie did all the actual policing while Kurt and Clive wore the uniform and needed to be led around like children. She let a small smile out at Freddie's consternation as he rounded on Clive. She did love it when he got surly.

"Because Riley Brent's death is clearly murder, you idiot. The accidental deaths have been bad enough, but that stuff gets left to us. Now there's been a murder, the States swoop in all shiny badge and glory, because hick police like us can't be trusted to investigate a real crime."

Clive nodded. "Oh, I see."

Holtz's shoulders slumped. "Fucking hell. You don't even understand sarcasm, do you." It wasn't a question.

"Don't I?"

Holtz looked at Val, raised his hands almost in surrender. She couldn't help a laugh escaping. "I'm sorry," she said, to cover it.

"Seems to me the States coming in is a good idea," Kurt said. When Holtz raised a questioning eyebrow, he added, "Too many people dying,

Freddie. I mean, accident or not, we just don't get this many deaths in Sallow Bend."

"Something is definitely up," Val said. "Four people have died since Thursday night. It's only Sunday morning, for God's sake."

Kurt turned to her, clearly desperate for support. "Right? It's not okay. My granddaddy told stories last night about times in Sallow Bend's history when there have been deaths like this, lots all at once."

Val had been prepared to shut Kurt up. Even if she agreed with him, she didn't want him to think her any kind of ally. But he'd caught her interest. "What do you mean?"

"He said to me that this is what happens here every now and then, and it's happening again."

"Okay, enough!" Holtz's voice was a whip crack in the room and all eyes turned to him. "We've all heard the stories. Sallow Bend has it's small town mythology the same as any other place. Children going missing in the old days, lunar eclipses where men die through weird and inexplicable accidents, strange beasts roaming the woods. It's all the kind of bullshit used to scare kids at night." He looked pointedly at Kurt. "It's clearly still working."

Kurt screwed up his face, looked away. "I ain't no kid," he muttered.

"I can't help keep coming back to Hester and her friends," Val said, surprising herself. She'd thought it on a few occasions, but always dismissed it as coincidence. She hadn't meant to voice it this time either, but something about Kurt's mood, Holtz's dismissal, triggered a kind of defiance in her.

"What about them?" Holtz asked.

"This all started when they went missing."

"Actually, it started when they came back," Clive said, once again displaying his remarkable ability to seem oblivious to everything yet occasionally make a razor-sharp insight.

Val looked at Clive, saw he had no idea of the implications of what he'd just said. She watched Kurt and Freddie, and they were equally unmoved.

"I guess," Holtz said. "But that's entirely coincidental. Let's not get carried away with any weird speculation. Three teenage girls are hardly the cause of a bunch of random accidents or one violent murder."

Val tried to grab onto the thoughts flitting around the edges of her consciousness. Every time she thought something concrete was about to come to her, it slipped away like a fish through a too-slow hand. Something about the girls. They went to school together, and Tim Daley was a teacher at the school. Reece Gossett had drowned and he went to school with the girls. Was there a connection to be had? But Kirk Branton had nothing to do with the school beyond having kids. Was that relevant? And hell, that poor bastard Riley Brent lost his own kid a year ago, so he and Tricia certainly had no connection to Sallow Bend High any more. Wait, though. Was there a connection between the girls and the Brent's missing son? What could that mean?

"Earth to Baker!"

She startled, looked up. Freddie was looking at her with concerned eyes. Kurt was grinning crookedly, entertained by her momentary lapse. Clive sat picking his fingernails. What had she even been thinking about? "Sorry, drifted off there."

"Daydreaming, Val? That's not like you."

She hated to look foolish in front of Holtz, but preened inside at his genuine concern. "Yeah, sorry. Not sure what happened. Go on."

"Well, I was saying I want you and Clive to partner up and spend this afternoon and this evening at the carnival."

"Oh man, really?"

"All the accidents I can write off, but Riley Brent was beaten to death. That's most definitely a murder. Those two carnies, the big black guy, Daniel Clarke, and the midget, John Barrow–"

"Little person."

"What?"

Val smiled. "Little person. We don't say midget or dwarf or any of that stuff any more."

"Jesus fucking Christ. Okay, so the big black guy, that okay?"

"Sure. He's big and black."

"Right. And the little person. They claim to have found the body up by the old cabin." Freddie held up hand to forestall Kurt. "I don't want to hear it. We've all heard those stories too. The cabin is where Daniel found the girls, he thought it was creepy and took Barrow up there to show him, and they found the body. That's what they told us, and honestly, I'm inclined to believe them. They have no motive for wanting Brent dead that we know of. Why would they have come and told us if they had something to do with it? There may be some beef we haven't heard about. There may be any of a million other connections. I just want a police presence at the carnival. We usually have one there anyway."

"Yeah, but you usually send Kurt and Clive. Why do I have to partner up with him?" Val turned to Clive, her cheeks heating up. "No offense, Clive. I don't mind partnering with you. I just don't like the carnival." She hoped he bought it. She could stomach the carnival if she had to, despite the heat. Hanging out for ten hours with Clive Taylor, however, was the definition of boring.

He shrugged. "None taken."

"I know," Holtz said. "Normally I would send Kurt and Clive together." His eyes were sympathetic as he looked at her, and she appreciated that. "But me and Kurt are going up to the lake to *observe* the State police dealing with the crime scene. I need to be there in person this time." His emphasis of the word 'observe', made clear his distaste that that's all they'd be allowed to do. "So you and Clive will have to take carnival duties. I want you to watch Barrow and Clarke. And just stay alert, get a vibe for any tension that might exist between any of the carnies, or between them and any local folk. You got it?"

"Sure."

"And no buying into this bullshit superstition or gossip. Let's just keep things safe, let the States take away the Brent thing, and we can get back to enjoying our peace and quiet."

Val thought maybe he genuinely believed what he said, but she couldn't shake off her own disquiet. Then she remembered something else. "You remember you asked me to check in on Old Man Wilson?" she asked Holtz.

"So I did. He okay?"

"Don't know, he wasn't there. His pick-up was, so maybe he was out in the fields somewhere. Could be anywhere in that sprawling land of his. You want me to check again?"

"Sure, if you get a chance. He's the busiest old man I ever knew."

Val nodded. "Okay." The thought of spending all afternoon and evening at the carnival weighed on her, but that was her job. She could check in on Wilson again on the way there. She stood, looked over at Clive. "You coming then?"

"Oh, now?"

"No, a week from next Thursday. They open in ten minutes."

Taylor pulled his slightly too heavy bulk up from the office chair and smoothed a hand over his balding pate before slapping his hat on top of it. "Let's go then."

28

S THE DAY drew into a hot afternoon, Caleb and Tricia stood outside the Sheriff's Office looking at the hand-written sign taped to the door.

Please call in emergency only – you will be redirected.
Office will be manned again tomorrow.

"I remember when they used to have a full-time secretary, always taking calls and radioing out," Tricia said.

"What happened?"

"Budget cuts, I guess. These days old Clive Taylor usually spends all day on his butt in there. I guess he's pretty much the receptionist now. It's some indication of how messed up things are if even Clive's out actually policing."

"You think… up at the lake?" Caleb asked.

Tricia nodded without looking at him. "I guess State police will come in, so they're all probably busy with that. I mean, accidents and suicides are one thing, but Riley was murdered."

Caleb watched a tear track over her cheek, drop down to the hot, dry sidewalk and burst there, like a wet sun. She sniffed, looked up.

"So what now?"

"Well, if the police are no help, maybe we should go talk to that carnie, Saul. Ask him for help."

"You didn't think he would be willing," Tricia said.

"And I still think maybe he won't, but what else is there? The way he looked at Hester, it's like he knew something was up. Like you said, if nothing else we need to find allies to confront Hester with numbers. It's the only way to maybe be safe."

Tricia nodded. "And some police will be at the carnival too, probably, so we can ask to talk to them?"

"Okay. And Tricia, we have to be really careful in case the girls are there."

"Hester wouldn't attack you in plain sight, would she? With me there too, we'd expose any move she made."

He shrugged. "We can't underestimate her ability to fool us both somehow. Let's assume she can and avoid her."

Twenty minutes later, Caleb walked along the midway with Tricia in step beside him. He did his best to tamp down the rising anxiety of the crowds. He'd spent more time among people in the last few days than he had in the last several years and had expected that his nerves would begin to fray from it. But he thought maybe he was finally growing used to it. The cumulative effect of so much activity was getting to him, but if he stopped and took a deep breath, took a moment to look around himself, the crushing hordes didn't feel quite as oppressive as they had. He found himself developing coping strategies and knew that was at least in part thanks to both Tricia's presence and her advice. He'd always tried to address his issues alone before, and failed. With Tricia's help, he thought maybe he'd made a little progress. He wondered how long he might live to enjoy it.

They passed the big flashy bumper cars arena, rock'n'roll music blaring from its speakers as people laughed and squealed. The smell of grease and popcorn, diesel and metal, ubiquitous as always. Nothing smelled, looked, or sounded quite like a carnival.

"You fucking sleaze!"

Over all the noise and music, the voice was stridently clear, high-pitched and furious. Several nearby heads turned. Caleb gasped to see Hester stood on the raised edge of the arena, yelling into the face of one of the young carnies who ran the bumper cars. He had his hands to either side, a condescending grin on his face.

"I'm only being friendly!" he said. "She's a pretty girl!"

Caleb and Tricia melted back behind the gathering crowd to avoid being seen, but stayed close enough to hear.

Another of the high schoolers, Caleb couldn't recall her name, stood beside Hester, face a mask of fury. "Fuck you, she's right. You're a sleaze."

"What, you don't like guys?"

"I don't like you!"

"Will she do something?" Tricia asked in a harsh whisper. "So many people are paying attention."

Caleb was frozen with fear, unable to really think, let alone act.

Hester stepped forward, shoved the guy in the chest. "What makes you think you have any right to touch her? To grab her ass? You fucking animal!"

"You'd be worth grabbing yourself, you know. Are you jealous? I like the white stripe in your hair."

Hester's face stilled, she tipped her head slightly to one side, as her friend made strident observations of what a pig the carnie was.

"All right, all right, let's all settle down." A local woman moved between Hester and the carnie. She began berating the young man, saying she would call the police, what he did was assault, telling the girls to step back. Others intervened, defusing the situation as best they could. A couple of guys, Caleb was pleased to see, also stepped in and told the young carnie to back the hell up and leave the girls alone, they were little more than children. Of course, that set the girls off again, protesting their adultness. But slowly the aggravation was averted and the crowds thinned. The carnie went back to work, looking entirely like a slapped puppy.

"He *is* a fucking sleaze," Tricia said with a grimace. "Such young girls."

"What's the bet he's the next to die," Caleb said quietly.

Tricia's eyes went wide. "Oh fuck. Look!"

She pointed out Hester and her friends. The rest of the group were back to talking and laughing, no doubt discussing the confrontation, but Hester stood a little to one side, watching the bumper cars intently. Caleb followed her gaze and saw the young carnie, hopping from one car to the next with practiced ease as they scooted around each other, helping out jams, leaning down to expertly steer cars from corners.

"We should intervene," Tricia said. "Distract her."

Conflicting emotions tore Caleb up inside. "But then she'd know we're here!"

"What will she do to him?" Tricia whispered.

"Other people are watching her still," Caleb said, nodding towards the ride. A few high school friends, and a few adults, were paying attention to Hester, and to her slighted pal, probably wondering if there was going to be more shouting. "She can't do much, can she?"

As the cars all slowed to a halt at the end of the turn, Caleb watched the offending carnie, looking out for that telltale glazed expression. But the young lad was grinning and hopping around, busy at his work.

Then right behind him Caleb saw a big bearded man in a lumberjack shirt and tight shorts. He recognized the guy he had bumped into a day or two before, a bear of a man with wide shoulders and arms as big as Caleb's legs. He had that expression in his eyes, grimacing like he was walking into a storm as he stepped over one bumper car and between two more.

"Look! See him?" Caleb asked.

Tricia scanned, trying to spot who Caleb was pointing out. Caleb had never felt so impotent in his life, knew he risked himself if exposed his presence to Hester. How could he distract her? He took a step forward, thinking to maybe yell out, warn the carnie. But he was already too late.

The bearded man grabbed the young carnie by one shoulder and spun him around, then slammed his other hand, fist clenched, into the young man's face. People screamed, ran towards the affray or away from it as the carnie staggered, but was prevented from falling by the huge hand gripping his shoulder. The bearded man punched him again, the young man's face awash with blood. He spat scarlet bubbles, his eyes rolling madly, legs like jelly beneath him. More people cried out, two grabbed the big man and tried to haul him off, but he was too strong. He turned the carnie around, held both his shoulders, and slammed him face-first down onto the rounded hood of the nearest bumper car. The carnie's body jerked and then lolled. More people ran in as the bearded man hauled the carnie back up, face-planted him once more into the bumper car. Blood spilled over it in rivulets dark against the sparkling metallic blue of its paintwork. The crowd finally managed to pull the big man away. His eyes still glazed, his face strained. It wasn't anger, or the effort of the beating. The poor bastard was trying to resist his compulsion yet completely unable to do so. Others rushed to the carnie's aid as more people pushed the big man away and out from under the roof of the dodgems arena. Then two police officers were there, Val Baker and the daft one with the big belly, Clive Taylor. Val was on her radio, the other policeman on his knees by the unconscious crew member.

Caleb looked from the mayhem to where the school friends had all been gathered and his heart skipped a beat. Hester stood staring right at him, pinning him with her eyes. She raised one eyebrow and her mouth quirked up at one side in a half-smile. He felt like a mouse in the claws of a particularly maleficent cat. Then she turned away and took her friends with her and they all melted into the crowds.

"Holy shit," Caleb whispered. Tiny knives of pain drove in behind his eyes.

Tricia gripped his hand, shook her head in confusion. "What can we do?"

Caleb couldn't still his trembling, tried to wet his suddenly dry mouth. He saw Saul from the Mengele's Secret sideshow on the edge of the midway, watching everything from the corner of a cotton candy van. Fear twisted the edges of the man's expression. Caleb pointed one shaking finger.

"Let's do what we came here for."

His feet were leaden as he trudged forward, but a sense of purpose gave him energy. Tricia trotted alongside, and the carnie looked up when they drew close. Caleb was no good at social interaction, but he knew people shook hands and gave their name. He stretched out one shaking palm. "Caleb Jackson."

The carnie looked at his hand, then at Tricia, back to Caleb. He took the offered hand and shook it. His grip was cool and dry. "Saul Fallon."

"Yes. You run the Mengele's Secret thing."

"That's right."

"We really need to talk to you."

"What about?"

"We think you can help us," Tricia said.

Saul narrowed his eyes, looked from them towards the bumper cars. The man had realized what they were about, and a sense of relief flooded Caleb. He saw recognition in the man's face, and that lingering fear. He hoped this strange carnie would be an ally.

"No idea how I can help you two," Saul said. "You're welcome to come by the Secret. It's open to everyone who pays the fee."

Disappointment replaced Caleb's relief. "No, you don't understand."

Saul wagged one finger. "Wait a minute. You two already came to my caravan. I remember you."

Caleb decided to take a chance. "You remember how we tasted?"

There it was. A brief flicker in the cheek and eye before Saul composed himself again. "Excuse me?"

"I think you know what I mean. There is something evil in Sallow Bend, you know that's true."

Saul shook his head, turned away from them. "I don't know any such thing. I think you need to leave me alone."

"You just watched her. You saw her make that man beat up your friend. You know that guy on the bumper cars, right? He's one of you." Saul flinched, turned back. Caleb pressed on. "Isn't that what you do? You guys look out for each other, right?"

Saul jabbed one finger painfully into Caleb's sternum. "You don't presume to tell me my business."

"Whatever is happening here," Tricia said, "it's happening to everyone. You and us alike."

Saul rounded on her, made her step back. "And what the hell do you think I can do about it?"

"I don't know," Caleb said. "But I get the feeling you're maybe the only one who *can* do anything. The rest of us are helpless."

Saul drew a deep breath in through his nose. "How come you two are so aware of what's happening? Seems to me like everyone else is oblivious."

"Whatever magic Hester's using, it didn't work on me." Caleb shrugged. "But it took quite a big thing to convince Tricia here. We can't try to persuade everyone that way. How come you can see her for what she is?"

Saul frowned, looked down at the ground for a moment. "I can't. I don't see whatever you do. But I feel something truly wrong with her, and I know something is up in this town. Hester's magic? Really?"

"You know Hester?" Caleb popped up one eyebrow.

"Well, everyone seems to know who she is. Bit of a town fixture, right? Everyone's favorite weirdo."

"How do you know that?"

Saul barked a mirthless laugh. "Exactly."

"So there *is* something different about you. What did you feel when she came into your sideshow the other day?"

"I felt like I needed her out of there as quickly as possible. I made it creepy but mainly boring and thankfully they didn't stick around long." Before Caleb could say anything more, Saul raised one finger. It shook slightly. "And that's how I plan to keep things. It's not my problem, we'll be moving on soon enough. Hester is Sallow Bend's problem."

"You think you and all your crew will last that long? You just lost one. I mean, he may live, but that was some beating."

Saul remained silent, shook his head. "I can't help you." He turned to walk away.

"Wait!" Tricia pulled a pen and an old envelope from her bag. She removed whatever was inside and stuffed it away, then scribbled on the empty envelope. “Here’s my name and number. Please, think about it and call me, okay?”

Saul took the number, stared at it for a moment, then folded it in half and tucked it into the chest pocket of his overalls. “Don’t expect to hear from me.” He turned and stalked off behind the cotton candy van, heading back towards his creep show.

“Now what?” Tricia asked.

Caleb had no idea. That had not gone in any way he’d hoped it would. “We have to have help in this. And Hester saw me just then, so we need to get out of here quickly. Let’s find somewhere to stay tonight and try talking to the police in the morning.”

29

SHERIFF FREDDIE HOLTZ walked into the his Office with trepidation. This last few days had become more of a burden than any small town cop should have to bear. He didn't sign up for this. He sipped takeaway coffee from Bella Donna's, breathing deeply of the aroma as he did so. Without coffee, life would be actually unbearable. He nodded to Kurt and Clive on his way through, then paused at Val's desk.

"He settle down yet?"

"Yeah. But he's one upset guy."

Holtz raised an eyebrow, remembering Jim Saddler from the day before. He and Kurt had had to rush back from their observations to see Val and Clive bring Saddler in, cuffed and raging, eyes rolling like a feral dog. He'd beat that young carnie half to death. Now he was upset? "Guilt, you mean?"

"Partly that. Go talk to him."

Holtz pursed his lips, watching Val for more, but she clearly had no intention of being any more forthcoming. "The victim?" he asked instead.

Val sighed, shuffled papers to find the medical report. "Still unconscious, coma. Fractured skull, broken jaw, broken nose, lost eight teeth. There's a brain bleed adding pressure, potential brain damage. They plan to operate this afternoon to relieve that pressure if the swelling doesn't begin to reduce on its own. Still listed as critical."

"Fuck me. He really did a number on that kid."

"A guy Jim's size, the rage he was in. And that kid is only seventeen, skinny little whip of a child."

"Why did he do it?"

Val shook her head, looked away. "Go talk to him."

"Any more from State on the Riley murder?"

"They're going over this morning to interview those two carnies…" She checked paperwork. "John Barrow and Daniel Clarke, and the boss, Ashley Strong."

"Okay. You see Old Man Wilson yet?"

"Not there again yesterday. Not like him to be so elusive, he's normally all over town."

"Yeah. Well, keep trying."

"I will. Go talk to Jim Saddler, Freddie."

Holtz stood for a moment, sipping at his coffee, then sighed and headed for the secure area. Jim Saddler was in the first of three barred cells, the other two empty and open. Jim sat on the edge of a small cot, head in his hands. His thick legs looked weird, great hairy limbs extending from the small shorts he always wore. It was a strange affectation with Jim, he wore shorts year round, even in the winter when he had a thick sheepskin jacket over his ubiquitous checked shirt, and heavy work boots. Holtz had known the man for decades, he was a gentle bear, a loving family man, a stand-up member of the community. Whenever there was anyone in need, Jim would be there. Natural disasters, vehicle breakdowns, charity drives, church vigils. Any situation Holtz could think of, Jim Saddler would be there, helping, that big smile bursting out of his thick, long black beard. If anyone in Sallow Bend was asked to name the town's good guys, Jim Saddler would surely be one of the first names out of their mouth. Jim looked up at the scuff of Holtz's boots, his eyes red-rimmed from lack of sleep, and puffy with tears.

"What the fuck, Jim?" Holtz said.

Jim shook his head, sank his face into his palms again. His shoulders shook subtly.

Holtz opened the cell and went inside, leaving the door open, confident Jim was not a threat for flight or fight. Not now anyway. He put one hand on the man's shoulder, feeling small beside him. Not many people made Freddie Holtz feel diminutive.

"What the fuck happened, buddy?"

Jim just shook his head, face still covered.

"Here's what I know," Holtz said. "Then maybe you can fill me in on what I've missed. Everyone at the carnival was having fun, business as usual, then that young carnie running the bumper cars, Victor Salzmann his name is, decided to grope one of the teenage girls. That started some outrage, a couple of the other girls yelled at him, he made some bullshit 'boys will be boys' excuse, then a couple of the adults stepped in and calmed everything down. That was the finish of it, according to the witnesses. The kid, Victor, went back to work. Then the bumper cars stopped, and you fell on Victor like a man possessed."

Jim flinched, glanced up at Holtz.

"What?" Holtz asked.

Jim took a shuddering breath, said nothing.

Holtz licked his lips, waited a moment, but the big man wasn't talking. "So what happened, Jim? You saw the guy groping the girls and it enraged you? You have two girls, right? Was one of them there?"

Jim shook his head, staring into nowhere across the cell.

"Your girls weren't at the carnival?"

"Both my girls and my son were there last night, but not at the bumper cars." Jim's voice was gravelly and thin, nothing like the booming confidence Holtz was used to. But at least he'd finally started talking.

"But what Victor did, that made you mad?"

"I don't even know what Victor did!" Jim looked up, his eyes haunted. "Until you just told me that, I had no idea he'd done anything at all. And now you've told me that, hell it's not much, is it? I mean, he's a shit for groping girls, that pisses me off, but all teenagers do it."

"They shouldn't though."

"Of course not! And I tell you, if I *had* seen that, I would have pulled him aside, told him to get his act together. I would probably have threatened to whip his ass to scare him decent. But Freddie, I didn't even know."

"So why'd you beat him up?"

"I don't know! You said possessed just now? That's what it was like." Jim stopped suddenly, stared off again at something only he saw. Holtz waited patiently. Now the man was talking, best to let him keep going, in his own time. Eventually Jim spoke again, his voice barely above a whisper. "I remember the ride coming to an end, all the cars losing power like they do, you know? We'd been having fun, I was barging around with a couple of buddies. Honestly, I was only killing time until ten when I told my kids to meet me back at the car to take them home. I wasn't there for me, I was taxiing them around." He drew a deep breath in through his nose, shook his head again. I stood up out of the car and for a moment I felt dizzy. I thought maybe I stood up too fast or something. Age, you know? Man, getting older fucking sucks. But then I was climbing over cars towards that young kid. Victor?" Holtz nodded. "I knew I was going to thrash him, Freddie. I didn't want to, I tried to stop, but I knew I was going to and I couldn't stop myself. It's like my limbs had a mind of their own. I was seeing all blurred, almost double somehow, I could hear and feel the blood pounding through my brain. I put every ounce of will I had into stopping, just standing still, but I couldn't do it. I'd already grabbed that kid and I was hitting him and slamming him down." Jim's voice devolved into sobs and he buried his face again.

Holtz let him cry, trying to understand what the man had said. It didn't make any sense. He could imagine some of the other residents of town making these kind of excuses, men who were always on the cusp of violence. Angry men, drinkers, stressed out husbands on benefits, maybe on drugs. But Jim Saddler was none of those things. Jim Saddler was a gentle giant, a stand-up guy.

"He's badly hurt, huh?" Jim pinned Holtz with his eyes, brooking no bullshit.

Holtz nodded. "Still in a coma, busted skull, possible brain damage."

"Ah, fuck me."

"You don't have any other explanation?" Holtz asked. "Jim, I don't know what to tell you. We have to charge you with assault. Maybe something worse, even."

Jim nodded into his hands. "I know. I don't know what else to tell you. I did it. I didn't want to, I tried to stop myself, but I did it."

Holtz patted his shoulder again. "Try to relax, rest. See if you can think of anything that might help me understand."

The big man looked up, brow creased. "You know one thing that keeps coming back to me?"

"What?"

"I was lost in that rage, and after they dragged me off I was distraught at what I'd done, felt like my mind was snapping. Then suddenly it felt like something detached itself from me, from my brain. Like a part of me whipped away, like a leaf in a gale. And I saw one of those girls in the group, that whacky Hester. You know her?"

"Of course. Everyone does."

"She was just staring at me, half-smiling, like she was so pleased at what I'd done. Even in my mania, I remember that face, her streak of hair. And she said, 'Good boy.' Like I was some kind of dog."

"Val said you were crazed and thrashing," Holtz reminded him. "She said it took three locals to hold you down while she cuffed you and then they helped muscle you to the patrol car."

"I know! And Hester was twenty yards away. But I heard her, clear as day. Like she was right inside my head."

Holtz looked at his friend for a moment. Perhaps the man was rationalizing what happened, imagining the approval of one of the girls Victor had harassed. He didn't blame Jim for trying to find some sanity in an otherwise entirely insane situation. He patted that huge shoulder once more, then stood and left, locking the cell door behind him. He passed Val leaning on the doorframe to the cells as he left.

"You hear all that?"

She nodded.

"Make any sense to you?"

She walked with him back into the office. "Freddie, nothing over the last few days is making a lick of damn sense to me."

30

ASHLEY STRONG STOOD once again on her trailer tailgate, surveying the crew under her command. She longed for the days when she would address them all with the standard speech right before opening at a new site, then congratulate them at the end. She didn't like gathering them over and over like this, they'd only been in Sallow Bend for five days. The crew were restless and rightly so, but she was about to disappoint them further. The general consensus that they should up stakes and leave had not passed her by.

"Everyone here?" she called out.

"Everyone still breathing is," someone yelled from the back.

Raucous chatter swelled immediately and Ash gritted her teeth, let them have at it for a moment. Sarah cast a concerned glance up from nearby and Ash gave a small nod of acknowledgment. John Barrow raised an eyebrow at her and she shrugged. Barrow put two fingers in his mouth and blew a sudden and surprisingly shrill whistle. Conversation died like a punctured balloon.

"You're all pissed off," Ash said. "Me too. But we have to push on."

"Do we really?" Saul Fallon said, his face creased in anger. And maybe some measure of fear, Ash noted, and that gave her the willies.

"We simply can't afford to move on. We're deep into Wilson for this pitch. And we have nowhere else to be until our next site." She didn't even dare mention the State Police who had interviewed her, Daniel Clarke, and

John Barrow that morning, and who had told them in stern tones to make sure they didn't leave town in the near future.

"And what about Vic Salzmann?" Fallon asked. "He gonna survive until the next pitch."

Ashley sighed. "I don't know. He's in a bad way. Still unconscious, fractured skull, we don't know yet how much more harm might have come to him. But we'll stand by him and see he's looked after." She raised a hand at the rising stir of voices to quiet them. "And the man who beat him is in custody. I don't know what got into that guy, but it's not like it's the first time we've had punters start a fight."

"Don't bullshit us, Ash!" Fallon yelled. "There is some evil shit going on in this town and you know it."

Ash stared, unsure what to say. She couldn't really argue with him.

Sarah stepped up next to Ash, her face a question. Ash blew air out, shook her head in resignation. "Why not."

Sarah smiled, then turned to face the crew. "We would be lying to ourselves if we denied that something is definitely up in this town."

"What are you gonna do? Smudge the whole town with bunches of fucking sage, you charlatan?"

Sarah scanned the faces looking for whoever it was who had spoken, ignoring the ripples of laughter, but no one seemed to be the culprit. She twisted a wry smile. "No, that's unlikely to work, and I don't have enough sage anyway. What I was going to say is that we just need to get on with our work and let Sallow Bend deal with its own problems. I agree with you all that we should move on, but I also know Ashley is telling the truth when she says we can't afford it. Who among you is willing to foot the bill of moving? Who even can?"

Nervous shuffling of feet and downturned eyes was all that met her question.

"I fucking thought so!" she spat.

Lots of eyes snapped back up, including Ashley's, along with a smile. She had never heard Sarah use language like that before, certainly not in public. She had never encountered an anger like Sarah now displayed. She liked it.

"We're a fucking team," Sarah said, her voice a whiplash to every crewmember. "So let's start acting like one. We have to look out for one another, we have to see out our time here, at least until the end of this week, then we get the hell out of town and go somewhere safer."

"The end of the week?" someone asked.

Ash stepped forward again. She had discussed this with Sarah the night before and Sarah had played the hand well, caught the entire crew off-guard. "If we work hard until Sunday," Ash said, "we can almost certainly cover all costs and pay ourselves a token wage. It will mean a very tight month, and we'll need to find somewhere to camp out before the next pitch. But if you are all on board, we can potentially pack up on Sunday and skip out. We'll have a break, then get to the next site on time. Leave all this behind."

"You think we can survive until Sunday?" Fallon asked. "Everyone knows John Barrow and Daniel Clarke went to that cabin and found a fucking corpse out there. You had the cops around again yet? It's not like just one of our guys got in a random fight."

Ash had managed to convince the State Police to conduct their interview in town, but she wasn't surprised word had got around nonetheless. Saul fucking Fallon stirring shit up again just as Sarah had brought people around. Fallon was definitely scared of something. She needed to talk to him alone. "Yeah, we all do know that," she admitted. "Some small town grudge bullshit that's nothing to do with us. The police are dealing with it. We stay until Sunday, then we pack up if you all agree to it. If things are going okay, we stay on like planned. We'll decide after we close on Friday."

"We gonna take a vote on that?" Fallon asked.

"This is not a democracy, Saul. I'm responsible, so I make the decisions. Now everyone, get back to work. We open at twelve like normal. We carry on until at least Saturday. Look out for each other, don't start shit with anyone. Be your best professional selves and we'll be fine. Go! Except you, Saul, I want a word."

Everyone slowly drifted away, talking amongst themselves in small groups. Saul stalked forward, face dark. Ashley wasn't surprised that Sarah and Barrow hung around too.

"You're signing death warrants for us all," Saul said.

"Am I? Tell me why. What do you know?"

"I don't know! I don't know *anything* specific. But you're a damned idiot if you deny something is going on."

"Watch your fucking mouth," Barrow said, stepping forward.

Ashley admired the small man's fire, but it wasn't necessary. For one, Saul would flatten him in an instant. More importantly, she didn't need a white knight of any stature. "You're not helping, Saul," she said, putting a hand to Barrow's shoulder to ease him back. "You're just whipping up more fear."

"There should be fear. The crew are right to be afraid!" He turned to Sarah for support and that surprised Ashley perhaps more than anything else thus far. "Tell her, Madame O'Reilly! Most of what you do is cold reading bullshit, but you're not entirely without talent, are you? Tell her!"

One of Sarah's eyebrow's rose. "Good grief, Saul, it must be serious. I bet that admission sticks in your craw."

"Just fucking tell her!"

"I have told her. It doesn't change the fact that we can't afford to move on yet."

Anger burned in Fallon's eyes.

"You go if you want," Ashley said. "You want to take whatever you've earned so far and hitch up your trailer and fuck off, then fine. Much as you piss me off, you've been a part of Strong's for a long time, and I wouldn't like to see you cut loose. But if you want to go, I won't stand in the way."

"Where would I go?"

"What, you can't afford to leave?"

"I can afford to leave." He looked away. "I just can't afford to eat until the next pitch in the meantime."

"One of the team, after all. We're all in the same boat, this is a hand to mouth life."

Fallon scowled at her and she felt a juvenile pleasure at having got him riled and trapped in a corner. But it was a short-lived joy. She shrugged.

"A couple of locals think maybe they have a better idea of what's happening here," Saul said, quietly, like he was reluctant to admit it, even to himself.

"You want to talk to them about it? I'm open to any suggestions right now, Saul. Any that we can afford."

He looked up, trying one last time. "We need to leave. All of us. If we stay until Sunday, we'll be several members fewer *at least* by the time we get out."

"We can't. We leave Sunday at the soonest. That's my decision, and I'm sticking to it."

"Fuck it!" Fallon turned on his heel and strode off towards the midway, staring at the ground, shoulders hunched.

Sarah put a hand on Ashley's arm. "There's no right decision here. You only have so many options."

"For what it's worth," Barrow said, "I think you're right."

Ashley shrugged again. "Right or wrong, I guess we'll find out. Go on, get ready to open."

They left her standing by her trailer alone, and she had never missed her father more.

31

CALEB WOKE ON the lounge room floor of a strange house, stiff and not particularly well-rested. Tricia lay beside him in her own sleeping bag, still dozing. The house belonged to her friend, Kathy Someone-or-other, who was away for a few days. Tricia had keys, as did Kathy to Tricia's house, a reciprocal agreement among many residents apparently, to water plants, look after cats, that sort of thing. Tricia had keys to at least half a dozen friend's houses, she said, and it meant they slept last night safe in the fairly certain knowledge Hester couldn't find them. But Kathy returned home today, so they'd need a new bolt hole tonight. It occurred to Caleb that perhaps they could simply keep moving around like this, perhaps even leave town for a week or two, until this latest event passed, as it seemed like all the others had. Maybe that would stop Hester from getting him. But it was a fundamentally selfish attitude. How many others might suffer in the meantime? And what about next time Hester came around, if that's really what was happening?

During the night he'd had an idea of something to take to Freddie Holtz, to help convince the Sheriff to help. It would mean dropping by the school. He should probably do some work around the place, if he wanted to keep his job. But during the holidays he was often the only one there and could get away with extreme laziness if the mood took him. Though it rarely did. Caleb was an honest and conscientious man, he believed in doing a good job of the tasks he was paid for. But right now there was no time.

Tricia rolled over, blinked as she came around. Her eyes were red, from tiredness, but probably also the grief of losing Riley, that still showed as a huge presence in every atom of her. So big, in fact, it seemed to eclipse her, unmanageable. Caleb anticipated she might collapse into some kind of breakdown once all this was over, her entire family gone. Assuming this was ever over. And assuming either of them survived. But if they did, he was determined to be there for her. Maybe no one else would understand like him. Much as he wanted to be left alone for any foreseeable future, he owed Tricia some allegiance. And in truth, her company was more bearable than anyone else he had ever known. It would be no chore. That revelation almost frightened him, but he chose not to interrogate it too deeply. Not right now.

"Morning, Caleb," she said softly.

"Hello. You okay?"

She smiled. "You're really getting the hang of this social interaction stuff. Yes, thanks, I'm okay."

"Good. Me too."

"We really going to talk to the police about this?"

Caleb shrugged. "What else can we do? We have to try to get some help."

"They'll think we're completely mad."

"But we still have to try, don't we?"

"I guess so."

"I need to stop by the school."

Tricia's eyebrows shot up. "Is that wise?"

"Maybe not. But we'll be in and out in no time. It'll be worth it."

Tricia nodded. "Okay, if you think so. Kathy won't mind us stealing a little food from her kitchen for breakfast as long as we tidy up. Let's eat and then get moving. But first, I need to get some coffee on." She pulled herself out of the sleeping bag and trudged through to the kitchen.

It was a little after ten by the time they arrived at the Sheriff's office, after stopping by the High School and finding it thankfully deserted. The specter of Hester hung like a weight on them, but for now she was mercifully absent.

They parked and stepped into bright sunshine and another day building up into a continuation of the heatwave.

"Storms forecast this afternoon," Tricia said.

"That right?"

"Yeah. Maybe the heat will break for a bit if we get one."

"Hope so. But they always forecast them and they never come around."

Tricia let out a small laugh. "We're killing time, huh?"

"I think so."

They went inside, saw Clive Taylor leaning back in his office chair, eyes closed. Kurt Janssen was nowhere to be seen, Val Baker sat at her desk, frowning at paperwork. She looked up as they entered.

"Help you?"

"Yes," Tricia said. "We wanted to talk to Freddie. Err, Sheriff Holtz."

"Regarding?" She licked her lips. "Trish, I'm mighty sorry about Riley."

Caleb glanced at Tricia, wondering what tack she would take.

Tricia swallowed, nodded shortly. "Thanks, me too. But I'm not here about that. Just about some other stuff happening around here lately."

"If you need help organizing the funeral, you can holler for me."

Tricia smiled, but Caleb saw it was forced. "Thanks. I don't know when the police will release the…" She swallowed. "Release his body. So I can't do much right now. But thanks, I'll remember your offer. That's very kind."

"You're welcome. We're a community, right?" Val stood. "This way."

She led them the three yards to Holtz's office door and knocked. When he grunted from inside, she opened the door and said, "Tricia Brent and Caleb Jackson to see you." She held the door open and followed them in, closed the door behind them and leaned back against it. Caleb assumed her curiosity was okay with her boss. It was okay with him too. There was something honest and genuine about Val Baker. She hid things, her face gave away thoughts she would never voice, but Caleb, in his few interactions with her, had never sensed malice there. He did see a powerful intellect, and respected that.

Holtz stood, forcing a smile. "Take a seat, please."

As Caleb and Tricia sat in the two chairs in front of Holtz's desk, he looked past them, raised a questioning look to Val Baker. She smiled, still leaning back against the door, showing no signs of going anywhere. Holtz sighed, sat back down.

"How can I help you two?"

"Too many people are dying lately," Tricia said. Caleb was surprised by the directness. He had expected some kind of prevarication.

"I'm very sorry for your loss, Tricia, but…"

"No, Freddie. Just listen to me!" Holtz's eyebrows leaped skyward, but he did shut up. "I don't know what happened to Riley and grief is eating me hollow from the inside, but that's not the point. Not the whole point, anyway. You have to admit some weird shit is going on in town right now."

Holtz nodded, flipping a pen end over end absently between his fingers. "Look, it's horrible, I won't deny it. But don't look for patterns that aren't there."

"People are doing crazy things in this town!"

Holtz barked a laugh. "They always have! For a small town, we sure have a large share of crazy."

"Not like this. Something else is going on." Tricia glanced at Caleb, looking for support. He was tense from the close proximity of people, the pressure of the subject at hand. But he owed her what back-up he could give.

"It's true," he said. He looked at Val, then returned hard eyes to Holtz. "You know it's true. You're police. You're trained to see things, to spot abnormal behavior. You can see it here, surely?"

"This town seems to have periods of strangeness," Val Baker said, but Holtz halted her with a raised palm.

"Yes, we're trained to see things," he said. "We're also trained to not jump to conclusions. To not overlay our own narrative on any given situation. I get that you're concerned. I get that accidents and weird shit makes people edgy. I get that you're grief-stricken, Tricia, and rightly so. But I won't have the citizenry stirring up panic."

Caleb became annoyed at that. "Stirring up panic? Let me ask you one thing, Sheriff Holtz."

Holtz looked at him, an angry challenge evident in his gaze. *Don't push me*, it said. *Don't make this worse.* Well, Caleb had every intention of making it worse. "How long have you known Hester Black?"

"What? I don't know. Years. She's always been here."

"Has she?"

Holtz's eyebrows drew together. "Everyone–"

"Everyone knows Hester? Since when Sheriff? Two girls went missing, Clare and Suki. *Three* girls came back. No one had ever seen Hester before that day."

"What the hell are you talking about, man?"

"There is something off with that girl," Val said.

Holtz looked up over Caleb's shoulder to pin an angry gaze on his deputy. "I won't have panic stirred up in this town! What the hell is a thirteen-year-old girl supposed to have done? She didn't drop a branch on Tim Daley. She didn't drown Reece Gossett. She didn't beat the shit out of… out of that carnie, Victor."

Caleb caught Tricia's wince from the corner of his eye when Holtz stumbled. Had he been going to say Riley Brent first? It didn't matter. Caleb leaned forward, drawing Holtz's attention again. "That's just it, Sheriff. I think she did."

"What?"

"Hester Black is unnatural. She's having an unnatural effect on this town."

Holtz's chair shot back and clanged into metal filing drawers behind as he stood quickly. "Enough. I know you're all concerned. So am I! But I don't have time to sit here listening to nonsense. You have to leave. I have work to do."

"Who were we just talking about, Sheriff?"

Holtz frowned. "What do you mean? You came here concerned about deaths in town."

"And what names were mentioned?"

"Tim Daley, Reece Gossett, others. The people who died. I get it, you're upset. Me too. So get the fuck out and let me do my job."

Caleb caught Tricia's eye and she nodded subtly, confirming that she'd noticed the Sheriff lose all memory of Hester's name.

"March, 1966," Tricia said. "A young couple were reported missing. The woman was eventually found, out of her mind, crazy. The man was never found. While they were gone there were at least ten deaths by accident, some reported as 'bizarre', and four suspected suicides."

"Tricia–" Holtz began.

She spoke over him. "February 1972, two missing girls, both found two weeks later. In that time, nine deaths."

"Tricia!" Holtz snapped. "I get you're traumatized, but I've heard all this before. Enough kooks in town look for coincidences and patterns. Maybe those extra suicides coincide with stock market slumps or something–"

"In Sallow Bend? Come on, Freddie!"

"Regardless! It's not helping. That kind of talk only stirs up fear."

Caleb decided it was time to play his trump card. "Sheriff, we were talking about Hester Black." Holtz frowned. "Bear with me! I want to show you something. Can I use your computer?"

Still standing at the filing cabinets, looking decidedly uncomfortable, Holtz gestured impatiently at his desk. As Caleb moved around it, he saw Val Baker's face, equally perturbed. He slipped a thumb drive into the port and pulled up the video footage from the school's CCTV he had collected on the way. The others moved around to huddle about the screen. "Watch, please."

The film was black and white, grainy from the darkness of the evening. It showed the play area and benches under the trees where Tim Daley had died, from a camera on the corner of the gymnasium. The school's back doors were visible, and the steps down to Caleb's room. Caleb forwarded through it, looking for the right moment. He paused, confused, when he saw himself emerge from his steps. That wasn't what he expected. "Wait," he said, backed up, played it forwards again. Once more, he emerged from his rooms. He looked at Tricia. "Where's Hester?"

"She should be there."

"What are you wasting my time with, Caleb?" Holtz demanded.

"I'm sorry, just wait, please."

They watched the footage. Caleb made his way to a saw horse under the trees. The noose he knew was there couldn't be seen from the high angle of the camera, obscured by branches and foliage. Caleb in the footage stepped up on the saw horse.

"What are you showing us?" Val asked, her voice low.

Video Caleb's movements were stiff and jerky as he climbed up. Even in the low resolution image, he saw his grimace of fear and impotent resistance. The others leaned in, straining to see, and though it was barely visible in the image, they could make out Caleb dropping the noose over his head.

"Holy shit, Caleb," Holtz whispered.

Then film Caleb staggered and wobbled, grabbed the knot of the noose and pulled himself upright as Tricia ran around the corner of the building, her arms stiff out in front of her. Then she stopped, stood rigidly staring.

Caleb looked over to Tricia as Holtz and Baker were transfixed by the footage, and Tricia gave him a sad smile, a small shrug.

They watched on screen as Caleb climbed down and moved toward Tricia. Then he raced forward a few steps before skidding abruptly and sitting hard on his butt in the dirt. Tricia staggered forward, rushed to help him up.

Caleb sighed, closed the video window and pulled the thumb drive free.

"Caleb, you want me to call someone for you?" Val Baker asked, her tone kind. "We have counsellors. You too, Tricia, if you feel like you need to talk to someone."

"No, thank you," Caleb said. He looked at Holtz, who returned his gaze with evident discomfort. "Who were we talking about before, Sheriff?"

Holtz shook his head. "The people who died? I get this is a hard time, but don't add to that number, Caleb. You're a good man. Was it that thing with Daley? Because I tell you, man, what you and I and Burt saw, what we did, it's been haunting me too. There's help if you need it. You and me, we can talk if you like. You want to go get a beer?"

Caleb took a quick breath. Daley's crushed body, that wet peel and slap. It had recurred to him a hundred times, it was there behind his eyes every time he closed them, but he had been pushing it out of his mind every time. Sure, it was haunting him, but it was over-shadowed by everything to do with Hester. He guessed Holtz didn't have the dubious luxury of that distraction. He was genuinely touched by the man's pivot from anger to honest support and friendship. "It's not that," he said.

It was pointless. While the police may well try to be proactive in protecting the town, they would be entirely ineffectual if they were incapable of even discussing the real threat. He thought the footage would be some kind of incontrovertible evidence, that it would break the glamor on the police like it had on Tricia. But Hester, or whatever damn creature she was, didn't even show up. Caleb felt powerless. Where did they turn now?

"Okay, folks," Baker said as she opened the door and gestured them out. "I think perhaps we all need to get on with our work. Are you sure you two are going to be okay?"

"Yes, thanks, Val," Tricia said. "I'm sorry to have bothered you. That's not the right footage, it's not what we meant to show you."

"You sure?" Holtz asked. "You sure you don't need someone?" He raised a concerned eyebrow at Caleb. Caleb shook his head, looked away. The Sheriff's perusal was too intense.

"We'll look out for each other, Freddie. Thank you." Tricia put a hand to Caleb's back, guided him around.

Holtz raised his hands, let them drop. Caleb saw his utter confusion, and his deep frustration at all the weird shit with which he was confronted. And the poor man didn't know the half of it.

Val moved aside to let them out, then accompanied them across the office. At the front doors she paused and put a hand on Caleb's forearm. "Something *is* very weird in this town," she said, almost a whisper. She shot a glance back into the station, but no one paid them any mind. "Every time I try to think about it, it's like my thoughts are smoke and there's a wind in my mind. It's disturbing the hell out of me, but I can't hang onto anything concrete. I feel like maybe you can."

Caleb simply nodded.

"Why is that?"

He had no idea what to tell her. "I don't know. But the spell can be broken."

"It's true," Tricia said.

Val looked from one to the other and back again. Eventually she shook her head and sighed. "I feel like there's not enough time. But this kind of thing, I think it *has* happened before. Perhaps you need to look into Sallow Bend history."

"We did. We spent hours researching." Tricia gestured back into the office. "I tried to tell him."

"No, I mean the unrecorded stuff that's passed around, stories from old-timers. Word of mouth, you know? I think there are some people who know more about this town than they're prepared to let on publicly. I know I'm a blow in, only been here a couple of decades, but I see what goes on. You know, Jerry Yonker said something interesting to me. He said he hadn't seen Old Man Wilson around for a while. I dropped in a couple of times, but he's not there. Or not answering–"

"Val, get in here! I got a job for you," Holtz yelled, hanging off the frame of his office door like a khaki-uniformed gorilla.

Val flashed a quick grin and ducked away. Caleb and Tricia walked out into the hot sunshine.

"Maybe we should have anticipated that," Caleb said, looking disconsolately at the thumb drive he still held.

"Yeah. But Val might have a point. Who can we talk to that might know more about the… I don't know. The folk history of Sallow Bend? You think Old Man Wilson is worth a try? He's ancient, after all."

Caleb opened his mouth to reply, but Tricia's cell phone interrupted them with a shrill tune.

She fished it from her purse, brow creasing. "Unrecognized number." She tapped the screen. "Hello?"

Her eyes widened, then narrowed again. "Okay," she said. "Sure, we'll come and meet you now. How about Bella Donna's Diner? Yeah, on Wilson Street. Okay."

She hung up and looked at Caleb with a mixture of elation and confusion. "Saul Fallon," she said. "Weird Mengele's Secret man."

"Yeah?"

"He says we need to do something because the carnival boss won't leave. He wants to know what *we* know about what's happening."

"So now he's an ally?"

Tricia shrugged, slipped her phone away. "I don't know about that. But like you said, the enemy of my enemy is my friend. And maybe with his help, we won't need to find out more."

32

BELLA DONNA'S WAS bustling with a pre-lunch crowd when Caleb and Tricia arrived. They ordered ice cold sodas to help against the heat of the day and took the last unoccupied booth. Caleb watched out the window as he sipped and spotted Fallon only moments after they'd sat down. The tall man stalked across the pavement, hunched as if the summer sun were a weight on his back. He squinted under his thick mop of dark hair, his navy blue overalls surely too warm for the climate. But Caleb had the feeling the man didn't ever wear anything else, whatever the weather. Fallon pushed open the diner door and Tricia stood, waved one hand. Fallon nodded and came over. Tricia moved around to sit next to Caleb and Fallon slumped into the seat opposite.

"Understand this is against all my better judgment."

"Straight to business then," Tricia said with a laugh.

The play of emotions across Fallon's face had Caleb intrigued. The carnie was scared and angry, that much was undeniable. But something else flitted and danced around the man's eyes. Something Caleb hadn't seen before and couldn't place. It was a flicker he couldn't describe, but it had no place on a person's face. Given the chance to sit and consider Fallon in detail, Caleb became quickly convinced the man was far from normal. Maybe even slightly removed from human. Whatever that might mean.

"Think you got me figured out?"

Caleb jumped, realized Fallon had been only too aware of his perusal. "No," he said honestly. "But you're different."

"You got that right. Tell me what you know about Hester."

Caleb glanced to Tricia, so she took up the tale. "Well, not too much. But we do know she can make people do things, make stuff happen. And it's all dangerous, everything she does." Tricia swallowed, shook her head. "She's killing people, Mr. Fallon. We don't know why, but she is, and she wasn't here before those girls came back from the woods and no one else seems to realize that. But we think she's been around before. Lots of times, years apart."

Fallon pursed his lips, stared at his pale hands resting on the table, fingers intertwined. "Oh, she's definitely been here before. Maybe not for a long time. But I think she comes around every once in a while."

Caleb's mouth had gone dry. What the hell could they do about any of this? These were beings and events well beyond the understanding of a man like him.

Fallon looked up, pinned Caleb with his gaze. "I would prefer not to take her on. Honestly, the best advice for any of us is to leave her the hell alone. But she won't leave *us* alone, and my idiot boss refuses to move the carnival on."

"So why don't you just quit? Take your trailer and go?"

"Because a job like mine is hand to mouth. Because I spent every cent I had on booze when we got here knowing I had more coming in. But I haven't earned enough yet to survive without the carnival. I gotta eat!" He puffed up and Caleb saw pride push aside the fear. "Besides, I can beat the evil bitch. I've been around a while too. So I'll face her, because she might take out a damn sight more of us before we get away if I don't."

A mild elation dared to raise itself in Caleb. "You can really beat her?" he asked, wondering how much of Fallon's claim was bravado. He saw a lot of conflicting emotions in the man's strange face.

"If I'm ready and in my own space, yes. I can prepare and set her up. The problem is, she has no reason to come to me again. The first time I shooed her and her pals out the moment I realized she was bad news."

"Does she know what you are?"

"Do you, son? What am I?"

Caleb looked away from the man's granite gaze, the familiar headache forming. "I don't know."

Fallon huffed a laugh. "Neither does she. But she knows I'm a threat and she's unlikely to come near me. And I wouldn't normally go near her, but believe it or not, I care about some of those fucking losers at the carnival, and I care about my ongoing living, and she might hurt those things. So I have no choice. But I can't take her on in the open. That's why I need you. You have to get her to me."

Caleb and Tricia exchanged another glance. "Us?" Tricia asked.

"You said yourself no one else knows what the hell is going on around here. No one else can do it, they'll forget as soon as you ask them. So can you do it?"

"The girls are always at the carnival," Tricia said. "Every night, like most of the kids in town. Hester is bound to be there with Clare and Suki."

"And can you get them to me? Into my tent?"

Tricia raised her hands. "I don't know."

"Yes, we can get her to you," Caleb told the carnie. "Tonight, maybe about six if she's there. In the meantime, it's best if you don't stay too close to us."

Fallon's eyes narrowed, then he nodded once and stalked away. He braced against the sunlight as he stepped out of the diner and hurried across the road.

"You really think we can?" Tricia asked.

Caleb shook his head, shrugged. "We have to, right?"

33

CALEB AND TRICIA spent the afternoon hiding out at the movie theatre in town, hoping Hester had no reason to come by and watch a film. Caleb tolerated a constant low-level fear that she *was* coming for him, would find him wherever he hid. *Watch your back*, she had said. Then that look at the bumper cars. *Who would believe you?* she had asked. Who indeed. Perhaps she was simply biding her time, safe in the knowledge she would get him eventually. The thought put a chill rivulet through his gut, made his hands tremble. A quiet life, that's all he wanted. It wasn't much to ask. He couldn't help thinking now that he was in his last days. Even with Fallon's help, could they really defeat whatever Hester was? For that matter, what the hell was Fallon? His rangy form, alabaster pale skin, dark hair, aversion to the bright sun. A cliché would make him some kind of old Hammer House of Horror vampire, but Caleb knew that wasn't right. He was something different, something less pop culture. But what? The man was entirely disturbing, that much was certain. And Caleb hoped the pride and bravado were well-placed. An undeniable power lingered about the strange carnie. Caleb hoped it would be enough. It had to be. Regardless, he knew now there were many things in the world he hadn't considered real before, and Saul Fallon was one of them. Maybe Caleb would never know exactly what Fallon was, and that wasn't so bad. Only a fool thought he had all the answers in the world.

In the darkness Caleb and Tricia had quietly talked about what they might do, how things might play out. But there were too many variables, too many unforeseen possibilities. It would have to be played as it came.

At five-thirty, Tricia tapped his knee and they slipped from the cool darkness of the theatre into the sweltering day, still bright but sliding towards twilight, and hot even this late. Tricia's eyes were wet, red-rimmed. Caleb saw the grief there, the pain. She had not had a great afternoon either. They climbed into her car and she started the engine.

"You okay?" she asked.

"Not really." He gave a weak smile. "This is all pretty messed up, huh?"

"It really is. Are you ready?"

"No. You?"

"Fuck, no! I'm terrified!"

Caleb nodded, looked away from her haunted gaze. "Me too. But what choice do we have?"

Tricia sighed, looked out the windshield as the day slipped duskily away. "I was thinking about what you said to Saul. About him just leaving."

"Yeah? He can't afford it, he said."

Tricia was silent for a moment, then, "I can."

Caleb looked over again, wondered how serious she was. It would certainly be the best decision for her.

She didn't return his gaze, still stared at the street ahead. "With Riley and Toby gone, why the hell do I stay here?"

"You could go. It would be smart. Take yourself away from these dangers."

She finally turned to him. "But what about you? What about… all this?"

"We'll cope. Or we won't. But you'll be free of it."

Tricia swallowed, shook her head. "It's a nice daydream. But I can't. I won't give up hope of finding Toby again, I can never leave while that's a possibility. I have to be here, at home in case he comes back. And this *is* my home, where I grew up. The people here matter to me. I have to help. But isn't it a tempting thought? To just pack up and leave, go somewhere new. Start again."

"I did. That's why I'm here."

Tricia tipped her head to one side. "Yeah?"

Caleb saw in her eyes that she was genuinely interested, concerned for him, not just gathering gossip as currency like so many people did. "It's a fairly simple story. I've always been overwhelmed by people and I was born in a big city. Grew up in a busy place, went to a school with hundreds of kids. It hurts me, that kind of relentless input. But I shut myself off. I had a reputation as the weirdo loner, and that was okay. I was comfortable with it, never joining in sports or clubs, keeping to myself and hiding in books. When I left school I tried to find jobs that meant I had little to do with anyone else." He paused, wondering how much to say. He thought he'd already said more in one go than he had to anyone in years. His throat tightened. She didn't need to know the details. "Then something happened. I was wrongly accused of a crime and it made life more difficult than ever. Even though I was cleared, parts of it stuck. I knew I needed to be somewhere with fewer people. Where it was easier to be alone. Far from there. This is where I found." He took a deep, shuddering breath, mentally exhausted from the monologue.

Tricia put her hand on his knee, squeezed. "Maybe one day you'll tell me what happened. What drove you away. Only if you want to. It might help."

Caleb smiled crookedly. Tricia was about the most genuine person he'd ever met, it was a pleasant surprise that such people really existed. "It might," he said quietly. "Maybe one day. For now, let's go."

"Okay."

They soon pulled onto the field already more than half-filled with cars and pick-ups. Even on a Monday night, it seemed everyone and their dog came to the carnival. The short drive over had been in silence, Caleb bereft of words for a while. Tricia pulled up next to a bright red Ford F-150 and put the parking brake on but left the engine running.

"So, are we going to do this like we said? Just double-team the girls?"

"Hester has very few weaknesses, but one of them seems to be Suki and Clare. She's attached to them. I can't figure out what it is, but there's a connection. I can't think of any other way."

"How do we do it?"

"First we'll go to Fallon and make sure he's ready. Then we find a way to talk to Suki and Clare, get them to follow us. Hester knows we're onto her, but she can only control one of us at a time. We'll have to see what happens, and hope she can't do any damage until we get her to Saul. Then you get Clare and Suki out of there while Fallon does whatever it is he thinks he can do."

Tricia frowned. "Seems a bit flaky for a plan."

"It is."

Fallon's attraction had a sign out front that said, *Closed – Back soon!* Caleb and Tricia ducked in anyway.

"Took your fucking time," Fallon said, from somewhere deep in shadows. "I'm losing money here."

There were no lights on inside the big tent, just a wan glow leaking from the trailer itself where it stood in the middle of the open space. Everything else had been cleared away, the small section at the back where Fallon lived closed off. As his eyes adjusted, Caleb saw the carnie on the ground beside his trailer. The grass had been trodden flat and dry by the passage of punters and the shelter of the big tent over the last several days, a strangely fibrous carpet. The earth beneath hard as cement. Fallon sat cross-legged in the center of a collection of unlit candles in glass cups that surrounded him in a weirdly geometric pattern. Something glistened wetly on the flattened grass between the cups. Fallon was naked. His pale skin like ivory, bony knees and elbows, ribs sticking out of his shallow chest like a dish rack.

"Don't try to understand or ask for any explanations," the carnie said. "There's power in ritual. I'm ready. You get her in this tent before my candles burn away, or we're fucked. When I light them, they'll burn for about an hour, no more."

"Okay." Caleb glanced at Tricia. She was looking anywhere but at the naked man. "We'll get them here."

"Fine. Whatever works. Will I light the candles now?"

Fallon's eyes glittered in the soft glow from the trailer. His teeth shone whitely as he grinned, clearly enjoying Tricia's discomfort at his nudity.

"Maybe we should check first if they're here," Caleb said.

"They might see us," Tricia said. "That could be a problem."

"They're here," Fallon said. "I saw them arrive. You've got one hour to get her to me."

There was a metallic click and then a flare of brightness as Fallon flicked a Zippo lighter into flame. He had one eyebrow raised.

Caleb nodded. "Okay, do it. I'll get her in here before an hour is up."

They wandered the midway and strolled between rides and attractions, scanning carefully. Caleb hoped desperately they would see Hester before she saw them. They used the crowds for cover, stayed close to people all the time. Several folks who knew him gave sidelong glances, no doubt wondering at he and Tricia together again, wondering why they seemed to stalk warily along. His whole life, Caleb had been the loner, the one people always avoided while also watching, as if he were a snake that might suddenly strike. Now he was hanging out with Tricia a lot, he saw the looks people cast at them together. They were different, while retaining what he was used to. Now they included the turning cogs of gossip machines pumping out all kinds of theories behind their eyes. And surely the word about Riley had spread far and wide by now. Maybe people wondered what Tricia was doing at the carnival, instead of grieving in the dark at home. Was that what people might expect? Whatever, let people wonder. The fascination with other folks' business had always mystified Caleb. He was interested to note that despite his attention to people, the familiar seemed weaker, less persistent than usual. Tricia's presence was armor indeed. Regardless, after about ten minutes he began to despair, thinking perhaps the girls had left again, or that Fallon had been mistaken.

Then he heard high-pitched, squealing laughter near the burlesque show tent that took up about three normal sized plots along one side of the site. A bunch of kids were gathered around the doorway, laughing and slapping each other on the back. A small man with dark hair turning iron gray hair at the sides, wearing an old-fashioned suit, was shooing them away, but he laughed as he did so. Caleb recognized him as the man with Saul that first day in the midway. It seemed so long ago. Tricia jabbed at his arm and Caleb nodded, ducking with her around a burger van out of sight.

"Get outta here," the little man said, waving both hands. "You're only here to giggle and cause trouble. It's an adult show!"

Among the kids were Hester, Clare, and Suki. She hadn't seen him yet. He risked a glimpse out from the side of the van and watched the group moving towards the midway. There were about a dozen of them. That was good. Clare and Suki chatted quietly to each other and Caleb was struck by how pale and drawn they looked, as if they were sick, or hadn't slept for days. Each day they looked worse instead of better. Someone called something to Hester and she moved to the front of the group, grinning and listening. She looked like the other teenagers on the surface, but her demeanor was entirely different, and Caleb realized what it was. She acted like an adult though she looked young. But he had no time to observe, this might be their only chance.

"Let's get to Clare and Suki," he said to Tricia.

As the distance between Hester and the other two grew to a dozen feet or so, he slipped from the side of the van, Tricia right beside him, and caught Clare's eye. She frowned as he gestured to her, opened her mouth to say something, but he quickly intervened.

"Clare, Suki, your parents are here. They need a word. Everyone has been looking for you."

Clare glanced towards Hester and said, "What for?"

Tricia stepped forward, smiled. "Everything's okay, but you should come now."

Caleb's heart raced, Hester would see him any moment. "They have something for you guys. Quickly, it'll only take a minute."

Suki shook her head. "What's with you two?" Her voice started to rise as she spoke.

Caleb panicked. He grabbed both girls, wrapping palm over each of their mouths and hauled them back behind the burger van, then around between it and the next stall. "You're in real danger!" he hissed. "Please, come with me for a moment."

"Jesus, Caleb!" Tricia said, running with him. "This isn't the way!"

"I don't know what is!"

Clare thrashed out of his grasp. "Let me go!"

Tricia grabbed Clare's arm before she could run back. "Please, Clare, come with me. It's really important."

Suki writhed in his grip, muffled screams pushing wetly against his skin. He gritted his teeth against a sharp pain as she bit him, but refused to let go. Tricia dragged Clare alongside them, stumbling. Fallon's tent was only twenty or thirty yards away, the thin gap between this line of stalls and the next empty of people. Cables and generators littered the way, made it an obstacle course, but they had no choice.

"I'm so sorry!" Caleb said. "You'll be okay, I promise."

They hauled the girls along as Hester's voice rang out. "Where are you?" The sound was like a thousand hooks in Caleb's skin. Grimacing with the effort, muscles straining, he stumbled his way between the stalls and burst out into an open thoroughfare. Fallon's tent was opposite, but a dozen people turned to look. Faces twisted in shock, eyes widened. All was lost, they'd be arrested for assault or worse.

He couldn't move.

Tricia grabbed Suki and dragged both girls to the flaps of Fallon's tent, her eyes wider than anyone's. "Everything's fine!" she said quickly.

The girls looked wildly around, bewildered.

"What's going on here?" someone called out.

"It's all fine," Tricia said, flashing a winning smile that to Caleb was fake as plastic. She put her arms around the girls' shoulders and turned them towards the tent. Both girls slapped at her, tried to move away.

"What's happening?" Suki asked, scared now as well as angry.

Caleb's heart slammed against his chest. As several of the shocked onlookers approached, firing questions at him, their eyes angry, Hester stepped out and stood in front of him. She cast a look around the gathering crowd and their faces softened as one and they drifted away like nothing had happened.

"Taking action?" Hester asked. "You're either very brave or very stupid."

"Hester?" Clare asked.

Tricia cried out and pushed both girls into Fallon's tent. Caleb thought his bladder would let go but for the vicelike grip on every muscle in his body. Would it be enough? Even if Hester killed him now, surely Fallon would get her next when she went for Clare and Suki. Only his eyes could move, and his lips quivered in a grimace. He knew he wore the expression he'd seen on Kirk Branton's face, and Tim Daley's, and the big bearded guy at the bumper cars. And on his own that night under the trees.

Hester looked from him to Fallon's tent and back again. "Teamed up with that predator, have you? I'd hoped to avoid him, same way a smart person avoids a bee's nest. No real danger, just an annoyance." She took a deep breath, shook her head. "You'll regret this. I should have let the mob have you, but that's no fun for me." She nodded towards Fallon's place. "I can't trust him, so you get another reprieve. But it'll be brief. I'll be back for you."

She turned away and Caleb's body fell limp as seaweed. He collapsed to the ground, gasping for breath as Hester walked confidently into Fallon's tent. Caleb dragged himself up onto hands and knees as a strangled cry rang out from the creep show. Tricia burst out, dragging Suki and Clare with her, all three with terrified faces, drained of blood in shock. Tricia didn't even notice Caleb as she pulled the girls away. Another cry rang out. Caleb surged to his feet and ran into Fallon's tent. He had to know what was happening.

Fallon stood in the center of his candles, his long body stretched tall, arms above his head. His teeth were gritted in a rage, a bright knife reflected brightly in one hand, blood streaked his chest from two long gashes, clearly self-inflicted. Hester stood facing him, arms out to either side, head tipped back to stare at the canvas roof above. The air tasted coppery with static, her dark hair writhed in a cloud. Her fingers clutched at nothing, her face taut with strain. Caleb pressed his back to the tent wall, mesmerized.

"Underestimated me, didn't you, bitch!" Fallon yelled.

"What are you?" Hester growled.

"Stronger than you ever thought," Fallon said. "I've fed on the energy of people for decades, and yours will last me a long time!" He began a chant of strange, clipped words that swam in the air like living things. The sound of his voice drilled into Caleb's ears, made him dizzy.

Hester laughed. "Feel it yet?"

Fallon's voice rose, a desperate edge creeping into it.

"I may have underestimated your strength," Hester said. "But you've mistaken me entirely."

The sensation of static in the space increased rapidly, made Caleb's teeth ache, his hair stand up. He sensed that drawing away again, like he'd felt the first time in Saul's attraction, but this time it was directed entirely at Hester, and it was huge. The tent sides billowed as if in a powerful wind. Hester lowered her head again, pinned Fallon with her gaze, and pushed her hands towards him. The two were locked in some battle of powers Caleb couldn't comprehend.

Fallon roared, dragged the knife across his chest again. "I am stronger than you!"

Hester screamed, staggered one step back, then leaned into her attack with renewed vigor. Caleb gasped as Hester's form wavered. Her left shoulder and arm shifted suddenly like water, the inside of her body dark silt instead of flesh and bone. A stink of stagnant lake and fetid mud rose, cloying.

"No!" Hester yelled.

The static in the room burst out, prickling across Caleb's skin like needles. He collapsed to his knees under the pressure of it, tasted bile forced up into his throat.

"NO!" Hester screamed again. She seemed to gather herself and drove forward towards Fallon.

He cried out wordlessly, an animal howl of pain. His candles began popping out and he went down onto one knee. Blood trickled from his nose, ran down his neck from his ears. He moaned again, constricted now, guttural and bubbling. "You're not even flesh!" he rasped.

A scream echoed from somewhere outside on the midway.

Blood leaked from Fallon's eyes like dark tears and Hester pressed forward again. Fallon collapsed to the grass and twitched, his candles all out. In the wan light of the caravan, Caleb watched the carnie shudder once more, then fall still.

Hester fell to her knees, breathing hard, head hanging. Her long black hair settled as the electric charge drained from the room, the white streak bright in the dim light. Caleb sat against the tent wall and shook.

"You made me kill her," Hester said, her voice low, strained.

"W… what?"

"You think it's easy holding this avatar together?" She turned to face Caleb. "I need their life force. Now there's only one." Rage burned in her eyes, and a kind of pain.

Shouts and screams sounded outside. Someone yelled for an ambulance.

Tricia pushed into the tent. She saw Hester kneeling, Fallon lying bloodied and still. Her hand clapped over her mouth. "Clare collapsed!" she said, tears pouring over her cheeks.

Hester pushed herself to her feet. Her face was down and she stared up at them through her lashes and the lank strands of her hair. She trembled, whether in exhaustion or rage, or both, Caleb wasn't sure. He knew he wouldn't live long enough to find out.

"I don't kill them, not the girls," Hester said in a dangerous whisper. "But you made me kill Clare. To beat that foul fear drinker, that ancient fucker, I had to take all Clare had to give. This is on *you*!"

Caleb had no voice, his mind empty.

"You should have let her live!" Tricia said. "You should have *gone*, left Clare alive!"

"Oh?" Hester gestured back over her shoulder at Fallon's corpse. "And let that live instead?" She stepped forward, leveled one finger at Tricia. "I'm too weak to do anything now, but know this. I will come for Caleb Jackson. His days are numbered. And Tricia Brent, I don't kill women, it's not my mission." She dragged in a deep breath, staggered slightly. "But I'll cause you pain for what you've done. Your Toby."

Tricia gasped. "What? What do you know?"

Hester grinned, callous. "I know the taste of his marrow. He was delicious."

"No!"

"I sucked that marrow from his bones just as he was on the cusp of manhood, about to become the beast all men are. Sweet childhood with bitter adult hatred just starting to turn the meat acrid. So good. Your husband delivered him to me and *his* despair was nectar. Now your son's bones are in the ground."

Tricia sobbed. "No! That's not true!"

"Oh, it's true. Your husband brought him to me. Two *men*, on an adventure, keeping secrets from you. They stumbled right into my web, and Riley lived with that guilt. Until he finally came back to challenge me. And I killed him too. I don't kill women, Tricia Brent. But I've taken everything from you. You know it's true. You *feel* the truth."

Tricia buried her face in her hands, wracked with sobs.

Caleb moved to her as she sank to the ground, put his arms around her. Hester stumbled past them. "I'll be back for you, fucker!" And she was gone.

Caleb pulled Tricia to her feet. "I'm sorry," he said. "I'm so, so sorry. But we have to go. We can't stay here."

He pulled her with him, out of the tent into the hot evening. People bustled everywhere, paying no attention as they were drawn to the crowd over at the midway. People called out, others were crying, several teenagers stood in a huddle, consoling each other. Through the feet of the crowd, Caleb caught a glimpse of Clare lying flat, eyes staring sightlessly at the indigo sky, Suki on her knees beside her friend. He dragged Tricia the long way around and back to her car, put her in the passenger seat, and drove them both away from the carnival.

34

VAL BAKER ARRIVED at the station early, coffee in hand. Slippery thoughts chased each other around her mind, darting away whenever she tried to hold onto one. She remembered talking to Caleb Jackson and Tricia Brent. Something about the weirdness currently dogging Sallow Bend. It had something to do with that strange girl, Hester. But what?

Her thoughts were interrupted when she saw Freddie Holtz, Kurt Janssen, and Clive Taylor gathered around Clive's desk, talking quietly. Their faces were serious, something clearly up. *Oh no. Another death. Has to be.*

"What's up, team?" Val asked, hearing the tremble in her voice.

Holtz looked up. "There you are."

"Everyone's in early," Val said. Holtz was often in before her, but Kurt and Clive never were.

"I called them in," the sheriff said. "I didn't bother calling you, you're always in early."

Val was mildly offended at that, but it seemed a petty way to feel. She pushed it aside, in favor of more important issues. "What's happened?"

"Clare Finlay died."

Val's stomach went liquid, the mouthful of coffee she'd just taken suddenly more bitter than reasonable. She swallowed. "What? How?"

"Collapsed at the carnival last night. Docs said it was a heart attack."

"She's thirteen!"

Holtz nodded, pursed his lips.

"How does a thirteen-year-old drop dead from a heart attack?"

"I don't know. The doc said maybe the stresses of getting lost, the attention, something like that. Said it's also possible it's entirely coincidental. Like she had a pre-existing condition and this would have happened anyway. Post mortem is hopefully going down today."

"That poor kid. And what about Suki?"

"Don't know. Reports are that she was right there when it happened, looked sick, but that's no surprise. Her parents took her home."

"And Hester?" The name tasted as bitter in her mouth as the coffee had become, but she didn't know why.

"No idea. That kid is tough as nails. She'll be all right."

Val shook her head, sat at her desk, stared at the screensaver sliding back and forth across her computer monitor. "So why is everyone in early?" she asked. "What can we do about it?"

Holtz came over, put a hand on her shoulder. An electric thrill buzzed through her at the touch, despite her horror at the little girl's death. *Control yourself, Valerie, god damn.* "No real reason," Holtz said. "I just figured we should all be here. The town is abuzz with tension, you must feel it."

"Of course. I've felt it the last few days. Only getting worse."

"Do me a favor?" Holtz asked.

"Sure, of course."

"Make a friendly community visit to Suki Tokugawa's place? Just enquire to her health, let the family know we care and we're here if they need anything."

Val nodded. "I can do that. Will it help?"

"No. But it's good community policing."

When Val knocked on the Tokugawa family front door a little after 9 am, she thought no one was going to answer. She checked her notes again. The father's name was Hiro, he was probably at work. But the mother, Hanae, and the older sister, Akiko, were likely to be around. Maybe they'd all gone out. Maybe they'd packed up and moved away, and Val couldn't blame them for that.

Then the door opened and Hanae Tokugawa looked out. Her eyes were drawn, dark bags beneath, like she'd hardly slept. "Yes?"

"Hello, Mrs Tokugawa. Can I come in?"

"Hanae, please. Why? What's happened now?"

Val spotted movement over Hanae's shoulder, saw Suki and Akiko in the hallway behind their mother, listening in. Suki looked pale as a ghost, more drawn than her mother. Her expression was slack, empty. Akiko's eyes betrayed a kind of contained fear. "Nothing has happened, Hanae. I just wanted to drop by. Sheriff Holtz wanted you to know the department is here for you. If there's anything you need…"

Hanae forced a watery smile, ducked her head once in a nod. "Thank you, that's good to know. But we just want some peace and quiet."

"Of course." A thought flitted across Val's mind. "Have you seen Hester today?"

She watched Suki as she asked and saw the girl flinch at the name.

"I'm sure she's back in her woods," Hanae said, a disgusted twist to her mouth. "Thank you. Goodbye." She gently closed the door.

Val stood on the step, replaying the moment. Suki's physical reaction to Hester's name. *I'm sure she's back in her woods.* What did that mean? Try as she might, Val couldn't hold onto the train of thought. All she knew for certain was that something was heavily out of kilter. She turned and walked slowly back to the patrol car, wondering what the hell she could do about it.

Sitting in the driver's seat, she pulled out her cell and scrolled through her contacts. She smiled when she saw a number for Tricia Brent's cell. Tricia answered after only two rings.

"Hello?"

"Tricia, it's Val Baker."

"Oh no. What's happened now?"

People kept asking the same thing. "Yeah, it's like that, huh? You heard about Clare Finlay, right?"

"Yes."

Val frowned. Tricia's voice was tight, as if with tears. Perhaps the two families had been close. Best to push on. "I just visited Suki's house, to offer support. I don't know why I'm telling you, I'm supposed to be the one to protect and serve for God's sake. But I feel like you and Caleb Jackson have a better handle on this than any of us."

"I might have agreed with you until yesterday. I think we're just making everything worse."

"What do you mean?"

"Nothing, go on."

"Well, I mentioned Hester, and Suki is downright terrified of her friend. And Suki's mom said something about Hester being back in her woods."

Tricia gave out a soft, humorless laugh. "I don't doubt it."

"So you know about that? About Hester and the woods?"

"Not really. Just suspicions." Tricia sounded dog-tired, washed out.

"Well, if there's anything you do know, maybe you can act on it. Because what I know for damn sure is the rest of us are helpless. Bad enough so many people keep dying, but two children now as well? First Reece Gossett, now young Clare. If there's anything you and Caleb can do..."

Tricia sighed heavily. "Of course, Val. And thank you. We're doing our best. You mentioned before that maybe we should seek stories from some of the old-timers. Any suggestions who exactly?"

Val felt like a heel. Since when did the police call regular citizens and ask them to fix things? She'd said the rest of them were helpless in the face of whatever was happening in Sallow Bend and she meant it. She'd never felt more useless in her life. "Try Old Man Wilson, like Jerry Yonker mentioned. I tried twice and couldn't find him, and that's weird in itself. But I reckon there's nothing worth knowing around here that he wouldn't at least have an opinion on."

35

JOHN BARROW STOOD outside Saul Fallon's tent, trying to decide if he really wanted to align himself with the man or not. He'd agonized over it all night, tossing and turning on the bunk in his trailer behind the burlesque marquee. Barrow had always stood by Ashley, often in the face of disagreement from everyone else. Almost always in the face of disagreement from Saul. Barrow wasn't so lacking in self-awareness that he didn't recognize the flame he carried for Strong's daughter. He also knew only too well she was almost half his age and his old yet undeniable desires would always go unfulfilled. But that's as it should be. Regardless, standing here, thinking of allying himself with her greatest hindrance, directly against her wishes? That stuck in his craw.

But a child had died. Simply dropped dead in the midway. No matter how much people talked about terrible luck, bad genes, awful coincidence, he couldn't ignore it. On the way through the quiet carnival in the early morning cool he had passed Daniel's van and seen the big man working out like he hated the weights, pumping them again and again, sweat pouring off his skin, face twisted in a kind of rage. That man struggled with events, it was written all over him. Daniel knew there was bad shit happening in this town and he hid in the effort of exercise. But it wasn't enough. None of it was. Damn the expense, they had to leave.

"Fallon, you there?" His voice punched uncomfortably loud through the still air. Maybe he should go around the back, to Saul's sleeping area and call him. But there was etiquette to observe in carnivals and his entering through the back before had been a deliberate act of disrespect. Barrow needed to rectify that, offer an olive branch. He called again, slightly louder. "Fallon, wake up!"

A sign hung on the post of the main tent flap, *Closed – Back soon!*

Fallon used that when he went out for food during carnie hours, or if he needed a toilet break. It didn't usually stay on all night. No one was here to see it. Barrow thought back, remembering the paramedics, the uproar around the girl's collapse. He'd come to see, as had most people before the majority slipped easily back into business as usual. He had glanced over as he passed and the sign had been up then. He assumed Fallon had hooked it up quickly as he came out too, to see what the fuss in the midway was all about. But Barrow hadn't seen the tall, pale man around the fallen girl.

An emptiness settled in his gut. He swallowed. He didn't know what he was about to find, but he was certain it would not be good.

"Saul, I'm coming in."

He pushed open the tent flap, stepped inside. As the canvas fell back, cutting off the light, an image stuck in his mind. A pale form lying on the floor by the old Eurostream trailer, jars scattered around it.

"Ah, fuck it." Barrow's throat constricted, made his voice tight and thick. "Fuck, fuck, fuck."

He lifted the tent flap again to let the light back in, stared, as trembling wracked his entire body. Fallon lay naked and obscene in death, eyes and mouth wide in something akin to raw terror. Blood covered his face and body, the whites of his eyes scarlet, crusted, scabbing rivulets snaking from his ears over his neck and cheeks. The jars were actually small glass cups of candles, some tipped over, wax in spilled rivers grown solid when they cooled.

Barrow barked a sound of dismay and disgust, stumbled back out into the succor of the mild early morning sun. "No, no, no." Bile shot up his throat and he slapped a hand over his mouth, swallowed it back down.

He stood, shivering, immobile for several seconds. They had waited too long. Damn it, Fallon had been right, they should have upped stakes and left already. Now Fallon himself was dead and that death was no accident, no coincidence of genetics. Whatever the fuck had happened in there, the police would get involved again and they would be trapped here, answering questions, filling in forms. How many more would die?

"Just what is happening here?" Barrow croaked to no one.

Daniel Clarke appeared around the side of a vendor's stall. "John? What is it?" Sweat ran over his face and naked torso, the jean shorts he wore soaked at the waistband.

Barrow shook his head, stuck for words. He gestured over his shoulder, managed to say, "Saul is dead."

"What?" Dan pushed past him, held the tent flap high to look inside. "Holy Jesus and Mother Mary!" He staggered back again, face suddenly ashen. He turned to Barrow, crouched and put his hands on John's shoulders. "We gotta talk to Ashley."

Dan's urgency spurred Barrow back into action, his head cleared. "Yes. Come on. But keep calm. Let's not scare everyone awake."

They walked as casually as they could to Ashley's trailer. Barrow climbed the steps, knocked on the door.

"What is it?"

"It's John Barrow and Daniel Clarke."

"Oh guys, come on…"

"Ashley, something *deadly* serious has happened."

There was a moment's silence, then scuffling from inside. Ashley pulled open the door, hair mussed from sleep, wearing only light shorts and a singlet. Sarah Carter sat up in the bed behind her, equally disheveled.

"I don't like the tone," Ashley said.

"You'll like the news even less. We have to come in."

Ashley saw Daniel waiting, nodded and stepped back. Barrow and Dan went inside, closed the door, while Ashley put a coffee pot on the small stove. Barrow knew there was no point in dragging it out.

"Saul Fallon is dead. Violently."

"What?"

"It looks, I don't know, fucking occult or something."

Sarah's face paled, Ashley sat heavily onto the end of the bed. Barrow told them all he could about what he'd seen. "This has gone far beyond anything normal," he concluded.

"No shit," Ashley whispered.

"But we can't involve the police," Barrow said.

Sarah sat up straighter in the bed. "Wait a minute. We can't cover this up!"

"We have to! If the police get involved we won't get away from this cursed town for days more, maybe weeks. If you tell the State Police where we're going they can keep track, follow up the whole Riley Brent thing. They'll let us move on as long as we tell them where, I think. As long as we stay in this state, anyway. But this?"

Ashley's voice snapped like a gunshot. "Quiet." She sat, lost in thought, for a long moment. Eventually she nodded, as if to herself. "My father gave me a sum of savings that I promised I would never use. It was a challenge to me, to take over this gig without needing his help. And I've done that, even if it has been week to week. Even if I've never had much in the way of savings of my own, I've never needed his money. But this is different. John's right, this is far beyond normal. I'll use my father's money to pay out Wilson and we'll quit. Leave today. I'll tell the State Police and they've got my cell for contact, and yours, John. I only wish I'd done it yesterday. Saul was right all along and now he's died for it." She became suddenly angry. "What the fuck did he know that we didn't?"

"Nothing," Sarah said quietly. "He was different, I can't explain how, sensitive to things. I felt it too. We all knew something was happening here if we're honest with ourselves, but we persevered anyway. No matter now. All we can do is act in the moment. I agree that we need to leave. But we can't cover up Saul's death."

Ashley shook her head. "We have to, at least in the short term. John's right, the police will make us stay if we report it, and if we stay more will die. We're family, we look out for ourselves. Always have, always will."

"But it's not right," Daniel said.

Ashley looked up at the big man, smiled sadly. "Sometimes things are wrong and right at the same time. Black and white, light and dark, good and evil, all that stuff is bullshit." She held up a hand at Dan's imminent protest. Barrow saw the light of determination in her eyes. He admired it, her strength of conviction. She had a plan.

"So how do we proceed?" he asked.

"We'll report Saul's death, but not here. We pack up, tell everyone we're leaving, but tell *no-one* about Saul. Only we four know. We'll pack his stuff up too, put his body in his trailer. Dan, you'll drive Saul's truck. What we'll tell everyone is that Saul isn't feeling well, he's sleeping in his trailer while you drive. We can pack up this morning, while I go and pay out Wilson. We'll leave this afternoon and put several hours between us and Sallow Bend. I'll let the State Police know where to find us if they have more questions about Brent. When we park up, we'll have dinner, then later tonight we'll *discover* Saul's body, he's died in his sleep or something, and report it to the authorities wherever we are. Not here. Okay? The main thing is that we're not here any longer."

Barrow nodded. "That's a good plan. That's smart. As long as the State Police don't make us stay."

"I won't tell them until we've gone," Ashley said. "I'll risk that problem to be rid of this one."

"Wait," Sarah said. "What if the authorities find something about Saul that's, I don't know, unexplainable? Time of death and stuff?"

"Let me worry about that," Ash said. "I'll figure it out. As long as we're away from here. Fuck Sallow Bend. We have to go."

"This ain't right," Daniel said. He looked close to tears, eyes cinched up.

"I know, Dan. But we have to look out for ourselves." Ashley rose to comfort him, but he stepped aside, looked to Sarah.

"I found those girls. This is my fault."

Sarah frowned. "What do you mean?"

"That little girl died, one of the ones I found. I saw that Hester leaving the carnival at the same time, she looked… broken somehow. She ran into the woods. Now Saul is dead."

"You think those things are connected?"

"I don't know! But all of this, it's at least partly down to me. I can't walk away from it. Sarah, you *know* I'm right. This *is* all connected somehow."

"Yes, I think you are right," Sarah said. "But I also think there's nothing we can do about it. I think if you hadn't found those girls then someone else would have. You're involved in this, but it's not your fault. Ashley is right. We have to protect ourselves."

Daniel shook his head, stared at the floor. "It ain't right. None of this is right."

"That's beyond doubt."

"But you have to help us, Dan," Ashley said. "Are you with us?"

Dan nodded and Barrow let out a sigh of relief. He'd thought the roustabout was going to refuse the plan, and it was a good one.

"Except I won't drive," Dan said.

"Damn it," Barrow muttered.

"Why not?" Ashley asked.

Dan looked up again, his face set. "I'll pack up for Saul, put his body in the trailer, make sure it's all under wraps. Your plan can go ahead. But you find someone else to drive him out. Because I'm staying here."

36

TRICIA STEERED HER battered Taurus up the long driveway to Old Man Wilson's homestead, her face betraying deep pain. Her knuckles were white on the steering wheel. Caleb sat beside her, watching from the corner of his eye. For all his frustration at her propensity for chatter, her silence now bothered him more.

He had driven them out the south side of Sallow Bend the night before, both of them in shock at the terrible failure of their plan. Their only hope in all this, the only person who might be able to face Hester, had died horribly. They reeled from Clare's death. Whatever else they told themselves, it was on them that she had died. His heart cracked at the thought and he knew it wouldn't heal. Tricia had that *and* she'd been emotionally smashed by Hester with that horrible account of Toby's death. Her grief, her guilt, must be a crushing weight and he had no idea how to alleviate any of it.

They spent the night at Sammon's Motel on the highway, empty. Tricia had curled up on the motel bed, shaking, crying silently, refusing to talk. Caleb had managed to get some fitful sleep on the fold-out couch under the motel's tatty curtains. They were shattered in every way.

Then Tricia had woken him in the morning and seemed to have gathered new resolve during the night, her face and demeanor hardened like rock. "Val Baker called me. She suggested we talk to Old Man Wilson. Maybe we should have done that before. So let's go. Get some answers. Get a new plan."

"You think there's a plan to be found?" Caleb had asked.

"Clare Finlay died!" Tricia shouted. "We cannot let that be the end of it. Toby-" She hitched a sob. "There has to be another plan. If not, you're dead once Hester regains her strength, so what choice do we have but to try?"

In silence, they left the motel.

As they pulled up outside Wilson's house, Caleb finally spoke. "What is she, do you think?"

"Hester?"

"Yeah."

Tricia shook her head. "I'm hoping we can find out here."

Caleb wasn't really afraid of death, though he would prefer to go on living. But guilt plagued him. "You think we might just make it worse though?"

Tricia rounded on him, her eyes flashing anger. "We already got Clare Finlay killed! That's on us. And that *bitch* killed my Toby. How much worse can it get? We might already be going to hell for our part in all this, but I will not walk away from it, not now. I'm going to fight that… creature, whatever she is, and destroy her or die trying. Nothing exists for me beyond that. You, Caleb, are dead anyway. She promised you that and I'm pretty sure you know she's not lying. So the only way for you to survive is to beat her. You either help me, or I'll take you home and you can sit there and wait to die."

Caleb weathered the tirade, unable to breathe. When she stopped, staring at him, he dragged air into his lungs. "Yeah. Okay. Well, I'll help."

"Good."

She got out of the car and strode up to Wilson's front door, banged hard three times. Caleb joined her, stood limply at her side. When no answer was forthcoming, she banged again, shaking the door in its frame. Still nothing.

"Maybe he's not home," Caleb said.

"You seen him anywhere the last few days?"

Caleb glanced at her face, twisted in rage. She was fueled by anger. But she was right. "No, I haven't."

"And he's always around town. Especially at carnival time, strutting up and down the midway grinning like he's the mayor or something." She hammered on the door again. Then she raised her voice to a shout. "I know you're in there, Wilson!"

A curtain beside the door twitched, and Wilson looked out, his face drawn with tiredness, long white beard in disarray. "I ain't taking visitors right now," he said, voice muffled by the glass. "Ain't well."

"Too bad," Tricia said. "We need to talk to you now."

"Nope." The old face vanished from the window and the curtain fell back into place.

"Fuck him," Tricia growled. She looked around the floor at her feet, then picked up an old leather boot from a pair on the step. She turned it to hold it by the toe and used the heel to smash out the window Wilson had looked through.

There was a yelp from the other side. "God *damn*, woman!"

"Open the door, right now."

"I'm sick! Go away!"

"I will smash out the rest of the window and climb in if I have to."

Caleb stood back, stunned at Tricia's ferocity, but impressed.

"I can't help you," Wilson said, but his voice was weaker.

"People are dying," Tricia said. "A thirteen-year-old girl, Clare Finlay. She's the latest. She died, Wilson. And you know something about it, right?" The old man said nothing, but Caleb heard his ragged breathing just beyond the curtain behind the broken window.

"We need to talk to you," Tricia said. "About Hester Black."

Wilson opened the front door and peered out, face pinched in a wince. "It's happening again, isn't it?"

"What is?"

"I can't help you. I don't know."

Tricia shoved against the door, made the old man stagger back. "We're coming in."

The inside of Wilson's house was dim and cool, old-fashioned in every respect. He led them into a kitchen with morning sunlight streaming through net curtains to fall across a scarred wooden table. He pulled out a chair and sat, gestured for them to do the same.

"What do you mean, happening again?" Tricia asked.

Wilson sighed. Despite his nickname, Caleb had never considered the man aged. Old, yes, but not diminished by age. Here, sitting with his shoulders hunched, wearing a stained singlet, beard and wispy hair disheveled, he looked every day of his years.

"I can't remember," Wilson said. "Not really. It's all… slippery in my mind. But I know something is happening here that has happened before."

"Why haven't you done anything about it?"

He looked at Tricia with a crooked smile. "Because I don't think there's anything anyone *can* do. I've just been hiding out, waiting for it to pass, because that seems to be the pattern. It passes."

"People are dying."

Wilson shrugged. "People die all the time."

Tricia's mouth fell open. "Clare Finlay died! She was thirteen years old. How can you be so callous? *Children* are dying. Hester Black killed my son, Wilson!" Tricia's eyes blazed. "I will see her finished."

Wilson's face scrunched as if he were straining to remember a name or a number. "A few times in my long life, something has happened to Sallow Bend. People disappear, too many people die at once. It goes on for a while, then it stops. I always forget about it, then it happens again, and I kinda remember that it happened before. And I remember how there's not a damn thing we can do. Then it passes. So it goes."

"So we just let her kill with abandon until some arbitrarily unspecified end?"

Wilson nodded. "You're safe, though. She doesn't kill women." His eyes widened, like he had surprised himself with that comment.

Caleb remembered Hester herself saying as much before she delivered the horrible truth about Toby, and their own research had proven as much. But sometimes you didn't have to take someone's life to kill them, to end them inside. He wondered if Tricia would ever recover from the last few days. Perhaps the only chance she had was from some kind of closure. And now Clare had died, so the rules were shifting.

“Regardless,” Tricia said, “I have a score to settle. What else do you know? Tell me everything.”

“What about?”

“Hester!”

Wilson jumped like he’d been stung. “Yes, of course. This is the problem, I don’t know!”

“There must be something.”

The old man’s eyes widened. “Wait. My grandmother’s journal. I forget again every time!”

“What about it?”

Wilson clenched his teeth, strained like he was lifting weights.

“Hester Black!” Tricia shouted. “Your grandmother’s journal!”

Wilson groaned, forcing memories out, veins pumped at his temples, his neck taut with effort. “My grandmother was only a child when it happened, but she saw it all.”

“Saw what?”

The old man’s face screwed up in concentration, like he was trying to resist a terrible pain. Once again, it was the same expression Kirk Branton wore as he put his head in front of the Ferris Wheel. The same as Tim Daley as he fought unsuccessfully to step out from under that massive tree limb. And Jim Saddler as he beat the carnie half to death. Hester’s influence was wide and strong. “She wrote it all down!” Wilson said suddenly. He looked up, eyes wide with realization, and one was solid red with blood. He gasped, chest pumping with short breaths like he’d been sprinting. His eyes went wider still and his mouth fell open with a rasping draw of breath. He clutched at his left arm, a soft whine escaping his lips. His face paled and he toppled from the chair to crash heavily, bone-jarringly, into the floor.

“Shit!” Tricia leaped up, ran around the table.

Caleb was in a position to see the man’s eyes, staring emptily across the room. Old Man Wilson wasn’t old any more. He’d moved onto the stage after that.

“The effort of resisting her,” Tricia said quietly.

Caleb stood, about to start searching through the house for a journal when there was a loud knocking at the door and a woman's voice.

"Mr Wilson? You home?"

Caleb froze, but Tricia appeared unconcerned. She stood from Wilson's corpse and moved along the short hall to pull the door wide open. Ashley Strong stood there, a large wad of money in one hand. She frowned. "Hey, Tricia." Then she noticed Caleb standing in the kitchen doorway. She leaned to one side and gasped, clearly able to see Wilson on his well-worn floorboards.

"Fuck," she said.

Tricia nodded. "You here to pay your rent?"

"That was the plan."

"I guess you get a free ride this time. Why don't you wait until the end to pay?"

Caleb guessed Tricia had already worked that out, as he had.

Ashley confirmed it for him. "This is the end. We're out, leaving today. This town is fucked up."

"And you're just going to run away?" Tricia asked.

Ash let out a humorless laugh. "Yes, we are. Not our problem."

"Your people are involved. Your guy found the girls, brought Hester back."

"Hester?" Ash said, aghast. "Fuck you. If it wasn't Dan who found those girls, it would have been someone else. You're welcome, by the way! I don't see what that has to do with any of this. This is Sallow Bend's problem, not ours."

Tricia nodded, eyes dark. "Coward."

Caleb was shocked at that. Hadn't they talked about leaving if they could? It seemed Tricia's rage was wide open, happy to collect anyone in its sweeping arc. But he saw something in Ashley's expression too, some reluctant knowing. Perhaps the carnie boss suspected more than she was letting on. Did she know about Hester? Or perhaps she'd simply made the connection that all this started when her guy found the girls.

Ashley looked once more at Wilson, then Caleb. Maybe she was wondering if they'd killed him. It looked like she didn't really care either way. She smiled stiffly at Tricia. "Good luck to you." She turned and walked away.

Tricia closed the door and returned to the kitchen. "We need to find that journal."

Much to Caleb's relief, the search didn't take too long. After going through a few drawers and desks, Caleb had wondered aloud if something like that might not be tucked well away, perhaps in an attic or basement. They decided on the attic first, found their way up, and discovered it was a mess. Decades, generations even, of junk. But an old steamer trunk at one end stood out, sealed with a relatively new-looking padlock. Tricia took a screwdriver from a nearby crate and levered off the entire hasp, padlock and all. On top of a bunch of old hardcovers and clothes lay a small leather bound book with ragged-edged paper. Inside was page upon page of small, spidery script.

Caleb pointed to the top line on the first page.

Hester Black is dead. It's not right. None of this is right.

Tricia nodded, looked around the gloomy, cobwebbed attic. "Let's get away from here."

"What about Wilson?"

She pursed her lips, then pulled her cell phone from a pocket, dialed. "Val, it's Tricia Brent. Yeah, we came to see Wilson, we had to break in. There's a reason he hasn't been around. He's lying dead on his kitchen floor." Pause. "I don't know, heart attack maybe?" There was another pause, then, "I don't know. We'll do what we can." She hung up without waiting for a reply.

They closed Wilson's door behind them, and climbed into Tricia's car. "Back to the motel?" she asked.

"I guess so, at least for now. I'll read while you drive."

Tricia turned on the dry grass in front of Old Man Wilson's house and drove back toward town. Caleb opened the journal. He took a deep breath, then read aloud.

"Hester Black is dead. It's not right. None of this is right. I need to write it down. No one will believe it, and everyone all agreed not to tell, but for weeks the guilt has chewed me up inside and I have to let it out. I'm one of the few who knows her letters anyhow. Perhaps the act of writing it out will help. Then maybe I won't feel the compulsion to tell someone else. Not that it matters. Plenty of people were there, pretty much everyone knows what happened, but now they all act like they forgot. No one says a word, but I see it in their eyes. The guilt. The horror.

"Hester was like a mother to us all, she cared for everyone. Healed folk when they was sick and injured. Delivered most of us. Delivered me, for the good lord's sake, and here I am, a party to what happened.

"I suppose I need to go back to when that strange fella arrived in town. He had long black hair, a sharp and hawkish face, but his eyes were like twin pits of hell, endless and disconcerting. I'm a young woman, strong and fit, and he was a wild and stringy old-timer, at least forty, but I was terrified of him. And so were most of the men, no matter how large or small. Seems none would tangle with him, all deferred. A kind of grudging, fearful respect took hold of everyone, myself included I'm ashamed to admit.

"He came to town and started offering healing and lucky charms and stuff like that, taking what little money folk had for his dark magics. Now we all know Hester had some magic in her and we just kinda ignored that because she only ever used it to help people. Of course, plenty of folk were afeared of her too, wanted her gone, killed or sent away. Unnatural, they said. But the majority were happy to take her services as long as she stayed far from town. That cabin out by the lake was removed enough for most folk and they went to her for help, or sent for her in the understanding she'd leave again once what needed to be done was done. And it worked like that for years. Since long before I was born anyhow.

"But that dark-souled fella arrived and it changed everything. Mister Crow they called him and lots of folks started talking about how a strong man like him was better than a witch. Perhaps he should stay and we should tell Hester to be gone. But others said Hester was the better of the two, cleaner and more godly than Mister Crow and his devilish arts. The town argued about it for some days, but in the end the two of them sorted it out for themselves. Hester had got word of Crow and she came to town. She challenged him, said he was evil and corrupt, that he should leave us all alone, go back to wherever he came from, or simply move along.

"There was a big argument and people took sides and it seemed strange to me then and still does now, how many folk quickly stood by Mister Crow despite Hester's years of caring for us all. But Hester demanded that Crow leave, and then she went back to her cabin. She told the townsfolk they would get no more of her help until Crow was gone.

"All of this story so far I know for fact, as it comes from interactions I witnessed myself, or was told by people I trust completely. The next bit is the best I can put together from hearsay and gossip, but I believe I have it all correct. Apparently that Mister Crow went out to Hester's cabin and tried to have his way with her. He wanted to punish her, drive her away, force his will upon her in that way men will insist upon so often. He meant to see her gone, but not before he'd sated his dark self in her virtue. And mark my words, for all the town's concerns, I believe Hester was a virtuous woman, even if she did have darkness in her ways too.

"We all know too that my cousin, Bradley Wilson, carried a torch for Hester. He seemed barely half her age, only a year or two older than me, but he would visit her cabin often, always be around when she was in town. It was an open secret and largely ignored. Most found it amusing, I think, though many think Bradley and Hester did seal their mutual attraction in secret trysts out in the woods. No matter, it was no one's business but theirs. But of course, Bradley had seen the challenge between Hester and Crow. And then he had seen that dark Crow head out into the woods, and he had guessed the man meant Hester harm. So Bradley followed.

"The next part of the story comes from Bradley's little brother, Jimmy, who followed Bradley out of innocent juvenile curiosity. When Bradley approached the cabin, Jimmy hid in the trees and watched.

"There was screaming from inside, Mister Crow raping Hester. Bradley strode into that affray and dragged Crow out, beating him something rotten. Well, Crow said some words that Jimmy couldn't understand, and Bradley began fitting, and foaming at the mouth. Hester yelled for Crow to stop, but the stranger was having none of that. He pulled out a knife and opened Bradley's throat back almost to the bone.

"At this turn of events, Hester screamed fit to split the sky and uttered a curse in a language foul and sharp. Jimmy said he pissed his pants just at the sound of her, frozen there in terror as he spied. Then she said, 'You will rot in hours though you don't deserve that swift a demise!' and Mister Crow, taken by surprise at her magical attack, staggered back and began clawing at his neck and face, gagging on words of pain.

"Now young Jimmy had just seen murder done to his beloved brother and Hester's revenge all too late, but he was terrified to move and could only watch. He said Mister Crow fell to his knees, but dragged in all his willpower and all his breath and cursed Hester right back. 'End me, will you?' he said to her. 'I give you a fate far worse! You will never die, and never again see your lover in the Kingdom of Heaven or anywhere else. Forever will you suffer here in grief!'

"At that Hester fell back like she had been struck a blow and she hissed at that stranger and said, 'So be it! I'll use my time well!' And she crawled back inside her cabin and left the stranger there while Bradley's corpse bled out. Mister Crow seemed too weak to move and his skin began to go gray and pustulent.

"Young Jimmy had seen enough, his fear-struck limbs were numb but they carried him once more and he ran all the way back to town in tears and reported what he had seen."

Caleb sucked in a breath, looked up from the journal. "This is horrible stuff."

Tricia's face was pale as she pulled into the parking space in front of their motel room, left the engine running. "And true, you think?" she asked.

He shrugged. "How can we know? But given what else we've seen these last few days, can we discount it?"

"Let's get inside."

They kept the curtains drawn in the small room and turned the air-conditioning on. Caleb sat in the small armchair by the window and turned on the standard lamp behind it. He blinked a few times, his eyes dry, then looked back to the journal. "Once Jimmy's story had been told, a posse gathered, carrying axes, hatchets, and knives, and went right back to Hester's cabin. Now all the next part I know for a fact as I was there to see it with my own eyes, though I still don't know if I believe it. A lot of the men tried to tell us to stay behind, no business for women they said. But many, my mother included, said this was town business and all should go along. So we did.

"It was nearly dark when we arrived and the first thing we saw was Bradley Wilson's body just like little Jimmy had described, his neck opened wide like a screaming mouth. Not far from Bradley, almost at the cabin step, was Mister Crow. Now I can't rightly say exactly what it was that had happened to him, but it seems Hester's curse was true to its word. The man was on his belly, legs kicking weakly as he clawed his hands towards her door. His skin was green and rank, the stench off him like weeks old rotting meat. The flesh in places had peeled wetly and split, ichor oozing through. His lips had gone, his teeth grinning like a death mask. His eyes rolled madly, shrunk and blackened, and mewling croaks and moans leaked from his scrawny throat.

"One of the men, I can't remember which, strode forward and hefted a mighty axe and took that Mister Crow's head clean off his neck to end the suffering and silence that terrible lowing. 'There is nothing godly about any of what's happened here,' Mister Willets said, and everyone knows Willets is an elder to be respected, just like Bradley's dad, my uncle, old Charlie Wilson. And then Uncle Charlie himself stepped up and agreed. 'We need to end all this,' he said. 'If Hester can do that to any man, we cannot suffer such a woman to live. We need to return our town to God.'

"It was like an unspoken agreement, right then. The posse immediately pushed into Hester's cabin and found her standing by her hearth, face set like stone. Of course, she'd heard everything that had occurred right outside. 'After all I've done for you?' she said. 'You'd turn against me now? Crow killed Bradley, not I!'

"But old man Willets had made his decision already, and Uncle Charlie backed him up, torn up with grief as he must have been over his eldest son. They strode over and both swung axes. Hester screamed as one took her in the top of the shoulder, severing her arm to hang only by strips of flesh and her plain white dress. She opened her mouth to speak and the other axe silenced her, the flat of the blade crushing her jaw, sending teeth scattering like frightened birds. Then a kind of frenzy took the mob. I stood back, staring through the cabin window, too petrified and sickened to do anything but watch as axes and knives rose and fell and Hester's body was rent in pieces. But those pieces kept on thrashing, her severed head would not stop screaming, though with her broken jaw she could form no words. That Mister Crow's last curse seemed to defy even dismemberment.

"The posse staggered outside, lost for further action. A hurried meeting was held there in the dark about what to do. Several people, myself included, said we should throw kindling into the cabin, as much as we could find, and burn it all down, burning the poor woman to ashes with it. Surely, no curse could defy fire if there was nothing left of Hester Black. But others were angry, that fury born of an inability to understand. Men fear that which they can't control and they could not control Hester nor their feelings about her. We had trusted an ungodly woman in our midst too long, they said, and we had been punished for it. Us! It seems to me that the only ones punished were Bradley and Hester, and they had done nothing wrong. A kinder man than Bradley Wilson I had never known. And Hester had cared for us all for years. But those scared men turned to cruelty. Let the witch suffer, they said. So they went back inside and using axes they levered up the hearth slab. They dug in the soft earth beneath until a makeshift grave was deep enough to contain all those writhing parts and they shoveled Hester in. Last to go was her head, kicked in atop her mutilated body by my Uncle Charlie Wilson, Bradley's father. His fear was, after all, soaked in grief, but even he had no excuse for that kind of malice. None of them did, it was sickening.

"But I remember Hester's eyes then, as her head rolled in and came to rest. Crooked it was, sideways, but her eyes stared hard at Charlie Wilson. Her screaming had ceased, her broken face incapable of expression, but those eyes were pits of hate.

"And Uncle Charlie dropped that hearth slab back into place above her and by then it was full dark outside. In silence, they buried the remains of old Mister Crow, and we walked through the forest back to town, Uncle Charlie carrying the body of his son. When we arrived, Uncle Charlie said, 'Only those of us gathered here know what happened, and that way it will stay. We will never speak of it to each other again. This chapter in our town is ended and tomorrow marks the dawn of a new history.' And everyone nodded and agreed.

"And so it has been. But at night I think I hear Hester's muffled screams drifting from the trees. Of course it's too far away, but my guilt amplifies the sounds I know must be there. Is she still alive? Is she still in that dark hole, in pieces, in pain, forever to suffer the cruelty of those scared and furious men? I don't know. But I have written down what happened and it's all true. May God forgive us for what we've done."

Caleb closed the journal and dropped it on the small table next to his chair.

"Jesus fucking Christ," Tricia said, her voice barely a whisper.

"This whole story," Caleb said, "deliberately forgotten en masse by the entire town. Only recorded here, but even Wilson himself would forget about it again and again. It's taken this long for someone, for us, to find it."

"Remembering this time killed him."

"Do you think she's still there?" Caleb asked.

"Well, something fucked is happening in Sallow Bend. And it's all because of Hester Black. She's not still there, Caleb, she's here, now. You saw her destroy that carnie last night. She killed Clare!"

"But that Hester is a child."

Tricia stared, shook her head, eyes haunted.

"I remember something she said when Saul died." Caleb's eyes widened, realization dawning as he spoke. "She said, 'You think it's easy holding this avatar together? I need their life force. Now there's only one.' So the Hester we see is not real. When Saul was hurting her, she wavered like mud and water before pulling herself together. She's using Clare and Suki to have a presence here. That's why Saul couldn't kill her. And that's why it killed Clare when Hester refused to let her avatar be beaten."

Tricia nodded slowly. "Hester was so angry that beating Saul had made her use too much of Clare and that poor girl died."

"But," Caleb said softly. "That means Suki is the only connection she has left."

37

SITTING ON THE edge of the bed, Tricia stared at Caleb for a moment and he became increasingly uncomfortable under that gaze. "What?" he said eventually.

"Caleb, we can't kill Suki."

He looked away. "Of course not."

"But Hester is hurt and weakened. She said so herself. She said she nearly killed Suki too when she was fighting Fallon, isn't that what you told me? This is the best chance we're going to get."

"To do what?"

"To finish her. That story, if it's true, is horrendous. I can't get my head around it. But given what else we know, the things we've seen lately, I can't help but believe it. And they *should* have burned Hester back then. That curse surely can't survive immolation of all her parts, her bones, her brain. The cruelty of burying her alive for eternity? That's atrocious. But she's weak, and we know where to find her body. We can end this."

"It's midday already." Caleb moved the curtain and looked out the window at the bright, hot day, but a chill tickled his insides nonetheless. "We'll have to hurry. I don't want to be there at night."

"We'll need help." Tricia shook her head, frustration written in the lines of her frown. "But who'll believe us? Who can we ask?"

"The police? Val Baker?"

Tricia barked a laugh. “They’d lock us up. Even Val had trouble holding onto thoughts about Hester.”

Silence settled on them for a moment, then Tricia looked up. “The carnies. We have to talk to them, get their help.”

“Will they understand?”

“They must have found Saul by now. I bet that’s why they suddenly decided to leave! We tell them what we know, come clean. Get a bunch of them together and fix this.”

“Okay. We can try that.”

They drove first back via Tricia’s garage to collect supplies. Matches and lighters, a five gallon gas can, three-quarters full. Caleb found a couple of long crowbars that he hoped would help lift the slab the journal had described. Tricia dug out a couple of sturdy flashlights. They packed what they could in an old canvas backpack, then carried the pack and the gas can out to the car. By a little after one pm they were driving north through town towards Gil’s Tavern and the carnival beyond. As they drove up Rose Avenue to meet the highway, they saw their salvation driving away. Tricia cursed as she sat at the stop line, watching trucks and trailers, flatbeds and utilities cruising past. The carnival had packed up and was leaving town.

“Fuck it,” Tricia said into the silence once the long convoy had passed. “I can’t believe how fast they did that. Now what?”

“Now we’ll have to do it ourselves.”

Sweat covered them both by the time they had trudged through the hot woods towards Hester’s cabin. Even in the shade of the trees, far cooler than under the blistering eye of the sun, the heat was enough to make Caleb feel weakened and irritable. Not to mention the crippling fear that threatened to fold his knees beneath him. Was he really going to face Hester? Would their new knowledge give them any advantage? The gas can was heavy, banging against his leg as he stumbled over the rough ground. He switched it regularly from one hand to the other and back again, but both palms were sore with blisters. Tricia wore a fixed frown of determination, hands hooked into the straps of the backpack she had insisted on carrying if he was going to heft the can. She leaned into her walk like she was facing down a gale.

Caleb nodded to himself. Regardless of what they now knew, Tricia had a score to settle. After what Hester had said about Riley and Toby, there would be no conversation. No attempts to mollify. Tricia was going to war. Despite the horrors of the story, despite Tricia's brief and no doubt genuine sympathy for what had happened to Hester, the vengeance was back in her heart.

Caleb's heart was hammering into his ribs, with fear as much as exertion, when they finally emerged from the trees into the clear sun over the lake. Hester's cabin stood dark and still. Tricia's face was pale, but still set.

"Come on," she said, and stalked along the lake side.

Hester stepped from the black doorway of her home as they approached. "You've got nerve coming here, I'll give you that." Her face betrayed a kind of strained exhaustion.

Caleb narrowed his eyes, saw that her features were shifted ever so slightly, as if they were wax and she'd been too near a fire. Or out too long in the sun. She was still weak from her battle with Saul Fallon. Still struggling without Clare's influence. Caleb wondered how weak Suki might be.

Hester's gaze fell on the gas can he carried, on the backpack Tricia was slinging off her shoulder. Her eyes narrowed. "What are you doing?"

"We're here to finish you!" Tricia spat. "You took my son!"

Hester rounded on her, face flashing fury. "Your son would be like all the others. Like the useless father who brought him here. They all deserve to die!"

"Toby did not deserve to die! Sure, it seems Riley was fucking weak. He let his son die and he struck at the slightest provocation out of guilt instead of confiding in me. But Toby was not like him!"

"He would have been. They all are in the end."

Tricia's face softened slightly. "We know what happened to you. We've heard your story. Mister Crow, the mob from town. No one deserves that. But your reign of vengeful murder is over."

Hester looked again at the gas can and her eyebrows rose. "Nothing is over!" she yelled. "All because he couldn't have me, that Crow. Like he was entitled to me! Then those other men who had always used me, no few of them raping me as well over the years, they cut me up. And in all this time, they haven't changed. Fuck them all. For eternity I will punish them. *You* don't get to decide where or how this ends!"

Caleb took a step forward, legs shaking, knees weak, wondering if he could push past her. But his limbs locked up as she drilled him with her gaze. The strain showed in her face, but she had him like a puppet. Tricia cried out his name just as a green blur flashed into his vision. Everything went black for a moment and he realized he was lying on the ground, head singing. A broken branch lay next to him.

As his vision settled back and he pushed himself into a sitting position, Tricia grabbed a crowbar from the backpack and rushed at Hester, the weapon raised high. Hester grimaced and Tricia screamed as her body slowed and froze.

I can only work one at a time.

Caleb drove himself to his feet, dizzy from the blow to the head, and grabbed the gas can again. He stumbled to the pack, aiming for the second crowbar. Hester howled as she held Tricia in place, frustration clear. She gestured with one hand and Caleb ducked just in time to avoid another tree limb cracking free from a trunk right by him and whistling past.

So she could only control one person, but she could manage her other tricks in the meantime. Tricia's face was frozen, but she let out a constricted howl. Caleb grabbed the crowbar, gas can in the other hand, and ran for the cabin. Another branch slammed into the ground beside him as he danced away, then another bent down, whipping and curling as though it were alive, a green and brown tentacle questing for his leg. He tried to side-step, but it wrapped over his shoe, bound painfully tight around his ankle and began to drag him backward. Tricia's wailing increased in pitch, Hester's face showed greater strain. Caleb despaired. Even this weak, she was more than a match for both of them. He put down the crowbar, scrabbled at the thin branch around his leg, but it was too tight to get his fingers under, too thick and green to snap away. Another branch bent forward, reaching for him.

Then Hester screamed, a wordless shriek of anguish.

Caleb looked up and started in shock. The big carnie, Daniel, had emerged from the trees. And he held Suki against his chest, one hand at her throat, the other across her chest. The girl's legs dangled like rope a couple of feet off the floor. Her face was pale and drawn, her eyelids flickered as though she were half asleep.

"Don't you hurt her!" Hester said.

Daniel shook his head, brows drawn together in sorrow. "She's already dead. I know it. Both those girls, they were already dead when I found 'em!"

"No, they weren't. And Suki isn't dead now." Hester swallowed hard, face stretched with effort. "You have to understand!"

With her attention drawn to so many vectors, Caleb realized the branch around his leg had slackened. He pulled it away, took up the crowbar again.

"They're already dead, and if I finish this one off, end her ungodly false life, it'll end you too."

Hester shook her head, took a faltering step forward. Tricia remained frozen in place, straining against her invisible bonds, but Caleb moved unnoticed, slowly, step by terrified step, toward the cabin.

"I just use their energy," Hester said, pitching her voice lower, cajoling. "I share it."

Daniel backed up a step, shook Suki like a doll. The girl looked tiny in his grasp. "No closer!"

Hester stopped, raised one palm placatingly. "When people sleep near me, on those rare occasions, I can use their life force to make an avatar. From the lake. For a little while I get to be free. Not of the pain, but of the prison, at least. Let her go, please. Don't hurt her."

"If I end her, it ends you!"

"That's true, but I'll make you a deal! I'll be honest. If the sleepers are male, I use them up, until they die, then I'm gone again until the next time. But when they're girls, I only use them as long as I can without killing them, then I quit, leaving them alive to recover. Put her down, and I'll give in now. Just let her live! Not another little girl. Please."

Caleb paused, halfway to the door of the cabin. There was the ring of truth in Hester's words. It sounded as though she really meant it. She would go and let Suki live. But then he saw the lie in her expressions, the misdirection in her eyes. She was lying. With her avatar gone, nothing could stop them burning her remains. She acted well, but there was no way she would give up her avatar for exactly that reason. She knew Caleb had her secret. She was playing Daniel.

"Don't believe her!" Caleb shouted.

The big man had his head tipped to one side, his grip on Suki loosened just a little. The girl's eyes flickered open, she looked around, confused, then seemed to drift off again.

"I'm not lying," Hester said, though Caleb knew she was. He moved again, slowly, toward the cabin.

"You weren't supposed to find them," Hester said. "I would have hidden them, kept them safe. Then they would have found their way home afterward and no one would remember my visit. It's happened that way so many times before. But you found us before I was ready, so we came back together. It was okay, it was working fine."

"The other girl already died," Daniel said, tears evident in his voice. "Right in the midway that girl died."

"I'm so sorry about Clare." Hester jabbed a finger at Tricia. "That was her fault, and her idiot man friend! I was lost in a rage fighting that bastard back there. But Suki doesn't have to die. I'll leave if you let her go."

Caleb moved again towards the cabin's open door and the darkness beyond it. Let Hester be distracted trying to urge Daniel to believe her, and he would get to her remains. Then movement in the trees caught his eye, gave him pause. Three people emerged. Ashley Strong, Sarah Carter, and John Barrow.

"Dan, what are you doing?" Ashley said.

"We heard in town that Suki had gone missing again," Barrow said. "We guessed it was you."

Ashley glanced at Tricia. "And even if it wasn't, we thought perhaps we owed something to this town."

Hester's face twisted in hate and anger. As Daniel looked to his friends, opening his mouth to say something, Hester made an expansive gesture with one hand. Caleb cried out a warning but it was too late. A tree limb whipped down from above Daniel, cracking into the side of his head, slamming him sideways.

Suki fell from his grasp, collapsed onto her knees, then looked up in surprise as blood flooded her chest from a throat opened wide. Daniel staggered back, shaking his head, holding up the small knife he'd had concealed in his palm the whole time.

38

HESTER SCREAMED. "NOOOO!"

As Suki pitched forward towards the dark earth, Hester spun around. Tricia, suddenly released from her invisible hold, stumbled forward in a run, and Hester ran right at her. As Hester's form wavered and slipped into wet mud, she splashed all over Tricia.

Everything froze for a moment, Daniel staring at the bloody knife in his hand, Ashley, Sarah, and Barrow staring at Daniel, Tricia trembling on the spot. Caleb paused, one hand on the cabin doorframe, watching it all. And a white streak appeared along the left side of Tricia's hair.

Tricia let out a cry, swatted at her face and head. "She's in me!" Then she shuddered and turned towards Daniel. "You'll pay!" she shrieked, in Hester's voice, and branches whipped again, battering the large man. "I can't stop her!" Tricia shouted.

"Help me!" Caleb yelled.

Ashley looked at him then Sarah said, "Go! I'll help here."

As the blonde woman began to incant in some lilting tongue, Caleb said, "I know what to do! Help me!"

He ran into the cabin and Ashley and Barrow followed close behind. Trying to ignore the shouts of pain from Daniel, the screams of Hester, Sarah's haunting song, he ran to the hearth. Sure enough, the base of it was one large slab of gray stone. He dropped the gas can and jammed the crowbar in between the slab and the flagstone floor.

"What the fuck is happening?" Ashley demanded.

"Trust me. Just help. We have to lift this."

Barrow had picked up the other crowbar and he began working at the other side. A high-pitched wail rang outside and Sarah's incantation ceased abruptly. Barrow grabbed Ashley's wrist.

"Take over, you're stronger than me. Taller. I'm better out there!" And he ran from the cabin, scrabbling in a satchel on his hip.

"Help me!" Caleb barked. "We have to burn her!"

Ashley grabbed up Barrow's discarded crowbar. "You better know what you're doing!"

As the large slab shifted and a foul stench belched up, a shot rang out in the woods. A scream, a shout. More screaming, another shot. Daniel yelling incoherently, trees cracking and whipping the air.

Caleb didn't dare consider anything that might be happening out there, he had to focus on one thing. Ashley put her back to the job as he did and with strained growls of effort, they heaved the slab up and over. And staggered back from what they saw.

A shallow pit beneath the stone contained bones, so many bones of all sizes, child to adult grown, all clean and white, with grooves like teeth marks in them. But worse, among the skeletal remains, ash gray fleshy parts writhed and slipped. Two hands with long, withered fingers clutched at the air, scrawny arms and legs flexed and twitched, all separated from each other, squirming as if with independent life. Then one hand pushed a head up through the pile, eyes glittering madly above a twisted and broken jaw, missing half its teeth and ragged. That jaw worked up and down hungrily, the eyes rolled, came to rest on Caleb as he stared, bile burning in his throat. He stood trapped in place, every muscle frozen and shaking with tetanic vibrations.

Then Ashley Strong stepped up beside him, the gas can glugging as she upended it, dousing everything in the pit. The mouth in that ruined face, framed with stringy black hair with one bright white streak, stretched wide in a soundless howl of defiance, and Ashley turned, swinging the gas can left and right, splattering the walls and floor.

Caleb finally found himself able to move and grabbed matches from his pocket. He struck one, it sparked, and snapped. Fell broken to the floor. With a wordless cry of anguish, he tried again, hands shaking, the next match flaring into bright life. Ashley turned and ran as he dropped it and pounded after her. At the door he paused, looked back to see bright tongues of orange and yellow leap and dance across the ground, then the hearth exploded in a blistering conflagration. An agonized, piercing wail split the air and he fell out of the cabin into the fresh air of the lakeside.

39

THE FIRST THING Caleb saw was Tricia standing tall and rigid, like she was being electrocuted, her face twisted in pain. A voice not Tricia's own cried out, "*I was not finished hurting them!*" Then Tricia fell to her knees.

She looked up, hair hanging limp, the white streak bright in the dimming light. "She's gone." Her own voice, but gravel and tears. She fell to one side and Caleb saw blood soaking the leg of her jeans. He ran to her and she pointed. "He shot me."

Caleb looked where she indicated and saw John Barrow lying flat on his back, a huge pistol loose in one hand. Blood covered his face, his eyes stared unseeing at the clouds above.

Ashley ran to Sarah, lying in Daniel's arms.

"She's okay, I think," Daniel said. "Knocked out, but okay."

As he spoke, Sarah's eyelids fluttered and she came around, one hand rising to press against the side of her head. She sat up to look in desperation about herself.

Ashley gathered her lover in a hug. "It's okay, you're okay." Then she looked over at the fallen Barrow. "Oh, John." A tear tumbled over her cheek. She squeezed Sarah into a hug, but her eyes stayed on Barrow. "John," she whispered again, and finally looked away.

"Turns out I'm a charlatan after all," Sarah said, with a weak smile. "I had no effect on her at all."

Caleb tore at his shirt, tried to bandage Tricia's bleeding leg. "Just as well the man couldn't shoot straight," she said. "Or I'd be dead. He just winged me. Hurts like hell though."

"But he saved us," Daniel said, crouching over the fallen man. "It distracted you. Her. And he paid dearly for it. She smashed him, but it gave me a chance to get Sarah away. And gave you time to do whatever you did."

Tears fell as Daniel closed Barrow's eyes then moved to the tiny form of Suki lying still in a pool of blood on the dark earth. "I killed this little girl though." He sobbed. "That was all me."

"No. That was Hester too." Sarah stood uncertainly, moved to put a hand on his shoulder. "It was her, Daniel. Those girls were dead since before you even found them, remember?"

She cast a meaningful look at the others. Ashley nodded subtly, Tricia managed a weak smile. Caleb saw through their lies, even if Daniel didn't, and he supposed the artifice of people sometimes was a better way.

40

HESTER'S CABIN BURNED brightly in the gathering night. There would be nothing left by morning. They decided to leave Suki's body on the shore of Sallow Lake to be found, or not, by others at some future point. No one knew any of them had been there. Who would believe any story if they returned now with the corpse of a little girl, her throat slit? Tricia cried quietly about it the whole way back, while Caleb ground his teeth. But it was done, he told himself over and over again. At such a price, it was finally done. There would be no more episodes like this for Sallow Bend.

Caleb carried John Barrow's body back with them through the woods, while Daniel carried Tricia, her leg bound up to stop the bleeding.

"We'll deal with him," Ashley had said about Barrow. "Carnie business, okay?" She had looked at him then, deep pain etched on her face, and Caleb knew she would never stop grieving for her friend. But he would remain in all their memories a hero.

It was full dark when they reached the edge of the trees, Tricia's car parked not far away.

"Our truck is near the bridge," Ashley said. "We'll leave you here. I don't know what the fuck has gone down, not really. I think we'll all be haunted by it for the rest of our lives. But thank you for what you've done."

"Thank you for your help too," Tricia said. "For coming back."

Ashley nodded. "We won't again. My carnival will find a new route. The people of Sallow Bend will have to travel to us from now on."

"Can't blame you for that," Caleb said.

Under a glittering dome of stars, the carnies walked off together towards the bridge, Ashley and Sarah arm in arm, Daniel carrying Barrow's body. Tricia leaned heavily on Caleb, turned and buried her face in his chest, and sobbed against him for several minutes. In the darkness, he put one hand on her back, offering what comfort he could.

Eventually she pulled back. "That crazy bitch was *in* me. I felt all her hate, her madness, her *age*! Her fury was almost blinding. And her pain. After all she'd done in her life, then those men treated her so badly, with such violence. How she maintained her avatar as sweetly as she did I can't imagine, with that rage burning like lava every second. I despise her for what she did to my family, to innocent people, but that poor woman!"

Caleb nodded, lifted the pale streak of hair. "She left a visible mark on you too."

Tricia looked sidelong, ran the white streak through her fingers. "Maybe I'll keep it, a souvenir of my revenge against Toby's killer." Another sob pulsed out of Tricia then, like a bird released, and she cried hard, pressed back into Caleb's chest. He held her, unsure what else to do but be there. "He's really dead," Tricia said eventually, wiping one forearm across her face.

"I'm so sorry."

She sniffed, nodded. "I wonder if anyone will remember her. The Hester avatar, I mean. You think anyone in town will have a clue about any of this now?"

Caleb pursed his lips to think about that. "I think people have an incredible ability to forget things they don't like, and to make the same mistakes over and over again," he said eventually.

Tricia smiled crookedly. "You got that right. Let's go."

She leaned in, using him like a crutch, limping as he walked her through the hot night. Insects buzzed and whirred in the grass as they made their way back towards Tricia's car, and the small, sleepy town of Sallow Bend beyond.

EPILOGUE

NEARLY TWO MONTHS after they left the woods, Caleb stood on Tricia's driveway, shifting uncomfortably from foot to foot. A huge removals truck stood at the curb, a bright *For Sale* sign in the grass of Tricia's front yard had a *SOLD!* sticker slapped across it.

"You're ready?" he said at last.

Tricia smiled, hugged him. "I am. I'm sorry I can't stay here now. Not since…"

"I know. You don't need to explain again. That little house you found by the ocean is lovely. You deserve it."

Tricia poked one finger into his chest. "And you *will* come to visit me there sometimes."

"Okay."

"Has there been anything? You heard any talk..?"

Caleb drew a deep breath, shook his head. "Only you and I ever say her name any more. It's like she was never here. All those deaths, they've just slipped into the fabric of town history, like it was nothing more than a strangely bad time. Suki's parents are packing up the same as you, by the way, but I think Clare's family are staying."

"Yeah, I heard."

"I guess it's hard for them to be neighbors now, since both their girls died. But at least Clare seemed like natural causes. The violence done to Suki has gone unexplained. Lunatics in the woods. People are already forgetting the details, or choosing to ignore them. But being next to each other must be difficult for those families."

Tricia grinned. "Look at you, understanding human interaction and shit."

His cheeks heated up with a blush. "Yeah, well. I've always understood. I just couldn't handle it. But you've helped me get better at it, so thank you."

"Don't endure this alone," she said, becoming serious again. "You have my new address and my number. Call to chat."

"I will."

"Bullshit. I'll call you."

He laughed. "Fair enough. You going to be okay?"

"Fuck, no. Not for a long time, if ever. But I'll work on it. You?"

"Same." Caleb had wondered whether or not to say anything about his recent visit, but thought maybe he should. "Val Baker came to see me."

"Oh, yeah?"

"She said she thinks I know something more about Sallow Bend than most. She's been having weird dreams, she said. About a girl with hair like Tricia Brent's." He saw the twitch of shock in Tricia's eyes, then it passed. "But she was too embarrassed to talk to you, she said."

Tricia ran a hand through the white streak over her left ear. She'd tried to dye it out, she'd told Caleb, but no color would ever stay. "Val was always a bit more aware than the others," Tricia said. "But even she couldn't hold onto it. Maybe some residual memory in there. What did you tell her?"

"I said I didn't know what she meant, but that Sallow Bend is a weird town so weird dreams are only to be expected."

"And what did she say to that?"

"She said maybe she shouldn't have come to me after all. Then she thanked me anyway and left."

A car horn beeped. Tricia turned and waved to her sister, waiting at the curb in Tricia's car. "Carol is impatient. She's having time away from the idiot she married and keen to enjoy herself."

"You're making a holiday of the trip to your new place?"

"Yeah, a couple of days, then she's staying with me for a while to help me settle in. I'll try to convince her to leave the putz while she's there."

Caleb raised an eyebrow, a subtle chill washing through him.

Tricia laughed. "It's all me, not her. Hester is long gone. But Carol's husband really is a dick. A lot of men are, Caleb. Not all of them, but far too fucking many. Carol deserves better. We all do. You just keep being one of the good ones, okay? Keep setting a good example."

Caleb nodded, lost for words.

She gave him another hug. "As for Hester, and Val Baker, and all the rest, better we let it all fall out of memory. Remember that journal, where that asshole said, 'This chapter in our town is ended and tomorrow marks the dawn of a new history'? Let's make it like that, but for real this time. And without any unfinished business."

He returned her hug. "Good idea."

Carol beeped again, grinning insolently from the passenger seat.

"So you'll come visit me!"

"I will!" He smiled, realized he meant it. Tricia was a good friend. "But school starts again in two weeks. Next vacation, okay?"

"I will hold you to that, Caleb Jackson."

He saw a deep sadness still in her eyes and wondered if it would ever leave her. If nothing else, at least she could rely on the fact that he knew everything about her story, even if no one else ever would. He wanted to remain that person for her, that friend. And she would be his only friend who knew everything too.

"Seeya sometime soon, then," she said.

"Definitely."

The driver of the removal truck slammed the back doors and walked over. "We're ready to roll."

Tricia smiled. "Thanks. Post the key through the door once everything's inside. We'll be a few days behind."

He nodded and clambered into his truck. Its engine rumbled into life and he backed off the drive.

Tricia planted a kiss on Caleb's cheek, then ran to her car. She waved from the window and pulled away. Caleb waved back and heaved a sigh. He actually would miss her. With a smile, he turned and walked back toward the school to enjoy the last couple of weeks of peace before the students returned.

END

ACKNOWLEDGEMENTS

Every book is born in the mind of a twisted soul like myself, created in darkness and isolation, but only sees the light of day with a concerted team effort. This book is no exception

My heartfelt thanks to Kevin Lucia and all at Cemetery Dance.

To François Vaillancourt for the amazing, creepy as hell cover art this book is wrapped in.

To Alex Adsett for tirelessly championing my nonsense.

My debt to David Wood, Angela Slatter, and Joanne Anderton is massive - all are beta readers of great insight and honesty. And especially to Michael Moshos, for his beta reading and in particular his help in ensuring I treated the character of John Barrow respectfully. Thank you for your consideration, Michael. Any mistakes I've made are entirely my own, and for those I apologise.

To my wife, Halinka, and our awesome kid, Arlo, thank you. For everything.

And of course, as always, my thanks to you, the reader. I greatly appreciate your time, and I hope you consider it time well spent.